Tempest

Also by Sofia

Dream Weaver

An Elemental Series
Terra
Torch
Tempest

Operation Kane Novella

Praise for *Terra*

"Prepare to be swept away by a unique and captivating fated mates romance that will enthrall you from start to finish. A fresh and imaginative take on the genre that is sure to leave you spellbound."

Judy Corry, USA Today
Bestselling Author
of Sweet Contemporary Romances

"With a Twilight feel, readers looking for a young adult urban fantasy will enjoy the hidden Elemental world of Terra. Excellent series for teen and up."

Morgan L. Busse, award-winning
author of the Ravenwood Saga,
Skyworld series, and the Nordic Wars

"Terra was a delightful surprise and kept me hungry for more. Weaving a tale of intrigue, romance, and danger, Sofia Simpson masterfully tugs on the heartstrings and crafts a tale of hope and redemption. A story to savor and an author to watch!"

Tara Johnson, Author of
To Speak His Name

AN ELEMENTAL SERIES

BOOK 3

Tempest

SOFIA SIMPSON

TEMPEST

Copyright © 2024 Sofia Simpson

Published by Starlight Books

First Edition

ISBN: 979-8-9874009-9-9 (ebook)

ISBN: 979-8-9874009-8-2 (paperback)

Cover by: EAH Creative

Editing by: Jessica Gwyn

Illustrations by: Joanna Hadzhieva

Map by: Sofia Simpson

To Sophie and all the ladies who
are fans I've never met,
I love that you love my books! I
only pray they teach you what
they taught me about our Jesus.
That He is capable of making
any change in our lives, no
matter how small or big.

N
W E
S
Borean
Borean
Neronian
Neronian
Neronian
Ner
Neronian
Festan
Gyan
Polar Bear Lo
Neronian
Festan
United States

Canada Clan Territories

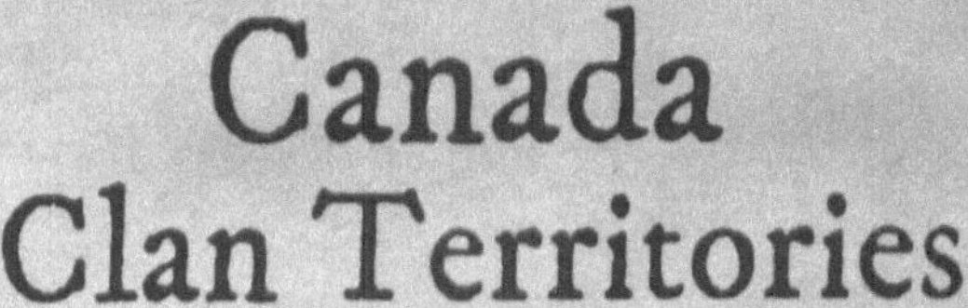

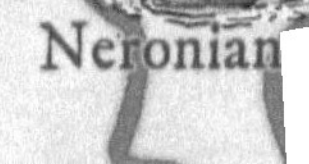

Vela

Linc

Rayne

When the day and night are of equal length, a
warrior star who will bear the child will rise.
Under the Winter Solstice, the Hunter will emerge.
He will capture the Goat under the Northern sky
and they will produce the one who unifies.
Though their elements are diverse, through them
the Child will command them all.

Unknown
Around 1600 AD

PROLOGUE

In this battle to the death, the man chooses to fight. To the final moment, he'll do anything for his wife and unborn child.

The horrifying reality that his wife continues to have labor pains doesn't change the fact that there's nothing they can do about them now. He ignores the cuts on his neck and arms, thankful he at least protected his eyes when the Extremists shattered the windows of his car.

Rain pours through the broken windows, and a hand reaches in, fumbling for the lock mechanism. The man tried to freeze the moisture in the air to bar anyone using the door handles, but with his windows broken open, the Extremist can simply reach in to open the door.

The man blinks rain and blood from his eyes and swipes a wind knife at the Extremist's hand, slicing into it. The intruder screams, pulling his hand out and kicks at the door.

His wife whimpers in the passenger seat as blood drips down her forehead and into her eyes. She chose to protect her stomach over her face when the windows exploded.

A firm resolve fills the man. They will not die today. He cranks the key again, praying the car will finally start, and issues a strangled thanks when it does.

Shouts fill the air. "He's trying to get away!"

The Extremist throws his upper body into the window just as the man presses the gas pedal to the floorboard. The Extremist lands punches to the man's head that dazes him, but he fights back with one arm while steering with the other. His car plows into more attackers, but he doesn't slow down.

The Extremist grabs the steering wheel, trying to wrestle control. Wrenching the guy's arm off the wheel, the man shoves the attacker as hard as he can out the window, but the Extremist manages to hang on, dangling by his fingertips as his feet drag along the ground trying to find purchase in the mud. With one last shove and smash on the gas pedal, the attacker flings off the car.

The man breathes a sigh of relief and then his wife screams, "Watch out!"

He wrenches the wheel just in time to avoid a shed. They narrowly miss crashing into the wooden structure. He careens the car around the building, and the car spits wet gravel as he drives it out onto the country road.

The woman moans, holding her stomach. He prays she can hold on for just a little bit longer.

The rain's coming down hard now, which might help or hinder their escape. He prays for the former. A car pursues them as they race out into the night, praying they escape their relentless attackers and have this baby somewhere safe.

1. Vela

I open my eyes to steep rock walls and blue sky impossibly far above. I shift from my position on the rocky floor of the ravine and look up at Rayne with wary eyes. My knee screams at me, my side aches, and I'm fighting dizziness.

My head swims from the pain, and then I remember why I passed out. *I'm the Chosen Child?* I shake my head. There's no way. I'm the mother of the Chosen one. My child will one day be in this esteemed and perilous role. It can't be *me.*

Ignoring that disturbing thought, I call out for Jack. I know he can't be in the ravine. There's no way he'd make it down here, but maybe he's close by. After a pause to listen intently, my shoulders slump. There's no answering bark. He's nowhere near me, or he'd answer my call.

Rayne looks down at me with a certainty that makes me nervous. His expression leaves no doubt that he firmly believes what he just said. That I'm the one, the Chosen Child the Elementals believe will one day unite our world.

"You're wrong, Rayne. You must be."

His eyes glint at me. "Why? Because you're afraid?"

I laugh harshly. "Are you kidding? Who wouldn't be? The Child is the most hunted Elemental on the planet."

He furrows his brow. "You're already in the safest possible place. There's no way anyone can find you out here in the middle of Canada."

I hold my leg, squeezing my thigh painfully to distract me from the agony in my knee. My heart lurches at his words. Why did he jump off that cliff with me? Hadn't we escaped the grolar bear? Is he hiding me down here? I look at my surroundings for the first time, my eyes passing over the vines trailing down the ravine walls and rocks that cover the ground.

"Was the bear right behind us when you flung us off that cliff?" I ask, piercing him with a glare.

His face is unreadable. "I don't know. But I heard something, so I reacted and found safety the only way I knew how."

"By flying us down into a God knows-how-deep-ravine?"

His eyes harden. "I did the only thing I could think of to make sure you were safe and not bear food. You don't get to judge me. I'm in this predicament, too."

My heart squeezes tightly. Is Linc okay? Was he the grolar bear's next meal? That bear is a deadly mixture of grizzly and polar bear. It's man-eating and my veins chill in fear at the thought of Linc facing it alone. There's no way to know what happened until we get back up there, back to the group. A resolve to find him immediately fills me. Did Rayne hide us so we could be alone? It hits me just then that I'm all by myself with someone I barely know, someone I definitely do not trust. A sense of loss rips through me that if my precious dog, Jack, were here, I would be protected.

But no, it's just me and I'm injured.

"Look, we need to get back to the others. I need to know that Linc's okay," I say, breathing in shallow breaths, trying to control the pain coursing through my side and leg.

I lurch back when Rayne kneels next to me.

"Relax. Is your leg broken?" He runs his eyes over my outstretched leg, and I'm thankful he doesn't touch it.

I shake my head. "I don't know. Gyans can't self-diagnose their injuries. I only know my knee is killing me."

He reaches for me and runs his hands over my shoulders and down my arms, squeezing as he goes. I lean back as far as I can from his probing touch. "What are you doing?" I hiss. I resent his touch as much as I do him and his thoughtless actions.

He glances at me but resumes his exam. If Jack were here, he would sense my discomfort and make sure Rayne stopped. I miss my furry buddy sorely. But it makes sense he ran off at the first sight of that grolar bear. I'm glad he didn't try to fight it. He knew a losing battle when he saw one.

Rayne moves from my arms to my left leg. "I'm checking if you're injured anywhere else." He starts at my ankle and gently squeezes it, then moves up.

His touch is disconcerting. No one has touched me like this, not even Linc. When he reaches my knee, I snap at him, "That leg isn't hurt, Rayne. Stop it."

He ignores me and continues up my thigh.

I've had enough, and I smack his hand off my leg. "I'm fine, Rayne. You don't need to grope me."

He scowls. "You're *not* fine. And I'm not trying to feel you up, Vela. Sometimes there's another injury that's masked by the primary one. I need to be sure there's nothing else."

Before I can tell him about my side, his elbow grazes it as he examines my hip.

I inhale sharply, wincing.

Rayne frowns. "What's hurt? Your hip or your side?"

"I think it's my ribs," I reluctantly say.

He turns his attention there and carefully places his hand on my right side. "I'm going to need to press down, just for a second, to see if it's broken. Are you having trouble breathing?"

Shaking my head, I say, "No. It just hurts. I don't think my lungs are punctured."

"Good. Brace yourself. I'll be as quick as I can."

I hold my breath and squeeze my eyes shut, preparing myself for agony.

I can't help but cry out when he presses on my hurt rib. I breathe in relief when he moves away from the injured one and probes all my ribs before he's satisfied and leaves me alone.

"Well?" I say, panting. Between my side and my leg, I'm struggling to remain coherent. Both injuries are on my right side. My body is angry with me for the fall.

He leans back and frowns deeply. He brushes his hands off and sighs. "I don't think it's broken, which is good. It's probably just bruised. That means we can move you without risking further injury to your lung. Let's get you up and see if we can find a way out of here." He stands up, and I look up at him incredulously.

"I can't walk like this."

He's looking around us with a critical eye. "You have to. This ravine fills up with water at some point in the day, and we can't stay here."

Looking around, I try to see what he does. I can't fathom how he could be right. We're nowhere near water. "I think you must have hit your head pretty hard when we fell. First you say I'm the Chosen Child. And now? What do you mean this place fills up with water? We're in upper Manitoba, the middle of Canada, not by an ocean."

He points at the walls on either side of us. "See those water lines? This place has a geyser somewhere that erupts throughout the day, maybe more than one for it to fill two feet up the floor of this ravine. That water is scalding hot, so we need to move so it doesn't cook us."

He turns to me with a hard glare. "And you *are* the Chosen One. You need to get used to the idea."

I huff and turn away from his gaze. "What makes you even say that?"

"I'll get into the details later. Right now, we have to go."

Worries assault me, especially how Jack is going to survive without me. I shake my head at the pointless thoughts. There's nothing to be done about it now. I guess it's a good thing Jack wasn't with me when Rayne flung us off that cliff. Jack would never have been able to follow us. I glance at the tall walls on either side of me. It's crazy to think the floor of this place will fill up with water, but with how narrow this ravine is, this reminds me of an oversized ditch. "Well, if we have to move, can you help me up?"

He walks behind me and slides his arms under mine. "Ready?" he asks in my ear.

If I turn my head, my mouth would be in line with his and I don't want that, so I nod curtly and suck in a breath. His breath teases my ear, and I fiercely stamp down the rush of *something* that fills me.

He chuckles in my ear, and before I ask why he's laughing, he pulls me up. I try to keep my whimpers in, but he's close enough to hear them. He slows down and is careful not to jerk my body into a standing position, which I appreciate. He moves to my left, one arm holding my side where the rib isn't fractured or bruised.

I take a moment to fight down the dizziness. Even though we didn't pop up quickly, my head still reels. I breathe in my nose and out my mouth, trying and failing to control the pain pounding through me. All the while, I steady myself, getting used to being on one leg.

"Easy, now. You can do this, Chosen One," Rayne encourages. His look is heavy, like he's found a precious jewel.

I scowl. "Don't call me that," I snap.

"It's the truth," he says easily.

"I'm not getting into this with you right now. Let's just concentrate on walking."

It's not easy, but when I can stand the pain, I slowly put my left arm over Rayne's shoulder and lean on him heavily. Sweat dots my brow, and I pant lightly.

Rayne looks around and sets his sights on the edge of the ravine, then turns to me. "I see a way out of here. It would be easier if I carried you there."

Instantly, I tense. "No, my side would kill me if you picked me up. I'd rather walk."

He sighs heavily. "Okay, we'll go slow. But we're going to have to climb out. I'll help you with that."

With those ominous words, I move my good leg and start the arduous trek out of this ravine.

2. LINC

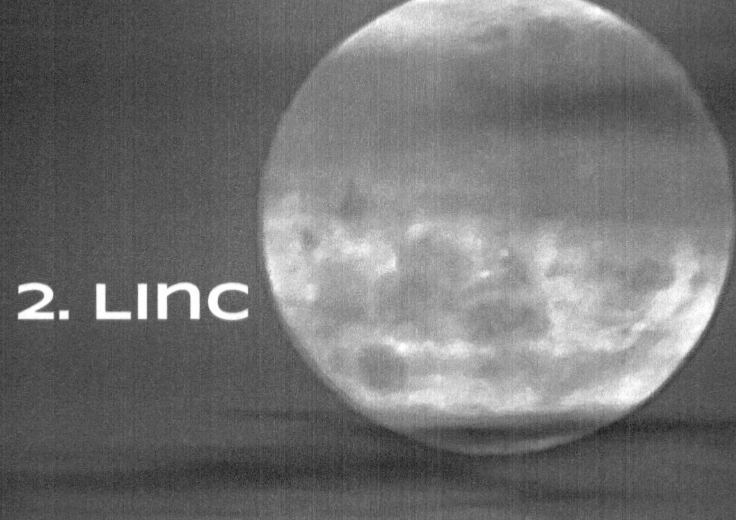

*P*lease *God, get Vela far away from here,* I pray as I race for my life from an enraged grolar bear. The massive white beast is hot on my trail, so I amp up my legs to run faster.

This bear is relentless. I jump over a bush and wish I had Vela's ability to move vegetation out of the way and clear a path. I force thoughts of her from my mind. If I think too much about her now, I'll be distracted, and this bear *will* eat me.

I don't even want to think about what that experience would be like. He or she, I'm not sure what sex this thing is, is hungry, that much is apparent. I don't really care if it's a girl or boy right now, just about getting far enough away to escape its attack.

Dodging massive evergreen trees and smaller ground cover, I pump my arms, forcing my body to a speed I hadn't known I was capable of. Just goes to show what a little adrenaline can do. I hear crashing behind me, and I throw a fireball, hoping it will set a blaze to something and scare the bear off.

I look back as I run and see my fireball landed in a tree. The fireball is too small to catch fire quickly. It'll burn, but not fast enough. That gives me an idea. I run to the nearest pine I can find.

They're easy to spot, and I pull out a final burst of speed, knowing I need to give myself a few seconds to get ahead of this bear. My lungs are burning, and my legs feel like they're going to fall off, but I get far ahead enough to enact my plan.

Skidding to a stop, I plant my feet and blast a decent sized pine with the hottest fire I've got. A whoosh of flames engulfs it in seconds. I skirt around it and hide behind the burning inferno. Pines go up fast, which is just what I need.

The bear catches up to me, but with the heat of the now burning tree, it rears back.

I watch transfixed as burning embers and ash fall onto the grolar bear's white head. It swings its head from side to side, almost as if shaking the ash off. Black ash sticks to its fur, staining it a sickly gray. I see the burns around its neck from our fire ropes earlier. They don't seem to have fazed this gigantic bear.

Inspiration strikes at how I can trap it.

I creep over to the right, slowly, so as not to attract the bear's attention. I advance toward another pine tree behind the bear, getting as close as I dare. Now that I'm no longer ensconced in the safety of the burning tree, my nerves kick into gear again.

The bear watches the tree and inches backward. It looks like it's going to give up and lumber away, but I can't have that. I need to trap it so no one else gets hurt. I think of Claudette taking a swipe to her back and pray she survived that hit. So far, it hasn't hurt Vela, and she's my priority. She needs to be protected from this man-eater.

I'm just close enough to the tree now, so I hold my hands out and send a rush of fire so hot even my hands feel the heat. I blast it as far as I can. I'm not as close this time, but thankfully my aim is good because that tree, too, erupts in an explosion of flames. Small trees next to both burning pines catch fire and soon there's a wall of flames. I turn and shoot fire at the two trees in front of me, and soon I have the bear surrounded.

The bear rears up on its hind legs and seems to know the danger it's in. It falls back to its feet and roars in fury.

The fire and smoke confuse the beast. I can't get any closer to it. I'm too close for comfort as it is, so I decide to let fate do what it will. The fire surrounds the bear and me, but it's not the fire that worries me. Which means I need to go.

Now.

Glad I have fire-resistant clothing, I sprint through the ring of fire and relish the brief energy the heat gives me. Then I try to figure out where I am. I need to see what happened to Vela and the others.

I pray everyone's safe. If I can make my way back to the main trail, I'm pretty sure I'll be able to locate the others.

As I run, I think of Vela and hope to God she's safe. I gave her to Raync to protect with his life. *Please, God, I hope he succeeded.* Rayne will have my unending gratitude if he got her away safely.

The trap must be working because it's keeping the bear from chasing me. As I run back toward the trail, I think about Rayne's pursuit of my Intended. He's been determined to attract her notice since we arrived at the Polar Bear. But there's something more lately, since he's considering the possibility that *Vela* is the Chosen Child. I think about Gene and Jerry, the two men from Saddleback who opened our minds to the possibility that she is the prospective hero of the Elementals.

They claim her birthday, her biological parents, her sign, everything points to her being the One we've all been waiting for.

And who the Extremists are desperately hunting.

When I first heard this line of thinking, I could hardly believe it. Vela won't either. We've considered that our future child might be this elusive hero. But not Vela. If it's true, I will do everything in my power to protect and support her.

When we left on this doomed hike to the other hidden Elemental community, she was furious with me for controlling her beloved dog, Jack, and forcing him to bite Rayne to win a mock battle. She still hadn't forgiven me, and it doesn't sit well with me that things are estranged between us. She is my Intended, my everything, and her silence and lack of trust twists my insides into a painful mess. I need to be back in her good graces.

But first, I need to find her.

Dark feelings of helplessness and worry slash at me. Guilt also torments me. I thought I would never do anything to hurt Vela and look at what I did. I've done exactly what I swore I never would. Abused her trust and violently attacked someone, all because I didn't like the attention he gave her. I'm not exactly proud of myself.

I backtrack to where I ran from the path. That's my best chance of finding everyone. We all scattered at the bear's attack, and it only makes sense for us to go back to where we separated.

I slow to a jog to conserve my energy. My thoughts return to Vela, as they always do. Her beautiful blue eyes and gorgeous face fill my mind. She's a golden-haired angel meant just for me. And she's not just physically stunning. Her heart, her mind, every part of her soul calls to me. I love every part of who she is and who she will be. She's young and has her whole life ahead of her. There's so much more she will do. And, if she really is the long-awaited unifier of our race, she'll have me to help her succeed.

At the thought of Vela's touch, I burn. She's the only one who's ever been able to slay me with just a smile. And her hand in mine, on mine, can stop every thought in my head. No wonder every poet describes love in flowery verses. She makes a kiss more beautiful than any scenic view in the world. I'd drop to my knees to beg her for just one more kiss.

And I wouldn't be ashamed to do it.

My thoughts and heart fill with the love I feel for my Intended. Even if our bond didn't make my heart race, it would anyway. There's no wonder people kill for love. It makes you desperate in a way nothing else can.

I hear crashing in the bushes ahead. I haven't made it back to the main trail, so I peer through the trees. Turning my senses on to feel the heat signature of whoever or whatever is approaching. I pray it's not the bear I left behind. I breathe a sigh of relief when I see who it is.

"Andy!"

The big man turns his head, wearing a look of surprise.

"Linc?" His look of happiness probably matches mine. He waits for me to reach him, then wraps me in a bear hug.

I laugh, wheezing as I slap him on the back. "Have you seen Vela?" I ask when I pull back.

He scrunches his eyebrows and looks around. "No. You're the first one I could find."

My stomach plummets, but I say with my hand on his shoulder, "Okay. Hey, it's good to see that you're alright."

"Do you know where the bear is?" He looks around this time with a nervous glance.

"Don't worry, he or she's way to the west of us. I lost it when I set fire to some pines. I trapped it."

"You didn't kill it?" he asks grimly.

"I'm not sure. I didn't stick around to see if the fire got to it."

"We better go then," he says, his lips pressed together. "Let's go find the others."

I agree. I need Vela in my arms right now more than I need air.

And I'd fight another massive grolar bear to do it.

3. Vela

Painstakingly, Rayne helps me walk to a rockslide so we can climb out of this death trap. Thinking of the boiling water that will soon erupt from this ravine is enough to keep me moving. Even so, each limping step is agony.

Rayne supports the left side of my body. His right arm wraps around me, and his hand grips my right hip as gently as possible. I know he's avoiding my hurt side, but I'm stiff as he holds me. I've only ever let Linc hold me like this, and I don't like that Rayne's touch is warm and not altogether unpleasant.

Every time I lean into him, I get a whiff of his scent, which reminds me of smoke and pine trees. I know it's just his homemade ash and pine needle soap that makes him smell so enticing, but I don't want to think of him in that way.

I need Rayne to be a crutch, and that's all.

I don't need any more confusing emotions roiling through me. First, he told me I'm the Chosen Child and then threw us into this ravine. Our lives are at stake with the threat of the geyser below us and, even when we escape the ravine, we're still stranded in the woods. And yet, my breath comes in a wheeze at the mere thought that *I* could be the Elementals' salvation, *me!*

It's laughable.

"How are you doing?" Rayne asks as he lifts my left side off the ground, leveraging me forward in an attempt to help me walk.

I drag my right leg to catch up to my left. "What do you think?"

He pauses, like he's measuring his words. "I'm not sure. That's why I'm asking."

"I'm just peachy," I snap. Stopping, I put my hand on his chest to stop him from thinking of moving. Panting, I judge how much further we've got to go to even reach the base of the rockslide.

We're about a hundred feet away, but it might as well be a mile.

My face must betray my bleak thoughts because Rayne looks at me sympathetically, then with resolve. "I've had enough. You don't need to suffer." At those words, he stoops and sweeps me up into his arms. Pain roars through my side and I moan, not able to keep it in.

"Sorry, Vela. I should have been more careful."

"I can walk, Rayne," I gasp. Being this close to him is making my senses swim. Before, I was only getting whiffs of his unique scent, but now he's all I'm breathing in.

Leaning away as far as I can manage while in his arms, I'm stiff as a board.

He squeezes gently and laughs. "Relax, Vela. I'm helping you. Not attacking you."

It doesn't feel like it. His nearness, his breath on my cheek, his scent, is assaulting me, and I'm trying and failing to not let it affect me. I can't help but notice his strong arms supporting me. It's like I can feel his every muscle. My heart kicks into a rhythm like I'm running at full speed. All I can think about is our last conversation when he purposely injured himself to be near me. That he wants a chance with me.

No way.

I can't turn my head to address him, or I'll just be that much closer to his perfect lips. So, I stare straight ahead and grit out, "I am relaxing. You're not giving me much choice."

"Should I have asked permission to carry you?" His voice carries a smile in it, so I turn to glare at him.

And find myself the recipient of honey brown eyes studying me with amusement. Flustered to be nose to nose with Rayne, I whip my head away to face our path again.

I wish I could hide my flaming cheeks, but my insides are on fire, too.

Why?

If I was a cursing kind of girl, I'd be a sailor right now. I don't know why Rayne affects me so much, but the fact is, he does. I can usually ignore it, but being this close to him, I can't pretend that Rayne's presence doesn't make my stomach flutter in ways I only want Linc to cause.

Oh, why didn't I forgive Linc before the bear attacked us?

Rayne chuckles and the sound of it makes me grit my teeth.

"What's so funny?" I feel him studying my face, but this time, I refuse to look at him.

"You."

"I don't see how this is in any way amusing."

"If you knew what I did, you'd think this is..."

I can't help myself. I turn and glare at him. "If you say funny, I won't be held responsible for my actions."

He shakes his head and continues to walk. We've almost reached the rockslide.

Thank God. He'll put me down, because there's no way he can climb and carry me, and I'll be able to breathe normally.

"Well?" I ask, grumpily.

"I was going to say interesting."

"Why would you choose that word?" I tense because there's no way he can read my mind. Is there? I wrack my brain for a Neronian or Borean's secondary gift. Please tell me they can't read minds. I come up with nothing.

He cracks a smile.

I bite my lip with worry. I see his smirk in the corner of my eye because I still won't look at him.

We reach the rocks, and I breathe a sigh of relief. I need to be out of these arms.

Rayne doesn't answer me, and I can only be grateful. I don't think I can take any more surprises today.

We face the slide of rocks that's our only saving grace. Now that we're here, it seems impossibly tall and very unstable. There's no way my leg will get me up this avalanche of rocks, boulders, and gravel. It might as well be a flowing volcano, for how hard it will be to ascend.

Rayne must come to the same conclusion because not only does he keep holding me, but he grips under my knees and takes a deep breath. He starts to climb.

I feel his muscles contract each time he places his foot. "Wait! What are you doing?" I splutter.

He ignores me and continues carefully choosing his path, stepping on the largest rocks he can find.

"Rayne, you can't climb this with me in your arms."

He balances on a rock and pants lightly. He ignores me. I tighten my grip on his neck and try not to move, so he doesn't lose his balance.

He jumps to another rock and says, "Vela, I think it's pretty obvious you couldn't climb this if your life depended on it." He pauses. "Which it does, by the way."

A gurgle sounds behind us, and I look over my shoulder. Steam rises out of the ground, warning us to hurry.

"That's my cue," he says, after turning to look at evidence that the geyser is about to go off.

"What do you mean?" Before the last word leaves my mouth, Rayne hikes me up, bringing me even closer to his muscled chest, and starts jumping from rock to rock.

"It's going to blow. We gotta get out of here," he says between breaths.

I squeeze my eyes shut, but curiosity peels them open, and I look over my shoulder to watch this geyser.

Water erupts from the ground in small bursts at first, but soon works up to a powerful explosion of steam and water. Power seems to crackle under Rayne's arms, and I realize his water gift has been boosted with the water now dropping on our heads. Even though it's sizzling.

But when Rayne said the water would be hot, I didn't expect this kind of heat. I flinch as each drop hits me. I feel it blistering my head, hands, anything that's exposed. I'm thankful I'm wearing a jacket and long pants.

I duck my head, trying and failing to protect my face while also craning my neck for a look. Thousands of gallons of water bursts from the ground in one, two, no, now three geysers. No wonder this place fills up with water.

Rayne inhales sharply as the water hits him, too, but he's gotten us halfway up the rockslide. Just when I'm amazed he hasn't lost his balance or tripped, his foot slips off one of the now wet boulders. He tightens his painful hold on me, and I grip his neck with alarm. I force my whimpers to stay in as his hand digs into my hurt side. He doesn't need the distraction of worrying he's hurting me.

He breathes heavily in my ear as he adjusts his footing. "Be as still as you can, Vela."

"Why don't you fly us out of here?" I ask in a tense voice, shaking the hot water out of my eyes. My face is burning from the drops now falling like a hard rain.

"I don't have the energy, or I would. Now, let me concentrate."

I stay still, wincing when the hot plops of water continue hitting my skin. I can only hope they're giving Rayne extra boosts of energy, which he obviously needs if his labored breathing is any indication. My clothes stick to me in a hot mess. I whimper at the burns that are now all over my face, neck, and arms. Though I've experienced worse in the past, these still hurt.

Rayne's chest rises and falls, but he continues his punishing pace, jumping from one boulder to another. He miscalculates the stability of one rock, and it moves as he lands. He squeezes me to him as he leans forward, trying to rebalance his foot.

My breath is squeezed out of me as I'm pressed to his chest. I don't know how much longer I can take it. He lurches to the left and right as he fights to balance us. I breathe again when he succeeds in finding a foothold. Then he grunts as he brings his back foot up to meet his other one and lunges again in a jump that I couldn't do in a million years.

I marvel at his athleticism and praise God that Rayne is as fit as he is. Now that the water has molded our clothes to us, I can easily feel every one of Rayne's impressive muscles.

The pain in my knee and side constantly reminds me why Rayne is forced to attempt the amazing feat of carrying me up these rocks.

I whimper as the scalding water continues to hit us. Two more lunges and Rayne brings us to the top. I look back, and my mouth drops open when I see how far we climbed. Well, how far Rayne climbed while carrying me.

His breath is labored as he pauses to gather the strength he needs to get us further away from the blistering rain. His face drips water, and his skin looks red and angry.

I look sympathetically at the angry welts. Wanting to gift him with something more than thanks, I lay my hand on his neck and infuse my touch with healing warmth. A strange ice coats my veins, and I feel a whisper of wind tickle my hand.

Rayne glances at me in surprise. I look at my hand like it's a foreign appendage.

"Was that..." Rayne asks as he stops midstride, breathing heavily.

Pushing the strange feeling away, I furrow my brows. "Please, just get us out of here."

He gives me a knowing look, but I don't want to acknowledge what we both suspect. I can't have Borean blood in me. As soon as I think that, I realize, I certainly could. I don't know the powers of my parents. Because I don't know who they are. That knowledge only cements that Rayne's assertion could be true.

Thankfully, he doesn't press the issue and turns away. My reluctance to talk seems to push him to walk more quickly. I look around us and see we're in a wooded area, and I'm only too glad to put that ravine of death behind us. I breathe a sigh of relief that mingles with his that we've reached dry land.

He sets me gently on the ground and flops down, putting both his arms over his eyes, blocking out the sun. He breathes heavily, and I look him over. His arms and face are covered in scalded skin.

"You weren't kidding when you said that water would be hot."

He nods but doesn't speak. I don't mind. I say a prayer of thanks and let my head fall back as I lean on my left arm.

I listen as the geysers shoot water into the sky and fill the rocky ravine floor. Now that I'm out of immediate danger, it sounds soothing in a way. The sun hits my burned skin, but I almost don't care. Rayne not only got us out of the ravine, but he did it in record time. But I'm completely drenched. I must look like a drowned rat. My hair is plastered to my neck and hangs limply around my shoulders and arms. My clothes are clinging to me uncomfortably, my pants soaked and heavy. I sigh as I look down at my jacket. It protected some of my sweatshirt, but most of it is wet.

I chuckle. "Nothing like geysers to get you moving."

He grunts but continues trying to get his breath back.

I sit, feeling guilty that I couldn't help get us out of that terrible situation.

"Rayne, thank you," I say with as much feeling as I can infuse into my voice.

His chest still rises and falls, but his breathing is calming down. He waves his hand in response, and I wait for him to be ready to talk to me.

I try not to despair over our situation. How are we going to find everyone else in the state I'm in? I can't expect Rayne to carry me everywhere.

Taking a deep breath, I refuse to allow myself to dwell on the overwhelming obstacles we still face. We're alive. The bear is nowhere near us, and we're out of that deadly ravine.

I'll count those as huge wins.

One thing I can do is start looking around at the plants around us. There has to be something I can use to help with the pain rocketing through me.

My heart squeezes painfully at being away from Jack and not knowing if Linc is safe. But I'm determined to make the most of this situation. I call for Jack again and hang my head when I still hear no barking reply.

4. LINC

"When did you last see Vela?" Andy asks me, his face pinched in worry as we walk in long strides back to where we lost the others.

I try not to let his worry transfer to me. *She has to be okay.* "I sent her off with Rayne, and they ran in the opposite direction, away from the grolar bear, away from me."

"You led the bear away from her," he says, nodding his head.

"As best I could. They ran east. That's all I know."

Andy's head bobs again, and he looks in that direction. "I haven't ever been in that part of the woods, so I don't know what's over there."

I shrug because I have no idea either. But my imagination goes wild. I picture a raging river carrying Vela off, wolves on the hunt for their next meal, even another grolar bear.

Shaking my head, I try to clear it of all worries.

"If she's with Rayne, I'm sure she's fine," Andy says in a reassuring tone. "He's capable of making it on his own. He'll take care of her."

Just as long as he doesn't take too good care of her.

My fear of Vela choosing Rayne over me crashes down again. Ever since I laid eyes on the guy, I knew he was going to be trouble. Anyone with looks like his is bound to attract all the feminine attention he wants.

Vela's different.

She wouldn't allow him to turn her head just because of his pretty face. She values honor and integrity over anything else. Two things I'm not sure Rayne has a lot of. He's got my hackles up, that's for sure.

I think that much was clear when I sicced Jack on him. I cringe when I think of what I had Jack do to my nemesis. I definitely did not plan for Jack to bite him like that. I allowed my anger and adrenaline to get fired up and it ended up really hurting the guy.

The worst part is that I lost Vela's trust. I can handle her cold shoulder. I had to for the first few weeks I knew her. It's disappointing her that's killing me. I let her down and in the worst way.

I'll get it back. If it's the last thing I ever do.

"Linc, did you hear me?" Andy asks, concern knitting his brow.

"Sorry, what did you say?"

"I said we have about a couple hours of daylight left. Let's hope we can find everyone before it gets dark."

I nod grimly. It will be difficult enough to round everyone up in the daylight, let alone in the dark. And I do not want Vela spending the night alone with *Rayne.*

At that disturbing thought, I pick up my pace; Andy matches my stride easily.

My ears strain to hear any other footsteps in this wooded area. I'm also half expecting the grolar bear to come upon us again, but I hope the fire trap took care of it. As much as I hate the thought of killing an animal with my fire, it's unfortunately the only outcome we can hope for. That bear is too deadly to be walking among us. I don't want to be hunted. I've had enough of that to last a lifetime.

Extending my senses, I try to pick up on any heat signatures. I come up with nothing.

"We'll hit some marshes soon. Let's hope no one got lost in one of those." Andy's deep voice carries his concern.

"The last time we went through one, we were in a Sherp," I say as I remember that terrifying ride getting Vela to Hannah in Polar Bear for healing.

Andy's lips compress into a thin line. "It's not easy to walk through. It can be done; you kind of have to jog over it lightly. If you try to stand still, you'll sink pretty quickly. Gene and Jerry were going to coach us in the proper technique."

"And now we're separated." I add, frowning.

"Right. Let's hope we find them before we come across a marsh."

I cast my senses out again, hoping...

Andy and I both turn to the left at the same time. "Do you feel that?" I ask in a quiet voice.

Several bodies are coming toward us. Andy must feel the same heat signatures. "I do. They feel bigger than wolves. I think."

"They're almost too far away to tell," I agree.

We start walking toward them. Andy is as quiet as I am, and when we get close enough, I can tell it's people coming toward us and not wolves.

Andy must be able to sense that too, because he breathes a sigh of relief.

"Let's hope Vela is in the group," I say, my heart in my throat.

I start running, Andy keeping up with me. After a minute, I see the people, but it's not anyone we know. They're all carrying rifles and notice Andy and I immediately.

We slow to a walk and Andy says, "They look like indigenous folk."

I nod, trying not to show my disappointment that we didn't find Vela.

Andy raises his hand to the four men, but they don't seem too surprised by our presence.

I study their features. Two have short, cropped hair and the others have long plaits. All sport smooth tan skin and intelligent eyes that seem to see everything. They wear jeans and coats, the same as Andy and me.

"Hello," Andy says when they reach us.

One of the men steps forward and clasps hands with Andy, and even I can see it's a firm shake. "What brings two Fire men out here?" the man's voice rumbles.

It's then that I reel back at the shock of feeling Elemental *and* human sensations coming from these four men. Andy has the same realization I do, and he steps back with wide eyes.

Two of the men are human, but that's not what surprises me. The leader and another are Elementals, except not like what I'm used to feeling. The usual sensations a Borean and Neronian would give are somehow diluted. That's the only way I can describe it. Instead of my blood icing over in the presence of a Borean, it just cools. Near a Neronian, my blood usually rushes through me like a river, but right now I'm only feeling a trickle. That can only mean one thing.

"How is that possible?" I whisper, shock clogging my throat.

The leader looks at us with understanding in his eyes. "You have never met a First Nation man before?" he asks with a wry grin.

Andy and I both shake our heads.

"Come, we'll walk and talk." He gestures ahead and we fall into step beside him.

The leader chuckles. "My people did not start such as yours did. We allowed humans to live among us, even marry and have children with us. My name is Waban. I am of the Wind, but I'm not like you. Not completely."

"We are Fire Elementals, but you are…" Andy says in an awed tone, like he's as confused as I am.

"My name means East Wind. For when I was a child, I created a great wind that blew from the east. It was stronger than what most of us with the Wind could do. So, I was named Waban."

"But you're not…" I start to say.

"I *am* of the Wind, but not fully. My mother was human. My father's mother, too, was human. It was my father who was of the Wind."

If we weren't all walking together, I would have stood in shock. Humans and Elementals intermixing and intermarrying? I had never heard of such a thing before. Neither, it seems, had Andy.

He splutters, "Your mother and grandmother are human?"

"Yes. I have some of your blood, you…Elementals," he says slowly. "But not all."

I turn to the other man, who is part Neronian. "And you have a similar story?" He nods.

The leader says, "Yes, but where I am of the Wind, he is of the Water."

I try to comprehend, but it's not easy. "We've done so much as a race to keep our powers hidden."

Waban nods, as do the others. One of the humans in their group says, "We have made a pact to never speak of our people's gifting to any other Non-blood."

"Non-blood?" Andy asks.

Waban answers this time. "Those without the Gift."

"Humans," I clarify.

They all nod.

I push all that they've told us to the back of my mind and refocus on our desperate search. Waving my hands, I ask, "Please, tell us, have you seen a teen girl with long blonde hair and a guy with short blonde hair?"

Waban looks at the others, but they all shake their heads. "What are you doing this far north? We have not seen any of your kind in a long time."

"We were hiking to a settlement to the west when we were attacked by a huge white bear," Andy answers. "We all split up to escape."

Waban's eyebrows lift. "A *white* bear? Like a polar bear?" He looks at us curiously, like he doesn't believe us.

"Yes, it's called a grolar bear," I answer grimly. "It's a mix between a grizzly and a polar bear. And it's vicious. It chased us all through the woods. I managed to trap it between some burning trees, but it might have gotten free."

Waban looks over his shoulder at the other men and looks back at me. "We have heard of this bear. We are hunting it but have not found it yet."

"You don't want to," Andy says in somber tones. "It's going to be very hard to kill."

Waban looks at us with a gleam in his eye. "I am a very good shot. All I need is one good look."

"Well, then I'm glad you're with us," Andy says. "I dropped my rifle and only have my fire gift to protect me and my friend."

Waban nods. "Where are you two going?"

I answer, "We're making our way back to where we last saw our friends. So, this way." I point to the north, and we all walk in that direction.

"We would like to help you find your friends, but we also must be sure the bear is dead. Our community is not too far away, and we don't want it to get too close."

"We understand," Andy's deep voice intones. "Linc, tell them where you last saw it and we'll be on our way."

I nod behind and to the left. "It's back that way. Look for the smoke from the trees I lit on fire."

"Thank you. If you come upon any of my people, tell them my name and they will help you with whatever you need."

Andy and I thank him as the men turn around in search of the bear. I shake my head, marveling at their bravery.

"They do know that thing's man-eating, right?" I ask Andy.

He nods grimly and we resume our trek. "They know. That's why all of them are armed."

I can only say a prayer for their safety as we continue our own search.

5. Vela

Soon Rayne has his breathing under control, and he looks over at me. "You're a Borean, or half," he says in a solemn tone. "I couldn't sense it in you until you demonstrated the gift, but I did. I felt it." He puts both hands on the ground and pushes himself into a standing position. "Sandy is a Gyan and her husband, James, is a Borean. Vela, that makes sense for you to demonstrate the wind gift."

I study the plant life around us, ignoring his statement.

"Vela, you can't hide from this."

"I'm not hiding, I'm ignoring. There's a stark difference."

He huffs a sigh.

I continue to evaluate the plants to see if there's anything I can use to alleviate my discomfort.

"What are you doing?" he asks.

"I'm trying to find something that can help me with the pain."

He puts his hands on his waist. "We need to talk about this new power you have."

I ignore him and continue to scan the ground all around me.

"Vela."

"How do I know that wasn't your power I felt?" I snap, quickly losing patience.

"I would know if I was expending my wind gift. I wasn't. That was all you."

Desperate to prove him wrong, I blurt, "It was too small of a breeze to say it was anything but the actual wind."

He pins me with a look that shows he doesn't buy my pitiful answer. "I sensed your gift. It was fleeting. But that's how it starts. I think you know what this means."

"I don't," I stubbornly say.

"Vela. The Chosen One will be a child of two elemental parents. It makes sense that your second gift would start emerging before your eighteenth birthday, if you have a Borean parent."

"But that's almost a year away! It couldn't have been me." I hold on to my refusal. I'm not admitting anything.

"That's about right. Small signs start appearing a year or so before your gift completely solidifies. Vela, you're also a Wind Elemental."

I stiffen in shock and shake my head. "I don't want to believe it," I whisper. Panic floods through me and my breath quickens.

He seems to take pity on me and changes the subject. "Well, tell me what plant to look for, and I'll help you search. But first we need to get out of these wet clothes. I have a trick that will dry them quickly. But we will have to remove them first."

I grimace, remembering I don't have any extra clothes. But then think of what the trick could be. He's a personal dryer with his wind gift. "Well, I dropped my backpack when we were running from the bear, thinking I could always go back for it. But then you had the brilliant idea to throw us off a cliff. So, I don't have any clothes." My voice is flat, and I hope it expresses my supreme displeasure at being stuck out here.

His backpack is still on his back, and he shrugs it off his shoulders and starts digging through it. "I can let you borrow some of mine."

I glare at him. "How do you expect your pants to fit me?"

With a flourish, he produces a rope, and with a lift of his eyebrow and without taking his eyes off me, takes his knife that's strapped to his leg and cuts off a section.

I stare down at my wet clothes and frown. *How am I going to get out of these skinny pants with my knee like this?*

Rayne seems to have the same thought, because when my face heats, he quirks a grin. "I can help," he says.

"With your wind gift?" I ask, my eyebrow raised.

He chuckles. "If I use my wind to dry your clothes with you wearing them, you'll blow away. No, I meant I could help you remove them."

"I'd rather sit here in wet clothes for days than have your help undressing."

A wide grin spreads on his face.

"Stop smiling like that," I snap at him. "And I mean it. You are *not* helping me change." Mortification swims through me, but another emotion tops it: resolve.

He chuckles at my embarrassment and says, "As much as I'd enjoy helping you, you need to change, one way or another. The temperature is going to drop soon, and you'll freeze to death in those wet clothes."

I stifle a sigh when I realize he's right. "Okay," I say reluctantly. I move to take my jacket off and hiss a breath of pain as my side erupts in pain too intense to ignore.

Giving up, I hang my head. "I'm useless." I mourn for the day I could move without pain ripping through me.

Rayne walks over and squats next to me. "Sorry, Vela." His eyes reflect sympathy, and his look practically pushes me over the edge.

I force down tears of frustration. They won't help me right now and will only remind me of my absolute helplessness. I fight for composure. "Can you at least leave the area so I can do this?" Even if he keeps his eyes closed, I don't want an audience for how much this is going to hurt.

He studies me, then nods curtly, putting his hand on my shoulder in comfort. Pushing himself up, he then walks over to grab the clothes he took out of his bag. He drops them beside me and leaves.

Once I'm alone, I study my predicament. I have skinny jeans on and they're wet. This is going to hurt.

Not having much choice, I start on my top. First, I shrug out of my jacket slowly. Then, taking a bracing breath, I carefully pull the sodden sweatshirt off. Agony rips through my side as I lift it over my head. I pant as I get my bearings again.

I breathe in and out of my nose and reach for Rayne's sweatshirt.

Rayne calls out from the trees, "Vela, how's it going? Are you okay?"

I don't want to lie, but I also don't want him to worry. "It's not easy, but I'm okay. I'm halfway done."

Sort of. I still need to put Rayne's sweatshirt on.

I hold it up to my chin, giving myself a well-needed pep talk. *I can do this. Once it's on, I won't have to do it again before we find the others and I'm healed.*

Thanking God for Tonya and her Gyan gift, I bury my face in the sweatshirt. I can't help but notice Rayne's scent as I breathe, and I take a minute to inhale deeply. It's almost like burning pine needles.

I can't help but think of Linc as I do and guilt washes through me. I should not be appreciating Rayne's scent. Besides, it's not nearly as good as how Linc smells to me. Nothing can compare to the fire and marshmallow I love to breathe in when I'm with my Intended.

An intense feeling of sadness rips through my chest. I miss Linc so much at this moment. Why didn't I make up with him on the hike to Saddleback? Now, we're separated, and I'd give anything to bury my face in *his* shirt right now.

Shaking my head and focusing on what I need to do, I take a deep breath and pull the sweatshirt on over my head in one quick motion. I can't help but cry out.

"Vela? Are you okay? What happened?" Rayne calls out from his hidden spot in the woods.

I take a second to call out, "I think so."

"What do you mean, you think so? You are or you aren't."

"Give me a minute," I beg as dots swim before my eyes.

I look down at my legs as I work on getting my breath back. When I think of taking off my pants, I cringe. If it hurt to take off my loose sweatshirt, what's it going to feel like to peel off my tight, wet jeans?

I know I have to do this, but I don't want to. I'm almost tempted to ask Rayne for his knife so I can cut these pants off me, but I know I'll need them when they're dry.

While I'm talking myself into what I have to do, Rayne calls out, "Do you need my help?"

Mortification fills me at the thought of Rayne taking off my pants. "No, I can do it."

I'm going to have to lie down all the way for this. Or else I won't get them all the way off. But when I slip my hands through the dirt to lean back, I cry out. My side screams at me and tears pop out of my eyes.

I hear Rayne swear in the distance. I take a full minute to let the pain ebb. My chest rises and falls in time with my harsh breathing.

Taking a deep breath, I pull the pants off in one quick motion, whimpering when they pass over my hurt knee, the motion shooting hot pain through my leg. I hear Rayne moving in the brush, and I look up to see he's walking toward me with his eyes shut, holding his arms out and walking blind.

"I can't not help you, Vela. You *need* me, so please let me do something. I can't sit there listening to you suffer," he says with his eyes shut.

He's halfway to me when I shout, "I got everything off! I'm *fine*, Rayne."

He's close enough that he can hear me breathing heavily, so I know he can tell I'm not fine. He pauses. "Just let me help you. I swear I won't look. I can't just do nothing."

"Rayne, this is something I have to do. I'm in pain, that's true, but there's nothing you can do to stop that."

"Fine. Just tell me if you need me."

Reluctantly, I nod. But, knowing he can't see me doing that, I say, "Okay, but whatever you do, don't open your eyes. No matter what you hear."

This time, his concerned face transforms into a smile. "Will you say that if a pack of wolves comes in here?"

I snort. "Okay, if my life is in imminent danger, I'll allow you to open your eyes."

"Thank you," he says sincerely. He stands with his arms at his sides, and I confirm that he still has his eyes squeezed shut.

It's much easier getting Rayne's pants on than it was to take mine off, and I finish dressing quickly.

I say, "You can look now. I'm dressed."

Rayne opens his eyes, walks up, and looks me over. He returns my smile with a wide grin of his own. "You did it."

"Just as long as you didn't look," I add, a smile on my face. "Thank you, Rayne."

His eyes twinkle, and I narrow my eyes.

"I mean it, Rayne. You didn't look, right?"

He shows his hands, his eyebrows flying up. "I swear, I didn't. Your wish was my command."

I look down when my insides go wild with butterflies or *whatever* this is I'm feeling. Rayne makes me crazy; I can't help having a visceral reaction to him. I ruthlessly stamp it down.

Rayne inhales deeply, and I peek up at him. His expression looks torn. He starts to walk closer to me, and I study him, curious at his reaction. But he just shakes his head and wipes all emotion from his face. Just like with a light switch, his mood changes. He quirks a grin. "I could very easily say a lot of inappropriate things right now, but I won't."

"I appreciate that," I say dryly. "But I am thankful."

"You would have appreciated me more if I had helped *more*."

I can't help it. I bark a laugh, but then hold my side and stop. "You just can't help yourself, can you?"

His eyes twinkle. "I guess not. Now, let's see if we can't get a move on. We'll need to make shelter for the night." He waggles his eyebrows. "To spend the night alone, together."

I throw a stick at him in response.

But he's right. I will be spending a lot of time with him, and I never wanted that.

One thing is for sure. He's more than proved he can be incredibly supportive when I need him to be. I shake my head. If that isn't confusing, I don't know what is.

6. LINC

For the millionth time, I wonder what Vela is doing right now. Is Rayne taking advantage of his time alone with her, trying to sway her emotions?

I scoff. *Of course he is.*

My emotions vacillate between anger and despair that he'll have who knows how long to woo Vela into forgetting about me.

I can't help but feel like I'm on a runaway train, careening wildly off the track with no control over where my thoughts carry me. Images of Rayne and Vela together... kissing... his hands all over her, assault me.

"Argh!" I hold my head in my hands to stop myself from going crazy.

Andy stops walking and puts his hand on my shoulder. "What is it? Are you okay?"

No. I lift my head and shake it. "It's nothing."

Andy studies the side of my face as we walk. "It doesn't look like nothing. You look worried."

Because I am.

He's quiet for a moment before he says, "It's better to let it out than keep it in. Things have a way of imploding on us if we aren't careful."

I'm going to implode alright at this rate. Preferably when I'm standing right next to Rayne.

I take a deep breath and pause for several minutes. I finally say, "Rayne has Vela all to himself and I *know* he's taking full advantage of it." I look at Andy meaningfully and his lips thin in displeasure.

"He knows you have an Intended bond with her. What could possibly compare with that?"

I laugh darkly. "Plenty. Have you taken a good look at him recently?"

I'd love to rearrange that pretty little face of his.

Andy smiles and squeezes my shoulder. "You have a claim on that girl's heart. There's no way she will just throw that away."

I hope so. "Yes, but he'll do whatever he can to win her. I'm worried about his methods."

Andy laughs. "Linc, if you could see Vela's face every time you walk into a room, you'd have no doubts about this. Trust me, my friend, that girl is yours. Forever."

She lights up when I'm in the room? How have I never noticed that?

We resume walking, and my spirits lift a fraction. He's right. Vela does love me. I can't hide the smile that takes over my face at the memory of when she told me. The night I proposed, when she promised to be *my* girl.

But that was before Rayne Williamson came into her life and tried to steal her from me.

My stomach clenches.

I try not to say anything more, but words spill out of me before I can stop them. "Of course, I'm worried! I know my Vela and I can tell, despite her best efforts, she's interested in him. His secret weapon is that he makes her flustered. That's his way in. If he didn't have any kind of impact on her, I wouldn't be the least bit worried. But he does."

With every word, my heart sinks further and further. I have to find her. I need to be there with her, if only to remind her of her Intended feelings when she's around me. She only gets those with *me.* I take ferocious pleasure in that.

"Okay, let's address each point you've made." His shoulder bumps into mine in a friendly reminder he's there for me. "One, they're alone. So what? She has an *Intended bond* with you and only you. And she's been alone with him before, yet she's still your girl."

He gives me a hard look, making sure I'm paying attention. I'm following every word, drinking them in.

"Two, he's a good-looking guy. Again, so what? His personality will soon show her who he truly is on the inside. That has discouraged many a romance, believe me, when someone gets to know the truth about a person."

I frown. *I don't like the sound of the word "romance," when it comes to Rayne and Vela.*

Then I lift my eyebrows. "Is he a bad guy, Andy? I hate him, but that's a given since he's trying to steal my girl. I haven't really gotten a read on him."

Suddenly, fresh worries assault me.

Is Vela safe with him?

Did I make the biggest mistake of my life sending her off with a dangerous person?

Andy waves his hand. "No, it's not like that. He has a good enough character, I suppose. I mean, that he will irritate her soon enough. He's full of confidence, rather cocky, which Vela won't be attracted to."

I can't help but feel relieved, but then irritation fills me. "Why not? Confidence is a good trait. Most girls love that."

I'm second guessing this pep talk.

He looks at me with a wry expression. "We're talking about Vela, right? She likes a confident man. You are a prime example. But overconfidence? No," he says, shaking his shaggy head. "She won't like that. Trust me, from what I've seen of Vela, she will not appreciate that side of him."

I muse silently. *Maybe he's right.*

She certainly didn't like it when I trapped her in the stairwell when we first met. It wasn't until I offered a way out that her eyes had lit up with interest.

"Okay. Maybe. The third point?"

He falls silent for a minute. "Hmmm, when you say she's interested, how do you know that?"

"If I know anyone on this planet, it's Vela. Rayne gets under her skin. He's like a maggot. It's only a matter of time before she starts to acknowledge he's turned her head."

Andy's laugh shakes me from my thoughts. The booming sound practically shakes the trees. "Do you hear yourself? She will enjoy a maggot getting under her skin? No, no, no. Listen to yourself." He stops walking and turns to face me, putting both hands on my shoulders. "That girl is in love with *you*. Rayne might be a blip on her radar, but you, my friend, are the only ship she notices. She will only see you and love you."

I slap my hand on his shoulder, bolstered, and we start walking again.

Oh God, please tell me he's right.

"How can you be so sure?" I ask, my nerves tied all up in knots.

Andy smiles again. "I may not have ever been married, but I observe those who are in a loving relationship. It's something I wish for myself, so I pay attention to the signs. Yours is one of those. Don't worry."

I fall silent and let his words sink into me. I wonder if I should bring up Hannah. It's so obvious he has feelings for her. Will he talk to me about it?

If Vela were here, she would definitely ask. Fine, I'll do it for her. "So, is there anyone in your life you'd like to be something more?"

He grins and pulls a branch half hanging off a tree and breaks it into smaller pieces. "There is. I would do anything to turn her friendly feelings to romantic, but I'm not having much luck." He throws the end of the branch away and sighs heavily. "Oh, I don't know. Maybe I'm meant to be a bachelor all my life. Because if I can't have her, I'm not sure there's anyone else for me."

I know how he feels.

This time, I lay my hand on his shoulder and squeeze. "Andy, if I know anything about women, you have to tell them you're interested. Make it clear."

He glances at me, then looks away. He laughs softly. "I've been that obvious, have I? You know who it is?"

I smile at him. "Well, to be honest, it was Vela who sniffed out your interest, back at your house when she first met you."

He barks a laugh. "Well, then everyone must know, because if Vela knew before she even met Hannah, then I'm doomed." He looks at me with his eyebrow raised. "If I'm that transparent to everyone, then what more can I do to get her attention?"

"When I say make it clear, I mean, bring gifts, show affection, *tell her* how you feel."

His face reddens, and he coughs a laugh. "I'm not good at those things."

I chuckle. "Most men aren't. That's why women are the queens of romance."

Have I done a good job of romancing Vela?

He nods. This time, he's thinking. I can see the wheels turning in his mind. I let him think over what I said, hoping his advice was as good as mine.

7. Vela

N ow that we've gotten that horribly embarrassing clothes changing situation out of the way, I can concentrate on finding plants that will help me with this throbbing pain. I would do anything for some wild lettuce or the bark of a white willow tree.

But first, I want to finish healing Rayne's burns. "Rayne, before we leave this spot, let me take care of those burns on your arms and face."

He turns from studying the plants and walks back toward me. I told him the plant to look for, so he was searching the areas I couldn't see from my position on the ground.

"Did you see anything?"

"Tell me again what wild lettuce looks like?" he asks.

"The easiest way to describe it is that the leaves look like maple leaves but a lot skinnier. And they'd be grouped together closely. See anything like that?"

He frowns and shakes his head. I notice his skin is redder in some areas than others, but it's clear it's uncomfortable for him. He rubs his neck where I healed it earlier. "I don't want you to heal my burns."

"Why not?" I look at him curiously.

He cocks his head and studies my face, looking at the burns I know I have. My face is tender to the touch, but it's nothing like the pain in my side and knee, so I'm easily ignoring it.

"It's not fair for my burns to be healed, and for you to continue to suffer. I won't do it. If you're suffering, then I will, too."

"Rayne, that's silly. Let me heal you."

"No." His voice is unyielding.

I search his face for misplaced sympathy but only see a grim resolve. A warm feeling comes over me at Rayne's unnecessary consideration.

"Rayne, I know you're just being nice," I say awkwardly, because I really don't know what to say.

"Why should you heal me when you can't heal yourself? Tell me how that's fair?"

My mouth opens and closes like a fish out of water. I've never had someone refuse healing before. But I've also never been in this situation. I grew up in a Gyan family. I've always been healed quickly. I look down, messing with the hemline of Rayne's huge sweatshirt. "Umm, well..."

"Anyway, I can handle a little pain. It really just feels like a bad sunburn more than anything."

I pick my head up. "How did you not get injured in the fall, anyway?"

Rayne hangs his head and puts his hands on his hips. "Vela, I need to apologize for your injuries. They're really all my fault. I dropped you at the last second when we landed, and that's why you're hurt so badly. I'm sorry, Vela."

His eyes beg me to forgive him for something that he could not control.

"Rayne, it was an accident. It's not like you meant to drop me."

"I know. You just slipped out of my hands." He hangs his head and shakes it.

I wave my hand. "It's fine," I say as reassuringly as I can.

He looks away for a minute, then turns back. "We really should find a better spot to set up camp for the night."

"Okay." I look around and see our spot is sparse with trees and, like the ravine, is rocky. Not a comfortable place to sleep, for sure. I inhale deeply and get ready for his help to stand. I remember all too well how painful it was the last time.

He moves behind me and slips his arms under mine. "I'll be more careful this time," he promises. The heat of his breath on my ear again sends a flutter through me, which I pointedly ignore.

He chuckles softly, again, and this time, I stop him. "Why are you laughing?"

He pauses. "No reason. Now, let's go."

Before I can comment, he eases me up, much slower this time. And, after a couple seconds of heart-stopping pain, I can breathe again.

"You, okay?" he asks, his voice sending a shooting thrill through me. He supports my waist, and his warm fingers distract me. I'm balancing on one foot, not wanting to put any pressure on my leg.

I inhale, deeply flustered. "This time was much better. Thank you." I hate that I'm noticing his touch. *I shouldn't. Even though Linc and I are fighting, I'm still his.*

He quirks a grin and moves over to my left side. He waits for me to lift my arm over his head, and I grudgingly comply. "You know, this really would be easier if I just carried you."

"I'm not going to allow you to carry me the whole time. I need to do some of the walking."

With my arm around his neck, I feel him tense. "Vela, there's nothing wrong with being injured."

I allow some of my frustration out. "Rayne, we have a long way to walk. You cannot carry me the whole way. I need to do some of this."

He's quiet for a moment. "You don't think I can."

"I don't think you *should.* There's a difference."

At that, he puts one foot forward, and I mimic him, wanting my steps to be in line with his. After that, it takes all my concentration to hold my side and drag my left foot.

It's laborious and slow going, but we get some distance behind us.

I'm doing everything I can to keep up with the snail's pace. I fight with my emotions as we go. Fierce resolve to keep up is soon replaced with an utter sense of loss at all I used to be able to do with ease. I'm using every muscle I own just to put one foot in front of the other. I won't allow myself to be more of a burden than I already am.

By the time Rayne stops, I'm breathing hard, and sweat drips into my eyes.

"I think I can make us a camp here," he says, not out of breath at all. *Smug uninjured person.* "I have food for a couple of days and water isn't a problem."

Right, because he's a Neronian.

We've arrived in a clearing with trees surrounding us and pine needles carpeting the ground.

I take my arm off his shoulder when he moves behind me. I try to get my breathing under control as the heavy panting only makes the pain in my side worse.

I can't help but feel a huge sense of frustration at my injuries and utter helplessness. A sob climbs my throat, and I push it down. Tears gather in my eyes, and I squeeze them shut to prevent them from slipping down my cheeks. But that only makes them fall, anyway.

Rayne moves to stand in front of me. I turn my head so he can't see my poorly concealed emotions. He must have caught a look, because he crooks a finger and puts it under my chin, turning my head toward him. "Hey," he says softly. "What is this?" He cradles my head and, with his thumbs, wipes my tears away.

When I look at him and see the compassion written all over his face, I burst into ugly sobs. I wrench my head away and bury it in his shoulder so he can't see my loss of control.

He holds me as I press my misery into his chest. He rubs his hands on my back in circles. "It's okay, Vela. Let it out. You'll feel better for it."

With his words of encouragement, I give vent to all my feelings. Being unprepared for this injury, fighting with and being separated from Linc, the bear chasing us down, being flung off a cliff, missing Jack more than I can breathe. It all rests on Rayne's soon wet jacket. I appreciate the feeling of comfort he gives. He's been wonderful through all of this. Besides his insane thought that I'm the Chosen Child, he's been remarkably understanding and supportive of my bad mood and outlook.

I pick my head up and swipe my arm under my nose. Rayne steadies me like before. I laugh softly. "I guess it's too much to ask for a tissue out here."

He bends his knees to look me in the eye. "I haven't said it yet, but I think you're doing amazing."

I scoff. "You're kidding, right? I've been one complaint after another since we ended up down in that ravine."

He smiles at me. "No, you've been dealt a harsh blow. And you've handled it the best you can."

I duck my chin so he can't see my flush of embarrassment. My cheeks warm. "Well, thank you, but I think I've been a bit of a brat. I'll make an effort to be better."

He pulls me in for another hug and rests his chin on my head. I let myself relax for a minute as I feel his voice rumbling in his chest. "Maybe you just needed to finish crying it out. My mom always says that's the best way to get your fight out."

At his words, I pull back and look up at him, my eyebrows drawn down. "Get your fight out?"

He grins. "Yeah, she's always said that when I cried about things and my dad told me to stop crying and man up." His grin slips and a look of pain crosses his face.

I put my hand on his chest. "Rayne, I'm so sorry. You were just a kid when he said that?" I frown in anger.

He laughs harshly. "Don't feel too bad. He toughened me up." He looks away, but not before I see another flash of pain cross his face.

"Hey, don't say that. It sounds like he was being incredibly unfair."

"Unfair or not, it worked. I don't cry much anymore. But when I did, my mom helped me through it."

I huff angrily. If a man needs to cry about something, he should feel the freedom to do it. I understand most men don't cry openly, but there's nothing wrong with it.

His face looks closed off when I glance up at him. I won't push him to talk about this. But I take it as a personal challenge to convince him that it's okay if a man cries.

"How about we find a comfortable place for you to sit down?" he asks, looking around where we stopped.

I smile up at him, my feelings conflicted. I'm angry at Rayne's father for making him feel like less than a man for showing his emotions. But I'm also incredibly thankful for

Rayne's support throughout this entire time. I marvel at the ability of the human spirit to be so compassionate and understanding, and I'm suddenly incredibly appreciative of Rayne. He's been himself, snarky and cocky, but he's also been more. When I needed him, he's been unflinchingly at my side. He'll make an incredible husband one day, of that, I'm sure. Just not mine, I tell myself firmly.

Why does the thought make me squirm uncomfortably?

Shaking off the thought, I push down my strange feelings and nod at Rayne. He moves behind me to help me sit down. "Let's do this nice and slow," he rumbles into my ear.

Again, I'm thrown off by the feelings cascading into me at his words and hot breath in my ear.

He inhales quickly, but he slowly eases me down onto the ground. I'm almost getting used to the pain in my side and my body goes limp in his arms. Suddenly I feel exhausted.

"Maybe help me lie down? I need to rest."

"Of course," he says.

Rayne is quick to brace me as I go into a halfway lying down position. It helps enormously that he's behind me as I do this; the pain is hardly even there. He sits down behind me, and I lean my back on his chest, sighing at the comfort of not doing this by myself.

He's suddenly stock still as I rest against him. Then he relaxes and puts his arms loosely around me, wordlessly supporting me.

Soaking in his comfort, I say after a moment, suddenly aware of how close we are, "Okay, I think I'm ready to lie down."

"You got it," he says quickly. He lifts himself into a squat, so he can brace me with his arms and lower me the rest of the way to the ground.

When I'm lying down on my back, I look up at the blue sky, and Rayne takes a shirt from his bag and cushions my head. It's damp from our wet clothes he stuffed in his pack.

"We should probably lay out the clothes that got wet," I suggest.

He smirks. "I'm going to dry them, remember?" He fishes out our sodden clothes and lying them on the ground, he stands on the edge of the first shirt, holds out his hands, and blows a strong wind at it. It flutters under his foot, and after several minutes, I can see it's dry as a bone.

I laugh in delight. "Too bad you couldn't do that with us wearing them."

He turns his head to look at me. "I would have blown you off your feet if I did."

I nod in understanding. He continues down the line of clothes until all the wet clothes are now dry.

When he's finished, he folds the clothes up and places them in his backpack.

"How are you feeling??" Rayne asks, turning to look at me.

"You know, if we weren't in the middle of nowhere and I wasn't in extreme pain, I'd say not bad."

"I'm glad to hear it." He sounds distracted, and I look over at him.

He's looking around at what appears to be an unremarkable wooded area. I can't figure out what he's so puzzled by, so I ask, "Everything okay?"

"Vela, when I told you that you're the Chosen Child, why were you so against being our hope?" he asks, a line forming between his eyes.

His light brown eyes spear into mine, and I glance away to avoid his attempt to look into my soul. "It's just overwhelming to even consider it. Does that make sense?"

He nods solemnly and says nothing.

His silence encourages me to continue speaking. "I've been a Gyan my whole life. And suddenly in less than a month, I have an Intended, I find out I'm adopted and now…" I say, my voice hoarse. "Now, I'm the Elemental savior?" I look back at him. "I can't wrap my head around it."

He nods again, studying his hands. "When I was little, that was all my friends and I would talk about. Leon made up stories about what he would do if he was the Chosen Child. I listened, but it was too fantastic for me to even consider. It was a dream. Then, when I learned I needed to have a certain birthdate, and my parents, too, and I knew it wasn't me, or any of my friends, I wanted nothing more than to find out who it could be." He looks up at me with yearning in his eyes. "Then you walked into the Polar Bear. I knew you were special from the first time I laid eyes on you. It did not surprise me in the least that everything about you matched up with the legend." He laughs harshly. "And it even makes sense for you to have an Intended, to have someone in your corner who would do anything to protect you."

I look out into the distance. His words feel like nails pounding into my chest. "I can't be the One. I can't, Rayne. I don't have what it takes to unite an entire race of people. I'm the worst person for such a job." Shaking my head fiercely, I say, "I won't believe it."

"Vela," he says in a serious tone. "You have the birthday. Sandy in the other camp, who might be your mom, has the right birthday, too. I've heard you look just like her. Her and her husband James's story match up to how the Chosen One's parents meet and marry. You're developing a second gift. The same gift James has. Soon, you'll have all of them."

I whip my head in his direction. "What do you mean, I'll have all the gifts?"

"Though their elements are diverse, through them, the Child will command them all," Rayne recites from the prophecy.

"That just means the Child will command the two gifts he or she inherits from her parents," I argue.

Rayne has a light in his eyes that I wish would go away. "No, I think that means the Child will command *all* the gifts."

I snort. "That's not possible." My expression turns hard. "I'm done with this conversation. I'm not the Chosen Child. I don't even know if James and Sandy are my biological parents. Drop it, Rayne. I mean it." Anger suddenly floods me. Every muscle in my body is clenched and strains to hit something. If he chooses to continue this conversation, I will lose it.

Rayne studies my face and seems to accept my anger.

That only makes me angrier.

He shakes his head and then picks up his backpack. He places it right next to me and says, "I'm going to go find firewood. I'll be back as soon as I can. I won't go far, so call out if anything happens."

I nod and then look around, praying no wolves sniff me out. Or maybe I want them to. It would certainly take care of this overwhelming urge to hit Rayne.

As I really have no other choice, I decide to relax as much as I can and stay still. Now that I'm out of imminent danger, all my aches and pains become much more pronounced. Not only are my side and knee throbbing, but the left side of my body is all out of whack after compensating for my strange gait as I tried to limit using my injured side.

I breathe in the clear early evening air and notice the sunset coloring the sky where I can see it between overhanging branches.

I might not be able to do much right now, but I can give this whole situation up to God. I desperately need His comfort and His help to cool my rage. I also pray for Linc, Jack, and the group's safety.

Surprising peace floods my body. There's nothing like taking your worries to your heavenly Father and letting Him handle them. Why didn't I think of that earlier?

At that, I close my eyes and bask in my newfound feelings.

8. LINC

Andy and I trudge along, trying to get back to where we lost everyone, when a sudden shout has us crouching.

Waban and his friends race toward us with wild looks in their eyes. "Run! The bear's right behind us!"

We hear crashing in the woods, and we spin around to race away for our lives...again.

Andy's right next to me, and I shout at him, "There's gotta be a way to stop that thing!"

"If there is, I don't know of one. We've tried everything," he calls back, huffing.

That's when the craziest idea I've ever had comes into my mind. I considered trying it before when I first saw the bear, but I never got the chance to try. I was too busy running for my life.

I take a look behind us and see that Waban and his friends are slowing down. They've probably been running for a while now, and they look exhausted. I'm not sure how much energy they have left.

That makes my mind up.

"I'm going to try something," I call out to Andy. I pull him to a stop and say urgently, "Get the others to safety."

Andy's confused look only spurs me to action.

I hide behind a tree and turn to Andy, who's still watching me, alarm taking over his face.

"Go," I shout at him.

"I'm not leaving you, Linc."

The others have caught up to us and they stop as well, sweat streaming off their faces as their chests heave.

"You...have...an...idea?" Waban manages to get out.

I nod. "Yeah. It's crazy. Not sure it'll work. You guys need to get out of here in case it doesn't."

He shakes his head. "No, we'll fight it with you."

"That's not exactly what I'm going to do."

Andy turns a terrified look at me, understanding in his eyes. "Linc, no!"

The bear is now in sight and charging toward us. Everyone takes stances in a semicircle around me.

I move away from the tree and raise my hands. I channel all the energy that I have, narrowing my eyes and focusing on the bear. If I could control a pack of wolves, maybe I can control one gigantic bear.

Pushing all my will into my thoughts, I look deep into the bear's mind and attempt to connect with it. I meet a mess of pure rage and what feels like a ten-foot wall between us. I attack it like a battering ram and try to push through. I widen my stance, bracing myself in case this crazy scheme doesn't work.

Waban sends a blast of wind at the bear, and it somehow slows down as it tries to push through.

It roars angrily, shaking its head as it walks slowly toward us.

Waban's friend also sends a rain shower into the bear's eyes. They can't do much, but they're trying. I have to be successful.

"God, help me," I beg.

Sweat drips into my eyes, and in the corner of my eye, I see that Andy is trying to help.

I don't know if the two of us can control the same animal, but we can try.

Breathing heavily, I fight the bear's resistance to give his mind over to me. I send a coaxing emotion through our tenuous connection, hoping sweetening it up works better than force. Now that I'm partially in the bear's mind, I can feel Andy's presence slamming against the bear's resistance.

The bear stops midstride and sways on its feet. Its eyes study first Andy, then me. We're confusing it.

"Andy, let me have it. It needs to be just one of us. I'm almost there," I call out.

Andy drops his arms and, with his presence gone, I can concentrate on breaking in.

Feeling a crack in its resistance, I dive in, praying I've made it. After a few more moments of resistance, I feel a sweet sort of release, and then the bear is mine.

I'm in its head, and I rear back at the enormity of this bear's power. I feel it fuel my muscles, and I've never felt more powerful in my life.

"I'm in," I call out.

I could conquer anything with this kind of power to command. Then its mind shifts. I see, through *her* eyes, two cubs she wants to get back to.

No wonder she's been so ferocious. There's a reason mama bear is a term used for enraged women.

She thinks we mean to harm her babies.

I send calming thoughts into her mind and a fierce desire to return to her cubs. I'm suddenly very happy my fire trap didn't kill her. That would have meant three deaths on my conscience.

"She has cubs," I say to the others. "I'm trying to get her to go back to them."

Understanding crosses all their faces.

I push every ounce of my gift into the bear's mind, encouraging her to go back to her babies. Pressing a sense of calm through my gift, I feel her will vacillate between anger at us getting too close to her babies and wanting to check on them. I coax her feelings of mothering, so that's all she sees and feels. She looks us all over and then huffs a big breath and finally turns away.

She ambles off, breaking into a run as she moves away from us.

When she's gotten too far for me to sense her, I release the hold I have on her. She doesn't turn back.

We all breathe a collective sigh of relief.

Now that I don't have the bear's power flowing through me, I'm suddenly exhausted. My shoulders slump, and what little energy I have drains out of me. Feeling dizzy, I drop to my knees on the forest floor, breathing hard.

Andy claps his hand on my shoulder. "You, my friend, are a genius." He laughs loudly and I and the others soon join him. We're all holding our sides and laughing together, celebrating this moment.

When I can breathe again, I ask Waban, "What happened? Did you shoot her?"

He's still recovering too, so he swallows and gets his breathing under control. When he can talk, he says, expressing himself with his hands, "She surprised us. We didn't hear her coming until she was right on top of us," Waban explains. "I got in a couple of shots, but they went wild."

"Us, too," the Neronian says grimly.

One of the humans adds, "We were so surprised, we dropped our guns. The only thing we could do was run."

Waban breathes a sigh of relief and looks at me with admiration. "What you did was incredible. I've never seen such a power."

"Do you have Fire Elementals in your community?" I ask.

He nods. "I don't know if they can do what you do. They, too, have both bloods. Human and Fire. I've never heard of this gift you have."

I shrug. "They might want to try with a small animal, like a bird or mouse. They shouldn't start with anything bigger."

He nods. "I will have them try." He smiles at me. "It's been an incredible experience meeting the both of you. We must leave and go retrieve our rifles. But our paths were meant to cross."

I smile tiredly. "Maybe our paths will cross again."

"I hope so," Waban says with a big smile. The others nod.

With that, they take their leave, going back the way they came.

I look over at Andy. "Let's hope we just don't come near that bear and her cubs again."

He chuckles. "Most certainly."

9. Vela

By the time Rayne returns, I've calmed down. I'm re-lieved that nothing tried to eat me. I got to rest for about an hour and start to wonder where Rayne is and why he's been gone for so long. When he eventually returns, the sun has gone down, but there's enough light for me to see him walk up.

"I was worried," I say after I've looked him over.

A huge pile of branches fills his arms. He cracks a smile. "Nice to know you've had a change of heart. And that some-one worries about me."

I frown. "I'm sorry I got so angry." I inhale a shuddering breath. "It's just a lot to take in." It's gotten colder since the sun set, and I'll appreciate a good fire. It'll be soothing at least.

He nods and dumps the branches on the ground. "I can understand that."

"I can't wait for the fire since it's getting chilly. Anyway, I'm sure your mother worries about you, too."

He gives me a wry look, but it's soon replaced with one more heated. "I did *not* mean my mother."

I blush and look down. "Oh, well, she would worry about you. Any mother of someone like you would."

He brushes his hands off. "What does 'someone like me' mean?"

I play with the hem of my sweatshirt. Words tumble out before I can stop them. "I mean, someone who looks like you surely has no shortage of female admirers, so yes, I would think a mother would worry about that very much."

He cocks an eyebrow. "Are you one of those?"

My breath stops, and I look up at him, my brain shutting down for a second. "One of what?"

"Female admirers." His voice has gone deep and gravelly and my stomach erupts in stupid flutters.

His mouth spreads in a wide grin at my silence.

"No," I finally cry out. "I am *not* one of those. I'm Linc's girl." I narrow my eyes at him. "You know that."

"Oh, believe me. I know." He scowls and turns, walking to his backpack. He fishes for something and pulls out a rock and his knife. He walks over to the edge of the clearing and starts gathering dry moss and brush. When he has a nest-sized pile, he comes over to me and stops an arm's length away.

"I'll make the fire as close to you as possible." He smirks. "I know you're used to someone just lighting a fire with a thought, but that is one gift I don't possess."

I throw daggers at him. "Yes, I am used to that. But you have your talents, too. Believe me, I've seen enough of them to know you and Linc are pretty even in the talent department."

He flashes a smile at me. "Thank you, Vela." He shakes his head as he pushes the brush into a neat little pile. "I didn't think it would be a compliment to be compared to your Intended. But I'm flattered, really."

I smile because I'm pretty sure he's serious. But it's hard to tell with him. "You're welcome."

He goes quiet and devotes all his attention to starting a fire.

"What's that rock?" I ask.

Rayne looks up surprised. "You've never seen someone start a fire with flint before?"

I shake my head and watch him curiously.

"Well, take notes because you might have to do this at some point." First, he arranges the brush into what looks like a bird's nest. Then, he holds his knife at an angle and strikes the flint with it. It produces a spark, but then he flips the flint over and strikes it again, this time without a spark.

"I thought you were trying to start a fire."

He looks up at me through the bangs hanging over his forehead. "I am."

"But you made a spark, then stopped."

"That's because I need to shave some flint onto the moss first. Once I have enough shavings on my pile here, I can light it. The flint will catch fire easily."

"Oh. That's pretty cool."

"Glad I can enhance your experience with fires." He flashes me a meaningful look, and I lose my smile.

My anger flashes again at his thinly veiled double meaning. I hold my relationship with Linc close to my chest. Rayne's not going to win any brownie points with me saying stuff like that.

"Watch it, Rayne," I warn.

"Hey, I'm just trying to widen your impression of the world," he says with wide eyes.

"I don't need you to *widen my impression* of the world, thank you very much. My view is perfectly fine the way it is."

He snorts. "If you say so. I thought you were mad at Linc, anyway."

I glare at him. "Just because I'm mad at him doesn't mean I stopped loving him."

He smirks.

I fume silently for a minute. "You know, for one second, I thought more of you. For your help and support in all this." I wave my arms at the fire and at myself. "But maybe I was too hasty. You are still a cocky, egotistical jerk."

He stops what he's doing and studies me. "I'm still that guy, Vela."

"Which one? The rude, conceited one? Or the gentleman?"

He throws down his knife and flint. "Both," he says gruffly. "I'm not your knight in shining armor. I am who I am. I thought you'd respect that, at least."

I look away and think over what he says. At my silence, I hear him pick up his tools and resume working on the fire. We sit in an awkward silence.

How am I wrong here? He attacks my relationship with Linc, and I'm supposed to be okay with that? No. I stand in the right. It's true when Rayne says I need to accept him for who he is. I can try to do that, even if he sends my heart beating a crazy rhythm when I don't want it to. But he needs to respect the fact that I'm in a relationship. He pointedly ignores that on a continuous basis.

I can't deny there's something about his brutal honesty though that catches and holds my attention. I can't help but like his ability to make me think more deeply about things. It shouldn't surprise me that he challenges my view on my Intended. It fits his personality perfectly to question everything. And if we're going to survive this trek back to civilization, we need to at least get along.

I sigh heavily. "Fine. You're right. I need to accept you for who you are. But that doesn't mean I'll just let you get away with rude comments."

He's directing sparks into the nest now and the brush is catching. He starts feeding it moss and small sticks, and the fire grows.

"I am a gentleman," he says, pausing in his efforts. "I wouldn't want any girl to think otherwise."

"I know. You are. I'm sorry, I shouldn't have called you all those names." I sigh and sit watching the fire steadily grow as Rayne adds more wood. The silence is easier now, the tension gone with my apology.

When Rayne is satisfied with the fire, he squats next to it. "I have some food, but it won't last us long. Without a gun, I won't be able to hunt, unless I can catch something with my hands."

I cringe at the thought of a small animal in his hands.

"I can set some traps, but that means we can't leave this area. The question is, do you want to stay in one place for a day before we try to travel again? It's really up to you."

"I don't like the idea of being out here with wolves and bears any longer than we have to. I say we travel and eat what we have and can forage."

He nods grimly, watching the fire dance in the night air. It's now completely dark. "Yeah, you're right. I don't want you in unnecessary danger."

I nod.

He stretches his legs out and sits down. Reaching for the backpack, he fishes out homemade granola and jerky, handing both to me.

I give him the bar back and say, "The jerky is fine. I don't want to go through the food too quickly."

He accepts it with a grim look on his face. He returns it to the backpack and takes only some jerky for himself.

"You should eat more than me, Rayne. You're supporting me as I walk, and it wouldn't surprise me if you just give up and carry me. As much as I hope that doesn't happen." I say with raised eyebrows.

He smiles but shakes his head. "Always altruistic, aren't you? Sacrificing for the greater good."

"No, I'm being realistic."

He turns to look at me fully. "Vela, I wouldn't let you heal me because you can't heal yourself. In what world do you think that I'm going to eat more than you?"

His intent look sends an unwelcome warmth flashing through me... again. I look away from him. For the first time, my mind goes blank, and I don't have a snappy comeback.

We sit in companionable silence as Rayne continues to feed the flames. I almost reach out to pet Jack when I remember he's not with me. I suddenly miss him and Linc even more fiercely as I watch the fire dance.

I decide to share my thoughts. "I miss Jack."

Rayne nods and smiles softly at me. "Of course you do. You two are inseparable. Where did he go, anyway?"

"You didn't see what happened?"

When he shakes his head, I explain how Jack took one look at the bear and ran in the other direction.

"So, you have no idea where he is?"

"No," I say softly. "He could be anywhere. I hope he's okay."

"Dogs have an innate sense of survival, so I'm sure he's fine. Why don't you call for him again?

I look out in the distance, fill my lungs and call out as loudly as I can, "Jack! Jack, boy, come here!"

I wait in anxious silence. When I hear and see nothing, I call him again. After a minute of long, quiet silence, only night noises filling the air, my shoulders slump. Hopelessness fills me.

Rayne says softly, "It was worth a shot. Why don't you relax? You have enough on your mind."

I really do. I wonder where Linc is and if he tracked our path to the cliff. "You know, even if the others follow our path through the woods, they'll never be able to find us since we went down into the ravine on one side and came out on the other."

"That's why we will find them."

"How are we going to do that?"

Rayne looks up into the night sky. "I've been thinking about that. There are First Nation communities all over the place. If we can find one, they'll help get us get back to the Polar Bear."

"So, Saddleback is out of the question," I say, sighing.

He looks at me with sympathy. "Vela, we need to find out what happened to the others and get you to Hannah."

"Yeah, I know," I say softly. Then I look back up at him. "First Nation? What's that?"

He grins. "It's not what, it's who. They're the local indigenous people who have made their lives out here for generations."

I raise my eyebrows. "Do they know about the Polar Bear? I thought it was meant to be a secret community."

"The First Nation has always kept our secret. They are the only ones besides the other off-the-grid Elemental communities who know about us. They sometimes help us get supplies. We trade with them, too. It's a give, give situation."

"That's wonderful! You think we can find one of their communities?"

He nods his head. "I do."

Suddenly, the thought of a rescue fills me with hope.

He looks at my stretched-out leg. "They might have a Gyan who can heal you, too."

My mouth drops open. "A Gyan? They're Elementals? Is it only Gyans?"

"No. First Nation Elementals have mixed with each other since the beginning. They don't have clan wars like everywhere else. They live like we should live. But the most interesting part is that humans live among them, too."

"Are you serious?" My mouth drops open.

He laughs. "Why? Does that surprise you?"

"Are you kidding me? Maybe because all I've ever known are clan wars and boundary battles. I was shocked when I heard about the Polar Bear and its mixed elemental residents. This is so much more, and with humans, too? How does that work?"

He grins. "Their powers aren't as strong as full-blooded Elementals, but they do have gifts. Inter-marrying with humans has sort of diluted their powers. But the heart loves who it loves. They don't discriminate in their matches."

I lean back and soak in all the implications of what he just tells me. "This is *amazing*, Rayne. I almost can't believe it."

He lets me think about it for a minute. "The important thing is, there should be a Gyan who has enough healing power to help you."

Hope soars through me. I laugh. "This changes *everything*." Now, my outlook has gone from bleak to promising. "I can trek around the world with this news."

He laughs. "Let's not go overboard. We just need to find the closest one."

I lean back on my hands and smile up at the sky. "I can do that."

And I really can. This adventure just got a lot more promising. Because these communities are really our people, just with some human blood. I can't wait to see what that looks like.

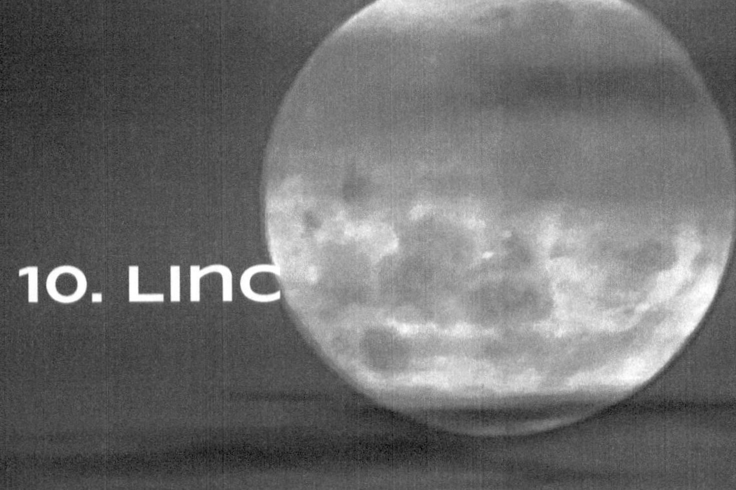

10. LINC

An Hour Earlier

Andy and I have been walking for about an hour when I hear the sweetest sound.

A bark.

Is that Jack? Does that mean Vela is with him?

I look in that direction and sense a dog-sized form running toward us. My heart jumps into my throat when I see two people following him.

Breaking into a run, I see Jack bounding toward me, barking happily. He rushes at me, jumping up onto my chest, almost knocking me over. He licks my face, arms, anything he can get his tongue on. "Jack, Jack! Good to see you, boy." Laughing, I rub his ears but can barely keep my hands on him as he wiggles hard in his excitement.

Nudging him away, I run to see if Vela is one of the people I sensed. When they come into sight, I see one person is being supported by the other. *Is Vela hurt?*

Jack runs with me as I skirt bushes and trees. I skid to a stop when I see who it is. My stomach drops in disappointment.

Jack runs to sniff Tonya as she braces Claudette, who's limping noticeably next to her.

My face must show my crushing letdown that Vela isn't with them.

"Don't look too excited, Linc," Tonya says dryly. She shakes her head and continues to support Claudette.

Andy's caught up to us by now and greets Jack, who's still too excited to stay still. "Claudette, are you okay?" he asks, looking her over and moving to relieve Tonya.

"I'm okay, thanks to Tonya. I'm alive." Claudette gives her friend a grateful look.

Tonya grimaces. "I'm just learning my Gyan gift and am not great at healing. But I did what I could."

"You were amazing, Tonya. I would never have survived that attack without your help."

Tonya smiles, but it looks doubtful. "You're a good patient. And very understanding."

Before I can burst, I ask, "Have either of you seen Vela? Or Rayne?"

Claudette looks around, shaking her head. "No. Jack found us about a mile back. You two are the first ones of our group we've come across."

Andy glances at me and when he sees my frustrated look, says wisely, "We'll keep looking. We don't have much time left before we lose the light."

I try not to burn with anger that Vela will be all alone with Rayne tonight if we don't find them. I shove those feelings aside. I don't even know if she's okay.

God, please tell me she's alive.

My thoughts must be all over my face because Tonya pats me on the shoulder as she, Claudette, and Andy walk slowly past me.

"I'm sure she's fine, Linc. Rayne's with her," Tonya assures me.

"And why does that mean she'll be fine?" I snap.

"Because Rayne is one of the most accomplished outdoorsmen I've ever met. And that's saying a lot. If she's with him, she'll be just fine," she says with a wry grin.

"Doesn't mean she's not hurt, though." When she arches a brow at me, I argue, "He's not a Gyan. If she's injured, there's not a thing he can do about it."

"True," she concedes. "But I doubt she's injured."

Andy changes the subject and asks, "Since you two came from that direction and didn't see anyone, let's go north. We should run into Gene and Jerry soon enough."

"And Vela," I say with a hard voice.

Andy puts a comforting hand on my shoulder. "And of course, Vela and Rayne."

Heat flares through me. "Do you not think we'll find them, Andy?"

Andy holds his hand up at my display of temper. "No, my friend, I do. It's just you said she and Rayne went east, so I think we'll run into Gene and Jerry first."

"Well, maybe we should go east first, then. You guys might not understand my reasons, but she's my *Intended*. I have to find her." I give them all hard looks, but it's Tonya who braves arguing with me.

"Linc, none of us understand an Intended bond. We wish we did, but the trail where we started is to the north. Rayne would bring Vela back to where we got separated. They might already be there."

Her words make sense, and I hold up my hand as I hang my head. "I'm sorry, guys. Having this bond with her is like a bone-deep need to be near her always. Not knowing if she's hurt, if she's even alive, is making me crazy."

Claudette and Tonya give me sympathetic looks but stay quiet.

Andy says, "Linc, we're here for you and will continue to be. But I agree with Tonya. Rayne would go back to the path to find everyone. Let's head that way. It's our best chance to regroup."

At those words, I look up at the sky to find the setting sun. When I spot it, I orient myself and turn my steps toward the north.

A half-hour into our walk, I'm fighting frustration that Claudette is slowing us down. Even though Andy is helping her, it's still slow going. I know she can't help it, but I clamp my lips shut to prevent a growl from escaping.

Andy is catching Tonya and Claudette up on what happened with the bear.

"So, the bear ran off, just like that?" Claudette says, her eyes wide as saucers.

"Yes, after Linc took control of her, he convinced her to return to her cubs."

"Linc, that's amazing! You're a genius," Tonya gushes at me.

I grunt in acknowledgement.

"I told him the same thing," Andy says.

I'm about to tell them I'll hike ahead of everyone when Tonya says, "I saw that Vela cleared a path with her gift when she and Rayne ran from the bear. That was pretty smart. It made their path much easier to run."

And to find.

I turn around. That just cemented what I'm going to do. "I have to go ahead of you guys. I'm going to try to find the path they made off the trail, and if Vela and Rayne aren't there, I'll track where they went."

"You only have a half hour of light, Linc," Andy protests.

I blaze my hands into two balls of fire. "I'll be fine."

He presses his lips together but doesn't argue.

"If you see Gene and Jerry on your way, tell them to wait for us," Tonya says with an understanding look.

"You got it." I douse my fire and walk through the smoke, heading to where I hope to find my Intended waiting for me. And the best part is that Jack follows.

11. vela

T he fire makes me sleepy as I watch its dancing flame. Rayne and I have been sitting in comfortable silence for a while, but one thought keeps me awake.

I decide to finally ask some questions. "Tell me again why you think I'm the Chosen Child and not his or her mother."

Rayne studies me over fire. "I don't think you're the Chosen One. I know you are." He holds up his hands and starts ticking off each finger. "First, your birthday is on the Autumn Equinox..."

I interrupt him, "Doesn't that mean I'm the mother of the Child? *When the day and night are of equal length, a warrior star who will bear the child will rise.* That's the Autumn Equinox."

He holds up another finger. "There's another prophecy about the Child that says he or she will have an Autumn Equinox birthday, as well."

I tense. "I haven't heard of another prophecy."

"It's out there. It says your birthday is the Equinox."

I scoff and raise angry eyes at him. "Stop saying I'm the One. You have to have more proof than that."

"I do," he says quickly. A third finger goes up. "The fact that your birth mother has the same birthday is also iron-clad proof."

I sit back, stunned. My mouth goes dry. "I don't even know who my birth mother is." My eyes start watering, despite my attempt to control my warring emotions.

He looks at me intently and it strikes deep within me. "I think you know innately that Sandy in the Saddleback community is your mother, and James your father."

"How can I possibly know that?"

He ticks off a fourth finger. "Gene and Jerry say you are the spitting image of her. How do you explain that?"

I shake my head. My heart is flipping in my chest. I inhale deeply, trying to get it under control. I look away from Rayne's piercing eyes.

Ticking off two more fingers, he says, "Fifth, James's birthday is the Winter Solstice. Sixth, he met your mother, and she agreed to marry him in the north. All fulfilling the first prophecy."

My head swims with all this information. I squeeze my eyes shut. "Stop. Just stop," I whisper. My emotions are out of control, like waves crashing on the rocks of my soul. A breeze lifts my hair into an ethereal cloud. It floats all around me, caressing my face. Opening my eyes, I hold my breath and stay perfectly still.

Rayne's eyes are delighted as he watches the display. He stays silent, his lips pressed together like he's trying not to spook me.

Too late for that.

I touch the swirling strands and will them to drop. The wonder of this moment isn't lost on me. Since this isn't the first time I've seen this, I must accept the fact that I have Borean blood. Once my heart stops galloping, my hair falls over my face in a golden sheet and I move it out of the way to look at Rayne.

A grin stretches his mouth wide in a display of intensity that makes me nervous.

"This doesn't mean anything," I say quickly.

"On the contrary, it only cements my thoughts and further proves I'm correct."

My breath catches. "Rayne…"

"Look, you'll be eighteen in less than a year. It's normal for you to show signs of your secondary gift like this. Let me help you with it. I am a Borean after all."

I can't deny I have the wind gift, so I can only nod.

"Be prepared to see unexpected breezes. And sometimes when you try to use your Gyan gift, you'll activate your Borean one."

My eyes widen. "Really?"

He shrugs. "Or they'll both happen at the same time. Until you master using wind, you could accidentally use one gift or both. It's perfectly normal at first."

"Normal," I breathe, thinking this is all so crazy. "What did you think when this happened to you?"

His eyes soften as he looks away, remembering. He laughs softly. "I had been waiting for my second gift to happen. Even so, when it finally did, it shocked the crap out of me."

I laugh. "Really? How?"

"Well, my dominant gift is wind, so when I was 17, I tried to activate the water in me and never could. Like I said, don't be surprised if you can't do it the first few times." He pauses. "But you know how it happens when you least expect it, when you're feeling particularly strong emotions?"

I nod, encouraging him to continue, thoroughly fascinated with his story.

He laughs. "Well, I guess I was innately wanting to cool off one day. I was chopping wood, and was crazy hot and sweaty, when in the middle of a chop, water dumps on me, like a mini rain cloud. I was so surprised, I let go of my axe mid-swing." He gestures with his hands, like he's chopping, and then mimics throwing the axe.

"I practically threw the axe across the field where other guys were working. It barely avoided taking Leon's foot off." He laughs, a fond expression on his face.

I can't help but full belly laugh at the picture he just painted. When I can speak again, I say, "You could have killed someone!"

He looks at me sheepishly. "I know. It was my first time using my second gift, so it surprised me."

"And Leon," I say, still laughing.

His face transforms into a serious one. "He practically knocked my face in for that. It was one heck of a brawl. Let's just say that never happened again."

I can't help but giggle, holding my stomach and grimacing when the pain in my ribs flares. "That's just hilarious."

"Once I got my full powers, it was like my whole world shifted. It came together, like," he pauses, searching for his words, "I finally felt complete. Until I got my second gift, I didn't realize I had been operating at half steam my whole life."

"That must have been the most incredible feeling."

"It was. It is." He looks out into the dark, his brow furrowed. "I know I'm an anomaly having two gifts, but I wouldn't have it any other way. My gifts are such a part of me, I couldn't imagine my life without both."

I sit thinking what it will be like having two separate gifts. Even though I've only experienced my Borean gift a few times, it's already becoming a part of me.

He turns to me. "Do you want to try to use your wind gift?" he asks, his eyes twinkling. "I promise I won't attack you if you accidentally hurt me."

I lift my eyes to his. "Should I really try?"

"If you want to. But don't be surprised if nothing happens at first."

"I don't have an axe in my hands, so I think you're safe. Okay." I blow my breath out slowly. Concentrating hard on my fingers, I hold my hands out, palms up in front of me. I wiggle them gently, digging deep into myself to produce a breeze.

Nothing. Not even a whisper touches my fingertips.

I try again. Squinting my eyes, I feel my palms warm, but instead of anything resembling wind, a small bush next to me suddenly explodes in growth instead. My breath whooshes out, and I look accusingly at it.

"It's okay," Rayne says gently. "Before you turn eighteen, it's difficult to produce your emerging gift with any measure of control. It usually just happens. Think of it like your gift practicing, trying out the feel of you."

I raise my eyes to his, my breath quickening at his words. I know he didn't intend to insinuate anything, but suddenly the air between us thickens.

His eyes darken, and it's like he's acknowledging the desire swirling through my veins. I force a blank mask of indifference.

Mercifully, Rayne brings the Chosen Child back up.

"So, does this mean you're more open to being the One?" as he throws a branch into the fire.

I've never been so happy to talk about something other than whatever this is I feel.

I blow out a breath. "If finding my birth parents means I'm the one everyone is looking for, then I'd gladly accept it.

It's what the Chosen One is supposed to do that scares me to death. I can't possibly unite all the Elementals together. I mean, how would I even begin to try something like that?"

Rayne studies the fire, feeding it more wood. He looks like he's choosing his next words carefully. Finally, he speaks, "I've thought a lot about how the Chosen Child would do what he, or she," he emphasizes while looking at me with raised eyebrows, "is meant to do. I've always thought it would be innate and that they would have a natural gift to lead others."

I start to protest, but he holds his hand up, stopping my words.

"Just listen. I'm not much of a believer in God, but if He exists, I think He would give our Prophesied One the gifts needed to bring our world together. This is bigger than all of us. I can acknowledge that. Can you?"

I think about his words and finally nod. "I've had similar thoughts myself. But I still can't wrap my head around the fact that it could be me."

"Would you like to find out if James and Sandy are actually your birth parents?"

"Yes, of course. It would be," I say, pausing for a moment, "like a huge piece of me finally fits. I'd be complete."

"Well, then, let them help you accomplish the goal of bringing our world under one banner instead of four."

"They would help me?" I ask before I can stop myself. It's like he's half convinced me of this insane idea.

"Of course they would. From what Gene and Jerry said, James and Sandy have accepted the fact that there's a strong possibility they are the parents of the Chosen One. They've been trying to find their missing daughter for years."

I sit, trying to process everything he says. As much as I'd love to think that Sandy and James are my birth parents, I can't bank on that. But, if I look just like her, how incredible of a coincidence is that? I can't just ignore the possibility, no matter how unbelievable it is.

Then my thoughts turn to the prophecy I haven't heard yet.

"Do you know the full prophecy about the Child's birthday?"

He shakes his head. "Not word for word. But I'm sure someone does at home. When we make it back, we can ask."

I sit back, disappointed. I hold my side at the movement and focus on that pain instead of the tearing in my heart at the thought that I could be the Chosen One. *I still can't believe it.*

I look up with pain-filled eyes. "Rayne, I seriously hope you're wrong about all of this. It's too terrifying."

Understanding replaces the confidence in his gaze, then brightens. "It might sound scary, but isn't it also amazing? We've been looking for the Child for centuries."

I look away and twist the fabric of Rayne's sweatshirt. "I don't know. Let me think about all of this."

He nods. After helping me lie down, he returns to his side of the fire, and I fall into a troubled sleep.

My dreams are full of Gyans, Boreans, Neronians, and Festans all around a fire, mingling happily. I'm sleeping as comfortably as I can when an overpowering feeling wakes me up. I inhale sharply and lean on my good side, panting heavily.

Linc is all I can think about. I can't shake the feeling that something has happened to him.

I look up and see that the sky is ablaze with gorgeous colors. The Northern Lights came while I slept. I blearily look up at them, finding comfort in their long green, blue, and pink wispy swirls while my thoughts are so scattered.

"What's wrong?" Rayne asks, his sleepy eyes looking me over.

My forehead is dotted with sweat, and all I can do is shake my head.

"Vela, did you have a nightmare? Something crawl on you?"

I squeeze my eyes shut, trying to banish the terrible foreboding I have that something is wrong with my Intended.

Rayne pushes himself up and comes over to my side of the fire. He looks all around me to find the critter that scared me. I wave him away.

"It's just this awful feeling." I can only whisper because of my dry throat. I swallow, trying to get some moisture. "I think something's wrong with Linc."

Rayne squats next to me, his forehead furrowed. "Do you get these feelings often about him?"

"No, never. What if he's looking for me in the dark?" I wouldn't put it past him. Terrified feelings grip my chest, and I massage the area. "I can't help but think he's in danger."

Rayne's silent for a moment. "Well, there's absolutely nothing we can do right now. Worry will only make your situation worse."

"I don't care about *my* situation, Rayne," I snap. "We're safe. I can't help but feel that he's not." I turn a wild eye to the wooded area around us. "What if he won't rest until he finds me?"

Rayne looks away and mutters something under his breath.

"What? What did you say?" I turn accusing eyes to him.

"I said," he says, turning to me, his eyebrows two light brown slashes, "then he's a fool."

"Why would Linc be a fool to search all through the night for me?"

"Because," he says with a hard voice. "There's a significantly higher chance he could get injured if he searches for you at night."

Concern blends with my terror. "I pray he's not."

"I suggest you do a lot of praying to that God of yours if you have a bad feeling about him. That is your only weapon right now. If you believe in that kind of thing," he adds under his breath.

Distracted, I ask, "You really don't believe in God, Rayne?"

He barks a laugh. "Why would I? For a god to leave me abandoned and stuck in the middle of nowhere, is the worst kind of punishment. The problem is, I didn't do anything to warrant punishment. And that's saying *if* this God exists."

My heart breaks for him. I can understand his reluctance to believe in a loving God. When he's only known the kind of love his father has given him. "Rayne, you're placing the blame in the wrong place." I modulate my voice to be gentle, not accusatory.

He snorts.

"No, really. Extremists have done this. They've made the choice to hunt anyone like us down. God's given us all free will, including them. This is what they've chosen to do with it."

He spears me with a hard look. "So, if your God is so big and powerful, why doesn't He put a stop to this group once and for all?"

"You don't know that He's not setting things up so they can be stopped, Rayne. We have to trust Him. Trust that He's got our best interests in mind. I believe we're meant to show His glory in everything we do. We don't know who

He's using to fight that group. We don't know His ways. They are as mysterious as the Northern Lights." I point up at the sky.

He lifts his face and studies the emerald, sapphire, and magenta colors snaking across the sky as he shakes his head. "I don't know if I can believe in Someone who makes His followers suffer." His face is bathed in the soft light from above. He looks so sad my heart clenches.

I sigh. "I understand. He promises there's a reason for everything. I choose to trust that promise. He knows, and that's what I hold on to."

"Well, then you're a fool," he says, turning eyes that reflect pain to me. "To blindly follow such a God is just childish."

"I am a child. I'm a child of God. It's with a child-like trust that I put my life in His hands. This has helped me remember what I've forgotten. If I don't trust God with everything in my life, I'm not being the follower I should." I hang my head. "I haven't been doing much trusting lately. So," I say, raising my head, "thank you for helping me remember that God is in control of every part of my life, including all of this." I wave my arm around. My heart cracks at my recent attitude.

God, forgive me for being so angry and resentful. Help me know You're here, like always.

Rayne scoffs. "Don't thank me." He picks himself up and returns to his makeshift pillow.

I settle back on my side, ignoring the sharp ache it causes. And I do just what Rayne suggests. I pray.

12. LINCOLN

I fight back curses when I finally admit that I'm lost. In the pitch black, I've somehow gotten turned around, and I've been wandering for four hours. Cloud cover has hidden the stars I would have navigated by. Not only that, but I know with absolute certainty that a pack of wolves is hunting Jack and me. I heard their howls earlier in the night and when they went quiet, I turned on my senses to find them. They're slowly, but methodically, surrounding us.

Usually, I wouldn't be overly worried. I can control a pack of wolves. I've done it before. But not tonight. I've been using my fire to light our way through the dark for these past four hours. In addition to the exhaustion from escaping the grolar bear, trapping it, controlling it, and searching for Vela, I'm also dangerously low on water, and I haven't eaten in a long time.

I'm drained and exhausted.

Before I realized the wolves were tracking us, I was ready to call it a night and get some much-needed rest. I debate if it would take more power to fight off hungry wolves with fire or to control them and drive them away. Jack growls in obvious awareness of his cousins hunting us.

They emerge from the mist, six wolves all hungry for a meal, growling and snapping their jaws. Ranging in color from brown to gray and black, they each look fearsome. As if trained by a marine unit, they fan out around us, about two hundred yards away.

Making a split-second decision, I press my lips into a thin line and plant my feet on the ground. I center my thoughts. Breathing in and out in measured breaths, I connect with each wolf.

One by one, I meld my mind with theirs. Their primary thought is deep hunger. I need to find them something else to eat.

My energy seeps out as I send out one command.

Stop.

I feel them all obey, but it's tenuous. I strain to strengthen the connection. I cast out my senses to find a caribou or something big enough to entice them to leave Jack and me alone.

As easily as snapping a string, one of the wolves breaks free of my bond and lunges toward me. With a fierce bark, Jack meets him in the air, and it takes everything in me to keep control of the other five wolves. My brain feels like a hammer has taken its anger out on an anvil as they fight to break free of me.

I can only watch the flashes of teeth and claws as the wolf and Jack tumble onto the forest floor. They roll around the ground, both landing bites that make me cringe. Jack's dark red coat and the wolf's black fur blend together as they fight for their lives in the darkness.

I hold out my hands and boost Jack's natural strength and skill, making him stronger and faster.

Just then, the wolf pushes Jack onto his back, and the bite meant to clamp onto Jack's neck meets air.

With renewed energy, my faithful companion twists his body, and with his back legs, thrusts the wolf off him. The wolf gets his feet under him and lunges toward Jack again. They meet in a tangle of legs and teeth, both vying for dominance.

With my attention diverted, I force myself to keep the connection I have with the other wolves strong. Jack does not need to be outnumbered. My breath saws in and out of my chest at my labors, but I can't let Jack down.

I see the wolf go flying in the air. Jack must have delivered a good hit. He lunges toward the wolf now lying on its back. He's on the wolf as soon as he lands, and Jack soon has his teeth clamped around the wolf's neck.

I hear a snap, and the wolf goes limp. Jack holds on for a moment before finally letting go. He returns to my side with a low, ominous growl at the other wolves.

With my arms outstretched, I fight to hold on to the connections, but the wolves fight me, too, trying to get to their fallen brother.

Snarling and yipping fills the air. Jack's growl grows louder.

Sweat trickles down my face and my muscles tremble as exhaustion hits me. My powers are stretched as far as they'll go. I haven't been this tired since the last pack of wolves I commanded. But that time I had Vela to give me added strength through our bond. That thought sparks the memory of Vela thinking I'd betrayed her to the Extremists. The ache of it hits me all over again.

Thinking about Vela distracts me, and another wolf breaks free from my hold. Determined to save Jack from another fight, I force myself back into the wolf's mind, just as he's ten feet from us.

Stop.

He skids to a halt. His body trembles as he fights my will again and I force what precious little energy I have left to subdue him. My arms ache as I hold them out. They shake with the effort I'm exerting.

Holding onto all the wolves, I scan the surrounding area to search for an alternate meat source. Jack will continue to try protecting me from the other wolves, but I hope to keep him from having to face them all.

Desperate, I expand my search. In a burst of energy, finally, I find something the wolves will drool over.

The tricky thing about convincing a wolf to leave one food source for another one is the lack of smell. They rely on their noses to find their meals for them, and the animal I've found is too far away for them to sniff out on their own.

I'm going to have to plant the idea in their minds.

Find meat.

They all turn their heads toward me.

Shoot. Wrong command.

This time, I force the image of a tantalizing caribou into their minds. It's not easy to do on a good day when I'm full of energy. With my dwindling strength, I send my last command to them.

Go east. Find meat there.

They fight my mental control and despite my best efforts, two slip loose. Free of my mind, they growl deeply and race toward Jack and me.

This time, Jack stands in front of me and barks at them wildly, warning them away.

I plant my feet further into the earth and pray that God gives me the strength to get us out of this. They prowl toward us more warily than the first wolf.

One of the free wolves lunges toward me, but Jack bites its leg and then resumes his guardianship. The bitten wolf backs up, limping to join the other one. They watch us with hungry eyes.

I'm too tired to reconnect with the two free wolves. But, if I want to survive this, I need to amp up my game. Instead of trying to get back into their minds, I'll play with a little fire. Using my dominant gift will be easier for me.

My head still screams in pain though as I create a firebomb in my hand. I throw it at the bitten wolf. It lands on the wolf's back, and it howls in pain and anger. I grit my teeth and create another one in my hand, and I reach my arm out like I'm going to throw it. The wolf looks at me warily, yelps, and runs off, not wanting to be burned again.

Jack growls deep in his throat at the other wolf, and I command Jack to stay, so he won't attack before I throw my second bomb. It hits the last wolf in the snout and, like the first one, it yelps, and with its tail between its legs, slinks away.

I squeeze my eyes shut, seeing black spots, fighting dizziness. I force myself to keep standing and hold on to the last three wolves with all the strength I have.

I'm perilously close to losing my ties to them when I remind them of my last command.

Go east. Find meat there.

After watching one of their pack get killed by Jack and two burned by me, they finally decide to agree with my suggestion and find easier prey elsewhere. One by one, they all point their noses east and with the last of my strength, I give them one final push as the three remaining wolves slink away.

I drop to my knees on the leaf covered floor, breathing hard.

That was way too close.

I'd like to move somewhere safe to camp for tonight, but I can't. My entire body is trembling and a limp mess.

Jack rubs his nose into my shoulder, and that little nudge sends me to the ground.

If anything sneaks up on us now, we're toast. With absolutely no energy left, I fall onto my back and blackness takes over.

I wake up to a wet nose pressing into my cheek. Jack's tongue soon follows, and I turn my head away from his sloppy kisses.

"Okay, Jack, I'm awake. I'm fine, boy." I examine myself to see if that last sentence is true. Besides muscle soreness and a headache, which always happens when I've burned out my last reserves of energy, I really am okay. I push Jack away when he continues to check me out.

"Really, boy. I'm good." I'm half tempted to take over his will and force him to leave me be. But because of my lingering headache from controlling, first the bear, then the pack of wolves, I resist doing it to Jack. Plus, I can't do that to him again.

As I push myself up, Jack circles around me and I half trip over his happiness that I'm up. But my first thought is concern for Vela.

Please God, I pray she's alive and healthy.

I have a grudging acceptance that Rayne is her one defender and pray that he is protecting her. As much as I dislike the guy, I was bolstered at Tonya's assurance that he's a capable outdoorsman and can keep Vela safe.

Jack barks, and I look down at him. That's when I see that he's been busy this morning. He's hunted down breakfast. A grouse, or a road chicken, as the Polar Bear residents called them, sits by my feet and my stomach grumbles in appreciation for this very welcome gift.

"Good boy!" I praise and rub his ears enthusiastically. "You're the best dog, Jack, really."

I drink the last of my water and hope I can find a stream soon to refill my canteen. Then I make quick work of finding small branches and moss to start a fire. I'm not hungry enough to eat this thing raw, and I hope that's never the case.

Within moments, I've sparked a small fire and built it up to cook this gorgeous bird.

I pluck all the feathers and promise Jack he can have half once I've cooked it. He'd have no problem eating it raw, but I want to cook the bird whole to contain the juices best. No sense in ruining my breakfast with dry meat. I dig out the entrails, kidneys, and heart, burying them so Jack can't get to it easily. He sniffs at the mound of dirt longingly, but I command him away from it. I don't know if any of that is good for him to eat raw.

After I've found a good branch to spear the chicken with, I set it over the flames and settle myself in to turn it as it cooks.

Jack lays next to me and I have to say, it's nice to have such a great companion. I see why Vela loves Jack so much. He's devoted and, as I look over our breakfast, very useful. I'm happy he seems to enjoy my company as much as I'm enjoying his.

The smell of our breakfast is hitting my stomach hard. After an hour, I take it off the heat and burn my fingers pulling the meat off to share with Jack.

My first bite is heaven, and I praise Jack again. "Jack, you are the best. Good job, boy."

He and I eat the bird in record time, and I put out the fire once we're done.

"Now, to find mommy," I tell Jack.

I pull on my backpack and we hike north. Getting lost last night has ruined my travel time. And I'm frustrated I slept in so late. It's already 11:00, and I'm just getting started. Getting a look at the sun, I now can find my way north.

Relatively quickly, I find the trail we were on when our group split up when the bear came upon us. I can see it's not exactly where we split up, but I'm close. I just need to follow it to hopefully catch up with the others. It seems I wandered pretty close to the trail last night before the wolves found us.

I'm also thrilled when I come across a small stream. Jack and I take long drinks before I fill up my canteen, wishing it were bigger. I don't know when I'm going to come across water again.

My heart lightens at the thought that I might find Vela soon. I need to find my Intended. I need to hold her in my arms to know she's okay. I have a bad feeling she's injured somewhere and there's not a thing Rayne can do for her.

Jack bumps my hand as we make our way onto the trail.

"I know, buddy. We'll find her. If it's the last thing I do, we'll find her."

I pray my words are true.

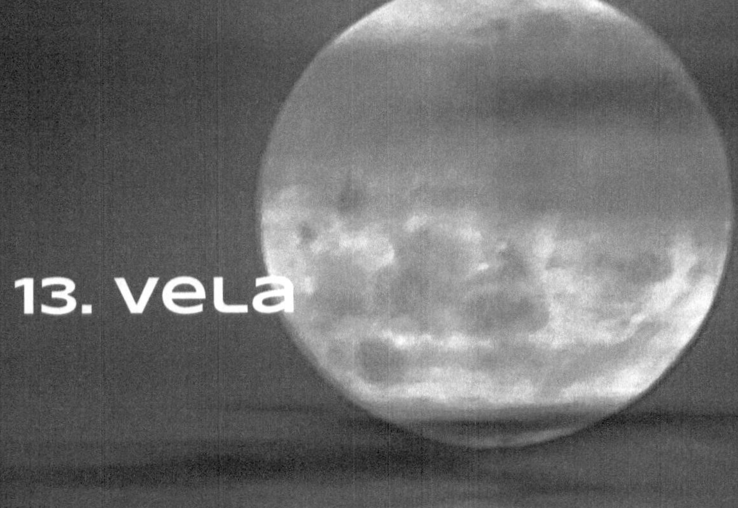

13. Vela

I slowly open my eyes to pink skies heralding another dawn. I thank God for giving me this day and ask that He help me overcome any obstacles and be a witness of His love and grace to Rayne. I also pray that Linc and Jack are okay. I hope that they've found each other at least.

Carefully rolling over, I turn to see Rayne getting up and busying himself by tidying up the campsite. I watch him, not announcing I'm awake, as he picks up the stack of firewood, bringing it closer to the ashes of last night's fire. I soon close my eyes, my heart clenched for him.

God, please give me an opportunity to tell him how much You love him. How can I show him who You are?

"I know you're awake," Rayne interrupts in a gruff voice.

I smile. Of course he does. He's as bad as Linc at reading me. Or, good, I can't decide.

Opening my eyes, I find him squatting next to the remnants of the fire, studying me.

"You seemed very serious just then," he says, waving his hand. "Before I said anything, I mean."

"I was. I'm very serious when I'm praying for someone."

His eyebrows raise. "Oh, yeah? Who, may I ask were you praying for?"

"You."

At my response, surprise comes over his face, but it's gone so quickly I'm not sure if I imagined it. His face soon twists in a sneer.

"Me? Why, in the world, are you praying for me? I thought you'd be praying for your precious *mate.*"

"He's not my mate yet. I prayed for God to show me how to tell you who He really is."

He huffs. "Good luck with that. I'm not very reachable."

My smile gets wider. "With God, all things are possible. He can reach you, if you let Him."

"Well, it's not happening today." He brushes his hands off and jumps up from his squatted position. "We should probably get an early start."

"Why were you starting another fire, then?"

He laughs. "It was habit, I guess. I'm used to having something to cook for breakfast. But, since we don't have anything but jerky and granola, there's no need."

"Okay. We should probably use as much of the light as we can today. It gets dark so fast nowadays."

"Yeah, the later in the year, the colder and shorter the days," he agrees.

"It's not too cold yet, at least." I hold my arms out. "Help me up, please?"

In answer, he walks over and, like he's done before, steps behind me, preparing to lift me up.

"One of these days, this will get easier," I say jokingly. I pick my head up and he slides his arms under me. He says in my ear, "We just need to get you to a Gyan healer.

I nod and he helps me up slowly. I must have a pained look on my face, because Rayne comes around and bends down to look me questioningly in the eyes. "It's okay. I'm okay." And slowly I realize I am feeling better than I did yesterday. It's got to be a good thing that my side doesn't ache as fiercely. It's a minor improvement, but I'll take it. My knee still throbs, but I'm so thankful for the reduction of pain in my side, I almost don't mind it.

"Thank you, God," I whisper, feeling such a feeling of gratitude, I duck my head.

Rayne makes quick work of stuffing his backpack. I hand him his shirt I used as a pillow and after it disappears into his backpack, he says gruffly, "I'm ready." He quickly walks over to me and braces me while I put my arm over his head.

It's painful, but bearable. I turn a smile to Rayne. "It's not as bad today."

His surprised look appraises me. "Your side or your knee?"

"My side. My knee is sadly, still pretty bad."

He nods.

We make our way slowly through the woods that surround our campsite. I admire the beauty of the place, wishing we had found a white willow tree among the poplars, evergreens, and maples.

"How do you know which way to go?" I ask, looking around.

"I'm following a trail. It must lead to a First Nation settlement."

I look at the ground, trying to see the trail.

As I limp along, he laughs softly. "You can't see what I do, can you?"

I shake my head.

"It's the small things. Crushed leaves, abandoned fox dens, animals staying as far away from us as possible."

I look around with new eyes and they widen in surprise at noticing broken pieces of foliage along the trail that I hadn't seen before. "How close do you think we are?"

He pauses for a moment, seeming to think. "A ways."

"That sounds suspiciously vague."

"That's because it is."

I glance over at his face to see if he's kidding with me. He's not. His face looks serious. "Why won't you tell me how far away we are, Rayne?"

He sighs heavily. "I'm trying to keep you from being discouraged."

My heart drops. I stop walking so I can look him fully in the face. "How far, Rayne?"

"I'd say at least a few miles." He avoids my eyes. "There will be more obvious signs of a trail the closer we get."

I rest my hand on his arm. It tenses under my touch. His eyes fly up to mine. And with my arm still around his neck, I can see his wariness easily. "Rayne, don't try to protect me from bad news. It's okay. We'll get there when we get there. Is there no hope of catching up to the rest of our group?"

He looks away. "I don't think so. Dropping into that ravine took us way to the east of the trail we were on. We were lucky to get out of it, to be honest, even if it was in the wrong direction. I think our best bet to get home is to find a First Nation settlement and someone who knows how to get back to that main trail. But first, you need healing."

He motions for us to start walking again. I just need to put my best foot forward to get there. Healing is in my future; I can feel it.

We're walking ridiculously slowly, because of my limp. When I stop to drink, I only take a few sips and then frown down at the canteen, because I'd like to drink a lot more.

"Why did you stop drinking?" Rayne asks.

"There's precious little water left, and we have to make it last," I say with a bitter tone.

Rayne looks at me with amusement. "I've told you I'm concerned about our food stores, but you're worried about our water?"

I look at him in surprise. "Oh, right? You're a Neronian." I laugh. "How did I forget that?"

He takes the canteen from me and, holding his hand above it, he fills it with beautiful liquid.

I take it from him and drink it down completely, handing it back to him.

He takes it back and, with an amused glance, uses his gift again.

I take a nice long drink until my belly's full of water. We continue walking on the small trail we've found. "Rayne, be on the lookout for a white willow tree. It's got a gray-brown bark that is really good for pain. I don't know if it grows out here, but it's worth a try."

He nods and we continue.

We walk, well, I limp, for another hour when Rayne heaves a big sigh and stops.

"What is it?" I ask, panting.

He slants me a look that's mixed with sympathy and frustration. "We're never going to get there today at this rate."

"Rayne, I'm trying..."

He interrupts me by raising his hand. "I know you're trying, Vela. You're being extremely valiant in all of this. But I want you to be seen by a healer. Today. So, I'm just going to have to do this."

Before I can ask him, 'What,' he stoops and slides an arm under my legs and another around my back and swings me up bridal style.

Pain tears through my side at the movement and I hiss. "Rayne, give me some notice you're doing that," I ask with a moan.

"Sorry. I thought it was better to ask for forgiveness than permission. You're incredibly stubborn. If I had told you what I was going to do, you'd argue, and we'd be even later getting some headway toward the First Nation encampment."

He starts walking, and I can't help but notice the strength in his arms. He lifted me so easily, like I was a ten-pound bag, not the 130 pounds that I am.

I blush at the feel of his muscles under me, and I stamp down the warmth filling my tummy. Looking at the side of his face, I marvel at truly how handsome he is. He's got perfect features. Nothing is wrong with his face.

Turning my head away from him so he won't see the burn of embarrassment on my cheeks and whatever *this* is I'm not wanting to feel. I chew my lip. Warmth fills me and my heart races at that implication.

I can't believe I'm attracted to him.

As much as I try to deny it, the feelings are there. I wipe all expression off my face so he can't see that I'm responding to him. But horror fills me that I'm feeling this way about Rayne. What about Linc? What about my feelings for him? They haven't gone away. So, I like two guys now?

He chuckles.

I whip my head toward him and ask, "What's so funny now?"

He sighs. "Oh, you, Vela. You're always a source of my amusement these days."

I sit in silence. Not quite fuming, but definitely unamused. I don't know what I did to warrant him laughing at me. There's no way he can know my thoughts. Or can he? What is his second Neronian or Borean gift? Can he have a second gift when he has both elements? I wrack my brain for answers but come up short. I almost ask him what it is, but I stop myself. I'm too embarrassed to ask. What if it's something like mind reading?

I remain quiet, stewing in my thoughts, refusing to let him know what I'm thinking.

We've walked about thirty minutes, and I can see from looking over Rayne's shoulder, he's covered twice the distance we had in an hour when I was limping along.

I sigh.

"What is it?" Rayne asks.

"I'm just so useless right now."

"You won't be forever. You'll be healed and back to your fighting self soon."

"Fighting?"

He slants an amused eye at me. "That's what we normally do. Fight. I'd like to get back to normal."

"So, you know, I've quite enjoyed seeing another side of you, Rayne. The nice side. And I don't think that all I do is fight with you."

He raises a brow at me and quirks a grin.

I frown. "Okay, so maybe I'm disagreeing with you right now. But I don't always."

He gives me the same deadpan look.

I laugh. "Well, maybe you're right. But it's not always my fault! You have a way of getting under my skin."

He considers me for a moment. "They say that opposites attract."

I look at him in shock, surprised at his comment. "Why would you go there?" I'm helpless to escape this conversation while held hostage in his arms. I want nothing more than to flee. Fight or flight instinct has just taken over. If I can't fly, I might as well do what I do best with him. Fight. Even if I am proving him right.

Half his mouth turns up in a grin. And I swear, his muscles flex under me. "Well, don't they?"

"Don't they what?"

"Don't opposites attract?"

"Yes, I guess they do. But that's not what this is!" I gesture between us.

"You say one thing, I say the other. You think one way, I think another. What do you call that?"

"Annoying conversation," I say in a dry tone.

He laughs, and I can't help but crack a smile.

We walk in companionable silence for some time.

Since I don't have to work so hard to keep myself upright now that I'm a passenger, I can notice my surroundings more. I see that the trail is looking more and more established. Like other feet have walked this way recently. It looks more like a path than it did before.

"We must be getting closer," I comment.

"Yeah, you noticed the trail?"

I nod. "I'm sorry you have to carry me all this way." I frown.

"It's no problem. You're not heavy."

I scoff. "Heavy enough. If you want to take a break, we can."

"Vela, I'm fine."

I start thinking about being carried into a settlement. I don't like the idea. "Rayne? How about when we get close, you let me down so I can walk in?"

"Why?"

"They're going to think I'm injured worse than I am, with you carrying me. I don't want to give that impression." Besides the fact that it'll look like I'm something more to him than I am. I don't say that, though.

"You are hurt, Vela. Badly. They'll see what they want to see, anyway."

"I'm not on death's door, Rayne."

"No, but you do have a bad injury, two of them. So, I'll be carrying you. End of discussion."

Anger flares up in me. "Remember when I said I liked the nice side of you? Make him come back. *You* are being annoying."

"Vela, I'm not going to take thirty minutes to walk to this place to get you the help you need when it could be done in five. That's ridiculous. All because of your pride? No. I'm not putting you down."

"It's not pride," I exclaim. "It's...oh never mind."

"What? Tell me what you were going to say."

I shake my head hard. I'm not telling him I think it's because it'll look like we're together. I can't say that, and I won't.

He shakes me. "Vela, spill it. Tell me what you were going to say."

"Ouch! And no."

He falls silent for a minute.

We walk, or he walks in a now uncomfortable silence.

Finally, he says, "I don't know what's going on in that head of yours, but if this is because you're worried people will think there's something between us, then put it out of your mind. I know my place with you."

If he said that then he can't know my thoughts. That's some relief, at least. But he sounds so final and curt. It's the tone that alerts me to his mood. He sounds unhappy and for some reason that makes my heart clench uncomfortably in my chest. I want to comfort him somehow, but I don't want to be anything more to him than a friend. So, I have to stay quiet. But surely, there's something I can say to lift this oppressive silence.

"You might find her one day, you know," I finally say softly.

He scowls and ignores me, but it's clear he knows exactly who I'm talking about.

"And when you do, you'll forget everyone else you've thought about that way. Trust me."

He's silent for so long, I'm not sure he heard me right. That is comforting, right? To find the one person meant just for you. Who wouldn't want that?

It's hard to be nearly cheek to cheek with someone who's not speaking to you. We're close, yet miles apart. When I think I'm going to scream just to change the air between us, Rayne speaks. "I don't want to forget, Vela."

I look at the side of his face. He's looking forward, but his jaw is jumping with how hard he's clenching it. "Rayne, I..."

"No, listen. I don't have many choices in my life. I'm forced to live in this backwoods settlement. Forced to hide who I am from the world. As much as I love my gifts, and they are a huge part of me, I didn't get to choose them either. I don't want to be forced into feeling things about a girl, too. *I* want to choose who I love. If I know anything, it's that I'll always choose to think of you and wish..."

When he doesn't finish, I say, "Rayne, you can't mean that." I shake my head, looking away, wishing I could describe the absolute need I feel when I'm around Linc. That he is mine, and that I'll always be his.

Rayne stops suddenly, his arms like two steel bands underneath me. "Vela, look at me."

I reluctantly turn my head and meet his darkening amber eyes. Now that I'm this close to him, I see that his eyes aren't merely honey brown. They have a depth to them I've never noticed before, with gold and green flecks.

"Don't tell me how I should feel," he says harshly, his eyes flashing. "I know my thoughts and no one, not even you, will ever change my mind."

My breath stops. "You don't understand, you can't possibly..."

"Don't you understand?" he growls. "*I* want to choose, and I choose..."

I stay silent, not wanting him to finish that sentence.

My heart sticks in my throat. He purses his lips and turns his head, walking forward again. "When you're ready to hear it, I'll finish telling you. Not until then. Let's just leave this conversation alone. I don't want to meet my Intended. She can't be that perfect. End of story."

I swallow my response because it's clear he doesn't want to hear it. But he couldn't be more wrong. She is more perfect than he could possibly imagine.

And it's not me.

Jack and I have been walking on the trail for an hour when I hear voices up ahead around a bend.

Picking up my pace, I run to see who it is. Two figures are hunched over a fire built just off the trail, and my heart flips in my chest. I think I see a blonde head, but when the person turns, it's Jerry, Gene's son. My stomach crashes to my feet in disappointment.

His face registers surprise, and he nudges Gene. Both stand up and walk toward me.

Jack reaches them first and greets both father and son.

"Linc! Where are the others?" Jerry calls out.

My disappointment at, once again, not finding Vela, is a tangible weight on my soul. So, it takes me a second to recover and say in a grudging tone, "Claudette, Tonya, and Andy are behind me. They'll catch up soon."

Jerry holds out his hand for me to shake, then pats my shoulder. "It's good to see you. We weren't sure anyone else survived that bear attack."

I rub my face and say without any preamble, "Have you seen any sign of Vela?"

Gene shakes his head. "No, and we haven't seen Rayne either. Think they're together?"

I nod. "I'm sure they are. I asked him to take her away when the bear attacked us."

"Okay. Do you know what happened to the bear?" Jerry asks. "Did someone kill it?"

"No," I answer grimly. "I thought I might have, but it got out of my fire trap and came back after us and some First Nation guys we met."

Jerry's eyebrows climb into his hairline. "Oh, really? How did you get away?"

I laugh. "I got into its head and convinced the mama bear to return to her cubs."

He whistles. "She had cubs? That explains her bad mood. Smart tactic."

"Yeah, that's one way to say it. Let's hope she and her cubs stay far away from us."

Jerry nods. "Definitely." He turns his head to look out into the forest. "Where could Vela and Rayne be, I wonder?"

I sigh heavily and put my hands on my hips. "I heard they went east. Tonya said she saw Vela forge a trail, so it should be easy enough to find it."

"You're planning on going after her?"

"Of course." I look at him incredulously.

How could he even think I wouldn't?

He nods. "I understand. Well, I know I'd get it more if it was my Intended lost in the woods. So, stupid question, huh?"

"Very." I give him a hard glare. "I was hoping she and Rayne would have made it back here by now."

"Sorry, man. Well, this was where we all split up. We figured it was smarter to come back here than to try to find everyone."

I nod. "Yeah, that's what everyone else planned, too. I can't believe she's not here, yet. I hope she's okay." I haven't quite gotten over Jerry's stupid question. But I blame my bad mood on not finding Vela and worrying about her.

"How is Claudette?" Gene asks. His serious gray eyes convey what we're all thinking. It'd be a miracle if she survived that attack. And it is. Thanks to Tonya's healing ability.

"She's okay. Tonya healed her. Well, as best she could. It's her secondary gift, so she's not as skilled as a full Gyan. But she saved her life, for sure."

Both men's eyes widen, and they smile in relief.

"Thank the Lord," Gene says.

"Absolutely. Now, I have to go and find the trail Vela blazed in her escape from the bear. Hopefully, I'll meet up with her on her way there."

"Shouldn't we stay together at this point?" Jerry asks.

I turn to glare at him. "I'm going to find my Intended. I'm not waiting. She could be hurt or worse. So, you can follow me if you want, but I suggest you and your dad stay together and wait for the others."

Jerry wisely stays quiet and nods after glancing at his father.

"We're going to continue to the Saddleback," Gene says. "Andy and the girls might end up returning to the Polar Bear. Will we see you at Saddleback?"

"I honestly don't know. I'll go wherever Vela does. If she wants to go to Saddleback, which I expect she will, since she wants to meet Sandy and James, then I'll see you there, eventually."

"Okay, my friend." Gene holds out his hand, and I shake it firmly.

"See you then," I tell them both. I flick my hand in a short wave and call Jack to me. Without resting, I turn to search for the trail Vela forged in the dense undergrowth.

I soon spot an opening to a fresh trail a hundred yards off the main path.

Jogging to it, I see that it looks exactly like the one she trailblazed when we were together in Colorado. I have to stop and hold my breath for a minute. My chest hurts so badly, it immobilizes me. I miss her so fiercely. To settle myself, I breathe through the rage that fills me at knowing I left her with someone I don't trust.

Why did I do that?

Then I remember. It was because Rayne can fly. He could have taken her to the sky and away from that maniacal bear.

Even so, he didn't do that. They ran like the rest of us. She could have done that with me. And I wouldn't be worried sick about her.

I breathe in and out of my nose to control my racing heartbeat. I'm terrified she's hurt and needs help. Forcing the thought from my mind, I do the only thing I can. Follow this trail and pray.

God, keep her safe. Keep her healthy. Keep Rayne's hands off her.

I shake my head at my last prayer, but I might as well be honest with God about what's on my mind. It's not like He doesn't already know. I am completely sincere about that particular prayer request.

Remembering the intoxicating scent Vela carries that signals she's just for me, makes me long to fill my nostrils with it right now. I love that she smells like my favorite scents: rose and honey butter rolls. It's how I knew immediately that she was my Intended.

That memory just never gets old. That was when I first figured out Vela was my soulmate. I can think of that all day long and relive it over and over again.

So, that's what I do.

Vela's trail is easy enough to follow, so I allow my thoughts to wander. As much as I want to find her at the end of it, I don't at the same time. Because that would mean something's wrong. That she couldn't leave for some reason.

A million terrible scenarios fill my head, and I come close to yelling at the top of my lungs to vent my frustration.

Why wasn't she at our meeting point? Where is she? How is she?

In order to keep myself from going crazy, I go back to that first memory and bury my thoughts in the beauty of it.

Jack barks at me and nudges my knee as I walk.

"I know, buddy. I miss her, too. We'll find her. Hopefully soon."

Or not. She should be far from the end of this trail by now.

Returning my thoughts back to that happy memory, I walk in silence with Jack trotting next to me.

I'm confused when I get to the end of Vela's trail. It ends at a ledge over a deep, narrow ravine. My stomach drops.

Don't tell me Rayne dropped her into that.

I race to the edge, hoping I'm wrong. Looking down, I see steep walls with nothing at the bottom but a rocky floor. Nothing could possibly grow in that space. It's all unforgiving rock. I kneel to get a better look and see vines that grow from here down the walls.

Did Vela and Rayne climb down those to get away from the bear?

No. Rayne must have flown them down. But how did they get out of that place? Did he fly them out, too? And why does the floor of the ravine look wet?

Jack barks at me, and I push him away from the edge. No reason for him to fall down in that pit.

I shake my head at the confusing scene I'm facing. I have more questions than I do answers, and that's driving me crazy. Why are there traces of water at the bottom of the ravine? There's no river nearby, so where did that water come from? And how on earth did Vela and Rayne get out of that mess? And why did they fly down there in the first place? The bear was chasing me.

That's when I spot a rockslide further down that leads out on the opposite side of the ravine. They could have climbed out on that.

Did Vela get hurt in the fall, or killed? Icy cold fear spears my chest.

No. I would have felt it she was taken from me in this world.

My heart hammering wildly in my chest, I look up at the sky.

God, please tell me she's okay. Protect her, Lord.

I quickly surmise that Rayne flew them down into the ravine, possibly to get them away from the bear. But the bear wasn't even that close to them, so *why* would he do that?

Either way, they must have ended up down there. Then they climbed the rockslide to get out. Or he flew them out.

My question now is how am I going to catch up to them? I can't fly down there like Rayne. And I don't think I'd catch up to them if I try to go around.

I pull off my backpack and fish out the rope that I packed, thanking God I did.

"Jack, come here, boy. You're going on my back."

In my mind, there's no choice. If I'm going to catch up to Vela, I've got to climb down the ravine and follow her footsteps. And Jack is going down with me. I can't leave him up here. If I, no, *when* I catch up to her, I need to have her favorite companion to greet her with. She'd love me forever for bringing Jack with me.

And I will receive major brownie points for the effort it will take to do it. I've grown very fond of her famous brownie points. She always rewards me with the most delicious kisses whenever I earn them. My heart pounds at the thought.

My mind made up, I know it'll take some maneuvering to get Jack to sit still long enough to tie him to my back.

After a frustrating ten minutes, I give up and reluctantly use my gift to subdue him. He's finally pliant as I wrap him securely with the rope, then tie him to me. I'm going to have to keep my connection with him as we descend.

I don't have a choice. He won't be calm enough and would end up wiggling himself out of the ropes halfway down if I don't. I cringe at the thought.

Remember, brownie points.

Smiling, I finish tying Jack to me, tightening the ropes as much as I can.

With my connection to Jack holding strong, I take a deep breath and whisper, "Vela. I'm coming, baby. I'm coming for you. Hold tight."

"You, too, Jack."

He doesn't like it. But he has no choice but to obey.

15. VeLa

My heart thumping excitedly, I point at the rooftops I see in the distance. "Rayne, is that it, the First Nation settlement?"

"Yes," he says, panting lightly. It took miles to happen but carrying me such a long distance has finally begun to wear his stamina thin.

"Will you let me down now?" I ask in an exasperated breath. I've been begging him to let me walk for a mile now and he's refused each time. He claims it's because he can more easily look for the willow tree if he doesn't need to support me on one side. But I don't buy that.

"We're almost there," he says tightly.

I can't believe he's being so stubborn about this. I can see his neck straining and feel his arms shaking with the prolonged effort of carrying me.

"So, no." I huff, frustrated. If my side didn't hurt so much, I would wiggle out of his arms, but he and I both know I could never manage it.

And now, he wins this argument, yet again.

"I can't believe we made it!"

"I told you we would."

"I know. But I never considered finding a settlement up here. Do you think they have generators like we do at the Polar Bear?"

"I think they might have solar panels. That's what I've heard, anyway. If this settlement is part of a reservation, residents would get rebates from the government for using them."

I raise my eyebrows and can't wait to see for myself how they live way out here. I was shocked enough by The Polar Bear and this location is even more remote.

Patiently, I sit still in Rayne's arms and brace myself for the questioning looks I'm sure we'll get when we're spotted.

As we walk, Linc suddenly fills my thoughts. I have a terrible feeling he's going through something, but there's no way to know what. I cling to my hope that he survived the bear attack. He and Jack. I send up a prayer that they're both safe. How is Linc handling my absence? I'm sure everyone reconvened back at the trail where we all split up, and he's panicking that I'm not there.

God, please give him peace about me. Please keep him safe. And Jack, too. Keep all of them safe.

Keeping my head bowed, I repeat that prayer over and over until I finally feel a fragile peace wash over me. I hold on to it, refusing to let any other thoughts rob me of my tenuous relief.

Because my head is bowed, I don't notice our entrance into the community.

"Momma, who is that?" a little voice carries to me, and I pop my head up.

A little girl with long black braids hanging over her shoulders points at me and tugs on the pant leg of a woman standing next to her. The woman hushes her, and they watch us walk up.

I can't help but blush at the thought of Rayne carrying me like a bride.

Rayne stops in front of the woman and asks with sweat shining on his forehead, "Hello. I'm Rayne and this is Vela. She's been badly injured. Do you have a healer? A Gyan healer?"

I look on with wide eyes at the woman, who I can sense is fully human. She looks me over with a questioning glance and jerks her head for us to follow her. Walking into the community of small wooden homes, much like ours at the Polar Bear, she holds her daughter's hand. The little girl keeps looking over her shoulder at me with bright, curious eyes. The girl, however, is not fully human. I gasp when I realize she's an Elemental, but I study her because she doesn't feel quite like an Elemental would. It's like her power is softer, not as powerful. She's a Borean, but instead of my blood icing over, it travels in a cool wave through my veins.

"Momma, who are they?" the girl asks in a clear, bell-like voice. She's shushed again, and I can't help but be reminded of Greta and Hannah. My chest clenches at how much I've come to care for them; I miss them terribly. This girl looks a little younger than Greta. I'm guessing she's six.

I wonder where the woman's leading us. As we walk, we attract more and more attention. People stop what they're doing to stare as Rayne carries me further into this quaint place. They are all dark-haired and have tanned skin. And just like I experienced with the little girl, some of them exude the same soft Elemental gifting. Others are fully human. I can't keep the shock from showing on my face. I never thought I'd be in mixed company with humans who know about our gifts.

The people study us with dark eyes. Most were doing various things around their homes. I see some standing with saws and hammers, working on projects.

I admire the community we've entered. It's charming. The homes are spaced farther apart than those at the Polar Bear and each has a nice yard adorned with flowering bushes.

When we've drawn close to the middle of the community, the woman stops at a home and knocks on the door.

As we stand there, the little girl tugs on her mom's hand and when she bends down, the little girl whispers something in her ear. The woman hushes her again, but the girl peeks at us, giggling.

I can't help but smile at her as we wait for the door to open.

"He likes you," the girl announces in her high, cheerful voice. "I can tell."

My eyes pop open at her announcement, and my face burns pink. I turn accusing eyes to Rayne.

He looks at the little girl with amusement flickering in his eyes.

"Rayne! Do you see what this looks like? Even a child can see it!" I hiss at him.

The girl giggles again.

Rayne turns his direct gaze to me, and my breath stops. "Let them think what they want," he says dismissively and looks away.

"Rayne, I don't want *anyone* to think we're a...we're a..."

"A couple?" he twists his mouth in a frown. "So sorry to disgust you."

"You don't disgust me," I say, sighing.

He rolls his eyes. "You keep telling yourself that."

Why would he think that? I've not given any sign of feeling like he repulses me. In fact, I've had to hide the opposite. Ignore feelings I don't want to really examine too closely.

He stands waiting for the door to open and soundly ignores me. I'm so mad, I could spit fire. Just when I'm about to bop him on the head, the door opens.

An older man with peppery short gray hair says, "Hello, Rima. Who do you have with you?"

The woman speaks in a soft voice, gesturing to us. "They asked for a healer."

He nods at her and looks me over. "Please come in." I can sense he's a Gyan, but like the little girl, the sensation pulses weakly through me.

My stomach drops in disappointment. Will he be able to heal me properly?

The woman tugs the little girl's hand, and they walk away. I'm sad to see them go, if only because they remind me so much of what I left behind in the Polar Bear. When Rayne walks us in, the man turns and says, "Please don't mind Rima. She's just lost her husband, so she's not very social these days."

Rayne and I nod, and my heart tightens at what Rima's going through.

The man rubs his hands together. "I'm Grey. I'm the town healer. We don't see too many strangers around here. I'm going to make a wild guess and assume you're my patient?" He asks me with a twinkle in his kind eyes, and I can't help but be instantly comfortable with him. He turns toward a closed door and gestures for us to follow him. "Please, come this way. Let's see what's troubling you."

Rayne's breathing has settled now that he's had a brief rest from walking. He carries me over to a twin-sized bed situated in the middle of the small room and sets me down carefully.

"Thank you," I say softly and sink into the mattress that feels like it's full of feathers. I marvel at how many birds it would take to fill this bed up.

Rayne doesn't step away. Instead, he gives Grey a hard look.

Grey laughs. "Don't worry, young man. I would never harm, only heal."

My mouth drops open at Rayne's protectiveness. "Rayne, it's fine. He's okay," I assure him.

He glares at the older man, then steps back.

I'm confused by Rayne's sudden attitude shift. He's the one who worked so hard to get me to a healer. Now that I'm with one, he's giving him the third degree.

I try to cushion Rayne's rudeness by giving Grey a smile.

He doesn't seem to mind Rayne's attitude; his mouth is turned up in a friendly smile. "I sense you are fully of the Healing gift. I feel it very strongly in you. It's too bad you cannot heal yourself."

I nod sadly.

"Okay, may I examine you?"

"She has a bruised rib and a hurt knee," Rayne says in a rough voice.

Grey glances at him, then turns to me. "Let me see for myself." He places soft hands on my side. I'm leaning on my left side to keep from hurting my right. He seems to understand that, and I feel a slight warmth from his hand on my injured side. He turns his head away and furrows his brow as he concentrates.

"It's not broken, which is good," Grey announces.

"Like I said," Rayne says gruffly.

Grey chuckles. "Yes, you did. Now, let's look at her knee."

I grip the edges of the mattress, expecting fierce pain as he examines me.

His hands are so gentle, I only experience mild discomfort, and slowly relax as he softly touches the areas around the part of my knee that radiate pain.

His hands are warm, like before, but he's not trying to heal, only sense the injury. I look at him in tense silence as he explores the extent of the damage.

"Well?" Rayne growls.

Grey stands up and breathes out slowly. "She's got a torn ligament. It will take more healing than I can give."

Rayne curses under his breath.

I turn disapproving eyes to him before I look at Grey again. "Can you heal it a little? Relieve some of the pain?"

He looks at me with sympathy. "I can help a little with the discomfort. And I will try to repair the tear, but I know my limits, and this is out of the scope of my gifting."

Rayne spins and turns, walking out of the room.

I absorb what Grey just told me. If he can help with the pain after trying to repair the ligament, I'll be grateful for that much.

Rayne stalks back into the room. "I'd like a minute with her."

I look at Rayne warily as Grey nods and leaves the room. "Rayne, if this is the best he can do, we don't have much of a choice and even a little relief will help."

"There's got to be someone else who can help you," he says, his eyes flashing angrily.

"There is."

When Rayne looks at me waiting, I finish, "Hannah can heal me completely. We just need to get back to her."

He nods.

"Rayne, we can't turn down what Grey is willing to do for me."

"I just wish I wasn't so useless," he says, in a low voice.

"Rayne," I say softly. "You're far from useless. Let him help me as much as he can and be *thankful*. Please?" I reach out and grip his hand, and he clenches it tightly and sits on the edge of the bed.

His forehead is scrunched, and his mouth is set in a thin, unhappy line. "I *hate* that I can't help you."

I squeeze his hand with both of mine. "Can you hear yourself? You carried me for miles. You got me out of the ravine before we were boiled alive. You've done amazing things. Now, can you let Grey back in here so he can fix all he can and give me some pain relief?"

Rayne grimaces, shame washing over his face, and stands up, making me release his hand. "Of course. I'm sorry. Vela, I'm sorry for all of it, that you're hurt in the first place." His fists clench at his sides, and I almost lean forward to hold his hand again.

The pain in my side stops me. "Don't think of it for a minute. You were trying to save me from a man-eating bear. Remember?" I smile at him, hoping he will really listen to me.

He nods curtly and leaves the room.

Grey walks in, smiling. "Are you ready?"

"More than I can say," I breathe and lean back on the bed. "And," I lean on my good side, "I want to say thank you from the bottom of my heart for helping a total stranger."

He smiles kindly. "I'm just happy I can do something. I can't help as much as I'd like, but I do what I can."

"Well, I thank you," I say sincerely.

"Tell me that when I'm done," he says, chuckling.

I lie back down, and Grey leans over me, starting with my rib. His hands warm as he lays them on my skin. I savor the feeling of pain disappearing. When he lifts his hands, the pain is completely gone. I'm so happy I can breathe normally; I laugh and enjoy it when it doesn't pierce my side.

"Now," he says, his breathing a little labored. "For your knee."

"Do you need to take a break?" I ask. "Maybe replenish your gift outside?"

Grey pauses and looks at me. "That's a good idea. I'll be right back."

Rayne walks in just when Grey leaves. "Are you healed? Well, for the most part?"

I smile up at him. "My rib feels much better, but he had to go replenish his gift before he starts on my knee."

Rayne's forehead furrows. "He's not done?"

I look at him sympathetically. "You're used to Hannah's full gift. Give Grey a break."

Rayne frowns.

Grey returns, his skin returned to its natural hue. "Okay, I'm ready." He reaches for my knee almost eagerly. It's obvious he loves his gift. I wish I could lend him some of mine. Alas, I can only do that with Linc. Grey places one hand on top of my knee, and the other on the side. I gasp at the warmth flooding my injury. After a few seconds, Grey sags and has to sit on the edge of my bed.

He's breathing heavily, and I wait for him to get his breath back.

When he's ready, he picks his head up and stands back up. He asks, "Can you bend your knee at all?"

I can already tell I won't be able to bend it much, but for the benefit of the exam, I attempt to slide my foot up the bed. I make it an inch before I have to stop.

I'm panting when Grey puts his hand on my leg to prevent me from trying any further. "I'm sorry that I can do no more for you, young one. I'll give you some crutches, but I'm afraid your injury will take time to heal."

Rayne grumbles quietly, and I flash a warning glare at him.

"Thank you, Grey. I so appreciate all you've done for me. You are a blessing. I'm feeling better."

He smiles tiredly. "I see you both also have burns on your face. They look like bad sunburns. Do you want me to heal them?"

Personally, I've gotten used to the burns on my neck, face and arms. And Grey looks like he's ready to drop, so I shake my head.

Rayne shakes his head, too, and Grey nods, leaving the room.

Rayne steps up to the bed. "I'll be back. I'm going to go ask how to get back to the main trail, so we can go home."

My stomach drops, not because I'd like to be healed by Hannah, but because my plan to meet James and Sandra, my possible birth parents, has been robbed of me.

I nod morosely and try not to let crushing grief over my injury, missing Linc and Jack, and my failed plans take over me.

Desperate to hold on to the blessing I just received, I bow my head and take my disappointments to the Lord.

16. LINC

S weat drips into my eye as I grip the thick vine with both hands, clinging to it like the lifeline it is. Thanks to my gift, Jack's handling the awkward descent down the ravine well, but I feel his heart pumping wildly through the back of my shirt. He knows he's not on the ground, and despite my firm control of his actions, his will is protesting our precarious situation.

I'm handling the descent fairly well, my strength coming in very handy right now. But it's awkward.

I transferred my backpack to my front, so I could secure Jack to my back more easily. I'm struggling to reach the vine and carrying Jack's weight plus mine is not easy to manage.

My legs are wrapped around the vine, and I thank God that it's holding. I tested it first by giving it a couple of hard yanks, but I'm still nervous and praying it holds.

We're now halfway down, and I'm tempted to slip down the rest of the way, but I'm afraid the landing will be too hard, and I'll break a leg and hurt Jack. So, slow going it is. Muscles trembling, my arms start screaming at me for a break I cannot give. I grip the vine tightly with one hand and reach down for another handhold.

Remember, brownie points.

That's all I need to think about as I do this. When Vela hears what I did to reunite her with Jack, she will definitely reward me. I smile, despite harsh breaths sawing through my throat.

One hand after the other. Keep control of Jack. One hand after the other.

Three quarters of the way down, I suck in a breath when the vine creaks loudly.

That can only mean one thing.

It's ripping from the root or breaking off.

I have to make a split-second decision, and I don't hesitate. I loosen my grip and slide down the rest of the way, with one eye on the ravine floor. The vine rubs my hands raw as I slide, and I grit my teeth as my skin tears. Right before I reach the bottom, I tighten my grip, squeezing as hard as I can.

I manage to hold on and just as my feet reach the bottom, the vine rips loose from its roots, goes limp in my hands, and comes crashing down around me.

Breath heaving, I reach up to dry the sweat off my forehead with my arm. Then I wipe my torn-up hands on my pant legs, wincing at the pain.

Even with my firm control over Jack, I can sense his impatience to be off my back and on solid ground.

Loosening the ropes connecting Jack and me is not easy now that my palms are raw. I ignore the sting and, with numb fingers, make it work. I stoop so Jack can slide off my back as I release my connection with him.

Jack slides off my back and shakes his body as if to rid himself of an unwelcome invader, which I guess I was. He runs in a circle, wiggling his body the entire time.

"I know, buddy. It's good to have your mind back. Sorry I had to do that."

Now that we're on the ground, I look around for any evidence of Vela and Rayne being here. I'm careful to study the ground for any traces of blood.

I'm relieved when I don't see any.

What I do see is as confusing as it was at the top of the ravine. The ground is wet in patches all around, and I cannot figure out why. I frown at the thought that the water would have washed away any signs of blood..

My brows shoot up into my hairline when I see water lines on the ravine walls, too.

This place fills up with water. How?

I decide not to attempt to make sense of this and just focus on tracking Vela and getting out of here. It's impossible to track anything down here because the ground is solid rock. Moss grows on the sides of the ravine walls and, of course, the vines trail down them.

A disappointed sigh escapes me as I come to terms with not seeing any proof that Vela was even here. I look up to where I climbed from and wonder if I made a terrible mistake.

What if she didn't come this way?

No, I tell myself firmly. Her trail ended at the edge, and I'm sure she reached this point. I won't allow doubt to make me question my decision.

With that thought firmly in mind, I call Jack to me and head toward the rockslide. I try to ignore the fire in my hands. I should be grateful that's all I'm feeling and not a broken leg.

I'm heading to the rockslide when I pass the answer to the riddle of why this place fills up with water. There's a huge hole in the ground, and I make sure to call Jack to me, so he won't accidentally fall into it.

It's a geyser.

Just when I figure it out, steam puffs out of the hole.

Alarm fills me, and I yell at Jack to follow me.

Jack and I run up to the rockslide, and I wonder if he'll be able to make it over the rocks. I assess them critically and decide they're big enough for him to get all four paws on.

But not if that geyser goes off. He'll have a hard time not slipping.

It takes some convincing, but I get Jack to follow me as I jump from one big rock to another. He makes his own way up the rocks, and I'm impressed again with his natural sense of survival. He even ran away at the first sign of the bear, so it's clear he's got good survival instincts. The way he's rushing up the rocks, I think he knows that the geyser is about to explode with boiling hot water.

We're making it up in good time when I hear gurgling. It sounds like it's coming from deep underground.

I look over my shoulder and see a thin stream of water explode out of the geyser. I won't take any chances of Jack slipping down the rockslide, so I hop over boulders to Jack and heave him up. I grunt when the first drops of scalding water fall on our heads.

Jack wiggles in my arms at the contact of the water, and I connect with his mind again. I have no choice; I need Jack to be still, so I can climb out of here. I have to take over his mind again.

In a final burst of power, water explodes into the sky as the geyser expels its geothermal charge.

Sizzling hot water falls on our heads in fat drops, and I choose the driest rocks I can find for footholds. Soon, all the rocks are rain slicked, and I do my best to traverse from rock to rock safely, all the while commanding Jack to be still.

My breath quickens when I hear another gurgling sound, and then another. *Three geysers?*

I wince at the blistering rain and hope Jack's fur protects him like my jacket is protecting most of me. My face and neck aren't as lucky, and I breathe through the scalding pain. Not sure how long I can take this water trying to melt my skin off, I climb as quickly as I can with a 100-pound dog in my arms.

Remember, brownie points. Vela's kisses are definitely worth this.

When I plant my foot down on the next rock, my foot starts slipping, and I tense my body, swaying as I try not to fall. I push my leg down, trying to find purchase and finally do. By the time my foot stops sliding, I'm in a full lunge.

Breathing heavily, I focus on bringing my front foot back to where my other one is. Afraid I'll slip again, I slide it on the wet rock instead of picking it up and placing it down. Once my feet are together again, I plant my feet solidly to avoid what just happened.

When I'm confident I have a good grip, I climb to the next boulder.

By this time, my neck and face are on fire from the scorching shower, but I ignore it and focus all my attention on getting up these rocks and out of the ravine.

With one final lunge, we make it to the top, and I jog out of the range of those hateful geysers.

Setting Jack down carefully, I run my hands over him before releasing my hold on his mind. After inspecting him without any yelps or cries, I release him, mentally and physically. His fur must have protected him.

Thank God.

He wiggles like before, shaking off my influence over him along with the water from our unwelcome and too hot shower.

I kneel on the ground and look at what just chased us up these rocks. Three enormous geysers blow water out at top strength. If I hadn't just been in their path, I'd say it was a beautiful sight. I try to catch my breath, my muscles spent from the descent down the ravine wall and carrying a 100-pound dog up a slippery rockslide. My arms are trembling, but I reach up and touch my face to see how bad my burns are.

I wince as I carefully pat my cheeks. Now that I'm out of the hot deluge, it feels more like a bad sunburn than anything worse.

Suddenly filled with gratitude for God's protection, I thank Him for keeping us safe. I bow my head and just revel in His presence. Awe fills me, and I take a moment to enjoy this closeness with my Creator. I felt His presence during the descent into the ravine and on the rocky ascent. And I feel Him now.

Jack barks, and I look up, expecting an animal or another geyser. But he just wants attention. I happily give it to him, smoothing down his sleek, wet face. I kiss his cheek, which he happily reciprocates.

"We've been through a lot together, haven't we, boy? First a man-eating bear, then a pack of wolves. Now geysers try to boil us alive."

He looks at me, his nub of a tail wagging and his tongue lolling out of his mouth, like he's used to life-threatening situations by now.

"Well, let's hope it's smooth sailing from here and it's easy to catch up to your mommy."

He just looks back at me as if to ask, *What's our next adventure?*

I look around and say the only thing I can, "We'll have to see, buddy. Let's hope it's nothing life threatening this time."

17. Vela

Rayne is only gone for about ten minutes when he walks briskly back into the room. "I found someone who can guide us back home." He walks up to my bed quickly and picks me up as easily as if I was a doll.

"Wait," I protest, "I thought Grey was giving me crutches?"

He shakes his head as he walks out of the room. "That'll slow us down too much. We're doing this my way."

"Rayne, I feel like I should have a say in this."

He continues to walk out of the house. We pass Grey, and I say a hurried goodbye. He returns it and we're out of the house before I know it.

Rayne walks purposefully down the street until he approaches a house with Rima's little girl playing outside.

Her eyes light up at the sight of us, and she jumps up, holding a homemade doll.

Rayne approaches the door and looks at me, tilting his head at the door. Rolling my eyes, I knock on it. We wait for a moment before a guy around our age opens it.

The teen looks at me curiously and with some amusement.

I swallow a disgruntled snort. If Rayne wasn't so freaking stubborn, I wouldn't have to be carried around everywhere like a child.

"Can I help you?" he asks Rayne.

"We're here to talk to Roland," Rayne says gruffly. He glares at the guy when his eyes return to me with interest leaking in his expression. I immediately sense he's Borean, like the little girl. Not whole, but partially.

"Yeah, come in. He's here."

We walk in and a man, older than the one who opened the door, but younger than I expected, glances up from the couch. He sharpens a wicked-looking knife. For some reason, I expected the guide would be older. This guy looks to be in his early thirties. He has long hair that is tied back with a leather cord. Rima walks into the room, drying her hands on a towel.

I wonder how they are related. Grey said Rima had just lost her husband, so who is Roland? He can't be her biological brother, since he's Borean, like her daughter and the teen guy. He must be her brother-in-law.

The teen guy says, "These people are looking for you."

I lean into Rayne's ear. "Let me down, please. There's no reason for you to hold me in here."

He hesitates as the teen turns and gives me a smile. I pinch Rayne's arm, and he shoots me a glare. I glare right back, and he finally sets me down. He keeps an arm around my waist, and I can't knock it off, because it's helpful to keep my balance.

"If you're looking for the Healer, he doesn't live here," the man says gruffly.

Rayne doesn't waste any time asking, "Are you Roland?"

The man nods sharply and runs a stone slowly down the blade of his knife. "Who are you?"

"I'm Rayne. This is Vela. We need to get back to the Polar Bear Lodge. Do you know it?"

Roland studies us under heavily lidded eyes, and I can't for the life of me figure out what he's thinking. He has the best poker face of anyone I've ever met. He finally nods. "I do. Why do you need to go there?"

"We live there. We were on our way to the Saddleback community when a huge bear attacked our party. Vela's hurt, and your healer couldn't heal her completely. We need to get back to the Polar Bear and the healer there."

"Did the bear do that to her?" He nods his head in my direction.

"No," I say. "We had to jump into a ravine. It was the fall that did it."

Rayne's face looks like it's set in stone, but I see him clenching his jaw. I know he feels guilty for my injuries, but I had to say the truth about what happened.

"Did you fly her down?" he asks Rayne.

Rayne's fist clenches at my side. "I tried. She fell when we landed."

Roland nods as if deciding something. That's when I wonder how much of his blood is Borean. I can't guess, only that it's stronger than Grey's, but less than Rayne's. He sets down his knife. "I will take you to the Polar Bear. But only if they are willing to trade my services for supplies my community needs."

"If we can part with it, we'll be happy for the trade," Rayne answers easily. "I'm sure we have something you can carry back."

Rima speaks up. "Is this wise to leave now?"

Roland gives her a look, and she falls silent. He returns his gaze to us and says, "It should only take two days to get there. Will you be carrying her the whole way?"

Rayne nods while I shake my head.

Roland looks between us, his eyebrows raised, and his lips looking decidedly unamused.

"Grey said he'd give me crutches," I say defiantly, putting my hand on my hip.

"She won't be using them. I'll carry her. It'll be faster," Rayne says, his tone firm.

Roland turns his gaze from me to Rayne. "It would," he agrees. "But only if she agrees. I won't have a woman forced into any decision." His eyes turn hard as he glares at Rayne.

Rayne inhales sharply, turns to look at me, and says under his breath. "Vela, don't be stubborn about this. Let me help you." His eyes beg me to give in.

"Rayne, I..."

"Please, Vela," he asks in a guttural voice.

A moment passes when I can hardly breathe under the intensity of his gaze. I finally nod, albeit reluctantly.

"Okay," Roland announces. "Let's look at a map. I'll show you how we are to travel."

Since I have no interest in studying a map and suddenly feel tired, I ask Rayne to help me to the other room.

I've completely forgotten the little girl until she pops up beside the chair Rayne finds for me.

"Hi," she says in a cheerful voice.

I look at her in surprise and smile at her. "Hi, what's your name?"

"Aponi," she says in the sweetest voice. "It means butterfly."

Her eyes blink up at me and I have to ask her, "How old are you, little butterfly?"

"Six," she says proudly, holding up one hand with five fingers splayed open.

I laugh. "You need one more."

She looks at me curiously with her head cocked.

"You need one more finger to be six," I tell her, trying to keep amusement from my tone. It's hard, though.

"Oh!" she says and adds another finger. "I just turned six, so I forgot."

"That's okay." I smile at her sweetly.

She regards me silently, and I'm suddenly at a loss for words. I want to ask her how she likes living out here, but I'm sure this is all she's ever known, like Greta. She probably has no idea what else is out there.

"You like him, too," she suddenly says, a mischievous glint in her eye.

My eyebrows pop up into my hairline. "What?"

"I can tell that you like your friend. Like, like, I mean." She looks in Rayne's direction, and I hold my breath. *Why would she say that?*

"No, I don't," I say slowly.

She bops her head up and down in a sure and confident way. "Yes, you do. I can tell," she repeats. I furrow my brows and fall silent. How do I argue with a six-year-old? I'm saved from trying when Rayne walks into the room with the teen.

"Sam here is going to get us more food, so we won't have to hunt on our way back," he says. He looks at Aponi and smiles thinly at her.

"You haven't told her, have you?" Aponi asks Rayne. She looks at him with a direct gaze that twinkles with merriment.

I'm amazed at how mature she's acting.

This time Rayne looks at her with surprise, which I'm sure my face still reflects, too. "Excuse me?" he asks.

Sam laughs and tells Aponi, "Hush, now. They don't need to know your secrets."

She laughs in a clear, bell-like voice. "It's not my secret. It's his." She points at Rayne.

Rayne looks at us with a confused expression. "I don't know what she's talking about."

"Yes, you do," she argues and giggles loudly.

Sam rolls his eyes and walks past us, ushering the girl toward the door.

"You need to tell her, you know," she orders Rayne before she's pushed outside.

I look at Rayne with confusion. "What is she talking about?"

A guilty look crosses his face before he smooths it out. "I have no idea," he says firmly. He leans down and swings me into his arms. I'm so relieved that my side doesn't scream at that movement that I forget for a second what Aponi said.

It comes back though when she's waiting for us outside.

I'm surprised when Rayne gives her a hard look when he walks past her.

"What was that look for?" I whisper to him.

"She needs to mind her own business."

"So, you do know what she's talking about," I whisper furiously at him. I look over his shoulder and see she's following us.

His arms tense under me. "She only knows what most of us do."

I furrow my brow. "That's not cryptic or anything."

He glances at me. "I said, most."

I blow out a frustrated breath. "Rayne, what are you talking about?" This time I nearly shout it instead of whispering at him.

Aponi skips her way up and walks beside us. "He knows you like him. And he likes you, too," she says in a singsong voice.

My mouth drops open in a surprised 'O'. "What? I do *not* like him that way."

"Yes, you do, and he knows it. He knows everything," she says in such a cheerful voice, I have to look at her twice. She's enjoying this. By the look of Rayne's twisted mouth, maybe it's him she enjoys making squirm.

"Rayne," I say, hitting him on the shoulder, "What is she talking about? Why do you look so guilty?"

"I'm not guilty," he quickly says. Then turns to Aponi. "Listen, kid. Keep your observations to yourself."

"Why?" she asks in an innocent voice. "It's true."

"It is *not*," I say forcefully.

Aponi smiles, then glances wickedly between us.

Sam, who's walking ahead of us, calls back, "Aponi. Stop badgering them with your gift."

Her gift? Her Borean gift? Is this the second gift I don't know about?

I whip my head to Rayne, and he turns his head to avoid my direct question. "Rayne? If you don't tell me what she's talking about, I *will* hurt you."

My heart is beating wildly inside me, and I look between Rayne and Aponi, dreading the worst.

"Can you read my thoughts?" I ask in a small voice.

He shakes his head hard as Aponi laughs out loud. She holds her hands up to her mouth like she's stopping herself from answering me.

"No, I can't. But I do have other gifts," he says in a reluctant voice.

"*What other gifts?*" I ask with clenched teeth.

He continues walking like this isn't a mind-blowing conversation.

"Rayne, stop. Stop walking," I order with pressed lips.

He does but looks straight ahead and refuses to meet my furious gaze.

"Tell me what she's talking about." I'm physically stopping myself from pulling a branch from the nearby tree and whacking him over the head with it.

He sighs heavily. "I honestly thought you knew. But then it became obvious you didn't."

"Know what?" I grit out.

He looks at me from the side of his eye and presses his lips together stubbornly.

Aponi bursts out like she can't contain herself, "I told you. He knows how you feel." Then she giggles so hard she bends over.

I turn astonished eyes to Rayne. "You can sense emotions?" I whisper with horrified lips.

He glances at me, then resumes walking. "Yes," he says curtly.

I can only stare at him, open-mouthed with shock. "All those times you laughed...reacted," I whisper, my throat closing in abject misery. "You knew?"

He glances at me with a semi-guilty expression and nods. He looks like he wants to defend himself, but not before I violently wiggle and squirm out of his hold. He's barely able to stop me from falling straight on my back when I heave myself away from him.

I land on my good leg and hold out my hands, turning murderous eyes at him. "*Don't* touch me, Rayne Williams. Don't you ever touch me again. All those times, you *knew*?" I screech.

"Vela, don't be like this. It's nothing," he says, his eyes hard.

"You call that kind of gift *nothing*? So, help me Rayne, if you come one step closer to me, I will not be held responsible for what I'll do to you."

"Is there a problem?" Sam asks. "Aponi," he complains, "what did you say to these people?"

"The truth," she answers just as quickly.

Now that my side is healed, I have so much more control over my movements. It's only my knee now that I have to worry about. Oh, and the murderous intent I have towards Rayne at the moment. I ask Sam, "Can you go to Grey's and ask him for those crutches he offered?"

"Vela," Rayne complains.

I whip my head to him. "Don't you tell me what to do, Rayne. I'm through talking with you and definitely done with you carrying me around. Can you feel that?" I direct such vitreous anger at him that it feels good when he flinches.

He looks away.

I turn to Aponi. "Thank you for telling me. I never would have guessed he could do that."

She looks at me, suddenly a sad expression crossing her face. "Does this mean you don't like him anymore?"

I flatten my lips and bemoan every time I felt something more for Rayne than I wanted to. But how do you explain those kinds of confusing emotions to a kid? So, I don't.

"Yes, that means I don't like him at all," I say instead.

"You're mad," she states with knowing eyes.

I marvel at her gift for sensing emotion. And it comes crashing down on me every time I felt an attraction toward Rayne. He could sense it. I think back over the past couple of weeks since I've been in Canada and in Rayne's presence.

He felt my emotions *every time*, every time my pulse quickened. And he didn't tell me. He said he thought I knew about his ability, but he clearly knew I didn't. He should have explained himself during our long hours alone in the woods. But what would he have said? That he could tell I liked him more than I should, more than I admitted? That wouldn't have been an embarrassing conversation at all.

It's no worse than how I'm feeling now, though. I lock down every emotion I have except rage, pushing embarrassment, and strangely enough, sorrow firmly down.

Why am I sorry, though? I'll examine those feelings later, when I can keep them to myself.

I turn to Aponi. "Do you have to be close to someone to sense their feelings?" I am going to find out every single thing I can from this precocious little girl before I leave.

She nods. "You have to be standing next to them to feel what they feel."

But then I think *Rayne's gift is stronger than hers. He might have more range.* So, I turn to him and ask with a bitter note in my voice. "How close, Rayne? How close do *you* have to be?"

He flicks a glance at Aponi and seems to understand my implication. He's silent for a moment, but just when I'm about to burst, he says, "About two arms lengths away."

"Is that the truth?" I ask with a hard edge to my words.

He nods and looks down, both hands on his hips.

I turn to Sam. "Would you please get the crutches from Grey? I'd really appreciate it if you would do that for me. I'm ready to leave. On my own two feet, well foot. I mean...whatever. Would you just please get me the crutches?"

He chuckles, then glances between Rayne and I finally nodding. "Be right back," he promises, then runs off.

I can sense the tension radiating off Rayne, but I ignore it. Rayne, Aponi, and I stand in an awkward silence as Sam retrieves the crutches.

I consider making small talk with Aponi, but I'm too angry to manage it. I stand on one leg in agony not caused by my knee. That's a constant throb I've gotten used to.

Memories of all the times Rayne must have sensed my errant feelings assail me. I blush deeply as humiliation races through me. I remember his reactions. Every time he laughed or responded, he had insider knowledge of my true feelings.

I hop back so I'm not anywhere close to Rayne.

The only consoling thought I have is that he also sensed the guilt I had at feeling any attraction to him. He knew I did not welcome, even was disgusted, by those feelings. *But still.* Why would he be silent about it?

He must have hoped to eventually wear me down and convince me to listen to my errant feelings. Well, that is *never* happening, I vow. He also clearly enjoyed having secret access to my private emotions. The thought makes my skin crawl and my stomach turn.

My heart is Linc's and always will be. What I felt for Rayne was only misplaced emotions taking over my good sense during a traumatic experience. He makes me think in different ways and I started to feel more for him than I should.

Well, that's over.

And if it kills me, I will control my feelings from here on out.

18. LINCOLN

I've taken a good look around, and I'm deliriously happy to find broken branches and crushed plants.

I'm going to believe these are Vela's tracks and not some strangers. Jack, too, has picked up a scent he's excited about. I'm positive it's Vela's.

The only thing I can do is follow the signs, so I trace the trail made maybe a day ago. These tracks look semi-fresh, so that fits the timeline of when Vela and Rayne would have been here.

As I walk, I see something that makes my heart lighter than it's been in days. I find two different footprints in the soft earth and when I examine them, one is significantly smaller than the other.

This must be Vela's footprint.

I lovingly put my hand in the dirt, knowing in my heart this is Vela's boot impression. But what confuses me is her next step. It doesn't seem to be a natural step. It's further back from the first one I found and my brow furrows as I see that it looks like the second foot was dragged up to the other one.

My heart freezes. Is Vela hurt?

I follow the trail that is as clear to me as day. Energized that I've found actual proof of my girl passing this way, I rush to track the odd footsteps. My chest aches at what I can tell was her painful struggle to walk. Her path continues this way for a while before the disjointed footprints disappear completely.

I look around wildly, trying to tell where she could have gone. It's like she just disappeared.

Jack doesn't seem to be too upset. He's continuing ahead.

Then I realize, Rayne must have picked her up. I easily see his footprints continuing and they look slightly more depressed in the earth than his previous ones.

My blood boils. Not only is Vela injured, but Rayne is holding her close. I look up and see hints of their trail continuing.

Wild resolve fills me.

I make a promise. Out loud where God and the whole world can hear me, "I'm coming, Vela, baby. Hold on. Hold on a little bit longer."

I start jogging then push myself to go harder, too fast to keep this up for long, but I don't care. Vela needs me and I am going to catch up to her. Jack happily keeps up with me, sniffing the ground every now and then as he lopes next to me.

I concentrate on my breathing as I maintain a steady pace. My chest is full of pent-up worry that slips away the closer I get to my Intended. *Nothing* will keep me from finding my girl.

And I'll find her a healer if it's the last thing I do. I wonder how she hurt her leg. Was it the fall down the ravine? If so, I'm going to bury my fist in Rayne's face.

If it wasn't for Rayne's footsteps, I might not have noticed when their trail turns into a well-traveled path.

Rayne must have the same idea I had to get Vela to a healer as quickly as possible. I wonder if the community they're headed to is another mixed-Elemental place. It can't be Saddleback, because that's west of where we were hiking. Vela and Rayne fled east from the bear.

So, this must be another place.

I lengthen my stride, determined to reach them before they leave. My racing pace starts to burn my lungs, but I push to go faster. If Rayne's carrying her, he couldn't have been walking too fast. I have a good chance of catching up to them.

My guess is they've made it to this community by now, and they'll get directions to Saddleback or return to the Polar Bear.

I can't help but consider what Vela must have been thinking through this whole ordeal. She's separated from all of us. We parted on bad terms. She has no idea what happened to her beloved Jack, and worse, she's stuck with Rayne.

As much as it pains me that he's carrying her so close, I prefer that to her walking on an injured leg.

Pride fills me that she tried, though. She is stubborn and strong. I can see her not even letting me carry her.

A white-hot rage fills me at the thought that Rayne might try to take advantage of his unavoidable closeness to Vela. *He'd better be the perfect gentleman.*

I'm heaving in breaths now and sweat is pouring down my face. I know I'm going to have to stop and rest in a few minutes. My muscles are burning at this point.

I'll pay for this punishing pace tomorrow, but by then I might have Vela in my arms.

That will make everything worth it.

That thought fuels me to keep going. I even pick it up faster, making myself proud.

When Vela told me to stay away after I controlled Jack, I thought that one sentence would kill me. But the thought of her being hurt somewhere without me is making me all kinds of crazy.

What kind of injuries does she have? Is she going to be okay?

When I picture blood running down her beautiful face, I have to stop or risk collapsing. My heart thunders even harder as I bend over breathing heavily, hands braced on my knees. I'm now terrified for my beautiful girl.

Jack is next to me as I heave in breaths, trying to control my inhales. Then I think of something that makes me feel slightly better.

I didn't see any blood in the ravine or around their trail through the woods.

I'm fairly positive she's not bleeding. It doesn't mean she's not hurt, but at least she's not in imminent danger of bleeding out.

At that dispiriting thought, I start running again.

I must find her. And I'm determined to do it today. If I have to run myself into the ground, I will find my girl.

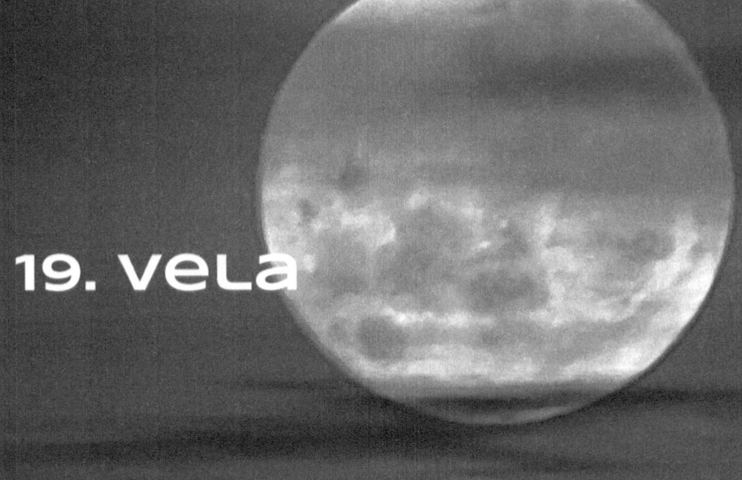

19. Vela

After waiting an hour for Roland to get his things together, I'm anxious to get started back to the Polar Bear. I'm ready to be fully healed, but more importantly, I need to be far away from Rayne and his intrusive gift.

He's left me to my thoughts and even Aponi wandered away, bored with my silence.

I watch with annoyance as Rayne plays with a water cyclone, jumping it from one hand to the other. Like he hasn't just gutted me with the revelation of his ill-used gift.

Sam brought me the crutches, and I'm thankful. I'm sure to stay four arms-length away from Rayne's mood sensing abilities now. I glare at him every now and then as I seethe about the humiliating information he gained.

He's loaded up with another pack full of food that we'll need for our trip home.

Home. It's hard to believe I consider the Polar Bear home now. I think about Linc and Jack and hope desperately they'll both be there when I return. He wouldn't have followed me down the ravine, would he?

I bite my lip in worry. Because if he is following me, I should wait right here for him to catch up with us.

My thoughts are interrupted when Rayne walks over to me. I give him a glare, feeding my burning anger and resentment so that it hits him full blast. His eyebrow twitches at the onslaught of emotions, but other than that, his face is smooth.

"Look," he starts out, "I know how you are feeling."

I bark a harsh laugh. "It's a little too late to tell me that now, Rayne."

He has the grace to cringe at that remark. "I know you're upset. But can you try to look past that to the bigger picture?" He fidgets with the straps of the bags over his shoulder.

"What are you talking about? That I need to get to Hannah or that I am forced to be in your company?"

His gaze hardens. "Both. Look, I *know* you don't want to be anywhere near me, but it makes much more sense for me to carry you. You'll get to Hannah sooner."

"Will you stop with that?" I snap. "I won't be within three arms-length of you for the foreseeable future. If you had been honest with me from the beginning, maybe this situation would be different. But since we're in this position because of *you*, I will deal with this my way. And my way," I gesture toward the crutches, "is staying as far away from you as possible."

"First of all," he grits out, stepping closer to me, so that he's invading my personal space, "How was I supposed to know you were unaware of the Borean secondary power of sensing emotions? It's not a secret, not like the Neronian gift."

I narrow my eyes at him, stepping a half step closer to him. I say softly, anger coursing through me, "And are you going to tell me what your secondary water gift is? Or are you going to make me guess on that one, too?" If I was his height, we'd be nose to nose at this point. As it is, I'm looking up at him, but his breath whispers on my forehead.

He presses his lips together in a thin line. He pauses. His eyes flash at me. "That's not something I can tell you. So, yes, you'll have to guess."

"So, we're back to square one, then? Where you keep secrets from me? Just tell me this. Can you read my thoughts?"

"No, I can't read your thoughts." He looks away, frustration leaking from him. "But I can't tell you the Neronian secret, Vela. It's heavily guarded and for very good reasons. As far as sensing your emotions, I guess I should have told you about that one as soon as I realized you didn't know what was happening."

"Yes," I say, stepping away awkwardly with the aid of my crutches. "You should have."

"Vela, when are you going to forgive me?" His eyes entreat me with an earnestness that surprises me.

"How can I possibly even begin to forgive you when you haven't apologized? Since I haven't heard one yet, I guess it'll have to stand like it is between us."

"*I'm sorry*, Vela," he says, both fists planted on his hips.

I raise my eyebrows at him. "And I'm just supposed to forgive you like that? Instantly?" I snap my fingers.

"Yes," he says solemnly, his eyes studying me, flashing frustration.

"Well, I can't. You'll have to wait for that to happen."

"Vela..." he growls.

I whip my hand through the air. "That's enough, Rayne. I don't want to hear anything more from you."

He curses and looks away, his hands clenching on his hips.

"That won't help your cause, Rayne."

He whips his head at me. "Maybe I didn't want you to know about my gift because it proved to me *over and over* you have more feelings for me than you're willing to admit, even to yourself."

My mouth drops open, and I gape at him as horror crashes over me. The fact that he'd say out loud what I've been feeling secretly is like a huge betrayal.

While I stand in stunned silence, he continues, "You can't tell me you don't feel *something* for me, Vela. I know you do," he says in a quiet voice, as if that tone softens anything.

I'm quivering with rage. I can hardly think straight. Blinking back tears, I throw my crutches down. I stand on one leg and fist my hands at my sides. Before I can talk myself out of it, I bring my hands up, ripping two huge roots up from the ground.

Whipping my arm over my head, one of the roots follows my movement and crashes right next to Rayne.

To his credit, he doesn't even flinch.

Deciding to do a better job with my other root, I fling it over Rayne and wrap him completely from his neck down to his feet.

He doesn't struggle. He could have used either of his gifts to stop me. But he didn't. And his eyes. They burrow inside of me and look deep into my soul, like he's okay with my anger and understands it.

That is not what I want. I'm suddenly deeply ashamed.

It saps the violent anger out of me. I'd rather he fight me. I need a good solid fight, not capitulation. Not surrender. And most definitely not understanding. That's what his eyes are saying to me right now.

I suddenly feel completely drained.

Panting, I notice it's gotten quiet. Looking around, I see Aponi watching me with large eyes. Roland, Sam and others all stand watching my attack on Rayne with serious expressions.

I look over the mess I made and see my attack for what it was. I might as well have stamped my foot and screamed for how immature I looked.

"I'm sorry," I whisper, tears leaking from my burning eyes. I call a vine back to me and stand it up so I can lean on it, letting Rayne go at the same time. I use the root to hop over to my discarded crutches.

With my emotions crashing around inside me, disappointment at myself and embarrassment at how I acted, I pick the crutches back up. I send my weapons back into the ground, cleaning up the mess I made. I smooth the ground over with dirt with a wave of my arm, erasing my embarrassing display. If only I could as easily erase it from my mind.

Mercifully, Rayne just stands watching me with clear, bright eyes. His look is non-judgmental and has a touch of sympathy in it. Can he feel my emotions swaying toward him? Am I close enough for that? It's like he's beckoning me over, and I forcefully push the traitorous desire to walk toward him firmly away.

I tell the crowd, "I'm sorry for that show of...anger. Please accept my apology." I direct my gaze at Rayne and nod at him, including him in that declaration.

He returns my nod.

I have to get away. I need some time to myself.

Using the crutches, I make my way over to Aponi. I ask her, "Do you have somewhere I can clean up?" I'm covered in dirt, and I'm suddenly tired of feeling dirty, inside and out.

She nods solemnly, looking at me with a bit of fear and awe.

I don't want her to be afraid of me, so I say gently, "I'm sorry for scaring you. I'm not normally like that."

"Why did you do it?" she asks in a small voice.

"I don't really know. I got mad at something Rayne said to me."

"What did he say to make you so mad?"

We're walking side by side, and I look affectionately at the top of her head. Her brutal honesty is going to do me in.

What did *Rayne say that made me so angry?* The truth, that's what. He didn't say anything that wasn't the glaring and obvious truth. I did have feelings toward him, *over and over*, like he said. I just didn't want to face it.

Finally, I answer, sighing, "He didn't say anything that wasn't true."

"And that made you mad?" she asks in a sweet voice. It makes me ache how innocent her questions are.

"Yes. For that I'm sorry."

"It's okay," she says, shrugging. "I get mad all the time. But I can't do what you did. My gift is…"

"Borean, I know."

She nods and we make it to a small house.

"I've been practicing," she announces proudly. Before she opens the front door, she whips her hand around and a small funnel spins on her upturned palm.

I gasp and say, "That's amazing, Aponi, good job!"

She smiles widely at me and walks in the front door. Rima greets her, looking at me with mistrustful eyes.

I know I look a mess, with traces of dirt smudged all over me. "I'm sorry to impose," I rush to say. "Aponi took pity on me and said I can freshen up here. I kind of made a mess back there."

"What happened?" Rima asks in a quiet voice.

"I got into an altercation with my friend Rayne."

"What's an al-ta-cation?" Aponi asks.

Rima glances at her daughter, putting her hands on her shoulders. "I don't like trouble coming into my home."

Aponi looks up in confusion from her mother to me. "Momma, the trouble is over. She got her friend good."

"Did you attack him?" Rima asks me.

I sigh and hang my head. "I really shouldn't have. I just got angry at something he said. I shouldn't have acted like that."

"Is he coming here to find you?" she asks me with a hard look. She pulls Aponi toward her.

"No," I assure her. "We're fine now. We worked out our disagreement." Well, I worked out my anger. Rayne just stood there and took it very gracefully.

She studies me suspiciously, then nods her head curtly. "You can clean up in the bathroom."

"Thank you," I tell her sincerely. "I won't be long."

She points toward a door and I get there without trouble. Once I'm inside the four blessed walls, I lean my back on the door and breathe a huge sigh. If I could, I'd sink to the ground and wrap my arms around my legs to nurse the wounds in my chest. But it would be too hard with my knee like this.

Rayne was right. I do feel something for him. But I don't want to. I knock my head on the door. What do I do with these unwanted feelings? I can't just turn them off, they return, staring me in the face every time I'm around Rayne.

But I love Linc. And I do, desperately. How do I have feelings for two people? Suddenly, feeling disgustingly dirty, I push myself away from the door, setting the crutches aside.

The bathroom is small enough that I don't have to step toward the sink. I can do a half hop and I'm there. I turn the faucet on and splash cool water on my face. I rub off all the smudges of dirt, telltale signs of my outburst. I rub my cheeks raw, trying to erase the proof of my immaturity.

Why couldn't I just have an adult conversation with Rayne? Why did I resort to such extremes?

I have no answer.

So, I clean up my mess as best as I can, hoping I can erase what I did as easily as the dirt.

20. LINC

B reaths sawing in and out of me, I refuse to slow my pace. Keeping up a seven-minute mile isn't easy, but I'm doing it. I'm close to this settlement. I can feel it and see it on the trail I'm following. It's well traveled, and I keep my eyes on the horizon, sure I'll see the tops of houses soon. Or some sign of civilization, maybe smoke from fires?

It's cold enough to warrant a fire. Since I make my own heat, I hardly ever feel the cold. And I especially don't feel it now that I've been running for over an hour.

Jack keeps up with me, but I sense he's getting tired, too. His sides are heaving, and his tongue is hanging far down the side of his mouth.

I'm going to have to rest soon for his sake. I've already rested a few times now, but I could keep going for another quarter of an hour at the pace I'm running. I praise God and my good training habits for my speed and endurance. For Vela, it's all worth it.

But I can't keep Jack going at this pace.

I send my senses far ahead of me, trying to find heat signatures. After a moment, I stifle my disappointment. Nothing so far.

I have my eyes trained on the distance, so when the trail dips, I look down and see a hole. But I'm too late to avoid it. My foot jams in it. I wind wheel my arms and my momentum carries me forward. I slam into the ground, my ankle twisting as I fall. I groan and turn my head, trying not to eat the dirt that my face is now planted in.

Jack comes back, inspecting me, whining softly.

Ignoring my sole companion, I push myself up, breathing hard from the run and the fall. Pain lances up my foot at the movement, and I suck in a breath.

No, I can't be injured. No!!

Holding my leg, I look back and see that my foot is wedged in the hole.

Why wasn't I looking where I was going?

Furious with myself, I twist my body, attempting to free my leg. It doesn't work. My foot is too tightly wedged. Breathing hard because that maneuver *hurt*, I look down at my situation.

My foot is just big enough to fit snugly into this hole. Blast it. I pound the ground with my fist.

Just my luck. When I'm trying to get to Vela quickly, I have to do something stupid like this.

I try to pick myself up so I'm on my hands and knees. I tug on my foot, but pain sears through my foot and up my leg at the attempt.

I'm going to have to stand up, I realize, and get my foot out that way. Getting my good leg under me, I use my quad muscles to push me up. Tired from sprinting for so long, they quiver in complaint. I stand up slowly. Balancing is a challenge, but I manage, swaying right and left to do it.

I swipe away the sweat falling into my eyes. This is putting a serious dent in me getting to Vela, and I fight the crush of disappointment at the result of my carelessness.

First things first. Now that I'm standing, I can crouch over this stupid hole and carefully maneuver my foot out. I use both hands to scoop my heel and pull that end of my foot up first.

I inhale at the sharp pain, but ignore it and push through because I feel my foot give a little.

Wrenching, I rip my foot out of the hole. Pain tears up my leg in a violent burst. I cry out and the movement makes me fall backwards onto the ground again.

But this time, my foot's free.

Jack pushes his wet nose into my cheek, and I breathe in my nose and out my mouth to control the pain shooting into my foot and leg. My ankle screams at me.

Pushing myself up with my arms, I bend my knee so that I can inspect what I did.

Running my hands over my boot, I can't see what's injured, since my ankle is covered.

I decide not to take off my shoe, because it's at least containing the swelling. From what I'm feeling, my injury is my ankle, not my foot, like I thought. I can't move my foot up or down without it killing me.

Looking around where I am, I sit and try to find a branch or stick that I can use to walk with. Either that or hop the rest of the way.

Spotting a good possibility, I pick myself up and jump to it on one foot. Examining it, I lean on it to see if it's a good height for me.

It fits well in my hand and seems strong enough to hold my weight, but it's far too long. It reaches over my head and bends to the right.

There's only one thing to do. I hold my hand over the place where the stick is at the height of my head. I turn up the heat and burn through the stick easily, throwing away the end I don't need.

I look over my handiwork and am pleased with the results.

Well, I'm as pleased as the situation allows. I'm not happy at all with my injury. I'm furious with myself, in fact. I should have been looking at the path and not obsessing about reaching the community and finding Vela.

Blowing out a breath, I calm myself down. Anger may fuel me for a while, but eventually I'll get bitter and despondent. I'm determined to give this new development to God. I'll give him my frustration and ask for peace and tranquility instead of this rush of self-pity and anger.

I give myself a minute to bow my head and ask God to handle this problem with me. He's a constant source of help and guidance, which I sorely need right now.

Help me get to Vela. God, I pray she's okay. Rayne, too.

I tack on the last part in grudging acceptance that he's a part of Vela's journey, and I need to be thankful for that and not resentful. It's not easy, though. In fact, I'm warring with my anger at this situation. I realize it's not permitting me to feel any peace.

I'm also so used to being angry at Rayne for trying to steal my Intended. A twinge of guilt pricks at me. Is God asking me to give up that anger?

Deciding to walk while I think, I test putting some weight on my right foot and am happy to discover that it can bear my weight, with a good deal of pain. My new staff helps. I take a few steps and call Jack to me. He went off to explore after getting bored with my inattention.

He bounds back to me, rubbing his nose into my hand. He seems very happy I'm on two feet again, well, two and a half feet.

"I'm okay, boy. Stay with me, okay? I guess you're getting the break you needed, aren't you?"

I huff a laugh. God sure has a way of slowing me down. I didn't want to do it for Vela's poor dog. Instead, I charged full power ahead so I could get to her faster, tried to do it on my own power.

Now, look at me. Hobbling forward, going so slowly, anything could catch up to me at this point.

God, let her still be at this settlement, please. I need to see her.

Then I stop praying. That last request gets me thinking. Maybe God isn't ready for me to see Vela. He's brought to my attention my anger towards Rayne and that takes some doing. Especially since I've been so desperate to catch up to him and Vela. Maybe God wanted to stop me in my tracks and point out my anger. I see that I've made Rayne my number one enemy. I've certainly attacked him with everything I have.

First, with that staff beat down I gave him. It felt good to best him despite his level of skill. But then it morphed into giving him more punishment. I even used Jack's bite to help me, albeit against poor Jack's will.

Shame fills me at the memory. I went way overboard, and Vela was right to stop talking to me for that gross abuse of her dog. What I did to Rayne was unforgiveable.

But I'm blessed to believe in a Savior who will forgive me for it. I'm not sure I've given that attack to God. I haven't asked Him for forgiveness or for help in controlling my anger toward a guy who's looking for love, just like I am.

I'm not proud of who I've become since I arrived in the Polar Bear encampment. I used to be pretty sure of myself. But since Rayne came into Vela's life, I've been an overbearing, controlling, angry man. I don't like what I'm now seeing. I've literally put Vela and my self-imposed struggle to command every moment of her attention, first in every area of my life. God does not like that. He wants to be first.

Looking down at my foot, I laugh softly. It took physically stopping me to give me this perspective.

Thank you, God, for showing me what I couldn't, or wouldn't, see. Forgive me for only now giving You my anger and rage. I tried dealing with them on my own and look where that's gotten me. Alone and miserable. I've put You on the back burner, when You should be front and center. God, forgive me.

I dwell on that for several minutes. I've become a cynical and angry person. I don't want to be that guy. I want to be the man God designed me to be. And that includes forgiving Rayne for his attempt to steal Vela from me.

Then, I almost stop in my tracks.

What if God's plan is for Vela and Rayne to be together?

My breath stops. Just because I have an Intended bond with her, it doesn't automatically give me rights to Vela's life, to our life as a couple. I thought it did. I thought that since God brought us together; it was absolutely His plan for us to be together for the rest of our lives.

I can see how I came to that thought. It's a God-given gift to find your Intended. It's a miracle actually, these days, since all the clans live apart.

But I can see now that God may have other plans for our lives. That thought feels like a knife stabbing my heart. I pray that isn't so. I love Vela. So much so that if it's God's will for her to be with someone else, I need to step back and accept it.

Tears rush to my eyes before I can stop them. The revelation fills me with crushing sadness. I need to give Vela to God. He knows the right plans for her. And I need to stop making Vela my only priority. God should be my focus, no one else. He's a jealous God, so it took some doing for me to see that I've put Vela in the place only God should occupy. God wants that spot. And I want to give it back to him.

So, I do.

God, you are my focus, my joy. Give those feelings back to me. And thank you for reminding me that You should be my focus. That You will give me the desires of my heart. I want more than anything for that to be Vela. But, God, if it isn't, help me with that.

I hope and pray fiercely that Vela's future includes me as her husband. I won't give up those dreams. I'll hold on to them for as long as I can until it's concretely clear that she's meant for someone else.

The important thing is that right now, I am acknowledging that I've given my life to the Lord and whoever else He brings into my life, which includes Vela. I know that if I have children, I will give their lives to God. I know that children are gifts from God, and their earthly parents are only caretakers. I need to fully realize that Vela is God's child, too. I've been claiming her as mine, and only mine, and that's not my place, ever. And certainly not before we're married.

If I hold too tightly to her, I might find her ripped from me.

What am I talking about? She has been ripped from me.

I'm trying to reach her now. But with a new perspective. I want what's best for her, not me. And God has been responsible for changing my mindset.

I will do everything in my power to be hers and for her to be mine. But I won't allow anger and resentment to take over me and my life again. I'm going to include God from here on out.

I know I will make mistakes in the future. I just pray that God will set me back on track, like He did today. And if He needs to practically break my ankle to do it, I'll welcome it. Because nothing compares to the peace and love flooding through me right now. I'll chase after this feeling every time.

Please God, give me the ability to ask for Your strength, not rely on mine. Keep me on the right path. And thank you for getting me here.

With that prayer in mind, I limp on toward a now much more peaceful future, which will hopefully include Vela.

I'm going to hold on to that hope with all that I have. I won't give up.

21. Vela

I leave the bathroom, wiping my face free of straggling tears and deeply ashamed of my actions. I can only pray that Rayne will forgive me.

He didn't seem too upset, in fact, he seemed understanding of my feelings. Still, I should never have reacted like I did, and I vow to be a better Elemental.

Aponi is waiting for me outside the bathroom. She jumps up from leaning against the wall and asks, "All clean now?"

I nod. "Aponi, I need to apologize for what I did to my friend. I never should have acted that way, especially in front of you."

We walk toward the front door, and she looks at me with a frankness that surprises me. "You said you were sorry, and I believe you."

Her childish innocence is so like Greta's, I hold my breath to catch my tears. I miss Greta terribly, and I'm suddenly so happy to have met Aponi.

"Thank you," I tell her sincerely.

"You're welcome," she answers with a big smile.

I shake my head at her maturity level. She's two or three years ahead of where she should be, at least. It must be living so remotely that does it. That's the only explanation I have at the moment. Greta is the same way.

Rima appears just as we approach the front door.

"Thank you very much for allowing me into your home," I say sincerely. "I appreciate getting the dirt off me. It's been quite a journey."

She studies me with serious eyes. "You're welcome."

I think I've found where Aponi gets her mature mentality. I don't see Rima babying her child in any way.

With a grateful nod to Rima, I walk outside with my crutches. Even in the short time I've been using them, my underarms are already sore. I suck in a breath. I'll just have to get used to it. I have a long way to go with these.

Aponi starts chirping as we walk together, telling me all about her friends, who I'm surprised I haven't seen.

"Where are they?" I ask.

"Oh, they're too scared to come out. They're watching from the windows." She points toward one house and sure enough, two little heads pop down when I glance that way.

We walk the short distance back toward where Rayne is waiting. As soon as we approach, I see that he didn't have the chance to clean up like I did. But, in sure Rayne style, he still looks good, like he just completed a grueling hike or something.

As I admit that to myself, I sigh. It's true, I find him attractive, and if I'm honest, there were times I felt more for him than friendship. The times he's been especially nice to me dominate those memories.

When we approach, his face flickers with uncertainty before he seems resolved to walk up to me. When he does, I see that he's careful not to come too close, being respectful of my desire to keep my emotions private.

"Are you okay? You look better." Frustration flashes across his face and he says quickly, "I mean, you looked fine before, but you got a chance to clean up?"

I nod. I take a deep breath and say in a rush, "Rayne, I'm so sorry for what I did. It was immature and irresponsible, and I really am sorry for attacking you the way I did."

He quirks a grin at me, but before he can respond, I ask, "Forgive me?"

"Of course." His lips turn down in a slight frown, and consternation fills his expression. "I thought about how I would feel if I didn't know about a gift like mine, only to find out later it was hidden from me. I'd be furious, too. I'm sorry, Vela. Do *you* forgive *me*?"

His face is so full of his earnest apology, I can't help but make my way toward him and put my crutches down before embracing him. I say lowly, "Of course I forgive you, Rayne. Thank you for forgiving me."

He rubs his whiskered cheek against my hair and that one little action sends a rush of heat through my middle. His day-old beard catches on my hair, and I can't help but enjoy the sensation. I push away from him, wildly uncertain, and make the mistake of looking into his eyes.

Standing so close, I know he felt my growing emotions and his eyes reflect a heat I don't want to acknowledge or respond to. His gaze flicks down to my lips, and I inhale sharply, confusion swarming my senses. I step away.

Looking down, I kneel to pick up my crutches and hop away from him, not daring to look at him again. I clear my throat and say, "I'm ready whenever you and Roland are."

"I've been ready for a while," Rayne says in a gravelly voice.

I look up to see him pinning me with a stare that floods me with an uncomfortable realization that we've crossed a line I wasn't ready to cross.

Despite not wanting to acknowledge what I feel for Rayne, I already have. Just the existence of my emotions has broadcasted how I feel loud and clear. If we were normal human teens, this wouldn't have happened. I could have hidden my feelings, but with Rayne's powers, I can't.

As much as that thought frustrates me, a small part inside of me appreciates the honesty. I'd rather things be in the open. My love for Linc makes me feel ashamed of feeling something for Rayne, but somehow that only draws me toward him, not away.

Why are these forbidden feelings so enticing? I'm sure, at this point, my emotions have loudly declared my confusion and frustration. Inside, I'm swimming in a rush of chaos. *I don't want this*, I cry in my mind! I glare accusingly at my source of frustration.

He reaches out a hand, his gaze unrelenting and aching with need. "Vela," he starts to say.

"Stop," I command. I step back until I'm out of range of his hand and his strange power. "Just stop, Rayne. I can't do this right now," I say in a hoarse voice.

Frustration replaces his expression of want and desire.

"I mean it. I'm not ready. You need to respect that."

God, help me right now. Help me figure out what it is I'm feeling and who I'm feeling this for. Rayne is not Linc, I can't confuse attraction with curiosity. Help me overcome these feelings, please, God.

I look back up at Rayne, who's watching with unabashed frankness. It's clear who he wants. Me. We've spoken few words, but oceans of feelings have happened in these short minutes. Aponi, who's been standing next to me the whole time, glances between Rayne and I in a child-like confusion. It must seem so obvious to her what we should do with our feelings, but I can't explain to her that what I'm experiencing is a betrayal to Linc. And I can't do that to him. I won't.

I clench the handles of the crutches, and I'm relieved when Rayne releases me from his penetrating stare and looks away. His jaw clenches, and I know he's fighting to keep from acting on his own emotions, which I can't feel, but can easily guess.

Roland, in all of his beautiful ignorance, chooses this moment to walk up to us. "Are you both ready?"

Rayne and I glance at each other and look away quickly. I can only nod curtly, but Rayne answers in a gruff voice, "Yes, we're as ready as we'll ever be."

"Good. I'm glad to see you got some extra food for the trip," Roland says, nodding his head at Rayne's burden. "Okay, Aponi, say goodbye. We need to take advantage of the light."

She turns forlorn eyes to me and, without hesitation, throws her arms around my middle and squeezes harder than I thought possible.

I laugh and let go of one crutch to hug her back. "It was so nice to meet you," I tell her.

She sniffs and says into my stomach, "I just met you; I don't want you to leave."

I agree. I don't want to leave her either. That and knowing Linc might be trying to catch up to me makes me want to stay here. But there's no way of knowing if he's on my trail, so I reluctantly let go of her and push her gently away. I tilt her chin up when she studies the ground and say, "I feel the same way you do. I feel like I've known you a lot longer than just an afternoon."

She played an important part in my admission that what I feel for Rayne isn't going away anytime soon. As much as I resent those feelings, I appreciate her helping it happen. She sees things in such a black and white way that I wish I still had that child-like ability. It seems everything nowadays is fashioned in gray. I prefer the simplicity of a child's mind to my own, which is a chaotic mess.

Sighing, I look up at our guide and say, "We'd better leave before this one convinces me to stay."

Roland nods and says goodbye to his niece. Rayne nods at her and ruffles her hair affectionately. "Thanks for everything, kid," he says, glancing at me.

His look is loaded with much more than a simple goodbye. It's saying everything I was thinking, too. She brought us to a point that we're going to have to face sooner or later.

Later, I think firmly. *Not now.*

After one last goodbye to Aponi, I lean on my crutches and start the arduous journey back to the Polar Bear.

We've walked for over an hour and a half, me keeping a good and healthy distance from Rayne and his powers, but it's painfully slow. I'm taking the longest steps I can, but I'm still slowing Roland and Rayne down significantly.

Rayne seems to respect my request for distance, because he stays just far enough away that I don't think he can feel a thing from me.

I take advantage of this time to examine my thoughts and feelings. To be honest, I am both flummoxed and frustrated by my feelings for the two men in my life. I love Linc; that's not a question. So I need to think long and hard about why I keep having these undesired feelings for Rayne.

I decide to take this to God.

God, I have no idea what is happening here. Why do I feel things for two different men? I don't like this. I feel like I'm dishonoring Linc's love by admitting feelings for Rayne. Lord, who do you want me to care for? Help me, God. I need you.

Roland has been glancing back at me, silently urging me to pick up the pace. I try, I really do, but I can only go so fast on three legs. At this point, I'm breathing hard, but I push through my discomfort for the sake of my two traveling companions.

So, we continue to trudge along at my pace. I'm still conflicted, but soon, pain pulls my focus. Every step is agony for my underarms. I've never been in the best shape, just good enough to keep up in my fighting classes back in Denver. This experience is forcing me to stretch my muscles to the limit.

Roland mercifully calls a break when he looks back at me and sees that I've slowed down... again.

I throw my crutches down and sit as gracefully as I can manage, with my good leg bent and my bad one extended. It doesn't throb like it used to, and for that I'm thankful. It's like Grey sped up the healing process by a few weeks, even if he couldn't heal it fully. I'm grateful either way. I throw my arm over my good knee and pant, trying to calm my breathing.

Roland squats on my left and looks curiously at Rayne when he chooses to sit a good distance away.

Roland turns to study me in his quiet, intense way.

"Yes?" I ask, curious about his thoughts. He's Borean, so he knows all about feeling emotions. He's probably reading mine right now.

There's nothing too revealing about what I'm feeling at the moment. There's a sadness that I can't shake as I think about Linc and Jack. But my dominant emotion is exhaustion.

"You two are making things too difficult," he states simply. He takes his knife and pulls a shapeless piece of wood from his pocket. He studies it and starts chipping away at it.

"Respectfully, this is our business and not yours," I say firmly. I do not need to explain my feelings to a complete stranger.

He brushes off my comment and says, "If we're going to be traveling together for a couple of days, we can't keep this distance between you."

"Why can't we? What does it matter? We're walking. Isn't that enough?"

He glances at me. "I'm your guide, but I'm also protecting you both, which is a lot harder when you're a hundred yards apart."

"Thank you, but I don't need your protection. I'm equipped to protect myself."

He purposely looks at my crutches. "Clearly," he says drily.

"That wasn't my fault."

"Whether it was or wasn't, you are not at your full strength. So, you're under my protection."

I bristle. "Rayne can protect me. You don't need to worry about that."

He raises his eyebrow and continues to whittle. "He can't do that from a hundred yards away either," he repeats.

I clamp my lips shut. He's caught me there, and I suddenly see how ungrateful I'm acting. He's right, I'm a liability.

Looking away, I feel my conscience prickle and guilt swarms me. I know God is reminding me of my manners. "I'm sorry," I say, breathing out heavily. I brush back wisps of hair. "Rayne and I are..."

Roland looks up at me with both eyebrows raised, waiting.

"Working through some things," I finish lamely. "We'll figure it out, eventually." I start working my long hair into a braid to keep it from sticking to my neck.

He nods and stands up, pocketing the piece of wood that looked like it had a head on it by the time we finished talking. "Fine, but at least stay close enough to me that I can step in if needed."

I nod grudgingly, tying off the end of my braid with a rubber band I've brought from home and managed not to lose yet.

"Ready?" he asks Rayne and me.

I nod again. Before I can figure out how I'm going to stand up, I see Roland and Rayne's hands both offering to help me up. I look between the two and grab both of them. They pull me up easily and Rayne hands me my necessary torture devices.

"Thank you," I tell Rayne and Roland as I get situated, ready to walk again.

I look up again, surprised when Rayne hasn't walked away and says, "He's right, you know."

I sigh. "Yes, but can we talk about this later?"

He looks at me intently, his mouth turned down in a frown. He finally nods curtly and walks over to Roland, who's waiting for us to finish talking.

I take my place at the end of the line and then remember I'm supposed to be closer to Roland. I limp forward, biting the inside of my cheek to help me ignore the pain the crutches are causing.

Better bruised than broken, which could be said of my brain, by this point.

I'm left to my thoughts as we continue.

22. LINC

I could crow in relief when I look up from my tortuous walk and see rooflines peeking over the trees.

Finally.

My heart kicks up in anticipation that I might find Vela in this town. Hope reigns supreme, and I pick up my pace as much as I can with my sore ankle.

"Come on, boy, let's go find momma," I tell Jack. Almost as if he knows, he lopes ahead of me, his nose twitching.

I'm reminded of my recent lesson from the Lord and try to contain my excitement. She might like this alone time with Rayne. I firmly tell my aching heart that if that's her wish, I will abide by it.

But with God as my witness, I'm going to remind her how great it is with me. I will respect God's plan for her, but I still believe her future is with me. I'll bow out of her life if I have to, but I'll wait until the last second for that moment.

So, with eager steps and many hops, I make my way to the settlement. As I near it, I make sure to keep an eye on my path. No sense in breaking my leg next.

People are doing odd jobs around small homes separated by nice yards. It's a little different from the Polar Bear, but it looks clean and well kept. The homes are built with logs, like the Polar Bear, but their style is a little different with flatter roofs and front porches held up with pillars. When I see that the majority of the people look deeply tanned, I realize I'm looking at a First Nation community.

I'm finally spotted and all work stops. A teenaged guy close to my age is the first to approach me.

"Hey stranger, what brings you out here?" His friendly face tightens a bit when he regards Jack warily.

"Don't worry. He's friendly," I assure him.

When he smiles in relief, it eases my anxiety a bit but doesn't erase it. "And what happened to you?" He looks down at my leg, searching for an injury.

"Twisted my ankle," I explain with a twist of my lips. "Wasn't paying attention to where I was going."

"Oh, ha!" he laughs, seeming to understand. "I'm Sam. We've had all sorts of injured visitors here lately."

Immediately, questions about Vela spill out of my lips. "Have two teens come through here? A girl with long blonde hair. I think she might have hurt her leg. And the other, a tall, blonde guy?"

Sam's eyes light up in recognition. "Yep! They've been here. Just left about an hour ago, I'd say."

My stomach plummets. Disappointment makes me frown, even as I try to maintain a friendly expression. I am encouraged that I'm closer to them than I thought I'd be.

"You trying to catch up to them on that leg?" he asks in a friendly reminder that I'm injured. I'm not catching up to anyone anytime soon.

Chagrin causes me to quirk up my lip. "Yeah, I guess so." But relief soon takes over. They only left an hour ago. All that running did help me get much closer to them.

"Well, you need to visit Grey. He can help with that leg. Or is it your foot?" He studies my leg, scanning it up and down.

"It's my ankle, I think."

"Oh, well, if he's not too tired from healing the girl, he can help you with that. I can tell you're a Festan, so I don't mind saying that he's a Gyan, well, part Gyan anyway. He'll help you if he can."

That's when I notice the slight gift he has. Like Waban, he's a Borean, but only partly. It's like instead of my blood icing inside my veins, it only cools. If a Gyan lives here too, then this community lives the way God intended. All together in harmony. Vela would love that.

"Do you know Waban?" I ask.

The teen's eyes light up. "You know him? He's from a neighboring community."

I nod. "I met him yesterday. They were hunting a massive bear that was too close to his home."

The teen laughs. "That sounds like him. He's a good man."

I agree, but what really captured my interest is hearing that Vela's been healed. A huge wave of relief fills me. "So, she's fine? Vela's okay?"

Sam's face twists in pity, and my stomach drops again. My insides are a right mess with all these tumultuous emotions.

"Well, our healer was able to help her injury, but not completely heal her."

"What do you mean, help it? What else was wrong with her?" I'm alarmed that she was more severely injured than I thought.

Sam raises his hands. "Hey man, I didn't ask questions. You'll have to ask Grey."

"Can you take me to him?" I ask quickly, needing answers.

Sam nods, and I give Jack a sign to follow me as we walk to a small home in the middle of the town. Knowing I was entering a home Vela had just been in shoots warm feelings through me. I'm so close to her.

Please God, let this healer be able to heal me so I can catch up.

I let my prayer rest as we wait. When a friendly man with pepper gray and black hair opens the door , I know I've found Grey. I can sense the Gyan gift in him. It's a subdued jolt of adrenaline, but it's there.

"Hey Sam, who do we have now?"

"Sir, I have some questions about the girl you healed," I say in a rush, hoping to get to the bottom of my search for answers.

"And he's hurt," Sam offers for me. "He knows Waban."

I nod my agreement, to my injury and to knowing the First Nation Borean.

"I can see that. Well, why don't you come inside instead of hanging around my doorstep? I can answer your questions and see if I have enough energy to heal you. Vela took a lot out of me earlier."

"When did you heal her?" I ask, impatient to know how she was.

"Come in, son. Come in," he repeats, with a friendly wave to come inside. "What's your name?"

I obey, if only to know what happened to Vela. "The name's Linc. Is it okay for Jack to come in with me?"

"Sure," Grey says easily.

Sam says goodbye, and I thank him before he leaves. Jack and I follow Grey inside and when he points toward a bed for me to sit on, I could weep in relief. I didn't realize how exhausting it was hopping and limping on one leg. It took more out of me than running a seven-minute mile for close to an hour did.

I sink onto the bed and my muscles thank me. I'm tempted to lie down, but I wait for Grey's instructions. Jack sits by the bed, watching Grey as he walks toward me.

"Is it friendly?" Grey asks, watching Jack.

"It's a he and yes, he's very friendly."

He grins. "Guess I should have asked that from the get-go."

I nod and smile. "No harm done."

"Now, where were we? Oh, yes. A strapping young man carried Vela inside, for it seems she had trouble walking on her own. Either that or he was being unnecessarily gallant. Either way, her injuries were severe." He fiddles with bandages, rolling up several as he talks.

"Severe? What were they?"

"Hmm?" He looks up at me. "Oh, she had a bruised rib and a torn ligament in her right knee."

He spouts off the injuries in such a detached clinical way, I have to squeeze my fist to keep from reacting badly and fire appearing. I don't know what I want from him, but a little sympathy for my Intended would be nice.

I need more information. "Was she in a lot of pain? How did you help her? How is she now?"

He puts down the rolls of linen and studies me with serious eyes. "Son, one question at a time, please. She's not fully healed. I couldn't completely repair the torn ligament in her knee, but I did what I could. Her rib is fine, though. I was able to heal that. I tell you, between you and that other young man of hers, she is a very well-cared for young lady."

I try to tamp down the burn of resentment at hearing Rayne referred to as her young man. I don't like the sound of that. But, like before, I give it to God. I will be a better man and allow God to help me rule my emotions in a way He'd be proud of.

Breathing in my nose to help me calm my pounding heart, I ask, "So, she's no longer in pain, at least?"

He frowns deeply. "No. I wouldn't say that. She's still in considerable pain, but I did help some. She needs a full-blooded Gyan to heal her completely."

I nod and remember to thank him, distracted in my thoughts about her pain level.

"I gave her crutches after her insistence for them. That young man seemed determined to carry her around everywhere. She allowed him for a time, but at some point, she asked for the crutches."

A huge sense of relief fills my lungs at hearing that, and I can finally breathe a full breath again. My chest had tightened at the former news, but at this, well, I'm elated, to say the least. It sounds like Vela prefers her space than to be carried around like a doll by Rayne.

"Now," he says, rubbing his hands together. "Shall we see what's going on with your foot, is it?"

"No, it's my ankle." I turn to bring my leg up on the bed, too anxious to get going to lie down completely.

He's careful as he unlaces my boot, and I appreciate that. As soon as the pressure of the tight lacing is released, I breathe an unconscious sigh. He tugs the boot off and even though he's being as gentle as possible, it still sends a jolt of pain through my ankle.

"Can I cut the sock off?" he asks. "I can always give you another one."

"Sure," I say, worried to see what the damage is.

He makes short work of getting the sock off when he produces a pair of silver scissors. I can see immediately there's bruising and swelling on my outer ankle.

Grey examines my ankle from every angle, then places his hands around it. I feel a low heat enveloping my injury and it eases the ache. I'm not sure he's trying to heal it right now, just determining what's wrong. But it's already helping.

He looks up after a moment and says what I've suspected, "Nothing is broken. Just a sprain. A bad one. I think I can help you."

I smile widely. "That would be really great. Thank you."

"How did you do this, young man?"

Eager for him to get started and to be on my way, I quickly explain what happened. I'm sure to be polite, but don't want to engage in a lengthy discussion over this.

He listens quietly, then nods. Placing his hands on both sides of my ankle, he furrows his brow, and a resulting warmth soon follows. The heat burrows deep into my injury, and before I know it, a pleasant feeling replaces the pain.

Grey lifts his hands, his shoulders slumping in exhaustion. I rotate my ankle in a circle, exhilarated to find I can do it easily.

"Thank you!" I exclaim, smiling widely at Grey.

He looks at me with tired eyes, nodding. "I'm happy I could help. I can't do everything, but a sprained ankle is well within my wheelhouse."

I lean forward when he goes over to the dresser and, after fishing inside, tosses me a sock. I'm quick to put it on and lace up my boot.

When I stand up, Jack jumps up and noses his way into my hands, seeking confirmation that I'm okay.

"I'm good, boy. Thanks to this amazing man, here."

I turn my attention to Grey and say, "I'm sorry to be healed and run like this, but I really am desperate to catch up to Vela and Rayne. Any chance you can point me in the direction they went?"

He squints his eyes as he looks away, and says, "I'm sure Roland left word about which way he went. It would be easy enough to find out."

When Grey motions for me to follow him out of the room, I give Jack the command to tag along. We find Sam standing nearby. After Grey talks to him for a moment, Sam approaches.

"Hey there. My sister will know exactly the route Roland took, so let's go talk to her," he offers.

I nod, and with Jack by my side, take care to watch where I'm going so I don't injure myself again. I'm only too happy to be back on two feet again walking normally and feel badly Vela had to leave a Gyan's care still injured. How she was that badly injured, I cannot guess. The only thing I can think of is the fall into the ravine, or maybe off the rockslide? I can't help the frown that takes over my face that Rayne allowed her to be injured like that.

We haven't gone far when we approach a home with a cute little girl playing outside. She looks at me curiously before asking Sam, "Did my friend really leave? Is she coming back?"

Sam gives her a sympathetic look. "She did and I don't know, little one." He ruffles the top of her head and lets himself in the home. He glances back at me before he steps in and looks down at the girl with obvious uncertainty if he should leave me alone with her. Or is it Jack he's worried about?

Jack approaches the girl slowly, reaching out with his nose to sniff her. She giggles and puts her hand out, which Jack immediately starts licking. She starts laughing outright, saying, "That tickles."

"He must smell something good on your hand," I say with a smile.

Sam must be assured she's safe with us, because after that interaction, he walks inside.

The girl beams up at me. "I just had a peanut butter sandwich. I must still have some on my fingers."

Jack soon cleans her hand thoroughly, then sits down right in front of her, like he expects her to pet him. She's happy to oblige, and I'm glad to see she's not afraid of the big dog. He can intimidate people with his Doberman looks.

She's scratching his ears when she looks up at me, squinting in the sun to size me up.

"You're a Fire man," she states.

I raise my eyebrows. "And you're a Borean...and human."

She nods happily. "My momma is a human, but my papa was of the Wind, like me."

I listen with fascination at how this place, or is it all the First Nation, integrates with humans. She says it so easily, but it's her normal way of life. I'm sure she has to explain it to visitors like me. That makes me wonder.

"Does your town get many visitors?" I ask, curious if many people come this way on purpose. It's definitely off the beaten path.

Her face drops, and I crouch down to her level concerned that I've made her sad. "What's wrong?"

Her mouth twists into a frown. "I don't meet many new people. And I met the nicest girl today, but she had to leave. She went with my uncle back to her home. I wish she could have stayed longer. She was nice."

My heart jumps because I know she's talking about Vela. Desperate for any news of my Intended, I ask, "Is she okay? This friend? Did she seem happy?"

The little girl's face scrunches up in thought, which confuses me because I thought that was a pretty simple question.

"She was okay at first, but then she got real mad about something and attacked her friend." She looks at me seriously. "She's really tough."

I straighten in surprise. "She *attacked* her friend? Her guy friend?"

She nods succinctly. "Yep. The one she secretly likes. She got real mad at him and wrapped him in roots from head to toe."

My heart squeezes at her words. "What do you mean, the one she secretly likes? How do you know that?"

She looks up at me like I'm dumb. "Because I can feel what you're feeling. I felt what she was feeling, too. I told her that her guy friend could do what I can do, and she got re-e-eally mad."

I lean back and think hard. Boreans have a secondary gift. What is it? That's right, sensing emotions. I forgot about that. *And Rayne could sense that Vela had feelings for him and didn't tell her he knew? Yes, that would enrage Vela.*

I stuff my hands in my pockets and fight back waves of despair. So, Vela does like Rayne more than she's told me. This is the news I've dreaded since I first laid eyes on the guy.

I can't help but be pleased as I think of her attacking him. *Serves him right.* It's small compared to the news of Vela's feelings, but I'll take it.

She must sense how unhappy I am because I feel the little girl's hand in mine. "It's okay," she whispers, her face set in a frown. "I'm sorry I made you sad."

"I'm not sad," I try to reassure her.

She looks at me knowingly. "You weren't sad before, but you are now. You know I can tell." She states it so factually, my heart wrenches.

I sigh heavily and rub my forehead with my free hand. "Yeah, well, it's okay. It's not your fault."

She regards me with uncertainty. "I know. But I feel bad for people sometimes," she says sadly. "I say lots of things that make people sad. Maybe I should keep my thoughts to myself."

I silently agree with her. It probably would be best if she kept her innocent revelations quiet. People hide how they feel for a reason. I'm sure she doesn't mean to upset people with what she knows, but it ends up that way.

"My name is Aponi. My friends won't play with me today because they're scared of so many new people coming here."

"I'm sorry about that. I'll be leaving shortly. So hopefully they'll come out when I'm gone."

She smiles widely. "You're probably right."

Sam emerges from the house. "Roland is taking them to the Polar Bear. He took the west trail at first. But, after that, he'll follow the south trail through the marshes. So, what you want to do is head right once the west trail meets the river."

I digest the news that Vela isn't going to Saddleback to meet Sandy and James, her potential birth parents. She must be disappointed. I'm assuming they're heading back to the Polar Bear so Hannah can fully heal her. Hopefully she can by the time Vela sees her. Some injuries are past even a full Gyan's ability. Then a practical thought hits me.

"Will I be following the river, or a stream? I'm out of water and won't make it far without filling up."

Sam shakes his head. "No, but I can give you some canteens to carry with you. Just give what you borrow back to Roland. We'll need them again."

I agree easily. "Sure, that makes sense. You don't have much access to supplies out here, do you?"

He laughs. "We barter. A lot. Trading with other communities gives us most of what we need." At that he leaves to find me the canteens.

I look down at Aponi, and it's easy to see why Vela made a friend in her so easily. She probably reminds her of Greta. Aponi is back to playing with a doll in her hands. She holds it like a baby and rocks it gently.

I suddenly long to see Vela doing that with our child. Wouldn't that be the most beautiful sight? I wrench my thoughts away from such a tantalizing dream. Vela isn't mine to think of like that, yet. *Especially if she has feelings for Rayne*, I think bitterly.

I then have a thought. *I really did think our child would be the Chosen One. But now I'm not so sure. Gene and Jerry made such a convincing case that Vela is the One.*

Shaking my head to clear all these thoughts careening out of control, I see Sam jogging over to me with five canteens hanging from leather cords. When I take them from his hands, I feel they're already full of water.

"Perfect, thanks, man," I tell him, situating them on my shoulder, adjusting to the weight.

"Hey, it's easy to give them to you, knowing Roland will bring back things from the Polar Bear that we need here."

"Absolutely," I say with certainty, knowing that anyone at the Polar Bear would be happy to give back to someone who helped one of their own. We shake hands, both squeezing firmly.

I feel like I've made a friend, and since friendships are hard to come by in this part of the world, I take it gladly.

"Take care, man," I tell Sam.

"I hope you find what you're looking for," he says with a sympathetic look.

Unable to help myself, since it's clear I'm looking for Vela, I ask, "What do you mean by that?"

Sam shrugs. "Hey, I'm just saying, if I were in your position, I wouldn't like it if my special girl was traveling with a guy like that."

I nod, urging him on.

"And," he continues after a pause, "there's definitely something there between the two of them. So, I hope things go your way."

What is with people butting into our business? First Aponi, now this guy.

My face must reflect my frustration, plus he's Borean so he can sense it easily. Sam puts his hands up and says, "Just giving you a little piece of advice, man. That's what I think, is all."

I've never hated an Elemental gift so much. I count to ten in my mind, slowly. I need to keep my cool. Why does it surprise me that God would send this stranger to me with words that slice so deep I'm not sure I'm in one piece anymore?

Inhaling slowly, I look up after a moment with God to help me stay calm. "Thanks, but I think I can handle what I'll find."

He studies me with an understanding that I really don't want to see. It just reminds me that Vela has feelings for me *and* Rayne. It's so painful, I almost can't breathe.

I turn before I can say something I'll regret. It's not Sam's fault I'm in this situation.

Looking over my shoulder, I say, "Thanks. It was nice meeting you."

At his nod, I start jogging, calling Jack to stay by me. It's time I found Vela and see what all this Rayne business is about for myself.

I break into a run.

23. VELA

By the time we've walked about two hours from the First Nation community, I'm thoroughly depressed. I'm disgusted with myself for my stupid, ridiculous feelings for Rayne. I love Linc and can't believe I'm also interested in Rayne. I'm about ready to wrench my heart out of my chest and stomp on it. I might as well, with how bruised and battered it already feels.

And every time I look back and happen to catch Rayne's eye, I'm ready to clobber him with the first tree branch I can get my hands on. It's his fault I'm feeling this way. If he respected my relationship with Linc and stopped gunning for me, as well as quit being so sweet and kind, I wouldn't be in this situation right now.

I can't blame this all on Rayne, though. It's me feeling things for him, too.

I wish I could happily be in love with Linc and *only* Linc and not have this crushing guilt weighing me down. Tears have threatened several times by now, but I've managed to keep them at bay. I don't want to be a sobbing mess in front of Roland and definitely not in front of Rayne.

I've been sure to stay far away from Rayne, but I wonder how much of my emotions he's been able to glean. They've been all over the place as I remember our journey and tender feelings take over before I can stop them. Memories of when he was understanding and supportive filter through my mind. And then I remember the many times he reacted whenever a surge of attraction filled me. I still can't believe *he knew* every single time. I feel my ears burning in embarrassment.

Why didn't he say anything?

Roland stops walking and waits for me to catch up to him.

"I'm going to scout ahead. You okay with me leaving you alone?"

"I'm perfectly fine being alone with Rayne," I say tiredly. But then I think, *am I?*

Being a stupid Borean, he reads me perfectly well and says, "You sure?" His eyebrows jut up.

"Yes," I say, exasperated at being read like an open book. "Go."

He looks uncertainly at me and nods. He walks to Rayne and tells him something, putting a hand on his shoulder and looking back at me.

Why couldn't I have supersonic hearing instead of this healing gift? Then I banish that thought, knowing I would never choose to part with my ability to heal.

See what I'm doing? Being completely unreasonable.

Rayne jogs until he catches up to me. I'm panting softly and wincing at how uncomfortable these crutches are. "You doing okay?" he asks, concern knitting his brow.

"I don't know. You tell me," I snap. I glare at him, knowing my anger doesn't change the fact that he will always be able to sense my emotions. Then I ask, "Can you turn your gift off for one minute? Is that possible? Can you choose to ignore what you feel or something?"

"Why?" he asks, pinning me with a stare. "You have something to hide from me?"

I exhale roughly. "I'd like *some* privacy, Rayne. Is that too much to ask?"

He furrows his brow. "I can't help who I am or what I can do."

"That may be, but it's an intrusion. And it's not fair. Just like I have no idea what you're feeling right now. It would be nice to know."

But I can guess. He's frustrated. That much I can see written all over his face.

"Why didn't you fight me back?" I stop and ask, needing to know. It's suddenly important I hear his answer.

He lifts his eyebrow, studying me. "Because I deserved your attack and anger. I wasn't going to fight you on it. I figured it was the least I could do to make up for what I did."

"You mean the way you deceived me?" Anger surges through me again at the thought of his secret. He kept it for days.

"I didn't deceive you. I hid my gift from you."

Same thing. "Which told you everything about me that I wanted to keep to myself. You stole that from me," I say with gritted teeth, clenching my fists.

"Are you looking for a fight now, too, Vela?" He cocks his head, considering me.

"Maybe I am," I growl.

"Why is it so important I fight back? Does it make you feel better about hurting me? You want me to feel pain, like you did. I hurt you by withholding my ability. I'm sorry, Vela. I am. I should have told you what I could do."

Again, his words crash into me, opening up deep parts of myself I don't want to examine too closely. I lose my breath and like before, all my fight leaves in a rush.

He takes a step toward me. I try to shuffle backward, but my crutches catch on a root, and I stumble.

Before I can fall, Rayne's hands are on my arms, steadying me. "How about some honesty, for once? No more hiding behind your walls. Come out and *talk to me.* Do that and I'll tell you what I feel. As if you don't already know. Unlike you, I've been pretty open about what I want."

I stutter at him in surprise. "I don't know what you mean." My face heats up at his nearness.

"How about telling me how you really feel? Be honest with yourself. For *once,* Vela." His hands still grip my upper arms, and he shakes me slightly. He leans closer, and his face fills my vision.

Emotions flood me, making my senses swim. Searing heat fills my middle, making my brain feel like mush. Everything flies out of my mind when his gaze lands on my lips.

"Admit it, Vela, out loud. You like me. You like being around me. You don't hate the thought of being with me."

I can't seem to stop watching his perfect mouth. It's mesmerizing. And what he's saying is making me come apart. Tears prick my eyes. His hands are squeezing me, forcing me to admit what I don't want to. I shake my head.

"Vela," he says in a tortured voice. "I swear I'll kiss you to prove to you this is true. Don't make me do it."

A squeak comes out of me. That's all I can manage. What do I say? That his brutal honesty has made me truly look at myself for the first time? That his gentleness has unraveled any defense I have against him? A tear slips from my eye.

He swears under his breath and catches it with his thumb, wiping it away. When I bite my lip, he switches his attention to my mouth.

He brings his now dark gaze back to my eyes. "Tell me right now you don't feel something for me. Deny it, and I'll walk away and stay out of your life forever. Tell me what you want, Vela," he growls darkly.

Somehow, I find my voice. "You want me to admit it? Fine, I admit it, I like you. More than I should."

"More than you...?" He looks at me in question.

"I shouldn't like you, Rayne, but I do. Okay? Are you happy now?"

"Tell me you don't want me to kiss you," he whispers. He's moved even closer, his lips a hair away from mine. I can practically feel them.

"I don't want you to kiss me," I whisper back, knowing he can feel the opposite is true. I lick my lips, hungry for a touch.

"Liar," he growls, and presses his lips to mine.

He brings his hands up to cup my face, angling my head so he can have better access. He moves his mouth on mine like an expert, knowing just the right pressure, just the right movement. The world could come apart, and I wouldn't know it.

I inhale sharply, forgetting I need to breathe. He takes advantage and kisses me more deeply. I hold on to him for dear life, because I can't stand on my own anymore. At first, I was so stunned, I just stood there, letting him kiss me. But the more he kisses me, the more I suddenly come alive.

I lean into him and drop my crutches, wrapping my arm around his neck, kissing him back. I explore his mouth like I've imagined.

He kisses me so deeply I only remember to breathe when all the air leaves my lungs. In a move that makes me moan in complaint, he tears his mouth away from me, putting his forehead on mine, breathing heavily.

"This is what I've wanted to do since I first saw you," he says hoarsely. He moves his lips to my neck, and I pull my head back so he can reach better. He kisses up and down my throat. When something bumps into my leg. I ignore it.

My head is swimming, and it continues to move in oceans of attraction. "Shut up and kiss me, Rayne."

He chuckles and does just that.

We stand there both exploring, getting sucked into a world of our own making, when I hear a throat clearing and a wet nose pushing into my leg.

I look around in a daze, expecting to see Roland. Except it's not Roland standing there watching me kiss the lights out of Rayne.

It's Linc.

24. LINC

The world crashes down around me when I come running around the bend and see a sight that will haunt me to the end of my days.

Vela, *my* Vela, is kissing someone else. And she's doing it with such passion that a hot knife cutting through my gut would hurt less than what I'm feeling right now.

Jack tries to get her attention, but she doesn't come up for air. Instead, she leans her head back to give Rayne what his lips are searching for, her neck.

And then when I think it can't get worse, it does. She asks him to kiss her again, which Rayne does, gladly.

It's like someone sucker punched my gut. I've got to stop this. I clear my throat, trying to breathe through the pain.

She finally turns her head to investigate the noise I made and what Jack's doing. She looks dazed and very, very kissed. Her eyes meet mine, and I swear I barely keep standing because I've only ever wanted that shine of desire to be in her eyes because of *me*. When she registers who I am, she jumps backward and pushes Rayne away.

He, too, looks up and when he sees it's me, he frowns deeply.

Jack jumps onto my stunned Intended, demanding attention. He's so excited his sleek red body vibrates with happiness.

I couldn't feel more opposite. In fact, the old, familiar feeling of rage rises up in me. It's a fiery storm, waiting to unleash a heat so hot my blood boils inside me. I close my eyes and send up a prayer, begging God to hear me.

God, help me! Help me control my rage. God, help me to forgive. I want to the be the man You've created, not fall into my old ways. But I need your help. Desperately.

After long moments where I breathe slowly, trying to control the hot blood pumping through me, I open my eyes. I see Rayne standing next to Vela, not moving, his eyes intently watching me. He clenches his fists, ready for an attack.

My old self wants to deliver a punishment so severe Rayne wouldn't recover quickly. Or at all.

I remind myself to breathe because that is not what I want. But my chest is on fire. I'm not sure how much of that is my gift reacting or my body wanting to erupt in a deadly mass of flames. "Oh, God!" I moan, burying my face in my hands.

I hear Vela crying. "Linc," she moans, "I'm so sorry."

I pick my head up, seeing Vela's face streaming with tears. I try to look away, but I worked so *hard* to catch up to her. I needed to reach her. And now I have. Only to witness the one scene I feared the most.

I'm not the Linc I was. God, help me be the man You need to be. Help me, God!

A wash of calm moves through my bloodstream, cooling me, tempering me. Taking away my *need* for violence.

Thank you, God. Give me the strength to have grace, forgiveness.

"Linc? Linc, are you okay?" Vela's trembling voice reaches me.

I look up, my arms trembling from the effort to contain my gift that wants to erupt in a vengeful inferno. I nod briskly, thankful to God for helping me.

"How? How did you find us?" she asks.

I find my voice or try to. I'm not only out of breath from running to catch up to them but also from the fight of my life to control my deadly impulses. If it wasn't for God lending me His strength, I'd be giving in to my urge to hurt Rayne. Badly.

My voice comes out hoarse, giving hints to my shredded heart. "I found your trail from when you guys jumped into the ravine. I've been trying to catch up to you ever since." I search her face for any sign that she's glad to see me, but all I see is guilt.

She cringes and looks away.

Rayne, surprisingly, is the next to speak. "You ran all the way here?"

Dark anger surges through me. "Yes, I ran here. I've been trying to catch up to Vela since the bear attacked us and you flew her down a ravine."

I force down words that spring into my head, angry accusations about their kiss. There's no sense in hurling words at them now. What's done is done. I need to move on from this.

God, give me strength.

Turning to Vela, I say, "I found Jack. I managed to get him back to you. I knew you would need him."

She looks down at Jack's wiggling body, her hand on his head. Her mouth twists in a small smile before her breath hiccups. Her eyes are swimming with tears when she looks at me, whispering, "Thank you. And Linc, I'm so sorry."

We all know what she's sorry for. A black emotion fills me as I wonder if she would ever have told me what she did with

Rayne if I hadn't seen it. Would I have found out if I hadn't caught them in the act? I force that despairing thought out of my head and again, give my anger and utter anguish to God.

I hang my head, shaking it.

"Linc?"

At the sound of my name in her broken voice, I bring my head up. My face is open in my grief over this situation and when Vela sees me, she breaks down in a sob, covering her face with her hands.

My gut squeezes at the sight and sound of her tears. Gritting my teeth, I keep myself away except every part of me wants to hold her. Despite what she did.

"I'm so sorry, Linc. I'm just so sorry," she whispers over and over into her hands.

I hang my head. I can't watch her breaking down like this. It's tearing me apart, and I'm in pieces as it is.

I hear Rayne curse and when I look up; I see him leaving.

She says in a tremulous voice, "I know I betrayed your trust. But I want you to understand. I love *you. I do.* I just came to know Rayne in a different way these past couple of days and he's been so kind. He brings out a side of me that I need to see. I don't know, I just came to appreciate him in my life, and I let myself get carried away." Her breath catches as she says the words that are like rocks shoved down my throat.

I nod. That's all I can do. For some reason God allowed Vela to be separated from me. She spent a lot of time with someone who's liked her since he first laid eyes on her. That much was always clear.

Forgive, my child. As I have forgiven you.

An overwhelming surge of love fills me at hearing God's words whisper in my mind. It reminds me of everything He taught me on my run to get to Vela. She's not mine, not yet.

I have to love her enough to let her choose, not force myself on her.

Without another thought, in two steps I'm at Vela's side and I wrap my arms around her. Clearing my throat, I say, "I don't want to *ever* see *that* again, but I forgive you. Vela, I've been so focused on you being mine, I forgot that it's you who needs to choose who to love. You have to figure out your heart and what it wants sooner or later. But, right now, I get it. Let it rest. Give yourself time to think. And don't worry about me, I'll be okay."

She looks up at me, her eyes streaming tears. She covers her sob with her hand. "Linc, how can you be so calm and understanding? I don't get it."

I gently push hair out of her eyes. I laugh hoarsely. "Believe me, I don't either. God showed me a lot on the way here, and I know that I have to let you go to have a chance to keep you. So, this is me letting you go. I've smothered you with my love. That was wrong. I see that now."

She tucks her chin to her chest, crying harder. "I don't want you to let me go, Linc. *I love you.* I'm just so confused."

I rest my cheek on the top of her head, my heart beating painfully in my chest. "I know you are. It wasn't easy to find you doing...what you did...but I had to remember what God has done for me, so I can extend that...forgiveness to you. I think that's why God prepared me for this moment. So, I wouldn't be a hindrance, but a help."

She wipes her wet face with her hands. "He has? I need that kind of help, too."

"Just ask Him to help you. He will."

I feel her head nodding.

"Believe it or not, Vela, things will work out. Just pray about your feelings and give them to God."

Jack has had just about enough of Vela's lack of attention. He barks and jumps on her.

"Jack? How are you, boy?" Vela says in a broken voice. Dropping down as much as possible with her unbending leg, she buries her head in his chest and wraps her arms around him, sniffing. "Oh, Jack, I've missed you."

Knowing we have a long road ahead of us, I say, "How about we start walking? We won't get your leg healed by staying here." I frown when I see that she can't bend her knee at all.

She inhales deeply and rubs her nose on Jack's coat. "Okay," she whispers. Then she looks around. "Rayne? Where did he go?"

I nod my head in the direction he left.

"Oh my gosh, what a mess," she moans and hangs her head again.

I allow silence to take over for a moment.

She nods again, this time grabbing her crutches and trying to stand up.

I hold out my hands to help her up. Once she's standing, I crouch and pick up her discarded crutches.

She gets situated, then looks at me. "It's good to see you, Linc. I was worried."

I force myself not to say anything about how she didn't look too worried when I found her. I give that dark emotion to God immediately. "The bear didn't get me, and when I found Jack, I knew it was even more important that I reach you."

Even catching her kiss Rayne, now that I've found her, all I want to do is to hold her and kiss her. I want it so badly I can taste her lips from memory. But I know now is not the time for that. No, I need to wait for that moment, and I will.

Because that's what Vela needs. She doesn't need more kisses; she needs space to think.

So, I give it to her with all the grace I can, as I thank God for giving me the strength to do it.

25. LINC

Vela almost seems broken as she clomps down the trail. It seems like she's struggling in both mind and body, and it's hurting me as much as it's hurting her. That compounds with my own sense of betrayal, making my existence a painful one.

I sense she needs time to think, so I leave her alone in her thoughts. But she asks, "How is everyone else? Did the bear hurt anyone?" Jack stays glued to her side, and I predict he won't leave her for a while.

I walk slowly beside her as I answer, "The bear took a swipe at Claudette, but thankfully Tonya was able to heal her quite well. I think she'll be alright."

"How did you get away?"

"I almost didn't." I tell her how I tried to capture the bear in a flame trap, only to be attacked again later. And when I explain how I got into the bear's mind to control her, Vela laughs. The sound is like a balm to my wounded soul. It's so good to hear her laughing.

"That's amazing, Linc. Why didn't you do that from the beginning?"

"Honestly, I didn't really think of it until the eleventh hour, and it was our last hope. She really wanted us away from her little cubs."

Vela's eyebrows shoot up when she hears that, and she laughs softly and nods. "She was a mama bear protecting her cubs. Makes sense."

With an aching chest, I think over everything I want to tell her. How I found her, how intent I was on catching up to her. I really wanted those brownie points when I climbed down that ravine wall to bring Jack to her. I decide to stay in safer waters and don't talk about my huge revelation. That's a conversation for another day. I tell her about what I found about Andy's romantic feelings for Hannah instead.

She sighs. "He does like her. I knew it. How did you get him to admit it?"

"It wasn't hard. He seemed ready to open up about his feelings. I even gave him some advice." *Which I obviously need for myself.*

Forcing down my bleak thoughts, I tell her next about my injury.

"You were healed by Grey, too?" she asks, her face open in surprise.

"Yep, and I met this adorable little girl by the name of Aponi."

At Aponi's name, her face lights up, then closes off after a guilty grimace. I wonder what that's about. And then I think, *of course, Aponi's the one who revealed Rayne's abilities. Should I ask her about attacking him?*

I feel like I'm walking on nails trying not to hurt Vela or scare her off, and it leaves me feeling unsettled, to say the least. I've become so used to being open and honest with her that this awkwardness is disorientating, and I long for a return to our usual ease *pre-kiss*. A surge of anger rises in my chest at the reminder of what she did.

I've forgiven her. Help me, God, to continue to forgive. I have to be patient and strong, I remind myself.

"Aponi," she says, wistfully. "She's so cute. Reminded me so much of Greta."

I nod sadly. "I knew she would. That's the first thing I thought of when she said she'd met you."

Vela's smile is sad also as she says, "For such a young girl, she's years ahead of her age." She stops and adjusts her crutches, wincing.

"They're the worst, I know."

After several minutes, she blows out a breath. "I've never had to use crutches before. This is torture."

I nod with sympathy. "I had a torn ligament once, and I despised them after the first day."

"I've been so adamant about having them, but they hurt so badly," she says, trailing off, looking ahead at the path ahead of us.

I guess what she's thinking. She's wondering where Rayne is. "I hear you were carried around a lot, before you got the crutches," I say carefully, tamping down the surge of jealousy that rises at that statement.

She glances at me; her face twisted in guilt. "I kept telling him to put me down, but he insisted that we'd go faster if he carried me."

I nod, looking down at the ground. "He was probably right. But he made it harder for me to catch up to you. I guess I feel better knowing you didn't have to drag your leg around with a torn ligament and bruised rib for too long."

She studies me with her crystal blue eyes. "Grey told you my injuries?"

When I nod, she says, "It wasn't too bad. Well, it was, but Rayne helped me a lot through it." At that she turns away, hiding her face, and I'm almost glad she does, because I can guess how he wormed his way into her heart. Anger fills my chest at the thought of what he did to get Vela to give in to him like he did. With gallantry like carrying her around, a girl could fall hard. Suddenly, I have to know how much of her heart has been stolen.

"How bad is it, Vels?" I ask in a quiet voice.

She looks at me quickly, a question in her eyes. "My injuries, you mean? They're much better than what they were."

"That's not what I mean," I say, and wince when I see something I don't want to acknowledge. She's trying to hide something from me. "And be honest with me, as much as you can be. Do you love him?"

She stops walking and gives me her full attention. She thinks for a minute and that moment is so full of pain for me it takes my breath away. I wish she would have denied it immediately, but she doesn't.

"I'm not in love with him like I am with you, but I do feel something for him. I just don't know quite what." She looks down and studies the ground. "I don't give my feelings away easily. I admit, though, I have feelings for him." She looks up then, her eyes shining with tears. "But I love you, Linc. I do. Just give me time to work this out in my mind."

I nod. That's all I can do. My throat is too closed up for words right now. Fire erupts out of my fingertips and with effort, I quench it quickly.

Vela looks at me with concern. "Are you okay?"

With gritted teeth, I answer, "Yes, I'll be fine."

We resume walking. I'm taking slow, measured breaths when I notice Vela adjusting her arms over her crutches again. I stop her. Grateful to have something to do, I say, "Here, let me fix those up a bit." I shrug the canteens and my backpack off and pull out two sweatshirts. Taking the crutches from her, I brace one on my chest and start wrapping the soft cotton over the armrests. I do both of them quickly and hand them back to her, but when I look up, I'm surprised to see Vela crying again.

I try to go to her, but she stops me by holding out a hand. Her other hand is over her mouth, trying to hide her sobs.

"Linc, I don't deserve you. I absolutely don't deserve someone like you loving me the way you do," she says in between hiccups. She gestures toward the crutches. "You only look out for me. You always have and look how I treat you? I kiss someone else." She starts crying harder. "I'm the worst...person!"

My heart is torn watching her cry. I don't know what to do. Do I ignore her protests and hold her, anyway? Or stay away? Before Rayne came into our lives, her life, I wouldn't have hesitated. I would have held her. Because there wasn't someone else vying for her heart. I was the only contender. But now... now, things aren't that simple.

I can't confuse her by holding her right now. Indecision wars through me. I watch her crying. Every sob rips into my heart. Finally, unable to stand it any longer, I reach over to her and pull her into my arms. She sinks into me like she was born to be here.

"Oh, Linc. I've missed you so much," she says into my chest.

I rest my cheek on the top of her head. "I think you know how much I've missed you," I whisper.

"I thought you hadn't held me like this yet since you found me because..."

"Of what I saw?" I finish for her, my heart squeezing painfully at the reminder.

I feel her head nodding against me.

"I hadn't held you because I don't want to confuse you," I say into her hair.

"I'm not confused about loving you. I know I do. I just...care about him, too, in a much different way."

My breath stops. I work hard at getting my heart to start beating again. It will *never* get easier hearing her say she cares about someone else.

She starts talking into my hurting chest. "I could feel you coming for me, you know. I know that sounds crazy, but I just knew you'd find me."

Why did she fall into Rayne's arms, then? If she knew I'd catch up to her, she had to know I might see her kiss him. At those angry thoughts, I give them up to God...again. And ask for forgiveness...again. This is taking the extent of my newly deepened faith and is stretching me to uncomfortable places.

At my silence, she continues talking into my shirt. "You know, last night I swear I could sense you were in danger. It woke me up out of a dead sleep." She looks up at me, her eyes worried. "What happened to you last night?"

The thought of the wolves trying to eat Jack and me comes to my mind. I smile softly at her. "Jack and I were hunted and attacked by a pack of wolves. You could feel I was in danger, really?"

She stiffens and nods. She looks up with shining eyes and asks, "Did you mind control them, too?"

I grimace. "I tried, but I was exhausted. And I didn't have the benefit of your presence to amplify my powers like I did with the last pack of wolves."

"How did you get away?"

"Jack. And a little fire. That and I convinced them there was better prey somewhere else."

She drops her head into my chest again, clutching my jacket. "Linc, this trip has been so hard. If you could only know what we've been through."

"I think I've figured out most of it. The geysers were a beast, weren't they?"

She looks up quickly. "Did they go off on you, too?"

I wince. "Jack and I had to hike up those rocks quick. I carried him for most of it."

"Have I thanked you for bringing him back to me yet?"

I look down at her, holding her waist and wish I could get the kind of thanks I'm deeply hungry for. But, again, I wait. *Now is not the time,* I remind myself. I'd like to erase her memory of Rayne's kiss with a few of my own.

"Yes, you did."

"Wait," she says, her face scrunched up in thought. "How on earth did you get him down the ravine? You couldn't fly him down like Rayne." She rubs Jack's head as she waits for my answer.

At that, I smile sadly. "That was one of my more brilliant moments. I strapped him to my back with a rope. I might have had to meld with his mind to keep him still, but I released him quickly after that."

She buries her face into my chest, squeezing my middle. "Thank you. You knew I needed him."

I accept her hug and absorb the wonderful, familiar feelings our Intended bond gives me. It makes my head spin, and I inhale deeply of her unique scent that I once thought meant she was only meant for me. Now, I hesitate. It does mean we have a bond, but that does not guarantee a life with her. I won't take for granted any time she gives me now.

She picks up her head and gives me a small smile. I smile back, happy to have made her happy. It's not the brownie points I wanted, but it'll do for now. I hope to be fully rewarded in due time.

Rayne has no idea how patient I can be. We'll see who has the gumption to wait for the girl we both want. I don't plan on losing that fight.

26. Vela

We've caught up to Rayne and Roland, who are both sitting on the trail ahead. Roland notices us first and he stands up, walking up to Linc, holding out his hand.

"Greetings. I heard we had another member join our group. I'm Roland. You're Linc?"

At his question, I look hungrily at Linc, who I still can't believe is here. I want so much to fall into his arms and never leave them. I wonder again, *Who is this changed guy in front of me?* But then I see Rayne watching me, a closed off expression on his face. My heart squeezes at the sight.

When did I start caring about his feelings so much?

The past two days have done a serious job of confusing my heart.

Linc nods, his mouth grim, and shakes Roland's hand firmly. "I am. I've been trying to catch up to these two for a while. It was quite a journey."

My throat closes at the thought of what Linc went through to reach me. And what he found when he finally did. The pain in my knee is nothing compared to the heavy and tortuous agony and guilt I'm feeling now.

Roland notices Jack sitting by Vela's leg. "Who's that?"

I speak up, "This is Jack. We got separated, but Linc brought him back to me. It was quite the job, too." I smile at Linc, and he returns a strained grimace. He's not looking at me, though.

I turn and see he's glaring steadily at Rayne.

"Rayne," he acknowledges in a gruff voice.

"Linc," Rayne returns in a similarly rough voice. His body is tense, and I can't help but notice his fists clenching and unclenching.

The air is full of tension. Roland looks between the two of them and asks, "Is there going to be a problem?" He's read the tension exactly right.

I can only imagine the feelings zinging through the air right now.

Linc's face contorts in anger, then, like a switch, he blinks, and the anger is erased. In its place is a peace I've never seen in him before. He's taken all of this so well, I almost don't recognize the person before me.

If I had to guess, I would have imagined nothing but bitter rage and resentment from him, but he's strangely calm about all of this.

What happened to change him so much? He said God helped him, but in what way? I need that for myself.

Rayne seems to have that same impression, because confusion crosses his face as he watches Linc warily, expecting an attack at any moment. He doesn't seem to know how to take Linc's grudging acceptance. He stands, hands ready at his sides for an attack. But none comes. And it doesn't seem like it will.

Nothing in Linc's body language says he's about to hurl a fireball or lunge at Rayne.

Roland nods as if he's got his answer and says to us all, "Okay, so let's get going. We've wasted enough light as it is."

I call Jack to me, and we resume our grueling trek. Linc is by my side and Rayne is up ahead a little ways. I know I'm close enough to Rayne for him to feel what I'm feeling, but I can't bring myself to care right now. I'm full of tumultuous emotions that seem ready to boil over. I never thought anything, or anyone, would come between Linc and me and look where I am now.

Torn between two guys.

Linc gives me time with my thoughts, and I wish he wouldn't. I'd welcome any distraction from the memory of Linc watching the searing kiss Rayne and I exchanged not an hour ago. It's all I can think about.

If Linc hadn't seen it, I would have told him anyway, so it was almost good to get it out of the way. But for him to witness my betrayal, that had to be his own personal brand of torture.

I glance at him and see him studying the ground, a small furrow in his brow. He worked so hard to catch up to me, to bring my precious furry sidekick back to me.

Wanting anything in my mind except the current drama, I ask, "Tell me what happened to everyone else."

He repeats some of what he's already told me, but I learn that he caught up to Gene and Jerry. It doesn't surprise me that they went back to where we all split up to wait for everyone else. I'm sure by now Tonya, Andy, and Collette have reached them and they're on their way to Saddleback.

My stomach drops at the thought. "I wish we could have gone to meet Sandy and James," I tell Linc.

He looks at me quickly, hearing the disappointment in my voice. "They'll be there when we can make the trip. The important thing is to get your knee fixed."

I sigh. "I know. But surely Saddleback has a healer, too?"

"I'm sure they have a healer, but one as good as Hannah?" He gives me a sympathetic look.

I nod. Because he's right. Hannah has a special ability to diagnose and heal an injury. My spirits raise at the thought of seeing her and Greta soon.

After about an hour of walking, Linc excuses himself for a bathroom break.

While he's gone, Rayne stands off to the side, looking out into nothing. Wanting to clear the air, or try to, I hobble over to him.

I stand, unsure what to say, when he surprises me by speaking, still studying the horizon. "Was any of it real?" His voice reflects pain, but that's all I can discern. He's so closed off that he's nearly impossible to read, and of course I don't have that handy, yet invasive, gift.

"Yes," I answer honestly. "It was real to me. But now that Linc's here..."

"Now that Linc's here, you're all his again," he says with such finality that I look at him sharply.

"I'm not all anyone's, Rayne," I snap. "I'm my own person, and I intend on being my own person for the foreseeable future."

"A future without me, you mean?"

"Why are you asking me that? Can't you understand I need time? Linc seems to understand that, in fact, he told me to take all the time I need."

"So, now you're going to compare me to him?" he says, turning toward me, spearing me with his gaze. He leans toward me, his eyes flashing amber as he continues, "I'd rather you hated me for the rest of your life than do that. Spare me your pity."

I step back. "I don't pity you, Rayne. I think I've been clear that I've admired your better qualities for a while now."

"So, you'll accept that side of me, and not any other? Should I just act like your prized dog and worship your feet in an attempt to earn your love?" He gestures toward Jack.

"No," I cry, "I don't want that. Ever. I admire many things about you. Can't you let me feel what I feel and not force your way into my life?"

He steps toward me. "I asked *you* if you wanted me to kiss you, remember? I didn't force anything."

"I distinctly remember saying I didn't want you to kiss me," I whisper, my heart kicking up speed the closer he gets.

"And you know that I can tell when you're lying. Don't forget you kissed me back, Vela."

"That was my mistake," I shoot back, glaring up at him. I'm desperate for some control. I don't like being on the defensive. I need to be on the attack, too.

He flinches like I hit him. "You liked that kiss. Or, should I say, kisses? Should I kiss you again to remind you how much you enjoyed it?" He towers over me.

Not wanting him to think I can be intimidated, I stand my ground and fill myself with as much antagonism as I can. I want him to feel how much I hate that idea. "No," I growl.

He laughs softly and leans in to talk into my ear. "I'll let you believe you don't want that, but sooner or later, you'll prove me wrong. One day, Vela, you'll beg me for another kiss. Or two."

I lean back and close my eyes, praying for the strength to resist him, unlike before. My heart kicks up such speed, it feels like I just ran a mile, instead it only took his words for that to happen. A resolve fills me after my quick prayer and I open my eyes and say, "If you even think of trying, I'll hit you with everything I have."

His eyes twinkle as he turns away, not looking the least bit intimidated. "That's a promise I hope you'll keep. Don't think I won't fight back if you do it again. I only have to wait and feel when you're ready. It'll happen. I hope both do," he says, walking away.

I want to hit him and grab him at the same time. He's just near enough to feel my emotions, and I hate it when he laughs softly as he walks on, reading me perfectly.

I turn in a huff.

He's so infuriating. His brutal honesty is going to be the death of me.

I fill my lungs with a bracing breath. I'll figure out my feelings. One way or another, I will, and I'll take them to God, since I clearly can't control them myself.

Linc returns, glancing between Rayne and me with a deep frown. He must have overheard some of our conversation. He strides ahead in long, angry steps.

My heart squeezes for hurting Linc...again. I follow Roland, who continues to lead us back to the Polar Bear. He's quiet. I can only imagine what he's determined about the three of us.

Knowing this is long overdue, I take my heartsick guilt to the One Person who can help me with it. And forgive me, too.

God, I confess my mistake to You. I shouldn't have kissed Rayne when I'm with Linc. Someone You bonded me with. Forgive me for kissing Rayne the way I did. I should have waited until I was sure of who You want me to be with. God, You know who I'm meant to tie my life to. Help me to not fall into his arms again if they're not meant to be mine. I'm so confused, Lord. Who am I meant to be with? Linc or Rayne? You've given me a bond with Linc, but does that mean we're meant to be together? If so, why would I have such confusing feelings for Rayne? God, help me choose the right guy for me. And help Linc to forgive my betrayal. Forgive me, Lord and give me strength to resist Rayne, until You show me who I'm meant to be with. Amen.

I continue my walk, my heart slightly lighter, but still heavy with unanswered questions. I avoid looking at Linc or Rayne, needing God's guidance more than I've ever needed it before.

We can't get to the Polar Bear soon enough. I need Hannah's comforting hug and Greta's unending monologue to fill my thoughts for a while.

27. LINC

My heart is so bruised and broken...and angry, I'm surprised it's not exploding in fire out of my chest. When I came back from my bathroom break, I couldn't help but overhear the last of Rayne and Vela's conversation.

He thinks she'll *beg him* for another kiss? That's the most ridiculous thing I've ever heard. But worry hits me that Vela would be tempted to do that. As hard as it is to admit, it's possible. He gave promises he intended to keep, but to my surprise, Vela was resisting. I should be happy about that, I guess. I can't help but want to nurse my rage, though.

Once again, God, help me with my anger. Help me forgive. Over and over if I need to.

One thing I do know is Rayne is going to fight for Vela, but so am I. And I know Vela better than almost anyone, so I have that advantage. I'll just have to remind her how good we are together. That shouldn't be too hard. I'm confident I can get her attention back. But will it be enough?

As much of a boulder-sized bur in my backside as Rayne is, I'll be generous and treat him how I'd like to be treated. What's the Golden Rule? Do unto others as you would have them do unto you. Yeah, that's it, and it's from the Bible, so it's legit true.

I stay by Vela's side, drinking in her presence. I hate that she's hurt and struggling around with those crutches. It's hard to watch. I see why Rayne just wanted to carry her everywhere. I'd do the same, but I can tell it's important to Vela to do this on her own.

She keeps looking over at me like she's never seen me before. I can guess that she's a little surprised at the change in me. I laugh in my head. Of course she's surprised. The last time I saw Rayne touching her, I sicced her dog after him, having Jack tear into his shoulder with a vicious bite. I sober quickly. That memory is not pleasant. Not my proudest moment, for sure.

I'm just thankful God produced such a change in me.

I catch Rayne's eye a couple of times, too. His is loaded with venom, which doesn't surprise me. I'm ruining his best laid plans with my presence. He probably thought he'd have her all to himself until they reached the Polar Bear, and maybe longer, if I guessed wrong and tried to meet them at Saddleback.

I scoff. He doesn't know me very well if he thought I wouldn't scour the earth to find my girl.

The image of their kiss suddenly flashes in my head again. It's on repeat over and over in my mind and I can't get it to stop. It feels like a high-resolution movie with special effects and music. I shake my head, trying to clear it.

"Headache?" Vela asks, looking at me with concern.

"Something like that," I say, not wanting to admit what their stolen moment has done to me.

The old me would have laid on the guilt trip so hard, Vela wouldn't be able to see straight. This new me is willing to let go and forget the whole thing.

How can I, though? And what if it happens again?

I shake those disturbing thoughts off, knowing they will only drive me crazy. I need to keep my head cool and show Vela and myself I'm a different man now. I can handle this problem. With God on my side, it's not impossible.

I know it will be beyond difficult as I'm not a superhero. I've got feelings, so I hope Vela is tender with them. But I've grown to trust that God will lead me through this. He doesn't promise I won't come out unscathed on the other side, however.

Desperate for a different conversation, I ask, "Once you're healed, you want to go straight to Saddleback? Or do you want to wait a few days to rest?"

She shakes her head. "As nice as it would be to be back at the Polar Bear, I want to meet my potential parents. I'd like to leave the same day if we can."

Rayne overhears and stops in his tracks. He waits for us to catch up, which is a full minute because of Vela's slow progress. He gives her an intent look and says, "Vela, you've driven yourself hard these past couple of days. You should take the time to rest. Saddleback will always be there."

I'm tempted to ask him what business it is of his what Vela decides to do, but I clamp my lips shut.

She seems to take his suggestion seriously, which is as much a surprise as anything else has been since I caught up with them.

"I don't know. I just want to meet them, you know? If they are my biological parents, I don't want to wait one more minute."

Rayne walks on the other side of her, and I'm reminded of our ill-fated journey to Saddleback just two days ago, before the bear attacked us. We were in this exact position, except Vela was healthy. Rayne on her right side, me on her left.

My chest burns with resentment. I'm in just as precarious a position now as I was then. Vela isn't mad at me anymore, which reminds me that I still need to apologize to her for taking over Jack. But it's just as tense and awkward as before, maybe even more.

She looks between me and Rayne, pinching her lips, looking stressed.

I want to wipe that emotion off her face, but this moment is strained.

To give Vela relief, I tell her, "There's something I want to ask Roland." I run to catch up to him a couple hundred yards ahead.

When I reach him, I say, "Roland, I haven't thanked you for taking Vela back to Polar Bear."

He looks over at me, his dark eyes scrutinizing me. Finally, he says, "I didn't do it for her. Our community could use some trade with those in your town."

"It's not really a town, more a settlement."

He shrugs, like he doesn't care what we call the Polar Bear.

"I hear Vela made good friends with a little girl named Aponi." I smile at the memory of the cute girl and her long pigtails. "She makes an impression, that's for sure."

He smiles. "She's my niece, my late brother's daughter. You made friends with her, too?" He looks at me with a new expression, his eyebrow hiked up.

This time, I shrug. "Kind of. I talked to her for a few minutes. She told me what happened with Vela and Rayne."

At that, he emits a long-suffering sigh. "Your friend..."

I interrupt him. "He's not my friend," I growl.

He smiles sardonically. "Not him, her."

"She's my Intended, much more than a friend," I say in a hard voice, despite the twinge in my chest.

He coughs, seeming surprised to hear that. "She's your Intended? Then why would she... You know what, it's none of my business," he says, looking out into the distance.

I give him some time to digest what I told him. It's basically unheard of for someone to reject their Intended. Not that Vela's rejecting me, I reassure myself. She's just exploring other options.

I hate that.

Once someone finds their true soulmate, they hardly ever look for love with anyone else. I completely understand Roland's outright confusion. What Vela is doing is strange, and a thought worms its way into my head.

Am I not a strong enough man to keep my Intended happy?

I refuse to believe that. Rayne had her to himself for two days. She was vulnerable, hurt, and very needy, and he definitely took advantage of the situation and caught her attention.

Well, now that he has it, I'll have to step up my game.

But how?

Again, I remind myself, I'll be me. That's all I can do. I know Vela would prefer me to be my genuine self. And this is who I am now, more understanding and compassionate.

So, I am a starkly different guy, I guess.

Still, Rayne was only alone with her for two days. Surely that doesn't erase the time I've had with Vela. Which has only been a few months, I remind myself. It seems like Vela's life has turned upside down for her multiple times in just a short time.

Compassion for her suddenly swells in me.

"How does it work for humans to live with your gifts?" I ask Roland, to get my mind off my Intended. I'm genuinely curious about how they keep their life a secret from the rest of the world.

He glances over at me and shrugs. "It's how we've always done things. Since the beginning. We try to keep our lines strong with the Gift, but if someone finds love with a human, it's nothing tragic."

"And the humans have never shared the secret?" I ask because that seems impossible.

His lips press together. "It is a sacred law for my people to keep our gifts from the world. It's an honor for them, and they do it gladly."

I nod. I know their culture is heavy on tradition. I can see their own following the laws they set out for hundreds of years of secrecy.

We walk in silence, and it's not uncomfortable. Roland is easy to travel with. He's not prone to small talk, which is fine with me.

My thoughts are full enough, and I turn my conversation inward and start talking to God about my grief and fear of losing my Intended.

It's all I can do. So, I pray.

28. VELa

At this point, I'm ready to throw these stupid crutches into the woods and leave them there. But that would require help from Linc or Rayne that I'm not ready to accept.

So, I trudge onward, feeling more and more sorry for myself. Despite my prayer, guilt for betraying Linc has consumed me, and I try reasoning with myself that the kiss was an innocent lapse of judgement. I know that's not true, though.

I'm not the kind of girl to just go around kissing guys I'm not dating, even ones I dated before Linc. And yet I kissed Rayne thoroughly.

He's walking next to me, glancing at me every few minutes. "I see he's improved your crutches situation," he finally says.

I nod, sighing. "Yeah, he didn't have to."

"He's different. I keep expecting him to come at me any minute. But he's so calm about all of this. I don't get it."

I shake my head. "He says God got ahold of him, but I don't know what that means. Believe me, I expected the same reaction you did, and I'm just as shocked it hasn't come yet. To the both of us."

He huffs. "He wouldn't hurt a hair on your head. It's me who should be concerned."

I look over at him. He looks wary and on guard. "He can't hurt me, you know, because of our bond. Well, with his gift. I guess if he wanted to hit me, that would be different, but we are physically incapable of using our gifts to hurt each other."

He grips the straps of his backpack and looks at me intently. "How strong is that bond, anyway? What's it like?"

Surprised he would ask these questions, I'm almost stunned into silence. He was so emphatic before that he wasn't interested in finding his Intended. I know she's somewhere out there, but he insisted he wants to choose who to love.

"Umm, well, it's pretty intense. His scent is unique to me, tailored to fit what I find most desirable. And my gift comes alive just being near him. Our gifts are amplified, too, when we're together."

He looks out into the distance. "Sounds amazing. Still, it can't be that great."

"No, it really is."

Suddenly, his mouth stretches into a wide grin. "So, the fact you're even interested in anyone else is kind of a miracle, right?"

I whip my head to look at him. *That's what he's going to fixate on?* "Don't be too proud of yourself. But, yeah, it's definitely unusual."

My chest feels like an elephant has just stomped on it. He might be proud of himself, but I'm certainly not. I feel like a parasite has taken over my body, making me do things I shouldn't do.

What made me kiss Rayne, anyway?

Now that it's been over an hour since *it* happened, I can look at it a little more objectively. I must have just gotten caught up in the moment. I do admire Rayne. He showed me the kind of guy he can be when we were alone.

"Were you only nice to get in my good graces?" I ask in a low voice.

He looks at me with confusion all over his face. "What do you mean?"

I sigh. "I mean, are you really that guy I saw the past two days?"

He frowns. "Well, I guess that's what you're going to have to decide for yourself. I'm not going to try to convince you I'm a good guy. But, for the record, no, I wasn't only nice to you to get you to like me. I'm a little offended you have to ask."

This time, a different guilt consumes me. I'm hurting people left and right, and that's not me.

"I'm not usually so... antagonistic. I'm sorry."

He's quiet for a moment before he says, "I'm sure it's not normal for you to kiss a guy when you're with someone else."

I'm so weighed down with a crushing guilt at his words, I can't respond. I just shake my head in silent misery.

"Are you two still together?" he asks. There's a note to his voice that makes me study him for a moment.

"I honestly don't know," I say quietly, looking at Linc's back, wondering why he left me alone with Rayne. Did he think we needed to talk things out?

He's right as usual. We did need to talk.

"Look," I say, stopping and putting my hand on his arm. "I care about you. But I love Linc. He's everything to me. You've just got me thinking that everything doesn't begin and end with my Intended. I need to be my own person and not just someone's other half. I almost lost my identity for a while there. And I have you to thank for helping me see that I need to be a better person. For myself."

He hangs his head, laughing softly. "I'll be honest with you. That wasn't my intention. But I'm glad I've had a positive influence on you."

I hesitate before I talk again. "As far as our future is concerned, I need time to think. You need to give me that."

His eyebrow lifts as he looks at me through a lock of his hair. "And if I'm not okay with that?"

"Well, then, that's your problem. Not mine. I mean it, Rayne. Don't push me. You won't like the results."

He laughs softly. "Wow. That's putting me in my place."

When I start to talk, he cuts me off by raising his hand. "I understand your need for space. I will respect it. But can we finally be friends?"

I resume walking, and he follows. "Yes, I think I can agree to that. But please, Rayne, don't ask for anything else right now.".

We've walked the entire day, and I'm beyond sore, my body hurting in places I didn't know I could hurt. Linc keeps giving me sympathetic looks, and Rayne has asked several times if he could carry me.

I shut him firmly down each time.

I know I didn't imagine Linc's relieved look. But more than that, I have to do this myself. It's important to me I stand on my own two feet, well, three technically. I feel a little guilty I've slowed everyone down, and we're getting to Polar Bear much later than if someone carried me.

But who would I choose to do that? If I could, I'd ask Roland. But he hasn't offered. Linc really didn't either, but I know he would in a heartbeat if I asked. Then I'd have to see Rayne's expression that I didn't take him up on his many offers.

So, I walk on my own, struggling to keep up with the guys' slow pace. It's one of the most physically and mentally taxing things I've ever done. I'm drained, and I just want to curl up in a ball and sleep for days. I'd give anything for a pillow.

At the end of the day, Roland finds a clearing that he says gives him a good view if anything comes sniffing around our campsite.

I throw my crutches down and stand there looking at the ground longingly. Sitting down is going to require my left leg to bear all my weight, and I'm not sure I can manage it after straining to walk all day. Jack is no help. He trots off to investigate something in the bushes.

A warm voice speaks into my ear. "Need some help?" Because I've experienced the rush of emotions and intense scent that comes with Linc, I know it's him. I'm suddenly very thankful for our Intended bond's reactions. If I had guessed wrong, I would have died of shame.

Instead, I smile and say, "Yes, please. Thank you, Linc."

He carefully avoids the sore spots where the crutches have deeply bruised me. I sink into his chest as he wraps his arms around my middle. Being this close to him is like coming home.

"Okay, on three, I'll ease you down. Just keep all your weight on me." Linc's deep voice rumbles through me, and I find it hard to breathe with the rush of desire that takes over.

I look up, unable to help myself and admire the lines of his jaw.

After he counts down, he gently eases me to the ground. Once I'm sitting, he crouches behind me.

"Want to lean on me? Or do you want to sit on your own?"

I'm about to tell him I'd love to lean on him when I catch Rayne's eye. He stands stock still, his hands fisting on his sides. His eyes are throwing daggers at Linc. Not wanting an elemental battle to happen, I shake my head.

"I'm good. I can sit on my own."

Linc sighs into my ear when he looks up and notices Rayne's angry expression. He stands up slowly, his arms loose at his sides.

I'm not sure if I could stop a fight from happening, the way Rayne is looking at Linc. I don't know why I didn't anticipate Rayne starting a fight. I only thought of Linc throwing the first punch, but it's clear Rayne is looking for trouble.

Linc still, to my surprise, has a serene expression on his face as he looks at Rayne.

Who is this new Linc?

I sit with my mouth open in shock. It looks like Linc will defend himself if needed, but he won't attack unprovoked.

From Rayne's murderous expression, I'm about to see a showdown.

Roland, however, has a different idea. He jumps in between them, one hand on Rayne's shaking chest and the other one outstretched toward Linc. "Hey, calm down, boys. Nothing is going to happen between you, right? Calm down," he orders in a firm voice. He waits for the fire in Rayne's eyes to cool.

Rayne's face changes from rage to cool indifference. "If he can keep his hands to himself, I'll be fine."

I seethe. He has zero right to say that. I'm about to tell him so when Linc says, "I think Vela can speak for herself. She doesn't need you to dictate every move she makes."

"I bet you'd like to do that for her, wouldn't you?" Rayne bites out.

I'm getting angrier and angrier the more I listen to this. Just because I kissed him does not mean he has a claim on me.

Linc agrees with me. "No, I wouldn't. Vela has a mind of her own. I'll never ask her to do anything she doesn't want to do. You should think about doing the same."

Roland gives Linc an exasperated look.

Rayne growls, "I've never made Vela do something, ever. What she's done with me has all been of her own free will."

And now he's talking about the kiss and not about Linc helping me sit down. I look at Linc's reaction quickly, hoping he can keep his cool, meanwhile trying to keep mine, too. He grits his teeth, his jaw clenching, but he stays levelheaded.

Roland is the one to break the silence. "Both of you sit down and stop antagonizing each other," he gripes, still standing between them.

Linc concedes first, which is becoming less shocking to me. He announces that he's going to collect firewood and walks into the woods.

Roland, assured Linc is gone, turns to Rayne. "That was incredibly stupid. You need to respect the fact that he has a revered bond with this girl. If you were in his position, you would be tearing the head off anyone who came between you and your Intended. Now, cool down and relax."

Rayne stays still for a second, still glaring in the direction Linc went. Finally, he huffs and stomps off in the opposite direction.

I'm wrestling with my feelings as Roland, shaking his head, walks in my direction. He glances at me. "I'm pleased to see that you stayed out of that."

"It was hard, I'll admit. Rayne thinks he has way too much say over me."

Roland nods and starts collecting rocks to form a firepit. "He seemed pretty cool and collected until the other one showed up."

I cringe. "You mean that display I made back at your house?"

He chuckles. "Yeah, I'm pretty sure I would have at least defended myself."

I look down and call Jack to me. When he comes, I bury my face in his neck, needing soothing. Turning, I say, "I might have gone overboard when I learned about Borean's second gift."

His eyebrows shoot up into his hairline. "You didn't know?"

"I grew up around only Gyans my whole life. There's a lot I don't know about the other clans."

He shakes his head as he stacks the rocks in a circle. "People of the Elements should live together."

"I agree with you. I've always felt so bad that I could only help the Gyans we live with. I hate that our territories are separated."

"It's not what the Maker intended."

"The Maker?" I ask, curious.

He lifts his eyes to look at me. "You call Him God; we call Him Maker. He is of the earth, water, wind, and fire. He is everywhere. He gave us these gifts."

I nod, agreeing completely.

Linc and Rayne come back into view from opposite directions, their arms loaded with firewood. I lean back on one arm, petting Jack with the other. I can only hope their tempers have cooled. Well, Rayne's at least.

They drop their loads on opposite sides of the campsite. Rayne is the first to carry wood over to where Roland has set up the place for the fire. He kneels down and takes his flint out of his backpack. He finds some nearby moss to gather in a nest-like pile. He's busy shaving flint into the fire when Linc interrupts him.

"You do know I'm a Fire Elemental, right? You don't need to go through all that effort."

Rayne doesn't even look up. "I'd rather freeze to death than sit by a fire you make."

Ooookay. He seriously hates Linc's guts.

Linc only laughs. He looks on with an amused gaze while Rayne continues his efforts to make a fire.

Roland is the one to comment, "You're wasting perfectly good materials when Linc can start it with just a thought."

This time Rayne looks up to glare at the man. "I don't care."

I can't help but think he's being incredibly childish. I'm about to say something, but I look up at Linc just as I'm about to make a rude comment. He shakes his head at me subtly, like he knows what I was going to say and that I shouldn't.

I swallow my words. But I do shake my head at the ridiculousness of what I'm seeing.

Roland has given up his argument at Rayne's obvious stubbornness. He opens his pack and brings out dinner. He passes out jerky and a bar that when I taste it, I'm pleased to find is made of fruit.

After a few minutes, Rayne's got a nice fire going, but I can't help but look at it with disdain.

Is he so threatened by Linc that he won't accept help from him?

Linc just shakes his head and sits down across from me. We all settle around the fire and a tense silence fills the air.

To lift the oppressive mood, I ask Roland, "Can you tell us about the origins of your people? Why did they never follow the other Elementals and split up?"

Roland loops his arms around his knees, and his face takes on a faraway look. "My people have always revered the gifts the Maker gave us. We treat them as prized pieces of our soul. Long ago, when the world started fighting and dividing itself up, we did not follow. We stayed together. We are family. We are one."

"And when did humans become a part of your people?" I ask.

He looks at me with his dark eyes. "They have always been a part of us. We are one, we are family, the ones who do not have the Gift and those who do."

I digest that for a minute. It's Linc who says, "That's pretty amazing. That's how our whole world should be. You guys have it right. We don't."

I nod, but sit, thinking it over. How different would our world be if humans knew about our gifts? We could help them in so many wonderful ways. It's something to really think about.

Rayne speaks up. I don't know if he's trying to be obstinate and get under Linc's skin, but he asks Linc in a derisive tone, "And what about the mixed Elementals? Where do we fit into this grand plan?"

Linc gives him a direct gaze. "You're an example of why Elementals should be united. Right now, you're an enigma because of your mixed blood. But, like Roland's people, we should all share gifts and live together."

Rayne's lip curls, like he'd rather chew nails than agree with Linc. But he says nothing.

The rest of the evening passes in superficial and stunted conversation. I'm relieved when I lie down to sleep.

I'm so happy to be reunited with Linc, but not under these circumstances.

I'm using my arm for a pillow when I feel something by my head. Linc's crouching next to me, handing me a sweatshirt for a makeshift pillow.

I look up at him, smiling. "Thank you."

He smiles down at me with warm eyes. "Anytime."

Rayne grumbles from his place by the fire, easily reaching our ears, "How many sweatshirts do you have in that pack? You seem to have an endless supply."

Linc looks over at him. "I came prepared."

Rayne snorts derisively.

Linc looks away from him and sighs as he looks down at me. "Sleep well, Vels."

I bite my lip. I'm still so shocked at this transformed man in front of me. I'm nearly speechless. "You too, Linc."

He stands up and walks over to his place by the fire, making up his own bed. I notice he uses a t-shirt for his pillow.

I almost point that out to Rayne. But I bite my comment back. Barely.

Sighing, I lay my head down. This is going to be a long night.

29. LINC

Every step we take is painful for me. Because I know they're nothing short of agony for Vela. I recognize the obstinate look on her face. Reluctant admiration for her swells in my chest. She won't give up, and she's determined to make it to the Polar Bear on her own steam. I've been struggling with my feelings for miles now. I'm determined, though, to forgive Vela, but I find that I have to keep doing it over and over every time I think of that moment I found them.

Looking around, I recognize where we are. Roland took us through the rugged wilderness, knowing his way around barely there trails. He got us through some wetlands that I had to carry Vela through. It was spongy ground that had to be jogged over. Even she had to admit she couldn't traverse over it with her crutches. The decision about who should carry her ended up being easy. I was closer, so offered first. I thought Rayne would come to blows with me over it, but he managed to keep his cool. But now, she's back on her feet, or foot, and we're on the main trail from the Polar Bear. We should be there in an hour or so, depending on Vela.

She seems to recognize her surroundings, too, though, because she's stepped up her pace.

We've walked in silence most of the way, each consumed with our own thoughts. That's fine with me. I don't want to start another argument with Rayne. It doesn't really bother me that he hates me so much. It's Vela who seems stressed by it. I don't want to cause her more discomfort than she's already enduring. But I admit, seeing her so concerned about another guy's feelings does make my stomach crawl.

It's weird. It's like the roles are reversed. I used to be the one who couldn't stand the sight of Rayne. Even looking at him would cause so much rage, I could barely see straight.

Now, he's the one who can't control his anger. He's pointedly ignoring me, but the few looks I've caught have been so full of vitriol I can feel his hatred aimed right at me.

I almost feel sorry for him. I remember what that kind of anger does to you, and it's not pleasant to live with. I'm so thankful God got a hold of me and released me from that deadening emotion. It steals the joy from your life. And it's totally not worth it. I would tell Rayne this, but I don't think he would receive it well.

Since we've already taken a break today, I'm surprised when Roland calls us to a stop. His hand is up, and he's looking intently ahead. I look to see what he's studying. He's stiff with tension, and when I raise my gaze to the horizon, my breath stops.

Vela's cry snaps me out of my shock.

Dark smoke curls up over the horizon into the sky in angry clouds. It spreads out in a way that indicates more than one building is burning.

The Polar Bear is on fire. How did I not see that earlier?

It's then that I notice the acrid smell of smoke. Roland sends out a sharp command, "I'm running ahead to see what's going on. You guys stay with her."

Rayne ignores him and argues, "I'm coming, too. That's my family!"

They both take off, and I go to Vela's side, letting her lean on me.

"Linc, no," she cries in a watery voice. "The Polar Bear is burning." She turns anxious eyes to me. "Carry me there? We'd get there faster. *Greta,* Linc," she says in a strained whisper.

I answer by throwing her crutches down and sweeping her up in my arms. I squat so she can pick them back up and lay them on her lap.

I'm up in the next second and we're running, Jack following behind. Vela hangs onto me, gripping my neck tightly. I think about all the people I've met at the Polar Bear who could be hurt, or worse, killed by the fire.

Those thoughts only make me go faster.

After a while of running, the smoke grows and fills the sky. It looks like it had just started when we first noticed the fire. Smoke now fills the air in a haze. Vela coughs and I do, too, since I'm pulling in heavy breaths from exertion.

Stopping for a minute, I try to get my breath.

Vela tells me to put her down so I can rest. "Please Linc, you need to be able to breathe."

"I'm fine. Just give me a second. We'll be there in five minutes."

She reluctantly nods.

When I've caught my breath, I start running again, clutching Vela to me closely. I don't want to take her into this burning fiasco, but I know she'd never let me leave her behind.

We finally make it to a point where we can see the fire between the trees.

"Linc, look," Vela cries, pointing toward the fire.

Suddenly, Roland appears, sprinting toward us. He's gesturing at us wildly, telling us to run.

I stand my ground because I need to know what's going on before I retreat.

Roland reaches us and, rather than talking to us, he pushes us back the way we came.

Vela cries, "Wait, what's going on, Roland? Please tell us."

He comes close to us and whispers, "The Polar Bear is under attack. Everyone is being captured."

"What? Why aren't they fighting back?" I ask, my chest tight with fear.

Roland shakes his head. "They're too busy getting people out of the burning buildings. A few are making a stand, but too many oppose them, and most have guns."

"The Extremists," Vela whispers, her white face turned toward the fire.

Roland snaps his head toward her. "Are you sure?"

Vela and I both nod. I say with gritted teeth, "They've been hunting any Elemental who could be the parents of the Chosen Child. They've been after us."

Vela turns tearful eyes to me. "They've found us," she whispers, choking on a sob. She turns to Roland. "We have to help. We have to do something."

"What we need to do is hide, Vela," he whispers urgently.

"I'm not running and hiding, Roland. That will not help our friends," she whispers back, her face lined with anger.

"He's not saying we should run," I say quietly.

"No," he agrees, his face set in grim determination. "We need to be strategic in how to help. Let's find a safe place to talk about this. For now, we need to be out of view."

"Wait, where's Rayne?" Vela asks, her eyes searching the way Roland had come.

Roland turns a disgusted look toward the fires. "He ran in fighting. He'll be taken soon. There're too many for him to fight. The majority of his people are in shock and unable to help."

Vela takes that news hard and her face turns even more ashen. I want to protect her. Protect her from pain and fear. But there's nothing I can do. Well, that's not necessarily true. My own heart is thudding hard, and it's not because of my run. I'm afraid. The Extremists are killers. I know what I have to do, but Vela is not going to like this.

We follow Roland, Vela gripping her crutches like they're weapons. Her knuckles are white with strain, and I want to reassure her, but I can't. This is bleak.

He takes us to a copse of small trees and holds the branches back for Vela and me to duck inside.

Once we do, I set Vela down and Roland talks in a low, urgent tone. "We need a plan. There's only three of us, well, two, really," he says, gesturing toward Vela's hurt knee.

"Hey, I can fight," Vela argues, indignant. "I just need a safe place to hide that's close enough, and my gift can do some real damage. I'm not helpless."

Roland nods at her in appreciation and then turns to me. "Right now, our plan is to get more fighters. We need to release those captured. As many as we can. We need to fight back."

I nod. "That's a good plan. I have another one." I look carefully at Roland, judging how he's going to take my idea. I decidedly ignore Vela, knowing what she'll say.

He gestures for me to talk.

"I used to be a spy in the Extremist organization," I say. "I can say I'm still in and that I want to help them. They won't have access to a phone this far out to check my story. They should believe me."

When Vela cries, "No!" in fury, I ignore her. She pulls on my arm. I ignore that, too. I look intently into Roland's eyes. "I'm very persuasive. There's a good chance they'll believe me. When they do, I'll incapacitate the ones guarding the Polar Bear prisoners and free them."

Roland keeps up with me easily. "It's a good plan. I'll stay close to help you take out the guards."

"Wait a minute," Vela whispers furiously. "This is a horrible plan. What if they don't believe you, and you become a prisoner, too?"

"I'll have to take that chance, Vela. We need to try this. It's our best chance. I'll study the Extremists and see if there are any who might recognize me and know I'm lying. If I don't see anyone, I'm going in."

Vela's face flushes with anger. I prefer that color to the extreme pale one she sported earlier. It means she's in a fighting mood. Right now, though, she's directing that toward me.

"You are not doing this, Linc. We need to stay together. You don't need to sacrifice yourself. Let's come up with a better plan."

To answer her, I grab her face in my hands and plant a hard kiss on her lips. She's too shocked to do anything before I let her go and run out of the trees.

30. LINC

I hear Vela's furious response to my plan, or maybe to my kiss, as I race toward the community. This strangely makes my heart light. The fact that it can feel anything other than fear is good. I need to fuel myself with Vela's love. If she didn't love me, she wouldn't be so angry.

And I know she didn't mind that kiss.

I keep behind the thickest part of the trees as I make my way toward the Polar Bear. Smoke clogs the air, and I start breathing through my mouth. It makes me very angry to see this precious community in flames. Those people have come to mean a lot to me, and I will do anything I can to help them defend themselves. I'm outraged at what they must be feeling. They were so proud of their homes and the community center.

When I get closer, I'm grateful to see that the big building Andy helped design has been spared, so far. My heart clench-es at the memory of when I gave Vela a sign of my love by sending her a whisky-jack bird in there. She had rejected it then; I don't think she'd reject one now. Shaking my head to clear the memories so I can focus on the task at hand, I carefully proceed.

And then I see why the building isn't burning. They're using it to hold the hostages. My breath freezes at the thought that they might plan to set the building on fire after locking prisoners inside.

I need to get there. Now.

I scan the Extremists herding the Polar Bear residents into the building. A boiling anger fills me when I see they're using zip ties to bind their prisoners' hands together. They don't want them to use their gifts, but it's like they're treating them like animals. I'm shocked to see a grim-faced Andy in the captured group. He came back here? Is the rest of the group I traveled with here, too? Hannah must already be inside. He wouldn't give up so easily if she was still free. I'm sure of it.

I'm disappointed to see the Extremists' guns. That's going to make this rescue mission harder, since they aren't just using their gifts. I decide that using smoke to hide will be the easiest, since there's already so much of it, so I make a smoky fire in my hands and use it to shield myself. Every time I reach a tree, I hide behind it to search the Extremists' faces to see if there's anyone I recognize.

After the best search I can do, I decide to just walk in. I haven't recognized anyone. Let's hope no one I missed remembers my face.

I walk in, my hands high in the air, when one of the Extremists holding a shotgun swings it toward me.

"Stop right there," he shouts.

I comply. When he gets close enough to me, I call out to him, "I'm one of you. I work under Greg Swanson. I've been undercover for a while, trying to ferret out the Chosen One."

His face is full of surprise as he continues to walk toward me. His expression soon turns to suspicion. "How do I know you're not lying?"

I shrug. "I'm sure you know the higher ups have planted people like me everywhere. I guess you're just going to have to believe me. But I know things I wouldn't know if I wasn't a United Elemental."

At my use of their cover name, he studies me but doesn't lower his gun. Only Extremists know they hide behind the name the Elements United. It's my best weapon. He gestures with the tip of his gun toward the community center. "Let's see what my leader has to say about this. Go inside."

I walk toward the center, still holding my hands up. I wear a confident expression that I hope helps sell my story.

The man shoves my back with his shotgun, pushing me to go faster. When I get to the doorway, I steel myself for the reactions of the Polar Bear residents to my made-up cover.

Immediately, I see that most of the fifty residents are in here. I doubt any are left fighting. Tonya and Claudette are here, so they came back with Andy. I don't see Gene or Jerry; they must have gone on to their own community. I also don't see Rayne, but I do spot Hannah. I knew Andy wouldn't give up unless they had her, but it's still hard to see her trussed up. I'm even more concerned when I don't see Greta near her.

At my pause, the man jams the gun into my back and shoves me inside. I scan the whole crowd of prisoners, hoping to see Greta's little face. Hannah notices me right away and her face reflects hope that I will know where Greta is. I shake my head at her, telling her I don't know. I wish I could ease her following worry. She looks behind me and when she doesn't see Vela, a confused expression takes over her face.

The guy with the gun brings me to a man standing at the front with five other Extremists. It's going to be tricky to get this guy to believe my story, but even harder to see Hannah's disappointment if they do. I resolve not to look at her. I send up a prayer of protection for Greta over my own safety.

Where can she be?

As I'm waiting for the leader's attention, I scan the captured group and see Greta's two little friends clutching each other, looking frightened.

"Who is this?" the leader barks out once he turns to me.

"He volunteered his capture, saying he's one of us," the guard says, digging his shotgun into my back, clearly not believing me.

Enough people are sitting close to the front that they hear this announcement. They gasp and start to furiously whisper to the others. In seconds, the whole room will think I'm a traitor.

I stand still, allowing the guard's aggression. Instead of defending myself, I nod my head.

"Really?" the leader says, but it's just casual enough to be dangerous. He doesn't believe me. This is where I'll have to convince him, which is where I'll shine. I'm very good at deception. With my parents, I had to learn fast. Ever since, Olympia. When my parents held me responsible for my little sister's death, I've had to become very good at pretending like I was okay. They wouldn't tolerate anything less.

I return my thoughts to the moment, not allowing myself to get lost in grief.

"Yes, my leader is Greg Swanson. He has a group of United Elementals based out of Denver. Ask me anything and I can prove my devotion to the cause," I say in a clear voice.

The room, by now, has heard of my betrayal and erupts in a chorus of angry shouts.

"Kill him!"

"Burn his body in flames!

"Take him out and shoot him!"

I flinch and turn to my friends, facing their outrage. The shout that hurts the most is the one for me to be set aflame, because a Fire Elemental can only be killed by the hottest fires of the most skilled Festans. It would be the most painful death I could ever experience.

"You know these people," the leader says as he eyes me carefully.

I don't hide the pain from the most enthusiastic shouters. My face contorts and I say, "Yes. I planted myself here, trying to find the Chosen Child."

"If I were to believe you, you'll join my cause?"

"Yes," I say quickly, and can't help but look directly at Hannah. She's the only one who isn't shouting. Instead, she's wrapped her arms around herself and looks confused, like she doesn't quite believe me.

I avert my gaze. It lands on Andy, who's watching me with murderous eyes. He must not have Hannah's guess that I'm lying. I'm pretty sure that's what she's thinking. I can only hope.

"If I don't believe you, I think I'll throw you to the mob. Sounds like they'd tear you to pieces," he says cheerfully.

I nod grimly. They would. Even with their hands tied. Guards are pressing in on them, forcing them back onto the ground.

Leon breaks free and rushes at me. I brace myself and dodge the roundhouse punch he's thrown with both hands fisted and tied together in front of him.

I'm going to have to make this look convincing.

I deliver a vicious uppercut, and Leon slumps to the ground. I watch him drop, trying to look disinterested. My insides are twisting. He's a big enough guy that he can take a hit like that and be fine. One of the other guards drags the limp Leon away.

The leader gives me an amused glance. "The name's O'Bryan. Grant O'Bryan. I think you'll do fine with this mission. Tell me, have you made any progress on finding the Child?" He waves his hand in the air.

"I'm afraid I have no news of that. I thought I would by living in this community, but no one fit the prophecy's requirements."

"Really?" he asks, sighing, looking out over the hostages. "I've had hopes, too, with all the mixed blood here." He looks back at me. "What's your name?"

This is promising. I'm pretty sure he believes me. Especially after what I did to Leon.

"Evan Smith," I answer in as low a voice that wouldn't be suspicious. I'm lucky that no one hears me. They're still hurling angry insults at me.

I can't let anyone from the Polar Bear give him my real name. There's no way I'm sharing that, especially because I'm sure Vela and I are the reasons he came to the Polar Bear.

He corroborates that he's here for that very reason. "Have you heard of Lincoln Stevenson or Vela Ashcroft?"

Hearing Vela's name on his vile lips sends a rage throughout me. I can't let him anywhere near her. Thankfully, Roland is guarding her. I'm sure he won't let her come close.

I spit out, "I've heard of them, but haven't met them." I'm hoping my anger shows that I despise what the names represent, not my consuming hatred for this man and his smug questions.

He quirks his eyebrow. "How is that possible? You say that you know these people. We know they've been here."

Protection for Vela surges through me. I'll say anything to throw him off her scent.

"I've just returned from a three-month trip to another hidden community. If they've been here during that time, I wouldn't have met them."

He hums and falls silent, looking out over the angry crowd. They're still shouting threats at me. The hate-filled gazes of Greta's little friends, Alisha and Betsy, strike sorrow, spearing my chest. I don't want to hurt them with my lies, but for their safety, I must.

I have to convince the leader I'm one of them, so Roland and I can disarm the guards and take back the Polar Bear. Or what's left of it.

Smoke is starting to billow in. A nearby building must have caught fire. Soon, this place too, will go up in flames.

"You say you just came back from another hidden community? No news of the prophesied one there, either?"

Grant doesn't seem too bothered that smoke is filling up the room. He is a Festan, so he has no fear of fire. But he's speaking so conversationally, I almost relaxed into thinking he's believing my story. I know better, however. My parents have taught me well.

I shake my head. I curse myself for mentioning that another place like the Polar Bear exists. I'll need to be more careful.

"Really? Why did it take so long for you to determine the Child wasn't at the other camp?"

I pretend to be embarrassed. "Uuuh, a girl there caught my eye. I'm sorry to say I got distracted."

Vela is *not* a distraction. She's hopefully my future.

Grant laughs. "Ah, young love. It's so elusive, but so encompassing. I almost forgot the way it consumes you." He puts his hand on my shoulder. "If you are going to be one of us, you'll need to learn not to allow such things to divert from our passion, our goal. You need to cling to our ideals."

It would be ideal to punch his face. I reign myself in. But barely.

The prisoners on the floor have gotten quiet with the presence of the smoke. Coughing is sporadic but will grow louder as it gets harder to breathe in here.

I have to get this show on the road. It's time for this man to believe me or not. I make plans in my mind in case he does throw me to the still angry prisoners. They're conserving their energy but watching me with burning eyes.

"So, may I join your cause?"

He eyes me, considering. An Extremist comes up and whispers into Grant's ear. Whatever the guy says makes him straighten, looking up at the roof.

Knowing fire so well has its uses. I'm positive that by now, the wind has carried embers up onto the slanted slope. I send my senses out and sure enough, I can feel the sparks resting there for now. Soon enough, most of them will catch the roof on fire.

"Please sir, let me help," I plead, trying to hide the desperation.

He must hear some of it in my voice, because he looks sharply at me. I make a point of looking up at the ceiling, letting him know I know what he knows.

"How about you come with me? We'll look for any hidden prisoners," he offers.

I'd normally jump on the chance to stay close to the leader, but I need to disarm the guards. I need to stay in this room.

"Might I stay in here and guard this building, sir?"

When he looks at me curiously, I say quickly, "As a Festan, I'll know when this building is a lost cause. I can do with the prisoners what you'd have me to do."

It's like a fist clenches my heart when I see the leader nod his head.

He is planning on burning all these people alive.

I force the trembling to leave my limbs. I need to fight so badly, I can taste blood in my mouth from biting my cheek.

Unable to help myself, I give Hannah a look that's meant to tell her to get ready. I feel the wind come in and ruffle my hair.

That breeze couldn't have come from any Borean in this room, since they're tied up, so I know that Roland just gave me a sign he's ready.

I pray that this leader will allow me to stay. Only God can intervene at this point. I've done everything I could, even gotten violent. But, oh, more of that will happen soon. Hopefully, in our favor.

Grant glances up at the roof and finally decides, nodding. "You can stay. But Alex here will stay with you until I've decided what to do with you."

He gestures to one of the guards and whispers into his ear.

As I wonder what he's telling him, probably to keep a close eye on me, a small face appears and disappears just as quickly in one of the bushes that I can see outside the door.

Greta.

Fear fills me that she's going to try to free everyone. I search for her again, but she's staying hidden. I add a prayer to my list.

Keep her safe. Keep us all safe.

I glance at Hannah and barely jerk my head towards the door. Her eyes widen, but to her credit, she doesn't whip her head in that direction.

Alex, by now, is standing next to me, glaring suspiciously at me. I turn away from Hannah, not wanting to attract any attention to her. My eyes land on Andy, who's been watching my interaction with Hannah.

I give him a burning look, trying to communicate to him I'm on his side. His face is now undecided. He casually looks out the door, and he sees something that makes him go tight with tension.

My guess is he caught sight of the elusive little Gyan.

He turns back, his mouth tightened in worry, even more so than before.

When Alex looks away, I nod at Andy, barely a fraction to let him know I know Greta's out there.

A relieved look fills his eyes, which he carefully hides by hurling insults at me again. He rouses the others next to him to join him, and I'm in awe of his brilliance. He's trying to create a distraction.

It's perfect.

Alex glances at me and gestures for me to follow as he heads over to where Andy and the others are, more and more joining their curses and shouts at me.

My guard turns to look over at me with disgust. "Why did he leave you in here, anyway? It's only making my job harder."

"The cause is worth it," I say smoothly.

He snorts and looks away, pushing down one of the prisoners who had risen to his feet, spitting threats.

When someone else rises, I act like a guard and shove him down, too.

That only provokes more of them, and the guards are soon busy keeping prisoners on the ground. I scan the door to see when Roland is ready to disarm the guards. I'm hoping Andy is on my side. It'll be essential to take the Polar Bear back.

But the fact there's only one door open is not good. It'll create a bottleneck situation for everyone to get out of this doomed building.

When a guard strikes a woman over the head with the butt of his gun, my decision is made for me.

As hard as I can, I elbow Alex's head in just the right place. He falls to the ground in a slump. I shout at Andy to take the other guard next to him. Roland makes his entrance in brilliant style. He follows a wind cyclone as big as he is, dodging left and right.

It's a good thing too, because bullets are flying at him.

I race to the front of the room, where a guard is about to start firing at the prisoners. He seems uncertain and I take advantage of that to jump over two people to tackle him to the ground.

I punch the back of his head, and he goes limp. I move to the next target.

The prisoners are all standing and fighting the remaining guards. With only five left, it's only too easy to take the building back, even with their hands bound. We secure the guards' hands with their own zip ties, and I make quick work incinerating the zip ties around the prisoners' wrists.

As I thought, the prisoners lunge for the door, which will create a huge problem as everyone tries to escape. Andy shoves his way to the front of the crowd and holds out his bound hands, barring the door.

He shouts at them, "We need to think this through! There's thirty of those Extremists out there and more will be in here soon. We can't leave yet and when we do, only a few of us can exit at a time and hide in the woods until we're ready to fight."

His voice carries despite his attempt to keep from attracting outside attention. Someone will check on the prisoners soon, which gives me an idea.

I run over to him and burn the ties off his wrists, then turn to the crowd. They watch me with distrustful eyes. It will take time to regain their trust.

I try to speak to them, anyway. "Let me continue pretending to be one of them. A few will leave at a time, like Andy says. The rest of you should stay on the floor pretending your hands are still tied. When enough of us have left to take over the Extremists, the final group can escape."

"Why should we trust you?" a youth calls out, his face screwed up in anger.

I'm about to say something when the old man Vela and I met, the one who lost his dog, calls out, "His plan is good. You people need to calm down. He's just saved our lives. Do what he says."

Roland has joined me, standing at my side.

"Who is he?" someone asks, pointing at Roland.

"A friend," I answer.

"How do we know he isn't an Extremist?" the same youth asks, his face screwed up in distrust.

"He's from a nearby settlement," I explain. "He's First Nation. Trust me. He is your friend." I turn to Andy. "We need to get everyone back on the ground. They'll be checking on the situation soon. We have seconds to get a few out."

Andy looks with pride over my shoulder. "Hannah is working on it. She'll get everyone in the right places."

My heart is much lighter than it was when I first came to this building, but knowing the danger we still face has me razor focused. "Andy, get the ten best fighters you know, and Roland and I will make sure you guys get out."

"And me," a small, determined voice says behind me.

I whip around. Greta is standing there with her hands on her hips and wearing a fierce expression.

Relieved to see her safe, I order, "Greta, you need to join the others."

"No, I'm helping," she shouts at me, her little fists clenched. "They can keep chasing me around. They can't catch me."

Roland, Andy, and I shake our heads. Andy reaches for her to haul her toward the group, now on the floor.

She evades him. "No! I know all the secret places no one else does. I'll take them on the chase of their lives."

At her voice, Hannah cries and stumbles toward Greta, hugging her fiercely. The little girl allows it, but then ducks under her mother's arms and scurries out the door before anyone can stop her.

"What is she doing?" Hannah cries, chasing after her.

Andy grabs her around her middle and forces her to stay.

She squirms in his arms and cries, "I have to go after her."

I know someone will come any second and so, say, "Hannah, you have to go sit down before someone sees you."

Our attention is drawn outside when, sure enough, an Extremist walks toward the door. Greta darts out from behind a bush to throw a pinecone at his head. He snaps his gun up and we're all about to scream at him, giving ourselves away, when Greta sticks her tongue out at him and runs into the bushes.

He's about to give chase when Greta pulls a stunt I'm shocked she can do. A root rips out of the ground, spraying dirt so high it showers on the man's head. It wraps him from head to toe. He falls hard on his side, and despite squirming, his breath is cut off from the root squeezing. He's soon silent.

We all look on with wide eyes, but Greta never leaves her hiding spot.

I'm about to fish her out of the bush when Hannah grabs my arm. Her eyes are wide with shock when she says, "She has a great hiding spot right there. They'll never find her. There's a fox den under that bush."

I study the guard who went after the little misfit, but when he doesn't move, we all heave a collective sigh of relief.

Turning to Andy, I say, "Get your fighters."

We don't waste any time. We soon have a lethal force ready to enter the fight.

Pulling the fallen bodies of our guards over to the back, we hide them under the stage. I pick guys who have the same size and coloring as the guards to replace them with our own men. We pull off hats and collect the guns, finishing setting up our cover.

I look over the group on the floor, meeting the eyes of Tonya and Claudette, both with burning eyes at not being selected to go out and fight first. Then I scan the "new" guards and inhale deeply.

We're ready.

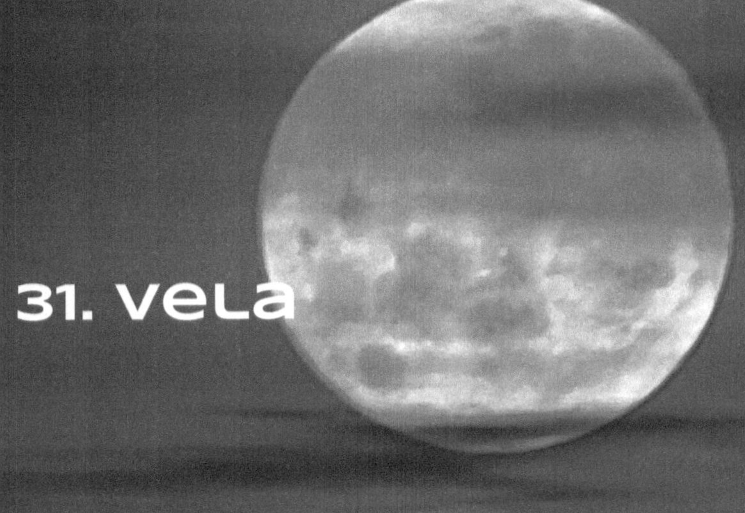

31. VELA

I'm stewing in my anger in the copse of trees Linc just raced out of. How dare he kiss me like that and leave on a suicide mission? When I see him next, I'm going to return his kiss, then I'm going to punch him in the jaw.

He'll deserve it too. Then I'll kiss his hurt away.

If he's alive for me to do it.

"How could you agree to an asinine plan like that?" I fire at Roland, who's busy looking inside his bag. He glances at me before he pulls out one wicked-looking dagger after another, some small, some large. They're all different. Some have sharp scalloped edges; others curve around his hand.

By the time he has a dozen or so knives laid out on the ground, I'm spluttering beside myself with anger.

"Calm down, woman," he says in a firm tone. "He did what he had to do. He has the best chance to get under the defenses of those people."

I'm surprised he's heard about the organization, being so hidden away from civilization like he is. When I tell him so, he looks at me with a sardonic eyebrow lifted.

"The First Nation knows the ways of the world, even if we're far from it way out here," he says casually and starts placing each knife somewhere on his person.

"You plan on killing that many people?" I ask, suddenly nervous. He looks absolutely lethal by the time he's stowed the last of his knives.

"If I have to," he says, shrugging.

Not wanting those souls on his conscience, I say, "Please don't. Incapacitate, don't kill."

His dark eyes look at me. "I'll do what I must. Those people shouldn't live."

"No, they shouldn't. But please. Just don't kill anyone."

He lifts a branch and looks out into the tree line. "He's had enough time to get there. I must leave now."

He starts to go when I cry out, "Wait, you're just going to leave me here?"

He turns, halfway out of our hiding place. "This is the safest place for you."

"I'm coming. Whether you like it or not." I hold up one of my crutches. "I have these to get me there. If you want to know where I'll be hiding to use my gift against the E.E., you'll need to take me with you."

He looks at me doubtfully. "You want me to carry you?"

I stuff my response down, because as uncomfortable as it will be to have a practical stranger carry me, I need his help. "Yes, please."

He looks down at himself. "I'm not sure I wouldn't stab you in the process."

"How about I carry the ones that might stab me? That way you won't worry."

He hesitates before ducking back into the hideaway. "Okay, let's get this over with."

Roland seems as reluctant as I am to do this, but there's no way I'm going to be left behind for Linc to single-handedly save the Polar Bear. He needs my help, and he's going to get it.

Once I've figured out how to hold three long knives and my crutches, Roland picks me up carefully and holds me away from his chest about an inch. I appreciate his care to make sure I'm not close to his other knives.

I hold the branches back while he ducks us out of the trees. Once free, he walks quickly, and I'm glad. It would be even better if he ran. But holding me while avoiding unnecessary contact makes it hard.

That's fine with me. I look down at my knee and wish more than anything I could heal myself. This injury has been one of the hardest things I've ever had to endure. Growing up as a Gyan definitely has had its benefits. I suddenly miss my mom so much. Not only her healing, but I want to talk to her about me and Linc...and me and Rayne.

What would she say about all that?

She'd give me her usual sage advice and wrap me in a hug where I could bury my head in her shoulder. She'd smell like lavender and vanilla. Like home. I didn't realize what a treasure she was until I left. I sigh. I didn't appreciate her enough.

I order Jack to follow, and Roland brings us closer to the burning Polar Bear. We're still far enough in the woods that we're hidden from sight. The smoke is heavier here, and I wonder how we're going to breathe if it gets much worse. He sets me down and waits until I've dropped the knives and balanced myself with my crutches. Jack stands by my leg.

Roland collects his knives and sheathes them, asking, "How close do you need to be to use your Gift?"

"I've never had to test my abilities with distance before." The only reference I have is when I strung those guys into the trees when they crashed into us on our road trip. Guessing, I say, "About twenty, thirty feet?"

He nods and looks for a place I can have a good vantage point but stay hidden at the same time. "It's too bad you can't climb a tree."

Coming up with an idea, I say brightly, "Actually, I can."

He looks doubtfully at my knee. "How?"

I touch the closest tree. "I'm a Gyan, remember? Trees do my bidding. Let's just find the right one." Looking around, I see something that will work. "See this balsam poplar? Let's pick another one that's a little closer."

He points at one.

"Perfect," I say, impatient to help my friends. "Go, I'm fine."

He crouches and runs toward the Polar Bear, and as I see the burning buildings closer, I clench my fists. I will do everything I can to stop the Extremists from hurting anyone.

I make my way as quickly as I can to the chosen tree. Jack follows and sits at the base. I command him to stay. Raising my hands, I connect with the tree and ask it to lower a branch. Settling onto it quickly, I flex my will for it to raise me off the ground. It's harder than I thought. It's one thing commanding a branch to do what I want, it's another for it to lift 130 pounds with it. Pain flashes up my leg from my knee when I sway and twist, trying to stay on. I'm sweating with my balancing act, my hands gripping the branch before I finally make it up.

I cough from the smoke tackling my lungs and start breathing through my mouth. I need to be hidden, not give myself away.

From my perch, I can see that I'm right behind the community building, which I'm relieved to find is not on fire. But the embers on the roof do not look good. I worry that they'll ignite soon enough.

Three Extremists step out the front door, and I wonder what's happening with Linc and Roland inside.

Movement to my right catches my eye. In the field of stumps where we did the mock battle, practicing our Elemental gifts, I count eleven Extremists who surround three Polar Bear residents. I don't recognize one of them, but my eyes widen as I recognize Rayne's and Grace's forms. Rayne uses both wind and water to beat his attackers off. Grace throws ice knives at her opponent. So, she's a Neronian. I wondered.

I smile as I crack my knuckles. I'm going to be the guardian angel they never asked for.

Moving a branch out of the way, my eyes widen when I see the end of it is on fire. Another branch catches in its blaze, the fire spreading.

I need to make this rescue quick.

Getting to work, I rip a net of roots up under three of the Extremists who are facing Rayne and Grace. They go down. I use a combination of strikes to the head and tripping them to get them on the ground. Using my gift so far away is stretching me in unpleasant ways. I grit my teeth and suffer gladly. Rayne and Grace are worth it.

Rayne looks up in surprise at the help, but not seeing anyone, simply takes advantage of the prone forms of his enemy. I see him using his wind gift to draw air from their lungs, making them pass out. Then he turns to the eight Extremists who are left.

I'm already onto them, too. Before I can take care of one who's sneaking up behind Rayne, I rip off a flaming branch coming toward me and let it fall to the ground. With my other hand, I take a root and wrap it around the sneaky Extremist's waist, yanking him back. He cries out, alerting

Rayne, who lifts him high in the air on the wind, then drops him. The man doesn't move again.

I bite my lip. I cover my nose with my arm, trying to see through the worsening smoke. I hope no one dies today, but with the Polar Bear in flames, and armed Extremists running around, it seems like that's their goal. At least my fighting would be in self-defense.

Before he turns to anyone else, Rayne looks wildly around to see who's giving him Gyan aid. Even though he can't see me, he seems to sense my presence, so he smiles in my direction and attacks Extremists who've ganged up two to one on the third Polar Bear member, who I don't know.

Seeing Rayne holding his own, I blink away tears from the smoke and focus on Grace, who's defending herself against a zealous Extremist. She's wielding ice knives left and right. Unfortunately, her attacker is using the same method. I see she's already gotten a few cuts from him.

I'm going to even the odds.

Pulling up a root, I knock the ice knife out of his hand. I wrap the root tightly around his wrist and whip it behind him, wrenching his arm back until he screams. He tries to use his other arm, but I take another root, repeating the process. Grace punches him in the throat when he leans his head back and screams in agony. He goes down. Seeing him incapacitated, I focus on another Extremist.

But why attack one when I can get three? Smiling, I open up the ground under the feet of Extremists who are unlucky enough to be standing close together and they all tumble in.

I'm so focused on my attacks that I don't notice when the limb above me catches fire. A blazing branch drops on my arm, and I lurch back, trying to get it off. After a few seconds of struggling, I fling the branch to the ground, but the damage has been done.

Grimacing at the searing pain in my arm, I look at my situation. I realize I have just moments to get out of this tree.

I look over at the last Extremist. When he notices his odds, he tries to turn around and run. He doesn't get far when Rayne wrestles him to the ground, punching him in the jaw. The man doesn't move.

Rayne's breathing heavily, looking down at the man he's straddling. Grace puts a hand on his shoulder, and he finally looks up.

All three Polar Bear members are bloody with various injuries, but after Grace says something to Rayne, they all look around the woods to see who their Gyan angel was who helped them.

I see a group of five Extremists who are about to come upon them, so I shrink back into the burning tree. I know I'm a sitting duck waiting to get roasted, but I can't run away with my knee that way it is, so I'm stuck where I am.

I need to alert Rayne and his friends of the approaching danger. I also need to stay invisible to be of any help to Rayne, who hasn't thought to look at my burning tree, accurately thinking no one sane would be there. I'm questioning my sanity, too. Half of the tree is on fire at this point, and I don't have much more time.

Rayne isn't deterred, however. He walks in my direction, looking up and down until he catches sight of me.

I need him to see the approaching Extremists, not worry about where I am, so I point behind him, and he turns to see the danger.

He flies into action against the five Extremists who have reached him.

Not able to stand the heat anymore, and with the branch I'm on now almost completely engulfed, I lower it to the ground while I still can and land in a heap of smoke and flames. I'm about to throw dirt on the flames closest to me when water douses it for me.

I look up, locking eyes with Rayne, who nods, smiling widely, and turns back to his opponent. It doesn't surprise me he wanted to return my favors.

Leaning down to pick up my crutches, I order Jack to follow me to another hiding spot, the burning tree behind me scorching my back. My arm is on fire, but it's not like I haven't experienced this kind of pain before.

I find a leafy bush, and work my way inside, ordering Jack to wait outside of the bush for me while I pull my crutches in.

Once I look back up, I blink through the smoke, wiping my eyes, when I catch sight of the most frightening thing. Greta darts out of the community building, running behind another bush.

How did she get free? What is she doing?

"Please hide, little one," I whisper, clutching the ground. I don't take my eyes off her hiding place and am so afraid for her I gasp when I see her dash out and throw a pinecone at an approaching Extremist.

He points his gun at her, and my vision turns red. Never will he hurt Greta. *Never.* I rip a root out of the ground so forcefully an explosion of dirt and rocks crashes down on the man's head. I wrap him up from his feet all the way to his head. He crashes to the ground like a fallen log. When he squirms, I squeeze. I wait until he stops moving before I search for Greta, who is nowhere to be seen.

I vow to find her when I see ten of our guys slip out of the community building and slink off into the woods. No sooner do they reach the safety of the trees when the three Extremists who left the community building return.

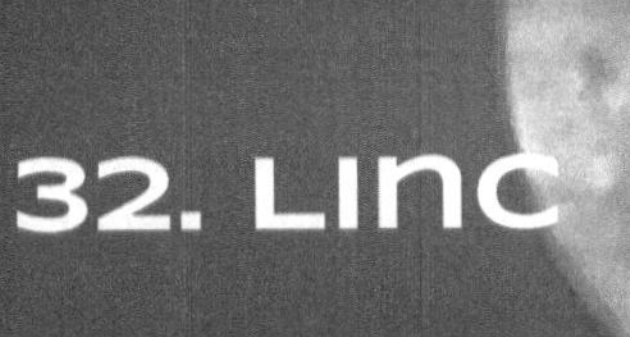

32. LINC

I'm so grateful that Rick and Gary have stepped up to our plan and help me get ten more guys out. A minute after we do, I spot the leader and his two goons walking back toward our building through the haze of smoke.

It won't be long before this entire place goes up in flames. I focus my attention on the roof and extinguish the embers slowly burning through the slats.

Now that the building is safe, I turn to scan our situation. I motion to our "guards" to turn their heads when the leader comes in. I'm trying to act nonchalantly, standing by the door when Grant enters. He looks over the group, and I count it as a huge win when he turns his attention back to me, disinterested.

"Any problems?"

I sneer. "No. It's been quiet."

"They're surprisingly easy to manage. I expected more of a fight, to be honest," he says, waving smoke away from his face.

I hide my clenched fist behind my leg.

If he only knew.

Hannah and Andy hurl insults at me, like before. I look at them with amused eyes, like I couldn't care less. Really, I'm proud to call them my friends. Others join them until the leader turns to me, saying, "You really aren't very popular, are you?"

I laugh. "It's one of my many charms."

He chuckles. "Well, once we've gotten everyone collected, I'll let you do the honor of torching this building. Will that be enough revenge for all these colorful insults?"

I look at him with my eyebrows raised, meanwhile my stomach churns with disgust. "That will be sufficient." I try to relax the tension in my body. I pray he doesn't notice the changed guards.

"We only have a few out there who are escaping us, but that will change soon." He looks back at the crowd on the floor with a sneer. "Then they'll all get what they deserve."

My blood is pumping and everything in me wants to sink my fist into this disgusting man's face. I wouldn't even categorize him as a man, but a monster, something vile.

He'll have more than he bargained for in a few short minutes.

"Where is Alex?" he asks, looking around.

I nod my head towards the door. "He wanted to be a part of catching one of the mixed ones. He should be back soon."

Grant hums and nods. "I think I'll do the same thing." He leaves, and when he does, my heart rests from its wild thumping.

Roland comes out from hiding among the crowd and he, Andy, and I immediately organize ten more fighters to leave. Tonya is one of them, and Claudette protests.

"Why didn't you take him out?" she asks, anger flashing in her eyes.

"We can't. Not yet. Let them think we're still contained. We need to get more out there before we fight back," I say, pinning her with a glare.

"Let me go next," she demands. "I want to fight."

"No, Claudette, you're still injured. Stay here," Tonya orders and leaves as quietly as the others, after we take a look around to be sure the coast is clear.

Claudette turns to Hannah and begs her, "Please heal me, Hannah. I need to be out there."

Andy speaks up, "Hannah needs her energy to fight with her Gyan gifts. She doesn't need to be drained healing you, Claudette."

Hannah gives her a sympathetic look and Claudette slumps. "He's right, sweetie. I need to be able to defend myself and Greta. We'll need your Festan and Neronian gifts soon. Rest until we need you."

I hear a whistle from one of ours out in the woods, and we get in position. The fake guards turn their heads when another visitor pokes his head into the doorway. He looks around and when he sees the same boring scene; he leaves for more exciting views.

I turn to the rest of the group. Andy selects ten more, a mixture of men and women for the next group of fighters. I'm surprised that some mothers separate from their kids.

One of them, Betsy's mother, says as she passes me, "Let me get my hands on those bloodsuckers. We'll stop them now that they don't have the element of surprise."

I nod and see that the group looks much more diminished. We won't be able to pretend much longer. Leon wakes up at that moment, inhaling deeply and springing up, his fists raised. He looks around for me and when he sees me, roars, rushing me again.

Andy intercepts him, using all his strength to hold him back.

While Andy's containing that situation and explaining what's actually happening, I get the rest of the fighters, leaving all the kids behind with a few adults.

Hannah puts her hand on my arm. She stops the fighters from leaving with a quiet command. "Linc, we need more protectors for the kids. Leaving only a few isn't a good idea."

I nod, agreeing with her. "You're right. They would use the kids to get us back in here. I'll leave twenty with them. Is that enough?"

She thinks for a minute. "I think so. We need to get the children out first, though. Let them hide in the woods with Greta. She knows all the best hiding places. Then once they children are safely hidden, the adults can join the fighting."

I squint my eyes to see through the smoke, looking out the door. "If we can find Greta again."

"I have a special whistle I use just for her. She'll hear it and come to me wherever she is."

"She's not still in that foxhole?"

Hannah shakes her head. "I saw her leave that spot a while ago. She's off to some other mischief." Her eyes are full of fear, and I vow to keep Greta and every other child safe from this bloodthirsty group.

After looking both ways out the door for Extremists, Hannah whistles a long, piercing call that Greta could hear even from the other side of the community.

While we wait for Greta to respond, we organize the kids and twenty capable fighters to leave with them. I give the adults one command, "Protect them until they can hide. Greta is coming. If the kids don't know a good hiding place, she will show them."

It's then that Greta bursts into the room, looking around with awe, her mouth open. "Where is everyone else?"

I'm beyond pleased she didn't see any of the escaped prisoners in her little jaunt through the community. "They've escaped. Now, we need you to help your friends hide." I put my hand on her shoulder, "Greta, it's very important you help them find the best places, so they'll never be found."

She nods concisely. "I can do that. Even though I'm going to give away all my best hide and seek spots." Her face scrunches up in a cute scowl. But she gets to work talking to the kids, telling them all her secret hideouts.

I tell the adults, "Follow Greta as she finds places for all of them. Make sure her spots are far away from fire and the community while we fight."

They all nod, and after a thorough search for Extremists, slip out into the smoke.

After watching them slink into the trees, making sure no one sees them escaping, I turn to find Hannah standing there with her hands on her hips.

"Hannah, I thought you'd be with Greta," I say, surprised. Before she can answer, I'm bowled over by Leon, who's a beefy linebacker of a guy. He grabs me by the shoulders before I can fall, demanding, "I need to fight. When are we taking over?" His blue eyes are hard as diamonds, and I'm shocked the Extremists were able to contain him.

Happy I'm no longer seen as his enemy, I say, "Now. We're getting the Polar Bear back." Rick and Gary step up, nodding their heads, ready for anything.

Rick's bald head is sweating when he says, "We have twenty fighters out there surrounding the buildings, plus the twenty helping hide the kids. They can fight once the children are safe. They're just waiting for our call."

Leon growls, "So, we're ready?"

I look at Andy and he nods.

"How many Extremists are there?" I ask Rick and Gary.

"About thirty," he answers. "All armed," he adds grimly.

"We're going to have to take those guns out," I say, and they all agree. "Do that first, then fight."

"Are we keeping any alive?" Andy asks.

I hesitate and avoid looking at Hannah. I couldn't bear it if she disapproved of my answer. I'm surprised when she answers instead, "We need to keep some of them alive, to question them and see what else they know. But we can't leave them in a place where they can just come back. This is war. Now, let's get our homes back."

She marches toward the door and stands in shock when the leader, Grant, pushes his head through the doorway, his eyes wide. We freeze at first, but then I come alive.

I rush at him with a roar, ready to tear his head off for his plans to utterly decimate this amazing community.

He turns and runs, calling out to his group, "They've escaped! Shoot to kill!"

That's when the Polar Bear explodes with elements firing back and forth and the sound of gunfire. The flames of their beloved refuge are the background as the Polar Bear members fight for their community and their very lives.

I can't chase after the leader because a Neronian attacks me. I disarm him and fight off the wicked ice spear that he's intent on burying in my stomach. From the corner of my eye, I spot Jack taking down another guy. After I tighten fire ropes around the Neronian's neck, squeezing until he's unconscious or dead, I'm not sure, I look wildly around for Vela.

Where is she?

I run over to Jack. "Jack, boy, where's Vela?"

"I'm here," she answers from deep inside a bush. I push aside the branches and see the loveliest view I could find.

She's smiling up at me, then she whips her hand at me, and I hear an anguished scream behind me.

I look over my shoulder and see that she's knocked out an Extremist with a big branch. I look back at her. "We're not just hurting them, Vela," I say with a significant look.

Her eyes widen and her face pales. "I'm not sure I can kill anyone," she whispers.

"I understand. So, just knock them out and we'll take care of the rest."

She swallows and then coughs, the smoke getting thicker and thicker.

"Are you going to stay in the bush?"

She puts one hand on her knee and holds out her other hand for me to help her up. Once I do, she looks at me, her eyes shining. "Good job with the kids. I watched you sneak them all out." She looks at me with glowing eyes, and I want nothing more than to snatch her up and kiss her senseless. I really like it when she compliments me.

She must see my desire, because she smirks. "Easy, Romeo. Don't you have some fighting to do?"

I snort. "I do at that. Later?" I ask, waiting for a promise to do more than just hug her.

She nods, her cheeks turning rosy, and I leave to join the fight of our lives, my heart lighter than it's been since I found her kissing Rayne.

Just that thought makes rage flow through my arms and I channel all that anger toward my enemy.

I'll use it to get the Polar Bear back.

33. Vela

When Linc extracted that promise from me, my heart leaped into my throat, and I couldn't do anything but nod. My heart's response had nothing to do with the pounding fear racing through my veins.

When I saw Greta leading away the little ones through the thickening smoke, then finding all of them hiding spots, I settled into a fierce calm. All my senses focused on taking back our precious community. Now that our little ones are safe, we can distribute pain to the ones responsible for the burning buildings. Amongst the fighting, some Neronians are already putting fires out. I love that I'm a part of this place. Most of all, I'm fiercely proud of Greta. She's a little warrior-in-training.

Speaking of being a warrior, it's time I join in.

Ordering Jack to stay by my side, and leaning heavily on one of my crutches, I hold my hands out to two Extremists fighting my friends, Claudette and Tonya. I'm distracted for a second that they're here. I open up the ground under their opponents and once they fall, Claudette and Tonya look around to see who helped them. I close the ground around the necks of the E.E. members and then I wave at my friends. They smile grimly at me, then turn to fight others.

I hear gunfire and spin in that direction on one foot. Two gunmen have shot down three of mine and rage tears through me. I'm thankful that Tonya and Claudette were spared that assault. My hair blows wildly when I raise my hands, breaking off small, sharp missiles from the nearby trees. I bring my hands down and whip the wooden projectiles through the air to knock the guns out of the gunmen's hands. Then I raise my hands again, bringing the sticks back up. I wave my hands around and aim. The branches fly as I drop my arms. Cries follow when they stick in legs, arms, and stomachs.

I'm not going for kill shots, but debilitating ones. I just can't deliver a lethal blow.

When I see what I've just done with the branches, I know that what Rayne has said about my second gift is true. I'm getting it in spurts. Wind definitely helped me just now. I'm just thankful I can use some of it when I need it.

Deciding to test the limits of my sporadic power, I hold my arms out toward the two guns laying on the ground next to the moaning Extremists I took down. Squinting my eyes through the smoke that blows in my face, I flex my fingers slowly up. I'm wildly happy when the guns both levitate. I bring my arms to my chest, calling the guns to me, completely unprepared when they whip through the air. The force of the heavy machine guns hitting my chest knocks me down to the ground. I'm on my back, holding on to my prizes, when Tonya and Claudette's faces fill my vision.

"Holy crap, Vela, how did you do that?" Claudette asks with a wild grin.

Tonya laughs and helps me up. "That was an awesome trick. I didn't know you're a Borean, too!"

I look at them in a daze, holding the guns to my chest, completely shocked at what I just did. "I guess it's my second gift. Rayne said I'd be able to do more every day, but I didn't expect to do that. Wait," I say, shaking my head. "What are you guys doing here?"

Tonya looks over my shoulder, whips her arm through the air, and clenches her fist, bringing it to her chest, and I hear a strangled gurgling behind me.

I drop the guns and look over my shoulder. A man with a bleeding forehead holds his neck, choking without air.

Tonya's eyes are fierce as she cuts off his air supply. He drops to the ground and after another second, she releases him, looking back at me, a wild look completely taking over her expression.

"I need to learn that one," I breathe.

She nods, pulling on my arm. "Come on, let's find a defensible position."

I plant my feet or foot, rather, and resist. "I can't really walk," I say with a twist of my lips. "I have crutches, but they're hard to fight with."

She looks at my bent knee and then sees my discarded crutches. "Oh, I see. Why don't we help you? That way, you have use of your arms to fight. Claudette, come on. You go on her other side." Tonya immediately comes to my left, and I put my arm over her neck.

Claudette holds her ribs and comes to my right side.

"Claudette, are you okay?" I ask, remembering the bear's swipe at her back.

"I can handle it," she says, tightly. She's at my side, and I put my arm over her neck. Seeing an ice knife come at us, I duck all of us down and Claudette's in action before I can react to the Neronian's attack.

Fire streams out of her fingers, meeting a wall of water and disappearing in a cloud of steam and smoke. I make sure we have Jack with us when we use the smoke to hide our escape.

"Wait, we need the guns!" I yell and Tonya and Claudette scoop them up.

With help from Claudette and Tonya, we run to the side of the Community building. Making it without any trouble, we lean our backs on the building and assess the scene.

Fierce fighting continues all around us. The ominous sound of gunfire carries from the other side of the community, sending spears of fear through me.

Are my friends dying?

Most of the smaller homes are on fire and my stomach twists violently. I look bleakly at the burning log houses on either side of me. I'm closer to the burning buildings than I've been, and I wince at the heat. The smoke is worse here, too, and I start coughing, worrying what the smoke will do to Jack's lungs. But he's lower to the ground, where the smoke is thinner. I think he'll be okay for now.

"Linc says to take out all the guns first," Tonya tells me as she coughs, too.

I nod my head. That narrows down who I need to help next.

I look for Linc's familiar form and my breath catches when I see him fighting for control over a gun. They're both wrenching each other to the right and left, so it's hard for me to aim any more homemade arrows at Linc's opponent without risking hitting my Intended instead. And I can't drop the guy in a hole, either. They're moving around too much for that. So, I use my trusty roots to trip him. He plants his feet, trying to get the gun from Linc, and it's only too easy to take him down with a well-placed root. Linc takes immediate advantage and knees the guy in the stomach, making him loosen his grip on the gun.

I look away when Linc points the gun at the guy's chest. I hear the gun popping two rounds and I know the Extremist is dead.

My face must register the shock I feel. I turn my head in his direction and Linc looks at me, his face set in grim determination. His expression shifts into one of concern when he reads the horror on my face.

Tonya shakes my shoulder, pointing at something else. When I look back to where Linc is, he's gone.

My heart squeezes at the thought that he'll have to live with what he's done here. Could I use my gift or gifts to kill someone?

I can't help but think about my second gift. The fact that I have it makes my blood pump wildly through me. It only makes what Rayne's said about me being the Chosen Child that much truer.

I can't think about that now. I have to focus.

Hannah comes into my line of sight when she runs past us. Blood streaks from her head down her face and she's limping. My sight narrows on her pursuer, who is lobbing fireballs at Hannah. They hit her back, making her cry out and fall to the ground. Red fills my vision and hot rage races through me. First, I use a root to trip the man. Once he's on the ground, I wrap his neck with the root, squeezing tight. He could have killed Hannah with that hit, and I want him to hurt like he hurt Hannah. All the times Hannah has been there for me fills my vision, and I squeeze harder.

"Vela, just knock him out. Vela!" Hannah is at my side, pulling on my arm. When I register that it's Hannah screaming at me and that she's alive, I tear my eyes away from the man's limp form on the ground.

My eyes widen at what I just did. Horror slices through me, leaving cold trails of dread. "Did I kill him?" I whisper, hardly able to speak, not able to take my eyes off the man. He's not moving.

Hannah runs over to him, putting her hand on his neck. She looks up at me. "He's alive. Don't worry. We need him alive. He's the leader." She opens up the ground with a wave of her hand and drops him in the hole she made, keeping just his head aboveground.

I'm standing frozen when Hannah gets up and runs back to me, limping all the way. "Vela," she says, holding my face in both of her hands. She forces me to look only at her bloody face. Her gray eyes are grim as she says, "You did what you had to do. He's not dead, but he deserves to be. We need to get information from him. But listen to me. Are you listening, Vela?" She waits until I give her a delayed nod. She says in a hard voice, "We are at war. We'll keep some of them alive, but don't be afraid to permanently put them down."

I try to shake my head, but Hannah tightens her hold on my face, not letting me. "Yes, you can," she says fiercely. "They have killed so many mixed elementals. They were going to put all of us in that building you're leaning on and burn it to the ground. They deserve nothing but death."

She looks into my eyes and when I take in what she says, a hot anger fills me to the point of bursting.

"Even the kids?" I ask in a shaking voice.

"Yes," she says with a dark look. "All of us. You're fighting for your life and the lives of the rest of us, too. Don't be afraid to take one."

I nod, trembling with rage, and I think, fear. I can't even begin to process all the emotions I'm feeling.

I'm suddenly so relieved Hannah is okay, I cry out and grab her in a choking hug. Her body is stiff, but she returns my embrace, then pulls back, looking at all of us.

"You girls stay together," Hannah orders. "You're safer in packs. Use all your gifts and these guns to take people out. Use the guns first, then when the bullets are gone, use your gifts."

Claudette, Tonya, and I look at each other, each of us with resolve on our faces.

"Wait, Hannah," I cry out before she can run off.

She turns to me with an impatient look, but with pained eyes.

"Let me heal your burn," I say quickly.

She hesitates, then she turns and holds up her shirt. I place my hand over her back, giving it a healing warmth. She'll scar badly, but I don't have time to try to do this slowly with less scarring.

She looks at me over her shoulder, with a manic grin, saying, "Thanks, Vela, I owe you."

I can only nod and watch as she runs off now with a slighter limp. Jack is restless with so much fighting all around us. I'm going to have to keep him close to me and use him only if necessary. I can't have anything happen to my faithful friend.

"Okay, then," Tonya says, and then she and Claudette grip the machine guns, and after exchanging a meaningful look, hold the guns up to their stomachs and start shooting. I stand, balancing myself on one leg and keeping an eye out on our surroundings. Jack sinks to the ground at the sound of gunfire and whines.

My stomach can't help but roil in nausea. But Hannah's right. We're at war. Death is one consequence of that. While my friends are trying to hit their targets, I look around for someone I can help.

I watch Roland fighting with his Borean gift and am impressed with what he can do with his element. He's using wind like he does his knives, almost interchangeably.

My gaze snags on a huge Elemental who's just ahead of me. He's hard to miss, a few inches shy of seven feet tall. Right now, he's got someone above his head and, with a roar, throws them to the side, like they were yesterday's trash. The body he throws looks broken.

My heart freezes in my chest, but my eyes narrow. I might be hurt, but I'm not defenseless. I look around to find a hiding spot where I can attack without him noticing me. Before I can, and probably because I'm with Claudette and Tonya who are mowing down Extremists with their guns, I look up and see that he's running toward us. He has his eyes set on Claudette and Tonya. He wants to eliminate their threat.

But he doesn't notice me. I'll take advantage of that.

I try to open up holes under him, but he nimbly jumps over them. I grit my teeth and try to catch him with a root. He dodges that, too. I find it lucky when I manage to grab him with one. He turns his attention to me, stops, plants his feet, and rips the root out of the ground with a flex of his huge muscles and a roar that could split my eardrums. After he throws my defeated root to the ground, he advances on me, a wild laugh spilling from his throat.

I swallow, my throat suddenly dry. I can't let him get close enough for him to get his hands on me.

How can I possibly defeat this giant?

"Claudette, Tonya! Take that guy out!" I cry, pointing in his direction.

They swing to shoot, but before they can press down on their triggers, he raises his hands, his wild eyes focusing on the guns.

Tonya cries out and drops her gun. It's red hot and smoking. Claudette is able to keep ahold of hers, since she's half Festan, but the man has ruined it, making it impossible to shoot. She throws it down, screaming in frustration.

The three of us face him. He calls out to two others fighting near him. The men he calls both backhand their opponents, my Polar Bear friends, almost simultaneously, dropping them to the ground.

With one word from the giant, the three Extremists set their sights on us.

Fear clogs in my throat, but I don't give up. To give up means death, and I'm not ready to die today.

"Jack, stay by me. And you guys," I say to my friends, "stay strong." I flex my hands at my sides, planning my next attack.

The three men advance on us, like demons coming from the depths of hell. Buildings burn to the left and right, making it look as if they are emerging from a fiery tunnel. It serves as an appropriate backdrop for their dastardly plans, our deaths. The giant tosses a fireball between his hands. The man next to him has torches on each hand. I can't see what element the third one has, but I want to bring it out in the open, so we know what we're up against.

I raise my hands and whip them down. Small branches break off nearby trees and fly through the air like arrows.

With a flick of his hands, the giant sets them all on fire, turning them to ash. The third man whips his arm in an arc, blowing the incinerated branches away with a gust of wind.

I know that Extremists would never invite members with mixed gifts, so we have a Borean and two Festans.

They're close enough for me to hear when the Festan giant says, "Look, boys, three snacks. I'll enjoy this. Should we play before we dine on their delectable delights?"

Tonya screams before she, with raised arms, creates a wind funnel, feeding it dirt. The men plant their feet to resist the strong winds, but her dirt is effectively putting out the fires the two Festans have in their hands. I absolutely love that she can use two elements against these men who hate what she represents.

The problem with her attack, though, is the third man. He takes the funnel from Tonya and easily controls it. Since he's a full Borean and an adult, it's like child's play for him to manipulate it. He turns it around on us.

I know that if I end up in that mini tornado, I'm as good as dead, or at least incapacitated and unable to fight.

"Tonya, help me," I cry out before I take roots from under the Borean's feet and wrap him tightly. Tonya does the same, and he's soon covered from head to toe. The funnel dissipates.

"Now that's not nice, pretty girls," the giant says with a wide smile. His face looks handsome enough, but I've seen enough to know that a monster resides under his pretty facade.

Claudette engages in a fire war with the second Festan.

"Tonya, keep an eye on the Borean. Keep him down." That leaves me with the giant.

Fury pulses through me, and I rip a root out. I use it like a whip and try to strike him with it. He dodges it and then, with a wild light in his eyes, he stands still so I can hit him easily.

He takes the hit like it's nothing. "You're only becoming more and more interesting, the more you fight dirty," he taunts.

Thinking I should take advantage of his monologue, I whip my root whip down as hard as I can. Just when the root connects, the giant grabs it. Under his hand, the root catches fire quickly burning. He drops it and walks toward me.

I limp heavily as I try to back up on one good foot.

He sets himself on fire, an inferno like my worst nightmare, my old fears of fire rising and chasing me down. Jack can't do anything with him on fire, so I force him to stay behind me.

In desperation, I open up the ground under him, but it's like he anticipates all my moves and just jumps. I'm out of options. I don't know how else to fight him, as he's only steps away from me.

I close my eyes, unable to watch the rest. But, oh, I'll feel it.

34. LINC

I catch sight of Vela trying to use a root whip on a giant of a guy. I race toward her, praying I make it in time. I dodge fights, lurching from the right to left, but I never take my eyes off my Intended. When the man grabs her whip, dissolving it in fire, I push myself to run faster.

She's trapped by her hurt knee, unable to escape the now burning Festan, who's fully engulfed, much like I was in our duel not so long ago. Even with the screams of all the fighting all around me, time seems to stop. It's like Vela and her attacker are in a bubble. I just need to reach them. So, I keep running, racing as fast as I can, my heart stuttering when I see her wait for a death blow.

With as great a lunge as I can make, I roar, jumping on the giant's back, my own fire matching his. I wrap my arm around his neck, choking him. He holds onto my arm and flips me off with a quick thrust down. I land on my back, but I'm up in a flash.

He shoots me a fiery grin, saying, "You've interrupted my snack."

At his words, I see red. Dousing the flames on my hands, I spot a weapon. I grab the staff, bringing it up over my head so I can get the velocity I need to break his head open. The giant dodges my strike and surprises me when he delivers a high kick at my face. I take the hit and stagger, but duck under his fiery roundhouse punch.

I come back up, swinging the staff with me and clock him under the jaw as hard as I can. It whips his head up, but he only laughs. I swing the staff back down, but he blocks the strike with his burning forearm.

Twirling the wood behind my back, I'm thankful the hit didn't set it on fire. I bring it back up to hit him as hard as I can, cracking the side of his face. He takes the hit, but before I can react, he's wrapped his hands around my weapon, this time succeeding in setting it on fire.

I wrench it from his grip, knowing I have moments to use what's left of it.

My next blows are blurs as I hit him in every place I can land a strike. He blocks most of them, but I'm satisfied that I manage to connect a few times. My staff is fully blazing now, looking like a furious, avenging weapon. It's appropriate, since that's how I feel. How dare this man try to hurt Vela?

Since the staff is full of the man's fire, the flames won't hurt him, but the force of my strikes can. I land a few before the staff cracks in half, the fire finally taking my bright weapon away.

I drop it and bring my fist into his stomach as hard as I can, but it's like punching bricks.

"What are you going to do without your little toy now, boy?" the man asks, sneering.

"I can think of a few things," I say, cracking my knuckles, trying to ignore my stinging hand.

"Do your worst," he says, holding his arms out like I'm welcome to give him my best shot.

I intend to.

Forming my hottest fire into a fireball, I feed it as much heat as I can in the limited time I have. Drawing my hand back, I launch it at the giant's face.

He stands still so he can absorb it, laughing loudly. But when the fireball hits him, his eyes widen, first in surprise, then in pain. He bends over at his waist, grabbing his face, screaming. He douses his body's fire; the smoke blooming at his feet.

I make another fireball, fully intending to again use every bit of my mother and father's strong Festan gifts. Before I can finish my next weapon, the giant roars and runs toward me, his head down like a battering ram.

It's only too easy to sidestep his attack, slamming the fire I'd prepared on the back of his neck when he charges past me.

He flings the fireball off him like an enraged bull screaming at the sky, with his arms flexing in front of him. Blood is streaming off his head, and even I must admit, he looks wild and dangerous.

He summons a firestorm in his hands that I can see I'm going to have to get creative to dodge. He throws, but I'm already moving. I jump backwards, landing on my hands, only to spring up in a double somersault. I spring into another backwards handspring until I'm far enough away to avoid his assault.

Once I'm upright, I can't help but smile at Vela's look of absolute shock. She looks so adorable it almost makes me lose my focus.

I turn just in time to bend backwards, avoiding a fireball that would have hit me in the face. I create two fire whips that I crack over my head. Even if the fire won't hurt this giant Festan, the strikes will. I advance toward him while he produces the same weapon I have.

I smirk. It's not my problem he can't be more creative. He's big and dumb. Typical.

When he cracks his whips at me, I aim mine and wrap them around his, tangling them together. I pull, but it's like trying to pull a wall down. I flex my muscles and lean back in my attempt to bring the man closer. What I didn't expect is Jack flying through the air behind the guy and jumping on his back, biting down.

The man roars in pain and knocks Jack off with one arm encased back in fire. Jack yelps and falls to the ground, not moving.

"Jack, no!" Vela screams.

I'm yanked forward when the giant pulls on our entwined whips, and I almost lose my balance. He's about to grab me, which would be a death sentence, when the ground rumbles.

I drop my whips and try to balance on the shifting earth. I'm shocked when I lock eyes on Vela, who's standing with her arms outstretched towards the ground, a fierce look of concentration and anger on her face. Her show of power is mesmerizing, and I can't stop watching her perform such an incredible feat.

By now, the ground is moving under me and when Vela shouts at me to move over; I don't hesitate. I leap to the side just as she opens the ground under the giant's feet. He's off balance with the ground moving, and it only takes gravity to help him fall into the crack Vela created. The ground splits in a line down from where the giant disappeared and stops when it reaches past me.

I'm watching to be sure none of ours go down with him, and I pull the back of Gary's shirt because he's on the edge and waving his arms to avoid falling in. Vela stops the quake with a drop of her hands. Once the ground stops rumbling, she looks up with tired eyes, panting heavily. I look down into the deep hole she created and realize I can't see the bottom of it. I'm staggered at her show of power.

She's so amazing, I can't resist.

Running to her, I fold her in my arms. I lean back to hold her face in my hands. "That was brilliant," I tell her before my mouth is on hers.

She tastes sweeter than I remembered, if that's possible. I pull away, knowing I don't have time to get lost in Vela right now.

"Later," I promise.

She nods and drops to the ground by Jack, running her hands over him. Healing him, I'm sure.

I spin around with my arms out to see who I need to fight next. Gary shouts at me, and I see him engaged against two Extremists.

I call over my shoulder, "Rest, Vela, if you can!"

Racing over to Gary, I produce fire whips and swing them over my head, whipping them around the neck of one of the Extremists. His screams are choked off when I plant my feet and pull. He fumbles at the whips, trying to claw them off, burning his fingers in the process. I'm relentless and don't let go until he stops moving. Gary finishes his fight and looks at me, breathing heavily.

"We need to assess and see how many are left," he says, looking around to make sure we're not about to be attacked.

I nod. "I need to get Vela in a safe place first. She's hurt, so she's at a disadvantage."

"I'll help you," he tells me, and we run over to her. She's in the same place I left her, looking so exhausted she could drop at any moment. Jack is sitting up beside her, panting, but seems to be okay. Thankfully, no Extremists are near them.

"Vela, we need to get you to a safe place," I say in a rush.

She looks at me with confused eyes. "And where is that, exactly?"

"How about in the trees?"

She winces. "Tried that and have the burns to show for it." She shows me her arm, which already had scars before, but now fresh burns ooze from her elbow to her hand.

Rage races through me. "Who did that?" I ask with gritted teeth. "What happened?" If I don't find out in two seconds what happened to my Intended, I'm going to lose it.

She looks guiltily at me. "I was up in a tree helping Rayne and Grace fight when the tree caught on fire."

"And you couldn't get out before you got burned?" I guess.

She shrugs.

Leon runs up, nodding his head at all of us. His eyes are wild when he says, "We need to get a move on. There are more Extremists to fight."

"Gary and I were just trying to figure out how many are left."

"Okay, but until then, I'm taking down as many as I can find." He leaves as fast as he came.

"We need to find Hannah, Linc," Vela says. "I need to make sure she's okay."

"I'm sure that Andy hasn't taken his eyes off her," I say with all certainty.

"They might need our help," she argues.

I look at Vela with a frown. "You're not exactly in any shape to fight, Vels," I say as gently as possible.

Like I predicted, she scowls at me. "I'm still able to fight, Linc. Don't you try to stop me."

I frown at her resilience. Did I really expect anything else? "Okay, but doesn't it help to draw energy from me?"

Gary pipes in. "I think that's what you should do, Vela. You need energy to finish out this day."

She looks at me in alarm. "But then, I would take from you. You need as much of your power as you can have right now."

I look at her with soft eyes. "I'd feel better knowing you had some juice left. I can recharge by using fire."

"Well, then I can do the same." She looks out into the trees.

"Here," I move behind her, putting my hands on her waist. "How about a bit of both? Take from me and draw from the trees nearest you."

She inhales sharply and stiffens, but soon relaxes when I imbue her with some of my energy. I watch the nearest tree's leaves wilt, but before she kills it, she stops. She straightens, putting her hands on mine.

"I think I'm good."

"Now, stay by my side the entire time, please."

"I can't exactly run anywhere, Linc," she says, frustration clear on her face. "I lost my crutches, so I'll need help walking."

Tonya runs up, her face shining with fight and anger. "Linc! You made it back!"

Claudette limps over, holding her side, her face screwed up in pain.

"Claudette, you need to rest," Vela says.

She only scowls at her and says, "So do you. We're not in a place yet where I can rest, so I'll fight till I drop."

I look on in pride at the Elemental girls defending this place with the last of their strength.

"We're finding out how many are left to fight," I tell Claudette and Tonya. "Do you guys want to stay with us or fight on your own?"

Tonya eyes Vela and Claudette skeptically and says, "I think it's best if we stay together." She motions toward Claudette, and, like a well-oiled unit, they go to Vela's sides, ducking under her arms. When they straighten, they look at me. "Okay, we're ready. Where to, boss?"

It's not ideal to have two injured people to protect while assessing the situation, but we don't have much choice.

Gary says, "I think we can best figure out what we're up against if we stay to the edges and away from the fighting."

I nod and we walk over to the tree line, Jack following us. I feel better knowing he's there to defend Vela's back if needed. I'm keeping watch for any attack, but so far, we've been spared since we came together. Tonya, Claudette, and Vela keep up with us, despite their injuries. Hiding behind trees, Gary and I watch the fighting, counting as we go.

At one point, I see Andy fighting next to Hannah, making an impressive stand together. Andy fights his attacker and sends streams of fire to the branches Hannah's using to attack, making them even more lethal.

We pass them, and at the halfway mark, Gary and I have counted eight Extremists so far. We keep going, and once we finish circling the Polar Bear, we've agreed there are about twelve left to fight. I'm surprised we weren't engaged in any fighting ourselves. I chalk it up to an act of God. We were very lucky.

We hide behind several trees as Gary, the girls, and I huddle to discuss what we should do. "Do we just let the fighting continue until they're all taken out?"

Gary shakes his head hard. "We've lost too many. We need to put a stop to this somehow."

I have an idea, but it's even more crazy than my first one, so I pause before I say anything.

Vela speaks up. "If we can get them together and pressure them to give up, then we can question them, like Hannah said."

"How are we going to corral them in one place?" Tonya asks, her face screwed up in worry.

"If I can get Andy's help, I have an idea," I say. "It'll take Andy, Gary, and I to do what I have in mind, but it'll work."

"Don't keep up in suspense, Linc," Vela says. A warning in her gaze tells me I shouldn't do something stupid and reckless. Again.

Too late for that.

"Okay," I say, inhaling deeply. "It's perfect that the three of us are Festans. We are going to start a *huge* firestorm at the edge of the fighting. We'll grow it with each loyal Festan we can find to help us, and we're going to push everyone from one side of the Polar Bear to the other. Everything's on fire anyway, so it won't do more damage that what's already been done."

"I can help," Claudette says, with her face set in a fierce scowl.

"Won't the Extremists who are Festans be able to withstand it?" Vela asks with a skeptical look.

I shake my head, while Gary nods, like it's been decided. "No, with enough of us, even three of us, the fire will be so hot, even the Festans will move away from it."

Vela shakes her head, looking uncertain. "I don't know. Then what? We surround them and they give up, just like that?"

This is the part I have to keep to myself. I need the element of surprise, from even my friends. It hurts to keep Vela out of the loop, but I'm not going to force her to act. Her reaction has to be genuine.

I say, "They'll surrender or fight. Either way, they'll be outnumbered. We've lost some, but we had more to start with, so we have more fighters. We just have to get us all together."

"I think it's a good idea," Gary says, clapping my shoulder. "Let me go get Andy. I'll be right back."

Vela is watching me with a suspicious look on her face. I smile at her and hide my guilt at deceiving her behind my anxiety about this plan.

Now, it's time for my acting skills to come out to play. Again.

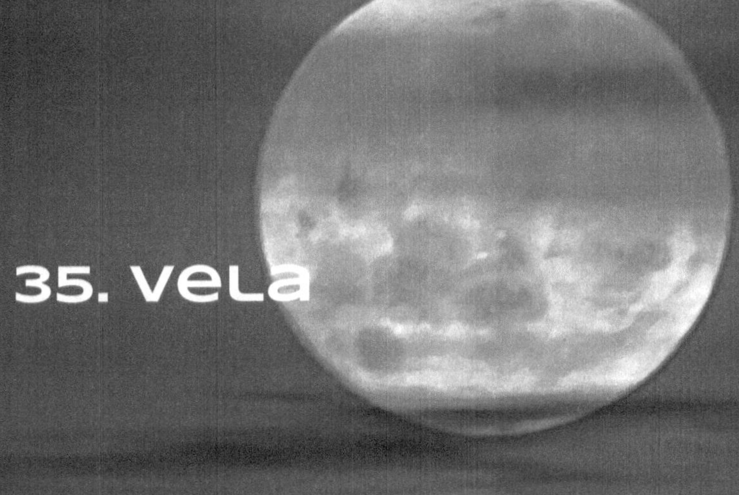

35. VELA

I'm worried. Linc's got that look on his face, like he's hiding something.

I can't imagine what it is. There's no telling with him, but I'm watching him very carefully from here on out.

I keep Jack behind me as we stay out of sight until we can enact this crazy plan. I wish I could use my wind gift at will, because wind would feed a fire storm with plenty of air, making it unstoppable. I'll try, even though I'm not sure it will work for me.

Gary returns with Andy, who's breathing hard and holding onto Hannah's hand, looking very much like he had to drag her here.

Hannah's eyes flash, and she looks at all of us. "What are you guys doing hiding out here? We need you to fight."

Gary explains the plan for us to get the rest of the Extremists in a group. "We need you guys who aren't Festans to pull our people away from the firestorm, so they won't get hurt. It'll take all of us for this to work."

Hannah and Andy absorb this news in two different ways. Hannah's face is thoughtful as she considers the possibilities of this plan working, but Andy is furious.

"I thought you said only the Festans can do this. I don't want Hannah or the girls involved. They need to stay safe," Andy says in a growl.

Hannah whips her head toward him. "Don't you try to control me, Andy Thompson. I'm helping, and you can't stop me." She has her finger in his face, which takes a considerable stretch since she's so much shorter than him.

He captures her finger in his large hand, holding it to his chest. "I just want you safe. Please, Hannah."

"No," she says furiously, yanking her finger from him. "I'm helping." She glares at him, daring him to argue with her.

He deflates and looks at Gary and Linc. "Okay, so let's get started."

Claudette joins them and the four of them step out from behind the trees to produce a fire twenty feet high. It could finish taking out the entire community in minutes if they're not careful. We gather Neronians to flank the fire and prevent it from causing any more damage to our homes. The Festans stand in a line, holding out their hands, causing the Hail Mary that will hopefully end this battle. It's like a huge, moving bonfire, without the wood.

Tonya helps me walk on the left side of the massive fire, while Hannah is on the right. It's our job to forewarn our people to get out of the way and help us corral the Extremists we're targeting. Jack is antsy as he follows me. I'll have to keep my eye on him.

We walk between burning buildings. It breaks my heart seeing them destroyed. When we approach the first fighting groups, Hannah successfully gets the Polar Bear members' attention. When they see what we're doing, they abandon their fight and run behind the fire, leaving their adversaries gaping at our storm. When they try to run in opposite directions, our people, who had just left the fight, force them to stay in front of us, using their elements.

The Extremists try to run, but they're forced back, and we continue to advance. We come upon three other fights and Hannah, Tonya, and I scream at our people to get their attention. As soon as they see what we're doing, they do the same thing the first group did. They join us and keep the Extremists they were fighting in front of our fire, not allowing them to leave. The Neronians among us keep the fire from further damaging buildings and trees as we pass.

I can't believe my eyes. It's actually working.

We continue along, the same scenario playing out over and over. We soon have a group of twenty of us and eight Extremists. More have joined the fire line, building it up to be a massive storm, capable of taking out anything.

It's actually frightening to watch.

The ones we've caught panic and attack the Polar Bear residents who are on the edges of our line attempting to corral the extremists.

Some try to extinguish the fire with their Neronian powers, and I order Jack to attack, knowing any ice spear they could shoot would melt into a harmless spray of water before they reach my precious dog. He leaps toward them, barking, and they back up, wary of Jack's bite. I call him back as Linc, Gary, Claudette, Andy, and the others advance forward. The Extremists scream at our line of Festans in frustration and are forced to retreat as the towering flames and overwhelming power of our organized gifts overwhelm them.

I'm extremely pleased at how well this is going. We're cutting off individual fights and rounding up these despicable group members.

It's jaw dropping to witness the enormous wall of fire floating off the ground in between burning buildings. This fits my idea of what an apocalypse would look like.

We've almost reached the end of the street when I warn the line, "Watch out for the big crack in the ground I opened earlier."

Listening to directions on how to avoid it, they walk around the large crack as one unit since the walking inferno blocks their view.

Tonya and I've have been relegated to the back of our group, where it's safer and others step in to take over our front-line work. I'm watching Linc, admiring his amazing idea and his abilities, when two Borean Extremists levitate toward me, dropping behind the fire line. Instantly, they hold up their hands to attack those producing the fire, but Tonya and I try to stop them by opening up the ground under them. Instead of dropping, they levitate again and turn around to take care of their threat.

Me and Tonya.

Jack barks wildly at them, growling deeply. The woman and the man narrow their eyes at him while they're floating. They turn to us, moving their hands to create a windstorm.

Tonya withstands it because of her Borean gift, but I'm sucked in and go flying into it. I'm whipped around in the violent wind, spinning wildly. The only way I won't be ripped apart is to go boneless. I learned my lesson the last time this happened. I allow the wind to take me anywhere it wants to. I don't think I could fight it, anyway.

But maybe I can.

I struggle to focus on the wind, trying to get control of it. I use all my strength and connect with its essence, commanding it to stop.

The wind suddenly dissipates, and I drop to the ground in a heap, moaning. Jack is growling fiercely when hot hands pick up my head.

"Vela, Vela, are you okay?" Linc asks, in worried tones.

I flop my head back on his palms while I enjoy the energy he's feeding into me. Everything is spinning, so I close my eyes. My knee screams at me, at the jostling it just received.

"Vela, please talk to me," Linc entreats.

"I'm okay, I think. Just really dizzy. What happened to the Boreans? Linc, the line..."

"Don't worry about that. Someone replaced me and the fire's still going strong. The Boreans were taken out by others. Jack is finishing them off. The important thing is you. Where do you hurt?"

"Maybe she should tell me that answer, Linc," Hannah says, her voice hard. She moves Tonya over, who looks on in worry. Hannah drops to the ground beside me. "Vela, where are you hurt?"

I take stock of my body, noting where I'm in pain. Everywhere. But with my boneless strategy, I avoided any major injury. At least in this particular incident.

I open my eyes to Hannah running her hands all over me, healing the burns on my arms as she hovers over my fresh injuries the windstorm caused. She stops at my knee, and I say weakly, "Don't worry about that one. That'll take too much to fix."

She looks up at me grimly. "Vela, what happened?" She shakes her head sharply, then says, "Never mind. You can tell me later." She looks up at our people standing guard over us and orders, "Keep us safe. This will take a few minutes." I see Rayne looking down at me and I'm happy he's with the group, not out in danger with everyone else.

He's glaring at Linc with hard eyes.

"Hannah," I protest, "you don't have to do this now. You need your strength."

She looks up at me with a fierce light in her eyes. "I can replenish my energy. You need to be on two feet." Turning her attention to my knee, she uses both her hands to send a rush of healing so sharp and quick I suck in a breath.

"What's wrong, are you okay?" Linc asks, still cradling my head.

"I'm fine, or will be soon," I say with some difficulty. Hannah is rushing this healing, much like I did hers earlier. After a few minutes, she slumps over my knee in exhaustion.

I put my hand on top of her head, wishing I could imbue her with energy, like I can with Linc. "Hannah, you need to replenish." I bend my right knee and am thrilled to find I can do it without pain.

I look up at Linc with shining eyes, and he smiles at me. "All healed then?" he asks.

"I'm good. Really good. Hannah, thank you," I say with all sincerity. I know it took a lot out of her to do this level of healing.

She holds up her shaking hand and draws energy from the nearest tree.

"Be careful of doing that too much," I warn. "You'll burn out if you do it more than a few times in one day."

Color returns to her face as the tree's leaves droop. She smiles at me, then gets up slowly, holding her hand out for me.

I'm almost giddy when I can put full weight on my leg. I look at what's happening and see we're still ensconced in our small circle of protection. Jack wraps himself around my legs, happy to have me up as I tap Rayne's shoulder.

"Hey, I'm good now," I tell Rayne and blush when he looks me over.

"Look at you!" he exclaims. "You're all better, finally. It just took the end of the world for it to happen."

"It feels like it, doesn't it?"

He hugs my side and moves so I can see what the firestorm is doing. It's still going strong but is much further ahead, almost to the end of the street.

"Come on," I cry to Hannah and Linc, grabbing both of their hands and pulling them into a run. Rayne follows.

We race to catch up, and I notice Hannah is quickly out of breath. I wonder how many times she's already replenished her energy. She's going to need actual sleep and soon. It doesn't surprise me to see Andy with us, one step behind Hannah. He must have been one of our defenders while Hannah healed me. Rayne is right behind, staying close to me, I note with a twist in my belly. It's like both Rayne and Linc are ready to defend me. I don't know how I feel about that.

We make it to the inferno, and it's grown, if that's possible. I race to the left of it and see we've captured almost all the Extremists.

I'm still holding Linc's hand, but I let go of Hannah's and we all look up at the firestorm, our mouths open in awe. Linc squeezes my fingers and then lets go so he can turn me to him, holding both my shoulders.

He looks intently into my eyes and says, "Now, what I'm about to do, just trust me, okay?"

"What else are you going to do?" I ask warily.

He brushes hair out of my face gently, almost reverently. "What I have to. Just know I have to say what I have to, no matter what it is."

Before I can agree or disagree, he walks off with purpose in his step. He goes around the fire, and I follow. Approaching Gary, he asks him, "Are these all of them?"

Gary turns to Rick asking, "What do you think?"

Rick's got a nasty head wound but otherwise looks good. He says, "I think that's everyone, but let me send some guys out to comb the area."

"Check the trees, too," I offer, remembering my former hiding place.

Rick nods and pulls several strong looking guys together, talking to them in a low voice.

"While we wait, I have something I need to say to the ones we've captured," Linc tells Gary in a strong voice.

What could he possibly have to say to these people?

"Wait," Rayne protests with a scowl, "why does Linc get to interrogate them? He's not even a part of our community. He's just a visitor." Rayne looks between Rick and Gary and a few others who've joined us. "I'd like to say a few words to these Elementals who tried to annihilate us."

Rick speaks up, holding his hands out, "Rayne, Linc used to be in this group as a spy. He has a distinct advantage we don't. He knows how to get them to talk. We need to find out how they discovered our location."

Rayne's face transforms into disgust as he looks at Linc like he's a parasite. "You? You were an Extremist? But as a spy? What makes any of you think he wasn't really a member? That he isn't currently a member?" He looks around at all of us with a deep frown.

Hannah calls out, "Rayne, Linc is as much a part of our community as you are. Don't doubt him. He must have had his reasons for being in the group in that capacity. He left them. That's all we need to know."

Rayne looks at Linc with distrust. He turns to Rick. "So, that's it? You're just going to let him lead this interrogation?"

Rick, Gary, and Hannah all say in unison, "Yes."

Rayne's face contorts in anger, but he falls silent, crossing his arms.

Gary finally nods and Linc walks up to the Extremists, who are all huddled together, fear and anger the dominant emotions on their faces. They try to look stoic as they're tied up. With their arms against their sides, so they can't use their gifts, they're forced to sit in a clump.

I'm happy that the leaders of this amazing community have so much faith in Linc. And I can only pray that what he has to say to these deranged lunatics will be worth our time.

With Linc, you never know.

36. LINC

Now that it's time for me to move forward with this part of my plan, I hesitate. I don't want Vela to think badly of me, but it might be inevitable.

I need to somehow get the Extremists to tell me their leader's name.

If I can get in their heads, I might be able to force it out of them. I don't think any one of my friends has the stomach to torture them for that information. At least I hope not.

But how? I need an explosion of temper, and I know just whose buttons to push.

Once Rick and Gary give me the nod that we've captured all the Extremists, I wave at the fire line, calling out, "You can put that out now. We've neutralized the threat."

The Festans feeding the fire look among themselves before, one by one, extinguishing their flames. A huge cloud of smoke billows up and around us all, joining the smoke from the burning homes. Everyone takes a minute to cough and try to clear their lungs.

I turn back to Rick and Gary. "How about we put out the rest of the fires?"

"Already on it," Rick says, coughing and waving smoke away from his face.

"Can we get some wind to blow this smoke away?" I ask our group.

A few Boreans start blowing air at the billowing smoke and within minutes, the air is as clear as it's going to be, considering the other fires still burning.

Roland comes to my side. He asks, "You have a plan for them?"

"I do, but it won't be easy," I say grimly.

"Nothing hard ever is," he says and steps back.

I fold my arms and face the group of the twelve Extremists who've been spared so we can question them. I study their faces but only recognize a couple of the guards who were in the community building and Grant, the leader. They must have regained consciousness and joined the fighting.

"Now, we have some questions for you who have been left alive." I want to remind them that they are completely at our mercy. I also need to give them a little hope. That would open them up far more than anything else I can do or say.

"I used to be a part of your group. I know why you're here. You think if you can eliminate anyone associated with the Chosen Child, our world can remain the way it is. You don't want our world to unite, because that would ruin your plans and your investments."

A murmur rises from my Polar Bear friends. I don't look back at them. I keep my focus on the E.E. members. They look at me defiantly. I need to up my game.

"You make good money from putting out fires and heal-ings and such. You use your elements to extort money from Elementals who are desperate." I nod my head. "I get why you're doing what you're doing. I do. But, if you could see what this community you just tried to destroy does when they combine their gifts, their strengths, you'd be convinced, like I am, that it's a good thing. They're doing every day what you pay people to do. They give their gifts freely. It's beautiful. In fact, you've seen it for yourselves, fighting against them."

The leader, Grant, who's covered in dirt, sneers, "Why should we listen to you?"

"Because I understand, more than anyone, who you are and why you've done all of this," I say, gesturing at this wonderful community now a smoldering mess of burned-out buildings.

"You think you're better than us, now that you've joined these mixed mutants," Grant says, his face twisting in hatred.

Anger roars through me at his audacity. It takes everything in me to deny my impulse to fry him. "I'm better for being on both sides of the argument," I tell him, clenching my fists to cool my rage.

"What makes you think we'd change our minds by observing this disgusting place?" he asks.

I shrug. "It's about perspective. Now, how about you tell us the name of your leader who found our hidden location?"

Grant laughs. "If you think any of us," he says, looking around at his fellow terrorists, "will divulge what we know, you are seriously misguided."

Here's when I need a loose cannon.

I squat down next to them. "Like I said, I understand. I'm only trying..."

"Are you serious right now?" Rayne explodes. In two lunges, he's towering over me. "Look at you, talking to them as if they didn't just try to exterminate us. You're being *kind* to them when they deserve nothing but death. You," he says, pointing his finger in my face, "you're still with them!" His face is red with fury, and he leans in, grabbing my shirt, hauling me up to his mottled face. "I don't believe for one minute that you didn't bring them here. Admit it. You're to blame for the deaths today. Admit you revealed our location. You're still an Extremist. Admit it all!"

This is the moment I needed. Good job, Rayne.

I announce to everyone, despite Rayne still being in my face, "I am the reason they're here."

The whole group of Polar Bear residents gasp, and their voices rise.

"Linc, no! Tell them that's not true!" Vela cries, Hannah holding her back from coming to me.

This is where I have to get the E.E. to give up some information. Forgive me, Vela.

I fight off Rayne's hold on me, holding my arm out at him, like I will attack him if he comes at me. I say, with my eyes trained on a murderous-looking Rayne, "But it is true, Vela. They were looking for us and found us here, so we are the reason for this tragedy today."

Vela shakes her head, and her voice chokes out in a sob. "No. We can't be the reason."

My chest clenches at the sound of her tears, but I need to continue. "Sadly, we are, even though we did not intend to cause this amazing place harm." I glance out among the E.E. and see their faces transforming into pure rage.

If I can get them to believe who I say I am, then let their anger speak for them.

"I'm Lincoln Stevenson. This is Vela Ashcroft. I understand you've been looking for us."

The reaction isn't surprising; the Extremists start fighting against their restraints, their faces contorted in anger.

The Polar Bear members shift and hold their hands out, ready to hold them back with their gifts if needed.

"Greg Swanson was my leader in Denver, and he would never have sent me and others to our deaths like your leader sent you," I say, not stopping my assault.

One woman screams out, "He didn't. He believed we could easily overpower the diluted blood of the ones who are hiding here like rats!"

So, the leader is a man. Good to know. I need more; I need a name.

"Oh, really? If you couldn't tell, and what your leader should have known, is that *diluted blood,* as you call it, gives you two gifts instead of just one. It makes you stronger, not weaker. And to send thirty of you against the fifty who live here? You think he believed you would survive that? Sounds like he thinks you're expendable."

Grant growls at me in response as the rest of them are silent, their mouths in grim lines.

"My leader cared about my group." I continue. "Cared about our ideals, wanted us to believe in what we were doing, not just be mindless little puppets. It doesn't sound like your leader cares about any of you at all."

Another Extremist, pulling against his ropes, snarls, "We know what we believe in. And it's not for some nobody little Child to come and *save us.*"

"That's too bad. I'm sure even you would appreciate the kind of life we could all have if the Child is revealed."

"And you think *you and her play any* part in the prophecy?" Grant snarls, glaring at Vela, who's openly sobbing into Hannah's shoulder.

I shrug. "We could. But like I said, it's too bad your simple-minded leader convinced you that you could stop the truth, stop the inevitable. If I could guess, I think your high and mighty leader has made enough money so far by skimming the profits you've made him. He probably doesn't care if the Chosen Child is revealed. Maybe, he wants the Chosen Child to come forward because he believes the Child could...what did you say? Save us?"

Just give me a name.

Grant, his face red and body quivering, shouts, "Lyle Weston cares more for each one of us, more than any of you could care about some sniveling idiot Child. He's the leader we should have. Not either of you," he snarls at Vela, who's leaning heavily on Hannah, her face set in surprised shock.

Finally.

The captured group all start shouting and the Neronians in our group ice their bound hands to stop them from trying to break free.

"He didn't know what he was saying!"

"That's not his name," another argues.

"He misspoke," still another shouts.

I turn to the Polar Bear group, supremely relieved I got the name from them. "We need to trace that name and find him."

Rick and Gary nod and both put their heads together going over their plan.

Rayne, who's remained next to me, growls, "Oh, no, we don't. You don't get to tell us what to do. In fact, you should be shackled with these people, Linc. You're one of them. I know it. I don't care what fancy argument you have. You admitted they came here for you. You brought them here. It's time you have the same sentence they have."

He reaches to grab me, but I twist, evading his hands.

"Rayne!" Vela calls, "Stop it, he's not an Extremist!"

He moves to face her. "How well do you know your Intended, anyway? How can you say that with all certainty? He's playing you, Vela. Open your eyes."

She approaches him, holding onto his arms. I growl, hating watching her touch him. "Rayne, I would just feel it if he were truly an Extremist. He was never a true E.E. member. He was a spy. That's all. Please, this is unnecessary."

"Why do you believe him so easily? How are you so blind? Maybe that's why he tried to kill me with your dog in the first place. He was just taking out a mutant freak, like they all believe."

She shakes her head hard. "No, he was jealous of you, that's all. I'm certain of it, Rayne."

Rayne's anger, instead of diminishing, only grows darker. "You're letting your love for him deceive you. It's your Intended bond making you ignore what's right in front of you."

Wind starts blowing all around and hail hits people left and right. Rayne is on the verge of losing it.

Ignoring the storm Rayne's creating, she says, "I wouldn't love an Extremist, Rayne. Do you think I could ever love someone who was capable of what these people did here today?"

Rayne's face contorts in anger and grief. "Have you thought for one second that I could love you, too? And even after everything we went through, you still love *him*?"

She stands looking stunned.

"You know what? Let me just finish this." He lifts his hands and ice knives form in his hands. "If you can't see it for yourself, I'm going to bring out the Extremist in him. Watch him try to kill me again."

I plant my feet, readying myself for his attack. It comes fast and hard. I didn't expect any less. He throws the ice knives at me so hard with his wind gift that it takes all my concentration to melt them before they plant themselves in my face.

Unlike before, when I fought with Rayne, I was on the offensive. Now, I'm completely on the defensive. I don't want to hurt him, especially when it would prove to him that I'm an Extremist.

He switches from ice to wind and I'm dodging wind knives. I weave left and right, barely missing getting sliced. Fire just passes through wind, so there's no defense other than evasion.

A wind knife slices toward my face. I bend over and swing my legs into a spinning kick, making me face Rayne again. I land on my feet, and put my hands up, like I'm about to use my gift.

"That's right, attack me, you miserable excuse of an Elemental," Rayne growls.

He throws down hail the size of snowballs. I sweep my hand up and melt them in the air before they can crush me.

"Rayne!" Vela screams. "Stop it! Just stop it!"

He ignores her, and I hope she doesn't try to intervene. She does not need to be between Rayne's rage and me.

He's breathing heavily with all the attacks he's giving me. I'll use his tiredness against him.

"You can't fight wind, can you?" he asks, a manic smile lighting up his face.

He starts swirling air around and it looks like he's going to use a wind funnel to pull my limbs apart. Before he can, I sweep his feet and jump on top of him when he falls. I hold my arm against his throat, cutting off his breath.

I should have expected it, but when he plunges an ice knife into my side, I grit my teeth at the searing pain and jump off him. He's just proved he's out for blood. He's trying to get me angry enough to kill him. I won't do it.

"Linc!" Vela screams. "Someone stop Rayne!"

I hold my side. Blood leaks through my fingers. The ice knife melted in my hot blood, so there's nothing to pull out. Rayne jumps to his feet in one fluid move.

"Come on. Fight me!" he roars.

I hold my pierced side and shake my head at him. Blood continues to seep between my fingers, but still, I won't attack him. It would only prove his point, and I refuse to do that.

"Coward!" he rages.

Rick steps in between us. "Rayne, it's obvious he won't fight you. You will stop this madness. Linc is not an Extremist, no matter what you believe."

Rayne stands with trembling hands at his sides. He glares at me with so much hatred, I resolve to always watch my back with him. Does he really think I'm an Extremist or is he just trying to get me out of the way so he can have Vela?

Either answer is grim. "I won't fight you, Rayne. You're wrong. Let's forget about this. I'm willing to," I say as calm as I can.

A man steps forward who looks like Rayne, but older. "Son," he says, "Let's focus on rebuilding our homes. Forget about the fight you have with this man. It's beneath you to act like this."

Rayne turns anguished eyes at his father. "It's beneath me to flesh out a traitor?"

"We don't know he is, son. Come on, drop this. We have more important problems to resolve. If Rick and Gary believe he is who he says he is, then that's good enough for me."

Rayne's eyes come back to me. They're burning with hatred. He allows his dad to turn him around, and I relax my stance and turn, thinking the fight is over.

I couldn't be more wrong.

In the corner of my eye, I see Rayne shake his dad off him and whip a wind knife with one long sweep of his arm. I move, but it's not fast enough. The knife slices across my throat.

I try to cover the wound, but blood gushes over my hands. Pain roars through me, and I stare into Vela's eyes, telling her

I'm sorry. Her face is frozen in horror. I drop to my knees, and everything goes black.

37. VELA

The whole world disappears. The only thing I can see is the blood gushing out of Linc faster than he can stop it, falling over his hands in a sick, crimson waterfall. He catches my eye as he falls to his knees. His eyes convey an apology as he slumps face down in the mud.

Hannah cries out and rushes over to him.

All my breath leaves in a rush. My mouth opens in horror as I wrap my arms around my middle, trying to hold my fractured soul together.

Linc's dead. He's gone.

Linc. Gone.

I fall to my knees, wind gusting all around me, nature bursting into growth. My soul splits in two, four, eight. I'm not whole. Not anymore.

Linc's gone. Taken from me.

The weight of that crushes all my breath. I choke as my throat seems to close.

God, help me. Who am I without him?

You are my daughter. I have created you for just such a time as this.

Sinking into the earth, I allow it to enfold me in its embrace. I close my eyes to my loss and my gain. The Lord is talking to me. I will listen. I have nothing else but Him. My pain numbs me into complete awareness of the Lord.

What time, Lord?

I am going to gift you with all the elements, my child. My Chosen Child.

Why? Why would I deserve this? And without Linc?

Pain crashes into me at the thought of doing any of life without my Intended.

You have faltered. You are not perfect. Lean on me. I will guide you.

Where, Lord? Where will I go?

Where I send you.

And Linc? What about him?

Start with Rayne. You know what to do. I've given you the gift you need. What you claim, you are to gift to another. May it be so.

As God does as He promised, I'm filled with such enormous power, I cry out and lift my head to the heavens. It's like a beam of light hits my face and spreads. I feel it rush to my fingertips, every bit of my body streams with this all-consuming, mind-numbing power. Heat, ice, and every sensation in between flows into me. I can move mountains. I can *fly*. I can burn. I can take. I know what to do.

I blink my eyes open.

Hannah is still bent over Linc. Is he alive? Could he possibly have survived such a wound? He's not moving. I turn to the one responsible. My blood boils as I'm consumed in despair. God told me to start with Rayne.

My emotions swirl like a tempest around me, causing an internal storm I can hardly contain. I've never felt such mindless black anger. The blood in my veins rushes through me, but it's not like the adrenaline I usually feel. It's different. It's like I have complete command of it. Of all the elements.

I stand up, ready to do as God commanded. Wind whips leaves around me, lifting my hair in a cyclone.

Responding to the wind, Rayne lifts his eyes from Linc's still form. When he meets my glare, his eyes widen in alarm. He holds his hands up, like he can defend himself from my next move. Like he can see the great and awesome transformation in me.

"Rayne, how could you?" I ask in a deadly, quiet voice.

When he doesn't answer, I raise my arm and whip it down, an electrical strike slamming the ground right next to me. Its white-hot heat seems to satisfy my thirst for vengeance. Just for a moment. Steam rises from the ground. Thunder booms all around.

"You killed him, Rayne," I say, choking on a sob. "You took him from me. For that, you will be punished."

I need him to fear me. Raising my other arm, I clench my fist and bring it down. Another strike sizzles, hitting the earth, chased by a boom of thunder. It's closer to my prey, but not close enough.

"Vela, calm down. He needed to be put down. He was the enemy. Can't you see that? He brought them here!" Rayne screams.

I shake my head as pressure builds inside; I shut my eyes, trying to contain it. I scream and my voice goes hoarse as I lament my horrible grief.

"Rayne, *I* brought them here. I'm the One they've been searching for. You've been right all along. You killed the wrong person. *I'm* the one responsible for today, not Linc."

Determination consumes my every emotion as I study my opponent.

My attention turns to Hannah who slumps to the ground, looking defeated next to Linc's prone form. I'm overwhelmed with such great sorrow that I scream again in raw despair. *She must have failed to save him.*

I turn burning eyes to Rayne. There's only him and me. Everyone else disappears from my vision.

God, help me. Show me.

Gathering every moment I spent with Linc in my mind, an avalanche of emotions pours into me. Sobbing, I feel tears stream down my cheeks. An overwhelming urge to take everything from Rayne, to leave him with nothing, fills me. I'm not sure I understand what this urge is, but I know what I'm supposed to do with it.

I just know.

Pointing my hands in his direction, I sling an air whip at him. When I feel it wrap around him, I hold him there.

An astonished look comes over his face. He tries to turn around, but I hold tight, digging my feet into the earth, letting it feed me strength: pure, raw power. God has given me an extra burst of Gyan power. I cling to it.

"Vela, no! Don't do this!" Rayne cries, struggling against my weapon.

Without hesitation, I yank the invisible whip back to me. An explosive force hits me, blasting me back. I land hard on my back, all my breath leaving me in a rush.

Screams fill my ears, but I don't think it's from me. It's coming from far away.

I can't breathe. I'm filled with such a staggering amount of unfiltered power, I can hardly feel anything but this new *something*. I hold my head, feeling like I'm going to burst with the amount of energy whirling around me. But that's not all. The blood throughout my entire body ices, causing a strong chill to encase me, kind of like what I would feel if I were near a Borean. My blood rushes through me in a torrent, like a Neronian, too.

Staggering to my feet, I draw in huge gulps of air. A great wind builds, and branches rip from trees, flying around our heads. Rain comes pouring down in sheets.

Though I stand with my hands at my sides, this storm reflects what I'm feeling inside, the very tumult of my soul.

God granted me all the gifts, but this is more. I can feel it inside my chest, whirling around, searching for a place to settle. Rain drenches me, but instead of just feeling wet, my hands tremble and then my body warms, like it does when I use my earth gift.

I stare down at my hands, like they're foreign to me. I bring one up and swirl it around. Rain transforms into a mini water funnel right before my eyes. I stare at what I've just created, hardly believing what I'm seeing.

"Vela, what did you do?" someone screams at me. Claudette pushes aside the funnel easily, like its child's play. Of course, it would be for her. She's half Neronian. She grabs my shoulders.

I look into her eyes and try to understand what she's asking me. It's like I'm in a tunnel and these new powers are drowning everything else out. Sound seems so inconsequential right now.

It's when she shakes my shoulders, screaming, "Vela! Snap out of it! How did you do that to Rayne?"

I look over and see that he's writhing on the ground, screaming himself hoarse.

Claudette fills my vision and says in a low voice, "You just used the second gift of a Neronian. No one knows about it except those of us who control water. Vela, you took his gifts for yourself. All of them. How did you do that? And it's supposed to be temporary, a couple minutes at the most, before they return to the host."

Tonya asks in the distance. "What's wrong with him?"

Rayne screams out in an anguished voice, "They're gone. They're all gone. She took them!"

It's almost with a detached fascination that I hear this. I look upon Rayne clearly suffering. Despite these new powers filling me, I feel strangely empty.

Rayne stumbles to his feet, staggering. He's holding his chest, his face set in agony so deep, I've never seen anything like it. His whole identity is wrapped around his gifts. Now that he doesn't have them, he looks lost. He looks at me with pain-filled eyes. "How could you do this to me, Vela? After what we went through together?"

I stay silent.

"You were everything to me...and you took from me everything I am."

"You used those gifts to kill my Linc," I say in a deadly calm voice. "So now they're gone. You don't get to hurt anyone, ever again."

He sneers at me with twisted lips. "I'll get even with you for this, Vela." He points at me. "I might not have my gifts, but I'll get them back somehow. Don't think this is over," he spits at me. Turning around, he lurches away into the forest, the rain pelting his body as he disappears from view.

Searching for Linc, I see his body lying in the rain. A few people are lifting him, taking him away.

I hold my hand out to him, reaching for him. But I'm paralyzed. Who am I without my Intended?

My heart cracked open when I saw him fall. But watching his limp form being carried away rips it apart into irreparable pieces.

Dropping to my knees, a keening comes out of my throat. I've lost him.

38. LINC

I float in a world so bright, my eyes burn from the impossible white. I have no idea where I am, but I feel safe here.

I have a feeling that, right before this moment, I was in terrible danger. The remnants of adrenaline race through my veins, as if I'd just fought for my life.

Am I dead? Or dreaming?

Is this heaven? I look around and see nothing but blinding white. I thought heaven would be more colorful. Streets of gold, right?

An empty echo resounds around me, like I'm in a figment of my imagination.

There's something important I need to remember. No, not something, *someone.*

A young woman whose long blonde hair waves in the wind appears in front of me. She wears a white dress and smiles gently at me. Her blue eyes twinkle with a secret I should know. She holds out her hand, but when I reach for it, she stands just far enough away that I can't quite touch her.

I step forward to embrace this beautiful girl. I get the feeling that she's mine to hold. It comes so naturally; I don't question it. But when I move toward her, she's still just a step too far. My heart tethers to hers and it pulses in my chest. It burns. But it's not in agony, it's a pleasurable warmth I recognize. A hot flash fills me, and I know it's my fire gift responding to my emotions. That's right. I'm a Festan.

I look up at the young woman.

Wait, I know her.

I step toward her again and again, but each time I put my foot down, she's too far away. Just out of touch.

"Linc, come back to me," she begs. Her face transforming from gentle happiness to concern and anguish.

I want nothing more than to comfort her. "I'll try," I say.

"No!" her eyes, like twin sapphires, send their will into me. "You will come back. Don't give up, Linc."

I just need to reach her. I need to prove to her I'm ready to obey.

But how? Where am I?

"Don't leave me, Linc," she begs, her voice lingering in the air.

I try to reach her again, but my feet are suddenly stuck in sand, sinking me into a soft, deadly prison. If I can't get out of this sandpit, I'll die. I know it.

"I need you," she says, her breath reaching my ear. It tickles my neck, but it feels like she's kissing me there. A hot pain flares through me at the touch of her lips.

But I only see the sand I'm sinking into. I'm in down to my knees. I start struggling, fighting for my life. I can't lift my legs out. I drop to the edge of the sandpit, reaching for anything that can save me, a branch or a root.

My hands slide through the sand. I'm digging furrows into it, doing nothing to save myself from sinking deeper. My thighs are fully immersed now.

"Help me," I cry, begging anyone for help. I suddenly remember the woman's name. "Vela, Vela, I need you. Help me!"

"Linc, I'm here. I'm here. Don't leave me." I feel a gentle warmth at my temple, like a kiss. Her voice is all around me. But I'm chest deep in this pit now.

"I'm trying, Vela. I'm coming! I'm coming." I spread my arms through the sand and wrench my legs up. It takes all my strength to do it. But I know if I don't, I'll be lost.

I start reciting Scripture I've memorized. "My flesh and my heart may fail, but God is the strength of my heart and my portion forever." (Psalm 73:26 NIV)

My son, I am with you. You are not alone.

Hearing God's voice gives me the strength to position my body like I'm swimming. Every move is agony, but with divine help, I push myself forward. I can finally move my legs, now that I'm horizontal. I kick as hard as I can. Pushing forward, I will my way toward the edge with every bit of energy in my body. When I move, it's like my blood pulses through me, sluggishly at first, but then quickens, the faster I swim.

The Voice distracts me, but then it fuels me to go faster.

I am the resurrection and the life. The one who believes in me will live, even though they die; and whoever lives by believing in me will never die. Do you believe this?

"Yes, Lord, I believe. But I want to live. I want nothing more than to get back to Vela. Lord, let me be in her life. In any way, whether as her Intended or as a friend, Lord. Let me live," I beg with gritted teeth.

Every reach is agony. But pain is worth it if it means going back to her. Vela needs me. I feel it more than the breath in my body.

I am your salvation.

"You are, Lord! You say in Psalm 9:10, 'Those who know Your name trust in You, for You, Lord, have never forsaken those who seek You.' Give me strength to overcome this pit! Help me, Lord!"

My arms are tired, my whole body is aching. I long to rest, but I keep going, keep fighting.

Be at peace, son. Go be with your Intended. Help her with the mission I have given her. She will need you.

"I promise, with all my heart."

With that vow, I feel fuel burning through my muscles, giving me a burst of energy I didn't have before.

"I'm coming, Vela. I'm coming."

And I will, if it kills me. No, death is not ready for me. Not yet.

39. VELA

"Vela! He's not dead! Vela, calm down!"

Lightning strikes left and right. The ground smokes next to me, like I'm about to be hit by an errant bolt. When raindrops hit the ground, they sizzle.

I'm kneeling on the ground where I fell after they carried Linc away. I can't face what life will look like without his solid, warm presence.

Hands shake my shoulders. "Vela! Look at me, look at me!" a hard voice screams in my ear.

Blearily, I look up, blinking away the rain. Through the wet hair hanging in my eyes, I see Tonya, whose face is so full of fear, I look around quickly, trying to find the threat.

"Vela, Linc's not dead, do you hear me? Hannah and the other Gyans are working on him. Stop freaking out!"

I'm the threat.

"We just got the fires extinguished. We don't need to deal with more. Stop the lightning strikes, please. And stop the rain. Man, girl, I've never seen anyone lose it like you are. Vela, he's alive."

I study her face for any trace of insincerity. When I realize she's not lying to me, I jump up in one fluid movement. I notice it's just her, Jack, and me standing in the rain. Jack and Tonya are the only ones brave enough to be near me. Jack is crouched on the ground, whining, so even he clearly isn't happy about my behavior.

Everyone else is standing far away, putting as much distance between us as they can.

Grabbing her shoulders, I shake her hard. "Where is he?"

She looks at me, sympathy chasing away the hope I just had soaring through me.

"You said he was okay," I say with gritted teeth. My heart slams into my chest with fear. The rain comes down even harder.

Her eyes beg me to stay calm. "I said he's alive. He's fighting for his life right now. He's with the healers."

"Where?" I ask in a hard voice. Lightning crashes down a few feet from me.

Tonya jumps in fear, looking at the smoking ground. Thunder booms so loudly my ears ring and Jack yelps. Tonya swallows. "In the Community building."

I let go of her, call Jack to follow and race as fast as I've ever run to the only building left standing whole and unblemished in this once beautiful place. I slide to a stop in the mud when Andy carries Hannah out of its only door. He stands under the overhang, protecting Hannah from the rain, and looks at me solemnly. He blocks the door.

"What's wrong with her?" I ask, my heart in my throat.

He slides his gaze over her face lovingly. "She's burned out. After healing Linc, she passed out. She needs sleep. I'm going to take her somewhere she can get that."

I nod furtively. I can't lose them both.

"Hey Vela," he says, capturing my attention. "How about losing the rain and lightning? Someone could get hurt." He smiles tiredly at me. "I know you have all these awesome new powers, but do we need to suffer for it?"

He doesn't know the half of it.

I slump my shoulders, looking at the rain still pouring down. It's only over me. Further down the street, the rain stops. I'm an Elemental Eeyore with a rain cloud following me.

"I don't know how to stop it," I say in a small voice.

"It's a gift. You know how to stop using a gift. You've done it your whole life. Just because you're using another one...or two, doesn't mean you can't turn it off." With one final gentle look at me, he tucks Hannah close to his chest and runs through the rain to the edge where the sun is shining. After he gets through the rain, he slows, walking carefully down the street. I have no idea where he will take her. The rest of the buildings are mostly burned-out shells. Maybe he'll take her in the trees and make her a shelter out there.

Facing the Community building, I vow to stop the elements I'm unwittingly causing.

I concentrate hard. The elements are raging because I am. The rain and the strikes are showing the world my turbulent feelings. But that's because I thought Linc was dead.

He's not dead. He's okay. He'll be okay. I have to believe that. God help me, please, help me calm down.

I inhale slowly, exhaling just as slowly, working to regain control of my emotions. If I can assure myself Linc is not dead, then I can be in command of my feelings. I repeat over and over in my mind that Linc is okay. Like a mantra. Closing my eyes, I say it like a prayer, but then it turns into one.

God spare his life and keep him with me.

My confusion about Linc and Rayne has vanished like chaff blowing in the wind. When Rayne tried to kill Linc, my attraction for him left so quickly I'm shocked I could have ever cared for him like that at all.

Rayne was a temptation, nothing more. It's Linc I need always and forever. Linc is who God intended for me. When my feelings settle and I feel I have control over myself, I raise my hands and bring them down in one hard motion.

All at once, the rain stops. Just like that, it's pouring one minute, sunny the next. Opening my eyes, I look around to be sure no more lightning strikes appear. Jack barks, happy I figured out how to control my newly discovered gifts and shut off the rain. He shakes his body in one long movement. I nod my head decisively, thank God for His help, and we walk into the building that holds the most important person in my life.

As soon as we enter, I'm assailed by the amount of activity this building is housing. Dozens of people lie on the floor in different states of injury. Every Gyan in the community is working on someone.

I grab the first one who walks past me.

"Please, tell me where Linc is?"

The woman furrows her brow. "You mean the fake traitor?"

I frown. I don't like that he's referred to that way. For the sake of time, I ground out, "Yes. Where is he?"

She points in the far back corner of the room and walks away.

I run over to him, dodging people on the floor and those walking around. I can't get there fast enough.

When I see him, I cry out and fall to my knees next to him. He's laying so still, an angry red line across his throat. Jack nudges Linc's face. Pushing Jack away, I cup Linc's cheek, relishing the feeling of warmth against my palm. I kneel and kiss him, running my lips back and forth over his stubbled face. Then I kiss his neck softly. As I do, I cast my senses out to figure out why he's not awake. *What's wrong with him?* I don't feel anything wrong in his neck or anywhere else. *Why isn't he waking up?*

"Linc, can you hear me? Linc, come back to me," Tears choke my voice as I wait for him to open his eyes and look at me.

He remains still except for his chest rising and falling in a slow, measured rhythm. I blink and tears fall, landing on his neck. "You will come back. Don't give up, Linc," I say with heat in my voice. He has to come back from this. He has to.

Knowing he got stabbed in the side, I check to be sure that's been healed. Lifting his shirt, my fingers glide over a new scar that shows the healers found and healed it. Satisfied that's been done, I sit back and pick up his hand.

"Don't leave me, Linc," I beg, my throat closing. His hand sits so limply in mine. I wish for any movement, no matter how small. When none comes, I sniff and look around for a healer. I wish I could talk to Hannah, but Andy just carried her out.

I shake off those selfish thoughts and catch the eye of a Gyan working on the man laying closest to Linc.

"Please?" I ask. "Can you tell me why he isn't waking up?"

She holds up her hand asking me to wait, and I do, impatiently. When she's finished with her patient, she gets up slowly, holding her head, like she's dizzy. I can imagine how overextended she is, with the number of patients lying all over the place. I should do my part and help, but first I need to see what's wrong with Linc.

The Gyan woman walks over slowly to me, her steps a little unsteady. She looks down at Linc with sympathy. "We can heal a wound," she says softly, "but we can't replace lost blood. If we had access to modern medicine out here, we'd give him a blood transfusion, but we don't have any way of getting it. He needs to regenerate some of the blood, and if his body can't do that quickly enough, he could stay in a coma. Permanently."

Horror overcomes me. Not wake up? Wait, what? I remember when Rayne sliced Linc's neck open. He bled so much.

"So, it's up to him?" I ask hoarsely, looking down at Linc's still form.

"I'm afraid so. We've done all we can. Until he wakes up, we can try to get him to drink to stay hydrated, but he can't stay in this state forever. Eventually..."

I raise my hand to stop her from saying anything else. "I understand."

She nods at me, her mouth grim, and turns around, walking away slowly.

Linc's not dead, I assure myself. But he's close to it. I swallow, my throat suddenly dry.

I lean down and whisper in his ear, "I need you," my heart breaking. It can't be as bleak as all this. I ghost my fingers over his neck wound that's completely closed now. It's so red, like the blood under his skin is reminding me how close he is to death. Even though the Gyan woman says it's useless to infuse more healing into him, I have to try. I concentrate, infusing as much as I can in him. Having four powers now is impossible for me to reconcile. I concentrate on my Gyan powers and pour them into Linc.

I watch with wide eyes as his chest lurches, like I've electrocuted him.

He settles, his breath a little quicker now, but otherwise nothing changes.

I sigh. I think of what God gifted me. And the fact that I took Rayne's gifts. All of them. The wind, its secondary gift, the sensing of emotions. I've been ignoring the emotions I've come across, because it's just too much to compute with the horror of Linc nearly dying. But I'll have to adjust to it, eventually. Right now, Linc's emotions are calm and placid. Like he's in a peaceful state. I'm glad for that at least. Everyone else is too far away for me to read what they're feeling and for that, I'm glad.

I think of taking Rayne's water element and its apparently secret gift, the ability to take others' gifts. God granted me that ability before I took Rayne's Neronian gift. God intended for me to take Rayne's gifts, which still sit inside me, waiting for me to distribute them as God instructed. The Neronian ability to steal a gift is supposed to be temporary. Yet I still have Rayne's gifts. Clearly, I'm supposed to do something with them.

Rayne tried to pound into my head this whole past week that I'm the Chosen Child. I sit back, playing with Linc's soft hair. The Child will have all the powers. The enormity of that thought shoots fear into my body. I shake my head. I cannot fully grasp the consequences of what God has done. Right now, I focus on Linc.

"Linc, I'm here. I'm here. Don't leave me," I beg, kissing his temple gently.

I blow out a breath slowly, singling out *my* gift. The one I know as well as the nose on my face. Even though it hasn't helped yet, I can't help myself. With my fingertips gently resting on Linc's angry scar, I send a trickle of healing into him again.

I imbue a will to live in my healing. I'm not sure if that's even a thing, but I do it anyway.

"Don't give up, Linc. I need you." I lay my head on his shoulder, soaking in the feel of him. I sit there for a while, barely noticing all the activity happening around me. Linc's body twitches, which pops my head up. But he doesn't wake up. It's like he's trying to fight his way back.

I pray, begging God for my Intended's healing and for him to come back to me.

My head is bowed, all my thoughts focused on Linc, when I feel his hand move. I snap my head up. "Linc? Linc, are you awake? Can you hear me?" I search his face for any movement. I'll take anything at this point.

His eyelids twitch.

"Baby, I'm here. I'm not leaving you. Wake up, wake up, please." My voice chokes off in a sob. Tears well up and slide down my cheeks as I lean over and kiss his lips. I lay my head on his chest. Jack nudges my neck, whining softly.

Linc twitches again. When I feel his movement, I lift my head quickly. Linc cracks his eyes open.

Overwhelmed, I cry out, "Oh, thank God," and lean over and kiss him, being as careful as I can. "Linc, you're back, you're back," I repeat over and over.

"Vela," he says, in a scratchy voice. "There's nothing better than waking up to a kiss. I heard you... in my dream."

I sit up, impatiently wiping away my tears, so I can see him better. "Yes? What is it? Do you need something? What hurts?" I sniff.

His eyes open more, and he looks at me, cocking his head slightly. "Why are you crying?" His voice is still hoarse, so I reach for a cup of water the healer left.

"Why am I crying?" I ask, forcing a laugh. "Oh, I don't know. You were unconscious, and they said you might never wake up. Is that a good enough reason?"

His eyes hold the same apology he gave me when he dropped to the ground.

"Don't look at me like that," I say softly.

"I'm sorry, sweet Vela. Are you okay?"

I laugh, sniffing. "I am now."

"Thirsty," he says, wincing.

I pick his head up and put the cup to his lips, lips I want to kiss so badly. His throat moves as he drinks deeply. "You need to replenish your fluids. Drink as much as you can," I instruct firmly. He pauses to breathe then obediently drinks some more.

When he's done, I put the cup down and cradle his face. Needing him to hear me, I pour my heart out to him. "Linc Stevenson, I love you. I'm sorry about Rayne. I never should have kissed him. I love *you* and *always* will." I shake my head, looking down. "I know you might not be able to forgive me for what I did, but I will prove to you that you're the only one for me. No matter how long it takes."

He tugs on my hair. I look into his eyes. They're full of love and swimming with tears. "Vela, I'm as in love with you as I've ever been. You never need to worry that you'll lose me or that you have to prove your love for me. You have mine, and that's forever. You're it for me."

Unable to wait any longer, I lean down and kiss his soft lips, lips still dripping from the replenishing water. I hold his cheek and move my lips with his as he kisses me like he never wants to come up for air. When he pulls away, I moan. In answer, he recaptures my lips, nudging my lips apart. I give him the access he wants and drown in the knowledge that he loves me and always will. Despite my actions, he still cares for me. The deeper and longer we kiss, the more my heart absorbs his unbelievable love and returns it. It cements the fact that my life will always be tied to his. I give my traitorous heart to him, thanking God for Linc's steadfastness.

We come up for air, and I look at him with all the tenderness I can express. If a glance could kiss, it would be right now. "I love you," I say and rub his nose with mine.

"You know I love you, Vela Ashcroft. Now, will you marry me?"

My eyes pop open with surprise. I laugh, not being able to contain it. "You're proposing minutes after you wake up from your deathbed?"

He grins and pushes hair out of my face. "I guess I am. There's nothing like facing death to show a man what's really important. You never know how much time you have left, and I intend to take full advantage of it. Anyway, I have a promise to keep. I figure the best way I can do it is as your husband."

"Linc," I say, leaning back, laughing deeply. When I get my giggles under control, I finish saying, "I'm still seventeen. How will that work?"

His eyes twinkle. "Is that a yes?"

"You're taking full advantage of your vulnerable state."

"Or yours. Either way, does it matter? Do you want to marry me, Vela?" He holds my gaze, intent on my answer.

I nod happily. "I do. I really do." I throw my arms around him. He kisses my neck, and I bask in his presence, that he's alive, and relish that he's mine, truly mine. He breathes in deeply, but I can't imagine what he smells. I'm covered in smoke and grossness. Maybe it's the floral and honey buttery bread scent he loves so much.

Jack barks, demanding to be involved in this momentous decision. Linc's and my hands intermingle as we pet Jack's smooth head. He licks Linc's face, then mine. I never want to leave this position.

"He seems to approve," I say, laughing into his neck. Thinking, I sit up and ask, "How does this work? I can't legally marry you, can I? Not until I'm eighteen."

He shakes his head. "I can't wait that long. We'll have to get your parents' permission. I told you; I have a promise to keep."

"To whom and what is the promise?" Did someone make him promise him something in the middle of the fight? I hold on to his hand, never wanting to let it go.

He crooks his mouth in a grin. "To God. I promised Him I would help you in your mission. He came to me when I was unconscious and tasked me to help you. Do you happen to know what it is? I have an idea, but I'll do anything. For you."

I look into his eyes, judging his response as I say, "God told me I am the Chosen Child. He gave me all four gifts. I'm meant to bring our world together." Just saying it makes it settle over me, like a weighted blanket. I thought it would be a crushing feeling, but it's a surprisingly comforting weight to carry. I'm at peace with it.

Linc nods, like I didn't just drop a bomb on him. He's not the least bit surprised. "I could sense them in you. I just don't know when it happened. Was it when I was unconscious?"

Just because I can, I lean down and kiss him for a long, lingering moment. "Can we not talk about that? It makes my heart freeze up every time I remember you falling face-down with your throat cut."

His eyebrow lifts. "What happened with Rayne? You didn't kill him, did you?"

I huff. "Worse. I took his gifts from him."

"What? You stole his gifts? How is that possible? Is that a Chosen Child thing?"

"Yes, and no. God gifted me all the elements, which gave me the secret Neronian power of stealing gifts. Apparently, it's supposed to be temporary, but because of my Chosen Child gifting, I've kept them longer than I understand a normal Neronian would. God told me to gift what I take to someone else."

Linc grimaces and tries to get up.

I push him down. "What are you doing?"

"Vela, we need to talk to Rick and Gary. Find out who knows more about these new gifts of yours. Now, help me up. Please."

I stare at him. "Are you being serious? Linc, you need to rest!"

"I can rest later. Vela, we need answers."

Grudgingly, I agree and put my shoulder under his arm, helping him into a sitting position.

He sits for a second, shutting his eyes.

"Are you okay?" I ask, worried.

He nods, then motions for us to stand up. Reluctantly, I do, taking most of his weight. Once we're standing, Linc shakes his head like he's clearing it.

"Linc, is this a good idea?"

"No, it's not," the healer I spoke to earlier says as she rushes to us. She puts her shoulder under Linc's other arm. "You need to rest. You were just very ill." She tries to nudge him down, but Linc stands his ground.

I'm shocked when I can feel her irritation at Linc standing up.

"I'm fine," Linc says with gritted teeth. "We need to talk to the leaders. It's urgent."

"Well, I can find them and bring them to you. You shouldn't be standing and certainly not walking around," she says in a firm voice.

"Look," I say. "My fiancé is determined to walk out of here. If he says he can, then we're going to have to believe him."

Linc turns a dazzling smile in my direction. "You said fiancé."

I smile back at him. "That's because you are, right?"

"Right," he says firmly, tucking me close to his chest, kissing the side of my face. He looks at the Gyan on his other side. "Did you hear that? She said fiancé."

The woman frowns. "Love-sick fools," she mutters, before she ducks out of Linc's arm. "If you're determined to walk yourself into the ground, then go." She walks away, shaking her head.

Linc moves and I have no choice but to walk with him. He's leaning on me, but really, he's walking under his own steam. I marvel at his strength and determination. His emotions are just as strong. I bask in feeling them. We step around the people lying on the floor and make it outside. Lingering on the landing, we look out over the devastation of the community.

Homes once whole are burned out, some down to the ground, others half gone. Black walls are all that's left of a once thriving community. Smoke curls lazily into the air like lives weren't just ruined. Now that the fires are out, the smoke isn't so heavy. The sight makes my heart squeeze so hard I can hardly breathe. This sweet, beautiful community is practically gone. And it's because of me.

"Jeez," Linc mutters as he looks around.

"I know. Linc, this devastation is my fault." A tear slips down my cheek.

He squeezes me to him. "Don't take responsibility for a group's grossly wrong choices. You are a blessing, been given a great blessing. Focus on that. All of this can be rebuilt."

My throat tightens. "What about the ones who they killed? Linc, how can I live with that?" I ask in an anguished voice.

He shifts and turns to me, facing me fully. Holding me by the shoulders, he says, "Baby, focus on my eyes. Focus, Vela."

When I turn my attention from the blackened homes to my Intended, he says fiercely, "This day has been a tragedy. One committed by a bloodthirsty group's misguided attempt to stamp out anyone possibly having anything to do with the Chosen Child: you. They are the reason for this devastation, for the loss of life, not you. Vela, remember, we saved the rest of their lives. Without our help, fifty people would have lost their lives today. Focus on what we did, not what happened. What the Extremists did is out of your control. What matters is what we do now, how you use the momentous legacy God bestowed upon you." His fierce resolve fills me, lifting my depressed spirits.

I nod, but my heart's crushed at the enormity that we lost good people today. I hold onto Linc's words, keeping me from sinking into despair.

People are walking around everywhere, some digging through the rubble of their homes, others choosing what to do next. I sigh heavily. "I wonder if they're going to rebuild."

"I'm sure they will. These are survivors."

"Won't they want to move to another location, now that this one has been compromised?"

He joins me in watching everyone around us. "I'm not sure. Come on, let's go find out. Rick and Gary are our best bet for that news."

Tucking myself back under his arm, I hug him to me, and we head out to find some answers. And hopefully someone will know more about these new powers I have.

40. LINC

My heart clenches at what Vela just said to me. She is not responsible for this day. The Extremists are. And I intend on finding the guy who revealed this precious location, if it's the last thing I do.

Jack's right next to me as we walk. I'm surprised he's giving me so much attention, but I accept his presence gladly. He must be happy I'm alive. *I'm* happy I'm alive. Turning to Vela, I kiss the side of her head and ask, "What happened to the Extremists we captured?"

"They're about twelve left alive. They're being held somewhere. That's the last I know."

"I have an idea of what to do with them," I say, testing my idea out in my mind.

Vela turns her delectable face to me. "Oh, yeah? What other brilliant idea do you have cooking up?"

"They must have come here on a plane, right? To get thirty people here, they didn't take ATV's and all-terrain vehicles. So, we'll take their ride and them back to Andy's hometown and turn them over to the Festans there. As long as one of them didn't sneak off and fly away with it, that is."

"And you're planning on doing that with just my help?"

"No," I say firmly. "We'll need help." I look around looking. "Have you seen Roland? Also, I'll ask Andy to come with us."

"The last time I saw Roland was in the middle of the fighting. I hope he's okay. He didn't ask to be a part of this fight."

"He knew what he was volunteering for when he helped us take this place back."

"That's for sure... about Andy, I don't think he'll go. It took everything in Hannah to heal you, and she's passed out somewhere. I don't think he'll leave her."

"Hmm, okay. We'll need some volunteers to come with us then."

"Mixed elementals will leave here?"

"Why not? They've already been exposed. They can come back if they want," I say, running through my mind those I think will leave with us.

Vela sighs heavily. "Only there's nothing to come back to." She pauses for a minute as we walk.

I squeeze her to me, hoping she's not spiraling into a dark place. I haven't spotted Rick or Gary yet, but I'm still looking.

"If what you said about us being the reason the Extremists are here, how can we protect these people in the future?" she asks in a small voice.

She sounds so vulnerable. I face her and kiss her forehead softly. "Learning how they found us is my next mission. I'll use every resource I have to find the one responsible and shut his cell down. Besides aiding you as the Chosen Child, it'll be my personal mission."

She sighs heavily. "The Chosen Child. It still sounds so weird referring that title to me. The man in charge, Lyle Weston, is it? You're going to track him down?"

"Not me, my mother. She'll find out exactly how he located this place."

She goes quiet as we resume walking, slowly, because I don't want to push myself too hard. I'm fighting dizziness, but if I keep my gaze focused on something in the distance, I can manage it. "So, what exactly happened with Rayne? What did I miss?"

Vela tells me of her new gift stealing elements and the threat Rayne issued as he ran away.

I listen intently. "So, you don't know where he is?" I ask, my palms suddenly sweating as my heart pounds. He has left a permanent impression on me, and I can't help but fear a repeat of what he did. I finger the scar at my neck and then check my side for that scar, too.

She shakes her head. "No. He could be anywhere." She looks around like she might see him hiding in the trees.

I study the trees, too. He's a dangerous liability, for me and Vela, especially after that threat. I imagine he'll stick close to her as he comes up with a plan to get his powers back. It took some digesting to understand that the secret Neronian power is stealing other elemental gifts. I can understand why they wouldn't want that to be widely known. But if it's supposed to be temporary, why does Vela still have Rayne's powers?

I can feel them in her now, sitting in wait for her to command. It's a strange feeling to sense four different elements in one Elemental. I thought two was awesome to behold in this community of mixed Elementals, but Vela housing all four elements is a power I've never encountered. But I would imagine the Chosen Child would play to different rules than the rest of us.

Looking around, I try to find Rick and Gary. I should be able to spot Rick's bald head easily enough. The sun is setting, but the light hasn't dropped yet.

"There they are!" Vela says, pointing toward the two leaders off to the right.

Rick notices us walking up first. He stops his conversation with Gary and nods his head in our direction. They hurry over and Rick asks, "Linc? You're okay! Thank goodness. It didn't look good for you." He turns to Vela, asking, "What happened to Rayne, to his powers?"

I look at Vela and wait to see how she's going to explain things. If she wants to keep her new powers to herself, I'll support her. My fiancée.

"I took them," she says boldly, grabbing my hand and squeezing it.

Okay then. We're going this route. God help us.

Gary's eyebrows shoot up, his face an open expression of surprise. "You *took* them?"

She nods decisively. "It's the secret Neronian gift. Not so secret anymore. I was able to claim Rayne's gifts because God gifted me with all four elements."

Gary puts his hand on Rick's shoulder, his eyes shining. "It's true, then. You're the Chosen Child. Rayne told us that before you left for Saddleback, but I didn't want to get my hopes up too much. It only makes sense for what you did to happen if you're the Child. Do you have the Fire gift, too?"

"Can't you sense all of them in her?" I ask them.

"Yes," he breathes. "The Chosen Child will command them all," Rick says, quoting the prophecy that's ingrained in my head. "And you're going to support her through this?" he asks me.

I squeeze Vela's shoulder. I love the idea of her producing fire a little too much. "Well, as her fiancé, I think I should support her." I can't help the smile that takes over my face. Vela finally agreeing to marry me will carry with me for the rest of my life.

"Fiancé? Wait, when did that happen?" Gary asks, laughing, his belly shaking.

"About five minutes ago. I'm a lucky man," I say proudly. I glance down at Vela, whose face is an adorable shade of red.

Rick looks between us, at a loss about which bit of news to comment on first, our engagement or Vela's new gifts. He takes the latter. "Vela, we will support you, too, in whatever you need. I can sense all four elements in you, so it's just a matter of time until you use them. How does it feel to have more than one gift?"

She clears her throat. "It seems I'm half Borean. My wind gift has been manifesting for some time now. I wasn't supposed to have it fully until I'm eighteen. But now I have all of it, along with my Gyan, and now Neronian and Festan gifts."

Gary says, "You're still a child technically, being seventeen. The Chosen Child will command all the gifts; it makes sense."

Vela's voice takes on a tentative edge. "For some reason, God has chosen me to bear this incredible title. He told me He would guide me and help me along the way."

Rick and Gary nod, holding onto her story, captivated.

"Afterwards, lightning came when I called. I'm not sure which gift even does that?" She turns a questioning glance at Rick and Gary, who both look away, considering her question.

Rick says, "Boreans can control lightning, but only the most talented."

"Well," Vela continues, swallowing noticeably. "God told me to take Rayne's gifts, to claim them and then to gift them to another."

I tug her into my arms closer, encouraging her to continue.

"After that, it's a blur. I held Rayne still with an air whip, and then I just took his gifts. They hit me like a Mack track. I already had my own wind gift, but it got exponentially stronger with his in me, too. And apparently for Neronians who can steal powers, it's a temporary thing. But these don't feel like they're going away." She rubs her head, strain showing in her eyes.

Rick answers, "The Chosen Child is an anomaly. God gifted you with special powers only you can have. But as far as still having Rayne's gifts, it seems you're going to carry them until you give them away to another Elemental."

Vela's face turns white. "I'm having a hard time thinking I permanently took an Elemental's gifts."

I speak up. "Vela, Rayne shouldn't have his gifts if he's going to use them to kill innocent people. He played judge and executioner trying to kill me for bringing the Extremists here and supposedly being one of them."

She whispers, "Didn't I do the same thing by taking what he values most? That was his whole identity, Linc."

I frown. "If he only lives for his element, he's not much of a human. And you didn't kill him, not like he tried to do to me."

She mutters, "He's not human, though, he's an Elemental." Then she says in a stronger voice, "I want to give them back to him."

Rick shakes his head. "I don't know if you can. These are uncharted waters. Vela, you need to really think who to give those gifts to now. How does it feel to have them?"

She hesitates. "It's a strange feeling. Like they're a part of me but kept in a separate compartment within." She bites her lip. "I think I can separate them, but I'm not sure how."

Gary says with a serious look on his face, "If you can gift elements like that, you'll be an extremely valuable commodity."

"Like being the Chosen Child isn't valuable enough?" Rick says, chuckling.

Gary nods. "It's just that everyone will want to be given more elements. She's going to be either hated or loved for this."

"Right," Gary says, frowning. He looks up, with a bright look, "She should practice on the Extremists we've captured. See if she can take their gifts."

"You want Vela to practice on members of the most dangerous group in our world?" I ask in a hard voice. I feel Vela's shoulders tense under my arm.

"Why not?" Rick asks, nodding along with Gary. "It could be a form of punishment. Take their gifts from them so they can't harm anyone else. What they did is even worse than Rayne."

"They can harm people with or without their gifts," I say in a hard tone. "You just said people are going to want to exploit Vela's gifts and then, in your next breath, you do just that. Suggest she use them to punish your captives." Protectiveness for Vela's mental health over such an act swarms over me.

"I can't think of a better punishment than that," Rick says, shrugging, completely unapologetic.

I huff and try to turn Vela away from this insane idea, but she resists me.

"He's right," she says, in a quiet voice, looking up at me. "They came here to prey on innocent people and to find and kill us. Linc, if I try taking anyone's power, it should be theirs."

I look down at her in surprise. I drop my arm and hold her shoulders, looking deep into her eyes. "Vela, are you sure? This will take a toll on you. You already feel bad for taking Rayne's gifts."

"Because Rayne was my friend. I'm not friends with the Extremists. Not by a long shot. What they've done is heinously evil. They need to be incapacitated."

"So, what? Are you going to take twelve more people's gifts from them? That might make you crazy with power, Vela," I say with heat.

She looks up at me, a resolve filling her eyes. "No. I'll do one and see if I can gift the power to someone else right away. Then if that works, I'd do another one, until I've claimed all their gifts. I'll keep Rayne's and when I see him, I'll give them back."

I sigh and run my hands through my hair. "Are you sure?"
She nods.

"I don't know. This is a crazy idea."

"That way," she says, gripping my arm. "When we take the E.E. back to Andy's hometown, they'll be less dangerous."

"They'll still be dangerous," I say, but I'm relenting. I can feel it.

"Wait, what? You're taking the Extremists?" Rick asks anger in his tone.

I turn to them, nodding. "I think it's for the best."

"*You* think?" Rick. "Since when are you the leader here?"

I look at him with hard eyes. "I am the Festan Grand Elder's son. I think that gives me the right to dispense justice."

Rick's eyes narrow at me. "What if we disagree with your methods?"

"And what would your methods be?" I ask in a deceptively calm voice.

"Death," Gary answers.

Rick nods, agreeing. "They took eleven lives from us. Eleven members of our community dead because of the Extremists' fanatical beliefs. So, we take one more than that from them with those who are left, to make up for it."

I can't help but notice Vela flinch at the number of those killed. Grabbing her hand, I squeeze it and fall silent, thinking. Turning, I say, "You realize my parents can facilitate extracting every bit of information? It would be senseless to kill the Extremists and lose the invaluable information we can gain about their organization."

Rick and Gary look at each other. Gary folds his arms over his large stomach, and says, "Say we agree? How would you get them to your mother?"

"They must have come here on a plane. We'll take it over and use it to take them back to the Festans in Winnipeg. My mother will instruct me where to send them from there. She will extract the information. You don't need to worry about that."

Rick snorts. "I'd rather they be punished with death, but if Vela can take their gifts from them permanently and gift them to some of ours, I guess that would be excellent justice as well."

Gary nods, agreeing.

I inhale deeply and look down at Vela, studying her reaction.

She nods. "Okay. I'm ready. Let's do it now."

"Wait," I say, pulling her back, stopping her from marching away. "We need to figure out who is going with us to watch over the Extremists first."

She turns to the leaders. "Who do you think would be best to help us get them to Winnipeg?"

Gary and Rick look at each other then turn and lean their heads together, talking quietly.

Rick turns back, saying, "Those who receive gifted elements will go with you. They might need to stay close to you to keep their gifts. Call it an experiment. We'll look for volunteers to not only take another gift but also go with you. Give us some time."

"Wait," Vela cries, her face screwed up in worry. "We don't even know if I can do this. We need to try it first."

Rick studies her with a serious intent in his eyes. "I have no doubt you can do it. But if you want to practice, I'll agree with that. Let me be your first volunteer."

Gary smiles at him. "What gift do you want, friend? You have your choice."

Rick inhales and straightens his belt, thinking. "Well, I'm a Festan. It would be nice to have water, too. But, with a Borean gift, I might be able to control lightning. Hmmm, it's a hard decision." His eyes fill with a fierce light. "Borean, let's go find a Borean Extremist. I'll be happy to take that ill-used gift off their hands."

He leads the way to the captives, bouncing on the balls of his feet in his excitement at the chance to acquire a second gift.

Vela and Jack follow, and I trail behind them. I can't imagine what's going through her mind right now. She's walking with her head held high, but I'm sure she's struggling with the morality of what she's about to do. If I know my Vela, I'm sure I'm right.

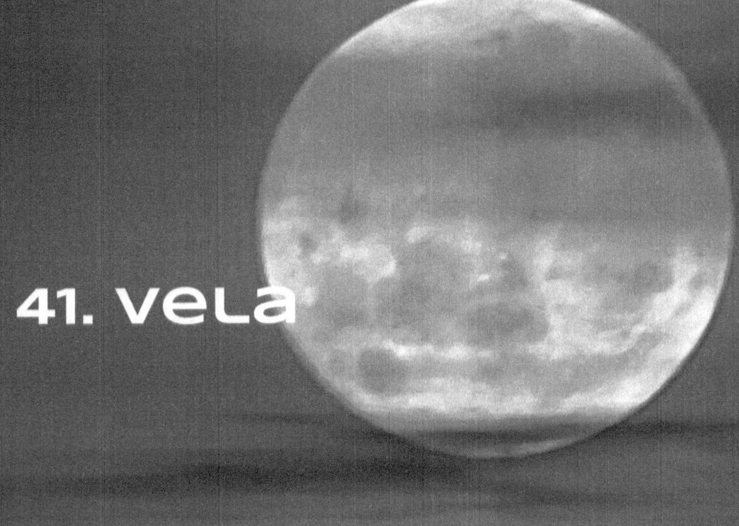

41. VeLa

What am I doing? Have I gone certifiably crazy?

I walk behind Rick and Gary, who are leading me toward the most impossible plan I've ever heard. Stealing gifts, then gifting them?

Do I really think I can do that? God told me I could. I need to be confident. Not doubting Him. I already took Rayne's. I should be able to do something with them now.

I had no idea Neronians could take power before that moment I took Rayne's. It's like I just knew when it happened. And I know I'll be able to do it now, too.

My hand warms, and I clench Linc's hand tightly. I can feel Rayne's gifts swirling around inside me, waiting for release. It's like my body is prepping me to host and dispense.

I can do this.

Jack is at my side, and Linc is behind me, where I know I have his support. He's worried, I can tell, but I don't know what to say to reassure him. One thing I do know is that he'll catch me when I fall, physically and emotionally. He's going to support me in any way I need.

Is this ethical?

I harden my thoughts. The Extremists took ethics out of the question by coming here to slaughter me and everyone else. *Even children.* They deserve this, and more. Besides, God commanded me to do it.

We reach the group of Extremists huddled on the ground. They look up at us with defiant expressions. Those looks will soon change once they realize what I can do.

Rick studies them, then walks into the group, hauling a middle-aged man by his arm to stand before me.

I look at the man, a Borean, who glares at me with his lips in a grim line. It's like he's accepted his fate. He thinks he's about to die, I'm sure of it. Why he thinks a seventeen-year-old girl would deliver such justice, I have no idea.

Thinking he at least deserves to hear why I'm about to do this, I say in a clear voice, "For crimes against an innocent community of Elementals, you are declared guilty."

He closes his eyes and with nothing else to say, I step back to around the same distance I was from Rayne when I took his powers. My chest warms with my intent, and I sling my arm back, then forward, wrapping the man with an air whip.

The man's eyes shoot open wide. I know why he's surprised. The whip feels warm, like my gift is energizing it. Air usually feels cold.

With all my strength, I whip the cord back at me, allowing it to hit me. Like before, it shoots me back. But, unlike last time when I fell to the ground, Linc is right behind me, catching me, holding me up.

I hear a hoarse screaming, but all I can feel is my breath sucked out of me. I feel a rush of hot energy filling me from my head to my toes. My blood soon ices, the same sensation I feel when I'm close to a Borean. It encases me in a chilly vice. My temples throb, and I wonder if I have too many extra gifts in me at one time.

"Breathe, baby, breathe," Linc coaxes in my ear.

I obey and suck in air greedily. I attempt to get used to the feeling of this power tucked into another compartment within me. I can feel its separate power swirling around, ready for me to do with as I will. Wind swirls my hair all around my head, and when I look, I see the tops of the trees are blowing, too. I can taste the extra wind in the air. It's cold, but I'm suddenly hot.

I push myself up from leaning on Linc, keeping my back to his chest, needing to feel his connection. With white knuckles, I grip his hands on my hips. He steadies me.

The now powerless man rolls around on the ground, screaming, holding his chest. He curls up in a ball, and I look on, dispassionately. He deserves this and more.

Rick looks down at the man and then up at me with bright eyes. "Are you ready to do the next part?"

I pant, getting used to air flowing back into my body.

"Give her a minute," Linc says firmly behind me. He squeezes my hips, saying in my ear, "When you're ready. Only then. Don't rush yourself because he's anxious for this to happen."

I nod, letting my heart calm down from its wild beating. I let go of Linc's hands and step away from him. I'm filled with so much power, I'm surprised it's not leaking out of my pores. Looking at the wind gusting all around us, I guess it is.

Examining my feelings, I think I can gift this element by touching Rick, but I want the Extremists watching to get the maximum effect. So, I sling an air whip at Rick, infusing it with the separate gift I've just taken. When the whip strikes him, he falls back, like I did.

His face is rapturous, though, as he absorbs the enormous rush of power I've just gifted him.

"What did you do to him?" a woman cries as she runs up, falling to the ground next to Rick. This must be his wife. I've seen him with her before. She turns her angry face to me. "Why did you attack him?" I realize just now that it did look like an attack.

Gary kneels next to Rick and the woman, saying, "Cheri, he's fine. He's better than fine. He has a second gift now. Vela did that. She took that man's gift and gave it to Rick." He looks at me with admiration and astonishment.

Cheri runs her hands over him. She's a Gyan, I realize, as she senses him for any injury. She won't find anything but a second gift. I know because I can sense it's gone from me. She looks up at me, her mouth opens in an O. "How did you…"

Linc comes close and puts his hands on my shoulders, which I appreciate. I'm suddenly so exhausted I would likely fall over without Linc holding me up. I need his bond to be near me. It's a comfort, because what I just did defies all logic. A faint headache blooms.

"She's the Chosen Child. She can do this incredible thing with her gift, Cheri," Linc says formally.

Hearing Linc say out loud that I'm the Chosen One is mind blowing. I still can't get used to it. But my new power is staring at me in the face. I can't deny the evidence before me.

The former Borean man has been taken back to the group, but he's sobbing into his chest. His friends look at him with horror, then at me with the same expression.

When they heard Linc tell Cheri I'm the Chosen Child, they all start fighting their bonds, their faces contorted in anger. The guards force them to stay on the ground.

Rick finally sits up, his face beaming. He holds out his hand and produces a mini cyclone. Looking at it with awe, he breathes, "This is amazing." He turns to me, saying with a wide grin, "You're amazing, Vela."

"It's God's gifting, not mine." I lean back on Linc's chest. Gifting Rick his new power took more out of me than fighting an entire day with my one gift usually does.

Rick stands with the help of Cheri and Gary. He rubs his hands together with a look of glee on his face. "Let's do another one." He looks over the group, then at Gary. "You want another power? I highly recommend wind."

I stiffen, worried. I don't think I can do it again so soon. My head starts to pound, fresh pain assaulting me.

I'm grateful when Linc says in a firm voice, "She's exhausted. If your overeager mind can grasp that. She needs to take breaks frequently. Don't push her, Rick."

He looks disappointed and says, "Of course, of course. When she's ready. It looks like we'll lose light soon, anyway. Come, Gary, let's get a group together who will take the rest of the Extremists' gifts."

Cheri looks at me with deference and a lot of awe. They walk away and leave me with Linc and the Extremists. They're being guarded by five Polar Bear members who are holding guns to the captured, but it looks like they're wondering if they should point them at me.

The captured Extremists start talking amongst themselves and begin to panic. They pull on the bindings tying their hands, but, they can't even lift their arms.

"You can't do this to us!" the Extremist leader, Grant, screams at me. "You'll pay for this."

"It's only temporary, Grant," a Neronian woman tells him, sending me a hate-filled gaze.

I shake my head. "We'll see. It's nothing you don't deserve if it is permanent."

The guards lift their guns and point them at the struggling group.

"You're a monster!" Grant screams at me, his face a mask of fury.

"No, you all are the monsters here. I'm just the one you've been searching for and trying to kill all these years. Well, I'm not dead. Not yet," I say and walk away, grabbing Linc's hand as I brush past him, bringing him with me.

I walk straight into the woods, needing to find a quiet place. And I need Linc with me. My head pounds, reminding me what I just did to Rayne and that Borean man. I know that Rayne is somewhere hiding out here, ready to take back what I've stolen, but I don't care.

Right now, I need to be alone with Linc. He's my sanity, my guide through this whole messy business. I'm starting to panic, and I don't want an audience.

Linc allows me to lead him and Jack to the copse of trees where we hid what feels like a week ago but was only a few hours. The sunset is brilliant against the backdrop of the trees, oranges and pinks glowing wildly and casting the trees in shadow. I wonder if we'll see the Northern Lights tonight.

Dragging my Intended past the low-hanging trees and bushes, I'm finally able to breathe once we're truly alone. I pace and blow out a huge breath. Running my hands through my hair, I turn to find Linc watching me, his arms folded across his chest. His expression is one of pure pride and love. He also looks confident. Is it me he's confident in? Or himself? Maybe both.

"Did that really just happen?" I ask, my eyes searching his.

He nods.

"I just took that guy's gift and gave it to Rick?" I need to hear him confirm what I just did. As if I wasn't there. It felt more like an out-of-body experience than something I'd done myself. Hearing God tell me to do this and doing it are two completely different things.

He nods again.

"I'm the Chosen Child?" Again, I need to hear him say it. He would never lie to me.

He nods and then takes several steps toward me and holds my face in his hands. "You, Vela Ashcroft, soon Stevenson, are the Chosen Child. And you are the most brilliant and amazing Elemental I've ever seen."

His eyes are blazing blue orbs as he utters these impossible words. I swallow and tears swim in my eyes. I accept his words as gracefully as I can. I've fought against the idea that I could be the Chosen Child since first heard it. My mind still struggles to embrace what I now know to be fact.

I hold Linc's hands and rest my forehead against his. "Will you be with me? Every step of the way?" I ask, needing to hear this answer.

"Of course, I will. You have me forever, don't ever doubt that," he says, sealing his promise with his kiss.

I luxuriate in the feel of his lips saying he'll be my support, everything I need. I break off, putting my forehead back on his. "God, help me. Guide me, Lord."

"He will," Linc promises, and I know he's right.

"I'm not supposed to know everything I need to do right now, right?" I whisper, feeling the enormity of the role I've accepted.

"No," he says, kissing my aching forehead. "Take it one step at a time. The next thing is claiming the gifts from the other Extremists and gifting them to the volunteers who agree to accompany us. Then we'll take the Extremists to Winnipeg. After that, we'll see what's next. But, first, you need to change into something dry. Your clothes are muddy and soaked through. It's getting cold. I don't want you to get sick." He chuckles. "Hey, do you think you could just blow your clothes dry with air heated by your fire? That would be a very useful trick." He frowns. "But the mud on them won't just go away, so maybe you do need to change."

I nod and he turns his cheek to rest it on the top of my head, hugging me tightly. I suddenly feel bone tired. "I don't know if I can do that. Rayne dried our clothes when they were on the ground. But Linc, I'm so exhausted. I can't even think of trying that right now. My head is killing me."

"Why didn't you say so?" he asks, leaning back to look at me with worried eyes. "Let me give you some energy. You're probably depleted."

When he cups both of my cheeks, my headache disappears as he feeds me restoring energy. He's right, that's just what I needed.

I sigh, gratefully, saying breathlessly, "That's so much better. Thank you." Leaning back, I say, "You know, it's no wonder God led you to me. I can't do this without you."

He smiles softly, brushing back my hair. "You would find a way, but I'm only too happy to be your support. You'll always have it."

I lean in to kiss him and say against his lips, "Thank you, Lincoln Stevenson."

Letting go, he inhales deeply and says, "As much as I'd like to continue that train of thought, let's do what we need to rest here." He picks his pack up from where he left it before the battle.

He fishes out dry clothes and hands them to me. I'm suddenly reminded of when Rayne did the same thing on our ill-fated trip through the woods. Sorrow and shame about Rayne fill me again. The thought of my betrayal makes me feel ill. Swallowing, I ask, "Linc, you really do forgive me?"

"For what?" he asks, his eyebrows lifted, like he's genuinely curious.

"Are you serious?"

A thoughtful look comes over him. "You're talking about Rayne?"

I nod, unable to trust myself to speak.

He sighs heavily and comes toward me, holding my arms. "Vela. The only thing you need to be worried about is me giving you your space. I've forgiven you. It needs to be forgotten now. God taught me an unbelievable lesson with that whole thing. I'm grateful for the experience, really."

"Grateful that I kissed another guy?" I ask, disbelieving.

His eyes harden, and he bends his head so he can look deep into my eyes. "No. That was definitely one of the most painful experiences I've ever felt."

I wince.

"But before it happened, God prepared me and taught me to put Him first, not you. I had you up on this pedestal that I would never have been able to reach. I made you my idol. Someone much more important than my Savior. God showed me what I was doing, and I'm grateful for that lesson. It just took what happened with Rayne for me to see I'd confused where my worship needed to be. Not in you, but Him."

I nod, leaning my head on his chest. "Well, I'm thankful for that, too. I would never want to be first. Only second to God."

He kisses the top of my head. "I'm straightened out now. Don't worry. Let's forget the whole thing, okay?"

"Okay," I say into his neck, breathing him in deeply. His scent of roasted marshmallows fills my nostrils, instantly calming me down. "We'll take the whole Chosen Child thing one day at a time?"

"Today is over. Rest, and we'll figure out tomorrow then. Remember when I said problems have a way of happening by themselves? Don't borrow tomorrow's problems. It even says in Matthew 6:34, Do not worry about tomorrow, for tomorrow will worry about itself. Each day has enough trouble of its own."

I nod and ponder his words. I think of him saying that exact advice so long ago. But really, it wasn't that long ago, just a world away from here. "Right. One day at a time." I give him one more squeeze, then go outside of the little hideaway we found and change into Linc's dry clothes, happy to be healthy and whole while I'm doing it. I return and dig into his pack for some jerky, because exhaustion isn't the only thing tugging at me. My stomach is suddenly ravenous.

I settle down to eat while Linc gets a spot cleared on the ground for a fire. I content myself with watching my gorgeous man take care of me.

And I know no matter what, he always will. He's proven that. Over and over. It's time I do it, too.

As I watch Linc put together wood for a fire, I reflect on my attitude that has been far from what I need it to be. I need to be confident in God's plan. In me.

42. LINC

After I share my meager dinner with Vela and Jack, she lies down by me, tucked under my arm. She's asleep in seconds, her breath coming deep and even. I'm happy she's finally resting. She's had a very full day and needs rest more than anything else right now.

The sky lights up in a brilliant display of blue and green wispy colors. The Northern Lights have come out to play, and I think of the folk lore that if you whistle and sing your loved ones will come visit with you. I wish I believed it. That I could bring the spirit of my sister with me right now, for just a moment, would make this moment perfect. I'd do it now, but with Vela asleep, I don't want to wake her up.

I'm deliriously happy to have her back in my arms. I had to give her up to actually have her and it took my near death for it to happen. I'd happily go through it again if it means this outcome. My wife. She promised to be *my wife*. My heart jumps at the thought, and I'm supremely satisfied with the sound of that.

As I watch the sky dance, I know we don't have an easy road in front of us. We're both young to be married, but that's the least of our worries. There's the unknown and serious business of Vela being the Chosen Child.

When I first heard Gene and Jerry's speculations that Vela was the One, I could hardly believe it. But knowing Vela's character like I do and her infallible sense of justice, it only seems right for her to be chosen.

I kiss the top of her head and pray God gives me the strength to be everything she needs and more. It's no surprise God gifted us with an Intended bond. I have high connections she will need to go forward in this path laid out before her. Us, I mean. Because she's not going to do any of this alone.

Unite the clans. I feel that phrase around in my mind, wondering how it will happen. I think it will start with the Festans. If not here, in the untamable wilds of Canada, then in California where my mother and father live and rule now. My mother technically reigns over the entire Festan clan, but we'd start in California first. Then we could work with the Gyans that have control of the southern portion of the state.

And here in Canada, word will spread of Vela's gifts and powers and then she'll have this country's support. The mixed Elementals will be ecstatic that soon they can come out of hiding.

There's another thing to consider. There will be a serious backlash from the Extremists. Vela's life is in terrible danger. They will want to eliminate her as quickly as possible. It's vital she's well hidden.

But she can't keep hiding out here. No, she'll need to be in the U.S. to do what she's been created for. We'll have to plant decoys. Girls who look like her will have to volunteer to be in different places to throw the E.E. off her scent.

And I need to find out who Lyle Weston is. He got our location from somewhere. I need to find out where.

I'm going to need my mother's help. I stifle a groan. She's a powerhouse I've avoided most of my life. But for Vela,

I'll brave it. My father will do what he can, but he's my indomitable mother's right hand, so I'll need her support first to get his.

We will need as many allies as we can get. I'm hoping we'll have Andy's help with my parents. He has a wonderful way with my mom that's always amazed me. But with Hannah pushing herself past her limits, I'm afraid he won't want to leave her.

I'll have to differ to the power of love in his case. In mine, too. I run my cheek over Vela's hair, breathing deeply of her scent that, when I first caught it, almost knocked me off my feet. Her beauty is reason enough but knowing I'm the only one who can smell the rose, honey-butter rolls perfume from her is enough to keep me happy.

Thank you, Father, for gifting me this treasure, this priceless gift I will never take for granted again. Help me to be there for her, however she needs me.

It's with that prayer that I fall into a deep sleep, with Jack already asleep on the other side of Vela. I guess he's had as rough a day as we did.

I open my eyes to empty arms and am instantly disappointed. I wanted nothing more than to wake up to Vela's sleepy eyes looking up at me. Instead, I get Jack licking my face enthusiastically. Not the kisses I wanted to wake up to.

"Jack, boy, okay, okay, I'm up," I say, chuckling.

Rolling up to my elbows, I see Vela behind me, putting together my pack. "Going somewhere?"

She jumps, startled by my voice. "You scared me."

"Sorry," I say with a grin.

"Are you?" she asks, her eyebrow raised.

"Not really. It's fun to see you shocked to see me first thing in the morning."

Her face colors and she mutters, "We probably should have slept on opposite sides of the fire."

I look at her contemplatively. "Why? Were you afraid you'd take advantage of me?"

She laughs. "How about the opposite of that? You could have totally taken advantage of my exhausted state."

I pin her with my most direct stare. "You actually believe I would do that?"

She blushes. "No, you were the one who said it in the first place."

I laugh and hop up. "I know. I'm just teasing you." I take two big steps and envelop her in a hug, burying my face in her hair. "I figured we were both too tired to be tempted to do anything much but sleep."

She melts in my arms but then stiffens and says with a deep sigh, "We should probably get going."

"Probably." But I stay still, enjoying her presence and delicious scent. Jack jumps on both of us, wanting to be included in this warm hug, and we both pet his sleek head.

She tries to pull back, but I resist. "Just one more minute, please. Let me hold you. I've been dying to do this for forever."

She relaxes and rests her head on my chest. She fits so perfectly in my arms; I cannot believe I'll be able to hold her like this anytime I want to once we're married.

I can't help but ask, "Are you really mine, Vela?"

She looks up at me, her blue eyes sparkling. "As long as forever," she whispers.

I lean down and kiss her soft, pink lips, not wanting to break the enchantment she put over me. Standing together in this glen-like place with birds singing around us and the morning light filtering onto her golden hair, I couldn't ask for a more perfect moment.

It almost erases the ugliness of what we're going back to in the burned-out shell of the Polar Bear. I kiss her soundly. She melts into me, and I force myself to step back. She's going to be hard to resist until we're married. But I will, because it's the right thing, what we've both agreed.

I inhale deeply, saying, "Okay, let's go. Before I'm not able to. You have some more gifts to steal."

"Claim, and give," she corrects, with a twist of her lips. She looks like she's unhappy that I stopped our kiss.

"Stop that," I order in a stern voice.

"What?" she asks, blinking up at me, all innocent-like.

"You know what. It's time for us to leave. Now."

She giggles, and I almost kiss her to stop that enchanting sound. She looks away and sighs. "I still can't believe I have all the gifts and that I can take them."

"I can. You're amazing in your new power and the fact that you're hesitant to acknowledge it just proves you're capable of wielding such power without it going to your head."

"You think so?"

"I do. Now, let's go."

We have a meager breakfast with the food I have left in my pack. After we finish packing up and putting dirt on last night's fire, we make sure all the embers are covered. This forest does not need more fires in the immediate future.

We leave our little nest, and I reach for Vela's hand, holding it tight. Just because I can, I infuse her with energy, which she'll probably need to get through today. Jack barks, noticing the exchange of energy. I'm always amazed he can feel that.

She smiles up at me, acknowledging my little gesture.

"I'll keep doing that for as long as you need today."

"Thanks," she says softly, looking resolutely ahead.

I study her for a moment. "What are you thinking about?"

She glances at me, then resumes looking ahead. "I can't get out of my head how painful and horrifying it must be to have your gift ripped out of you."

I squeeze her hand. "It has to be hard to be the one administering justice."

She nods. "It is. I can hardly believe I'm in this position."

"Would it help for you to see Hannah before you get started today?"

"Yes," she says. "That would be wonderful. I could use her insight."

"And motherly love," I add, knowing how Hannah has become like a surrogate mother to Vela.

"She really is. Have you seen Greta?" she asks, squinting up at me through the light shining in her eyes.

"The last time I saw her was when she got the kids out to hide them."

We've reached the remains of Polar Bear and see that most everyone is already up and salvaging what they can from the burned buildings. I glance over at the captured Extremists and count to make sure they're all still there.

Good, no one escaped. Vela commands Jack to stay by us when he looks like he wants to investigate the captured Extremists.

"Vela!" a little voice screams behind us and we spin around. Greta is running full speed towards Vela, who braces herself for impact.

Greta plows into Vela, who catches her up and swings her around. They both laugh while Greta squeals.

When Vela sets her down, Greta buries her head in Vela's stomach. Jack licks the side of the girl's face like a lollipop. She greets him then gushes, "Vela, I was so worried. Everything is gone, well, practically everything. And my little animals. Some didn't survive the fire. Then I heard about you being The One. I couldn't believe it."

Vela smiles down at her and pets her hair. "I know. I couldn't believe it either."

Greta looks up at her and beams a great smile. "Does that mean I can live anywhere I want to now that you're here? We don't have to hide anymore? Even though I'll have two gifts?"

Vela shakes her head and frowns. "No, little one. You can't leave the safety of this place yet. I have some work to do first." Her face twists in worry, and I can imagine the enormity of her new role hitting her hard.

"Vela," I say gently. "Remember, take one day at a time."

She smiles at me and looks back down at Greta. "Give me some time, okay? Eventually, it will be safe to leave this community and see the world."

Greta beams up at her. "Wow, that sounds awesome! I want to stay with you, can I?"

Vela laughs softly. "I'm afraid your mom would miss you terribly. Speaking of her, where is she?"

Greta looks toward the Community building. "She's in there. She barely leaves it. There's a lot of people she's trying to help."

"Of course she's there. Want to come with me to see her?"

Greta scrunches up her face. "No! She'll give me an errand again. I'm hiding from her right now."

Vela musses Greta's hair. "Well, then go hide. Because I'm going to go see your momma."

"Okay," she says, disappointed. "But can you tell me the story later of how you took the powers and gave them away? That's just awesome!"

Vela gives a quick nod, and Greta scampers off after saying goodbye to Jack. Vela has to command him to stay with her when he tries to run after Greta's retreating form.

"You have a lifetime devotee on your hands," I tell her as the three of us walk toward where Hannah is busy healing.

"I know," she says with a sigh. "I take comfort that we were friends first, though."

"Of course."

We head to the Community building, giving a wide berth to the captives who hurl a few names at Vela. The guards soon quiet them down.

I stop her with my hand on her arm. Roland approaches us with a determined stride. I'm happy to see he's uninjured. "Hey, it's good to see you. Thanks for your help getting this place back in the right hands."

He furrows his forehead over his dark eyes. "They should not have attacked. Of course, I helped. But it's time I make my way back."

"Can we give you anything for your trip?" Vela asks. "I know you wanted to trade guiding us back for supplies."

He shakes his head hard. "Everyone here needs their supplies more than we do."

"Oh, sorry."

He studies her. "If what I hear is true, it will have been well worth it to help the Chosen One."

Vela blushes.

He crooks a small smile, his gaze amused. "Be well and believe in yourself."

She looks up at him with surprise and just nods.

He returns it and glances at me before he turns and heads off toward the woods carrying the canteens I borrowed. *Where did he find those?*

"He was a huge help. I'm sorry to see him go." Vela slips her hand into mine and leads me toward the community building. When we walk in, she immediately spots Hannah healing someone on the floor.

They've made progress since we were here yesterday. There are fewer patients. That means the others were either healed or buried. I tuck that grim thought away and follow Vela to Hannah's side.

She waits for Hannah to finish what she's doing. When Hannah looks up, she cries out and jumps to her feet, hugging Vela's neck fiercely. Jack nudges Hannah's leg, wanting to greet her, too.

She laughs, kneels down to give him love and exclaims, looking up, "Vela, you're okay? We were worried about you. I heard about what you did last night. Where did you go afterwards? We searched for you but couldn't find you!"

Vela blushes, which makes me giddily happy for some reason. "Linc and I passed out in the woods."

"And that makes you blush?" Hannah asks, standing, her eyebrow cocked, and her arms crossed.

Yep, she's a mother hen to Vela, all right.

"No! We were...nothing happened...I mean, we just slept, I swear," Vela stammers and blushes a deeper shade of red.

I only smile, a contented one at that. Hannah should be worried about me being alone with Vela. She knows how I feel about her.

Hannah looks between me and Vela and says grudgingly, "Okay, I guess it's alright. So," she says in a business-like tone, "what's next for you two?"

"Vela and I will be married as soon as we get her parents' permission," I announce before Vela can speak.

Hannah's eyebrows shoot up in surprise.

Vela laughs and puts her hand on Hannah's arm. "Hannah, your face! He's right, we're going back to the States after we take the captured E.E. to Winnipeg and hand them over to the local Festans."

"But first you'll take their gifts from them, right?" Hannah asks in a hard voice.

Man, I do not ever want to be on this woman's bad side.

"Yes, and give them to those who you guys choose," Vela answers.

"And then?"

"Then we go to Denver," Vela says, looking to me for confirmation. When I nod, she says, "We'll get my parents' permission to marry and then, I don't know."

"Vela, only certain states do that. Most require a court order for a minor to be married," Hannah says.

Vela shrugs. "We'll go to another state if we have to."

"Then we'll go to California," I say with a firm voice.

"Why?" Vela asks, looking up at me. "We don't need your parent's permission, you're already eighteen."

"Not permission for that, but to start uniting the clans, you'll need their help. My mother, as the Grand Elder, can do a lot to get you started."

Vela's face turns white at the thought. But I don't know if it's the idea of meeting my mother, which she should be nervous about, or assuming the duties of the Chosen Child that worry her more.

Hannah says in an awed voice, "So you really are the One."

I nod. Vela looks down, like she's embarrassed. Hannah takes the hint she doesn't want to talk about it.

Hannah looks between us. "And when in all these grand plans is the big day?"

"Big day?" Vela asks, her mind probably still on being the Chosen One.

"The wedding?" Hannah asks with a laugh.

"Oh! I don't know. I haven't gotten that far yet."

I have. "I thought we'd have something small and private and soon, in the next week or so. I guess after we get the court order."

This time, Hannah outright belly laughs. When she's done laughing, she says, "You aren't in any hurry or anything."

I give Vela a look that speaks of my deep desire to marry her. She blushes.

"Okay, that answers *that* question," Hannah says with another huff of laughter. "Vela, what do you have to say about all of this?"

She looks down, like her wall of hair can hide her embarrassment. "I'm fine with being married soon," she says quietly.

My heart soars at her words. I reach for her hand and squeeze it.

"We haven't really talked over this, Hannah. So, please don't pepper her with questions. We're taking it one day at a time," I say.

"But you're getting married," she says in a disbelieving tone.

Vela nods and I say, "Yes," in as firm a tone as I can manage.

"Okay, you two. If you're both sure?"

"I am," we both say at the same time, and then look at each other and laugh.

Then I turn to Hannah. "Do you know where Andy is?"

She blows out a breath and looks around. "He was around here, but he must have left. You'll have to hunt him down outside. I'm sure he's working to rebuild this place."

"Is that the plan?" Vela asks. "You guys will stay here despite the location being compromised?"

Hannah gives Vela a frank look. "Once word spreads that the Chosen Child has revealed herself, we won't need to stay in hiding much longer. We hope to rejoin the rest of the world soon. So, yes, we'll rebuild here until that happens."

"Hannah, I don't know when those things will happen," Vela says, two worry lines forming between her eyes.

"It will when the time is right, nothing less," I say firmly, locking Vela's gaze with mine. I give her an encouraging look and say to Hannah, "We're not borrowing tomorrow's problems for today."

Hannah nods and says, "Truer words have never been spoken. Vela, you have yourself a good man, right here. I know he'll be a good support for you. And, like I told you a while back, we've always believed here at the Polar Bear that if the Chosen Child comes from our ranks, which I consider you a part of, then we'll support you and protect you in any way you need. If you need me and Greta to come with you wherever you go, you just say the word. We'll make it happen. A lot of us feel the same way."

Vela answers by throwing her arms around Hannah's neck.

Hannah laughs and hugs her back. Vela says something low I can't hear in her ear and Hannah grumbles, "You know I would tell you if I didn't approve."

Vela lets go of her, and Hannah takes one look at me and wraps Vela and me in a hug. "I'm so happy for you two. You're young, but it sounds like Vela can use all the support she can get."

I pull from the group hug first and then smile as Hannah releases Vela and leans back, moving hair out of her eyes, like a mother would. She's so good for Vela. I hate to take her away from Hannah, but unless she decides to come with us, it's inevitable.

"Vela! You're okay!" a voice screeches from behind us.

A small girl comes flying from my right and hurls herself at Vela, almost knocking her over.

"Grace! You're okay, too!" Vela says, laughing. Jack jumps up, wanting to be a part of any reunion Vela has.

Grace pulls back. "Is he upset with me?" she asks nervously, eyeing Jack warily.

Vela pushes Jack away, saying, "No! He's just excited, is all."

Grace nods and says, "Vela, you save my life, then everyone else's, then you disappear?"

Vela looks at her with a confused look on her face. "I didn't save everyone's life. What do you mean?"

Grace puts her hands on her hips. "You aren't the Chosen Child? I heard wrong? That sounds like you're saving all of us by uniting the rest of the clans and not leaving us up here in hiding like rats. So, yes, you're saving our lives, Vela."

Vela's eyes grow big, and she looks overwhelmed.

I step toward them and tuck my poor Intended under my arm, hugging her close to my side. "Let her take that kind of information in pieces, Grace. It's kind of a lot."

Grace has the, well, grace to look chagrined. "Sorry, Vela. I was just so surprised. And thankful. I'll tone it down," she finishes in a whisper. That's more like the Grace that Vela and I know. Not that I don't like seeing more of her personality.

Vela seems to feel the same way because she says, "Grace, don't worry. Linc is just a little protective of my sanity. As much as I appreciate it," she says, looking at me with a narrowing of her eyes, "I can handle things better than he thinks."

"Good," Hannah says, "because you're about to have more company." She points behind us and I see Rick and Gary marching toward us with determined strides.

"Are you ready for this?" I ask in Vela's ear.

She just nods as we wait for them to approach.

I give them a warning glare to not overwhelm my Intended, but I'm not sure how far that will go. They look like they're ready to conquer armies. With my Vela, I'm positive they could.

43. VELA

As I wait for Rick and Gary, I have mixed feelings. I rub Jack's head, needing soothing. I'm ready to complete the task of claiming and empowering gifts, but I'm not sure about anything else.

I turn to Linc and say, "I want to do something."

He looks at me, his eyebrows raised, and asks, "What would you like to do?"

"This," and with both hands, I produce both fire and a waterspout. Laughing, I play with them, moving them around and then wanting to add flare, I combine them, squealing when the water fizzles out in a hiss of steam.

Linc looks on in amusement and says, "Are you finished?"

In answer, I drop my hands, banishing the fire only to raise them, creating a small wind funnel and watch as I send it outside. Since I'm indoors, I can't play with my earth gifts, but I've done enough with that gift over the years that I'm satisfied with playing around with my new gifts. "Now I'm done."

Linc laughs and wraps his arms around me, squeezing. "You're amazing, my sweet Vela."

I enjoy his show of love but pull away when Rick and Gary reach us. Rick speaks first. "Vela, that was impressive, to say the least. Are you ready to do more?"

"To do more what?" Linc asks in a warning tone.

Gary glances at Linc with appropriate wariness and says, "We have eleven volunteers who will not only gratefully accept a new gift but will also go with you to guard these people on the journey to Winnipeg. We don't know if you need all of them, but they're willing."

Linc relaxes next to me and since I'm tucked into his side, I can feel his guard go down. He's going to be my dedicated defender. I appreciate his devotion. It helps me to mean it when I say, "I'm ready." I have Jack and Linc to help me do this next thing on my Chosen Child checklist. I really am ready.

"Good. Hannah, everything going well in here?" Rick asks.

She nods. "We're working on the worst cases. I don't think we'll have any more fatalities." She scowls in the direction of the captured Extremists.

I wince when I hear the word, fatalities. That means we lost some of our own to the Extremists' attack. I heard from the leaders that we had deaths, but to hear from Hannah makes me want to hurt something. I channel my anger into a controlled burn in my body. I'll let it fuel me when I do the business at hand.

Burning up, I lead the way outside. Everyone, including Jack, follows me out the door and to the captives. Walking up to them with my fists clenched, I must look like I'm out for blood, because the faces of the E.E. are full of fear when they catch sight of me. It could be that they know what I'm capable of, too, though. Either way, I gladly accept knowing they're feeling even a portion of the fear they inflicted on so many innocents over the years. They need penance for what they've done. I pray no child was lost, because if I hear that, I might go into such a rage, nothing will bring me back from ending all of them.

Giving Jack to Linc's care, I ask in a cold voice, "Who's first?"

There's a crowd around us, who I realize are the volunteers Gary mentioned. Rick pulls one of them over to me and says, "Josh is the first one you're gifting." I barely glance at the red-haired man before I turn my glare to the E.E.

"I meant them," I say coldly.

Rick pulls one of the captured to her feet and forces her to stand in front of me. "Josh requested a Festan."

Not needing the theatrics I used the first time, I reach out and grip the woman's shoulder. The burning anger I feel transfers to my hand. I mentally reach into her and yank. I'm hit with a Festan heat so hot, I stagger. Again, Linc is behind me to prevent me from falling.

I rest against his warm chest and try to contain the energy coursing through me. The woman's Festan gift isn't foreign. I recognize the feeling since I now have my own portion of the Festan gift. I gasp, trying to control the flood of power. I compartmentalize the extra Festan gift in me.

I'm panting when Linc whispers, "Are you okay?"

I nod and stand up, leaning against Linc for a minute. When I feel I can, I step toward Josh and place my hand on his shoulder. I exhale a breath and with it unleash the Festan gift.

Josh gasps and staggers back, hitting the ground hard.

Gary laughs while the E.E. all start shouting and fighting their bonds. A guard has to hit one of them on the back of the head, making the captive slump over. They quiet down, but only to lower their voices to angry murmurs.

"Guess we'll have to stand behind them and catch 'em, so no one gets a concussion," Gary says, going over to Josh to check on him. When he inquires, Josh sticks his thumb up, but his chest is rising and falling quickly, like he got the wind knocked out of him and he's trying to catch his breath.

"Next," I say, still burning with anger. Jack whines, but he stays next to Linc, allowing me to do this.

Rick brings me someone else and so it continues. I manage to take and gift seven people before I'm forced to stop. Linc tried to get me to quit after a few, but after drinking some water, I pushed through my exhaustion.

I feel as if I've been stuffed like a sausage, then gutted seven times. If it wasn't for Linc telling me how many I had done, I would have lost count a while ago.

"Vela, that's enough." Linc says in a worried voice.

I'm barely standing, trying to overcome the pounding headache, dizziness, and blurry spots in my vision when Linc takes one look at me and sweeps me off my feet, carrying me away.

"Where are you going?" Rick asks.

"Away. Vela needs to rest." Linc growls as he walks with determined steps to our little nest in the woods, and I call Jack to follow.

I close my eyes and enjoy the feel of Linc's strong arms around me. Resting my cheek against his chest, I listen to the beat of his heart and say, "Linc, thank you."

"Thank *you*," he breathes, kissing the top of my head.

"I didn't..."

"Don't even say you didn't do much. You know that's not true."

He's right. What I just did was incredible. "I couldn't have done it without you," I mumble, letting the bliss of sleep come closer.

"Hush, just sleep. I'm here, Vela. I've got you. Sleep."

I'm only too happy to obey.

It's morning when I blink awake. I'm tucked against Linc, and I snuggle into him, enjoying his closeness. Jack's wet nose pushes into my face, and I let him kiss me before I push him away. I see the remnants of a fire, which Linc must have made when I was asleep. I also see half of a road chicken keeping warm by the embers. A roaring hunger fills me at the sight, and I move to get to it.

But when I try to sit up, arms tighten around me. "Where are you going?" Linc grumbles in my hair.

"I'm hungry," I say, laughing, attempting to get up again.

At my words, he releases me, and I fetch the bird and start picking meat off the bones, stuffing my mouth as fast as I can. "Tank you mor a 'ome-cooked meal," I say, my mouth full of this glorious breakfast.

Linc raises up, leaning on his elbow as he lies on his side. He chuckles at my exuberant eating. "Of course. I'm glad I found it. I thought all the animals would have been long gone with all the fire. They say these pheasants are stupid, but this takes them to a whole new level."

Jack comes over and begs for attention and food.

"This chicken didn't get the memo there was a fire close by, obviously," I say as I give pieces to my hungry dog.

"No," he says, smiling. "I made good use of it, though."

"Yes, you did," I agree as I continue to devour the meat. I haven't been this hungry in a long time. I reach for Linc's pack and dig out his water canteen. Noticing it's not very full, I frown down at it.

"What's the matter?" Linc asks.

"It's almost empty."

"So, fill it up," he says, smirking, leaning on one elbow as he watches me.

I look down at the canteen with wide eyes. He's right. I have the Neronian gift now. Narrowing my eyes at the water container, I feel my hand grow warm. Choosing which gift to use takes concentration and obviously practice, because a sudden gust of wind nearly blows the canteen out of my grasp.

Sighing, I drop my hand and find Linc trying not to laugh.

"Hey! This isn't as easy as it looks."

"I didn't say it was. Try again," he says with an amused look in his eyes.

I frown down at the canteen and focus. When I feel my adrenaline rise, I force it down. I don't need my Gyan gift right now. Instead, I imagine the rush of water flowing through my veins, and I look on happily when water overflows the canteen spilling onto my hand.

Laughing, I cry, "Aha! I got it!" Linc laughs with me as I hold the overflowing canteen away from me so my borrowed clothes don't get wet. I finally stop the water and hold it to my lips, taking a deep drink.

"Alright, are you ready?" he asks after I hand him the water and he takes a drink. He picks himself up and holds out his hand.

"For what? World domination next?" I ask with a smirk.

He snorts. "Worse. I need to call my mother. Let's hope the satellite phone wasn't destroyed."

Instantly, I stiffen. "Do you want me to talk to her?"

He nods. "I think it's important. She'll want to speak with you, now that your role is set."

I take a deep breath. Everything I've heard about this woman strikes terror in my heart. She's the leader of the entire Festan clan. Linc has never said anything remotely warm about her. She blames him for his sister's death. She sounds peachy. "Okay," I say reluctantly.

Linc picks the rest of the meat off our breakfast bird and then he, Jack, and I walk back to the Polar Bear in a calm silence. I attempt to gird myself to talk to a woman who probably eats people like me for breakfast.

"What's your mom's name?" I ask, clenching my trembling fist.

"Mom," he says with a smile. "She will be your mother-in-law soon, so just get used to calling her your second mother."

I shake my head. "I don't think I can call her that, Linc. It'll take a lot of time and trust to go that far."

He reaches for my hand, shaking it. "Don't let her intimidate you. You're her equal in every way, if not more."

"Don't say that," I say quickly. "I'm still me."

"With three extra additions that make you the most powerful Elemental our world has ever seen."

"Linc," I complain.

"Hey, the sooner you accept it, the easier it will be to speak with Elizabeth Stevenson."

His warm voice tries to soothe me, but I only panic more. "She shares the name of the most powerful monarch in England's history. Linc, how can you expect me to feel better knowing that?"

He laughs. "It's just a name, Vela."

"Look, you're taking this all well and all, but even you have a difficult time dealing with her."

He stops suddenly and yanks me to him and brushes his lips across mine.

I gasp and reach up, running my fingers through his soft hair, and pull him to me for a much better experience. I move my lips across his, firmer than he did to me, but just light enough to tempt him to kiss me better. He takes the bait brilliantly.

"Vela," he breathes and crushes his mouth to mine.

I get lost in his arms for a full minute before I yank myself back, breathing heavily. "Linc," I say breathlessly. "We have to stop."

"Why?" he growls and buries his face in my neck, running his lips up the sensitive skin.

I take a deep breath and force myself to take a full step back. "Because," I say, looking away from him toward the community, blinking at it, "We can't get too carried away. We're not married *yet*."

Linc moans and drops his head.

We're close enough to the community that I see two people I don't recognize. "Linc, who are they?" I ask, pointing.

When he turns, his face drains of all color. He pulls away but tucks me next to him like he needs comfort.

The woman is looking over Rick's shoulder and meets Linc's gaze. She gives him a small smile and says something before she starts walking toward us. The man with her follows.

I reach down to hold Linc's hand at my waist and feel his palm sweat. He clenches mine tightly and says in the corner of his mouth. "Vela, please relax."

"Me relax? Who is that Linc?"

The woman, an attractive brunette close to my mom's age, reaches us and, to my surprise, leans in and kisses Linc's cheek. "Hello, son. You've been very busy, I see."

My mouth drops open, and I shut it before I look too foolish. Linc's mother's *first* impression of me is watching me make out with her son. *Great.*

"Are you going to introduce us?" the woman asks him, looking at me with piercing green eyes.

By this time, the man with her earlier has reached us. He reaches over and sticks his hand out to Linc. "Son! How are you? Good to see you well." I see the resemblance quickly.

"Dad, Mother," Linc finally says, glancing at his father before he turns his gaze on his mother. "I'd like to introduce my fiancée, Vela Ashcroft."

Silence fills the air, and I watch several emotions cross Elizabeth's face. I barely notice Linc's father because I'm so fascinated by what I see in his mother. Shock, hurt, and finally, determination settles in her eyes.

"Fiancée? Isn't it a little soon to tie yourself down?" she asks with a bite.

Indignation roars through me. I squeeze Linc's hand, letting him know I'm here, and I'm not going anywhere. I will try my best to be nice, but we're not starting on a good foot. I stamp down the rush of power that follows my strong emotions. Grass spurts up at my feet, but I stop at that and contain the fire, wind, and water surging to come out.

He responds by first returning my gesture, tightening his fingers, his hand hot, saying, "Mother, I'm not tying myself down. I'm forging my life with the love of my life. You know she's my Intended."

"Son," his father interjects, looking flustered. "We had someone else in mind, that's all. You know this. We didn't expect you to jump the gun and get engaged so soon after meeting this girl."

"What?" I ask in a hard voice. I'm surprised I didn't shriek it. Jack barks and I rush to pet him to help calm him and myself down.

Linc looks as uncomfortable as I've ever seen him. "Vela, I was going to tell you..."

I take a step away from him, dropping his hand. "Your parents planned to marry you off to someone else, and you haven't told me that?"

He barks a laugh, running a hand through his hair. Hair I just ran my hands through. "I never accepted it, Vela."

"That's not true," Linc's father disagrees. "You were considering it."

"That was before I met my Intended," Linc grits out, his lips pressed in a thin line.

"Linc, you've known your duty for a long time now. Don't pretend otherwise," Elizabeth says in moderate tones.

Linc flashes her a glare, then turns to me, stepping closer. He holds out his hand like he's cornering a wild animal. "Vela, please listen to *me,* not *them.*

Maybe I am a wild animal. My blood is boiling inside me. I can hardly contain my powers, all four of them now. I take short breaths trying to control my anger.

I bite out, "Were you going to tell me, Linc? Your parents' *plans* for you?"

He blows out a breath and looks into my eyes, saying in a soothing voice, "You have a lot going on right now, Vela, wouldn't you agree?"

I nod, not trusting myself to speak.

"Okay, so I was waiting to tell you later. Before you met my parents. But they showed up here and surprised me, surprised us. Vela, I'm sorry. I would never even consider anyone else now. You're it for me. I've told you that."

His words soothe the angry edges of my soul, ease the fierce desire to use every element to annihilate the danger his parents represent. I realize they're trying to rip us apart. I turn my attention to them.

"This girl," I say in hard tones, "is not going anywhere." My blood pumps through me in righteous anger.

"You might think so, but my son has been known to get bored with his attachments quickly," Elizabeth says in chilly tones.

"Really?" I know she's trying to get under my skin and dang it if she's not succeeding. *Still. I'll be strong.* "Well, I will not walk away. Your son is my Intended. Do you mean to separate us? Do you know how painful that would be for him?"

She shrugs. "He would get over it."

"No, I wouldn't," Linc says heatedly. "Mother, why are you here?"

She inhales deeply, looking away from me for the first time. She looks around. "We received a call this place was under attack. We came to be sure the proper steps are taken."

"And what is your decision?" Linc asks.

I look at Linc and the angry set of his lips. What does he mean, her decision? Is the future of the Polar Bear up to her?

"Until the Chosen Child is found, the people here will stay and rebuild."

"What?" Linc asks, outraged. "You know Vela is…"

Elizabeth's face hardens, and she resumes studying me. "Yes, I heard everyone here thinks she is the One. But that is yet to be determined."

Linc splutters. "What do you mean? Can't you sense all the gifts in her?"

She sneers. "Any Neronian can steal a gift."

"What about keeping them?" I ask, in as steely a voice as I can manage. "How do you explain that?"

She lifts an eyebrow. "That you have an exceptionally strong Neronian gift."

Fury races through my veins. "And how do you explain that I come from a Gyan and Borean?"

"Are you sure about that?"

Frustration fills me. "No, but that doesn't mean..."

"That means everything, child. You have no idea who your parents are. You must have inherited the Neronian gift. Any more questions?"

I stare at her in disbelief. Do I explain how I heard God's voice? Would she believe me? From the look on her face, no, she would not.

"May I suggest," I say in a surprisingly calm voice, "that you investigate this a little better than you have. I am the Chosen Child and nothing you say can refute that. Maybe you don't like having someone who's more powerful than you are standing right in front of you. And engaged to your only son. But get used to not being in control of everything. I will never be someone you can push around. And it's time you stopped doing that with your son. He's mine, gifted to me. I intend to enjoy that gift. And marry him as soon as I possibly can." I tremble with fury, but cold resolution fills me.

Clapping fills the tense air. I turn to see Hannah and Andy enthusiastically showing their support for my declaration.

Elizabeth turns her sneering frown to them before she resumes her glare at me. "You are even more ridiculous than I expected."

"And for that, I'm extremely grateful. Something tells me that your approval is the last thing I'd want."

"Elizabeth," Linc's father says, coughing into his hand. "Let's leave this for the time being. There is much to be done around here. We're needed elsewhere."

She sniffs then turns, leaving with him, looking just once over her shoulder. She delivers a look so cold, I'm shocked I'm not in a block of ice where I stand.

I lunge into Linc's arms, tucking my nose into his neck. "I'm sorry, Linc. I just made things so much worse than they should be."

He hugs me, squeezing me tight. "No, Vela. You were incredible. I have never seen anyone stand up to my mother that way. You're perfect."

"I don't know about that." I breathe in his unique scent, reminding myself he's truly meant for me and me alone. I take solace in his embrace and sweet and smoky flavors swirling around my head. "It's a good thing we don't need her permission to get married."

He chuckles and kisses my cheek. "That wouldn't stop me, believe me. I would find a way."

Andy interrupts our chat by clapping Linc's back with his big hand. "Linc, my friend, you have yourself one powerful young lady. You sure you can handle her?"

I laugh and lean back, but still in Linc's embrace. "If he could handle his mother his entire life, I think he can manage me."

"Don't be too sure of that," Hannah says, laying her hand on Andy's arm. "We women have a way of keeping our men on their toes." She looks lovingly up at Andy, and he returns her gaze so warmly that I could melt in the heat they're giving off.

"Wait, are you together?" I ask, untangling myself from Linc.

Andy laughs and puts his huge arm over Hannah's shoulders, holding her carefully, like a doll. One he's crazy about. "The only good thing about this whole crazy battle was fighting with and for this lady. She finally realized she couldn't live without me." He turns a beaming smile to her, and she blushes.

"I guess I was blind to how he felt about me," Hannah says with a chagrined look.

"I don't know how you didn't see it!" I say with a laugh. "I've never seen anyone more smitten."

"Except me," Linc says, nuzzling his nose into my hair, wrapping his arms around my waist.

We all laugh and Linc lifts head up and says indignantly, "You don't know what I went through getting this girl to realize she couldn't live without me."

I sober at that. "He's right," I say quietly. "I almost had to lose him to truly make him mine."

Linc squeezes me. "I know the feeling. I had to do the same thing."

"Well, then, now that we're on the same page, let's never look back." I turn in his arms and pull his head down to my waiting lips.

As I breathe in roasted marshmallow, Linc's delicious scent, I think that this is one place I never want to leave. It'll take the end of the world for me to come back from this.

Oh, yeah. We're at the end. It took centuries to find the Chosen Child. We're in a new age and now that I know I'm the long-awaited uniter of the clans, the one God destined to do the work, I don't want to hide anymore. I will no longer be lost.

Only lost in love.

So, that's where I'll stay. With my Intended by my side, I know we can face whatever the broken world throws at us.

A NOTE TO MY READERS

I'd like to say one thing about the characters in this book. It was an honor to write about the First Nation people of Canada.

Of course, all the elements I gave them are all made up and are a figment of my imagination. They do not follow a "Maker", that is also in the threads of my made-up story. The reason for this note is that I want to share the reasons for why I diluted their powers. It was for the simple reason that they intermarried with humans, which made their "gifts" less powerful, since humans in my story do not have elemental gifts.

I, in no way, meant for them to appear "less than" the other elementals.

In fact, I imagined they would take the higher road and not allow prejudice and fear to control their marriage customs and would allow humans to intermarry with elementals.

I have a great respect for this great Canadian nation and only wanted their characters to fit into the storyline of my book.

They have achieved far more in their culture and longevity than I could possibly describe.

Free Book!

Receive a free novella, Operation Kane, from the Terra, Torch, and Tempest world if you join my newsletter!

Elia will do anything to get her best friend's older brother to notice she's a woman now, even become a spy.

Dive into this world of Elementals, unrequited love, and the power of hope. Enjoy the best friend's older brother, forbidden love, fake dating, and friends-to-lovers tropes in this powerful story of faith and young love.

Go to: www.sofiasimpson.com to find this charming novella. Connect with me there if you'd like to have me on your podcast.

And if you enjoyed this book, please leave a review on Amazon, Bookbub or Goodreads, or if you're especially generous, all three! It means more to us authors than you know.

Fill your rooms with the delicious scents of my book candles!

Vela, Honey Butter Rolls
Linc, Roasted Marshmallows
Rayne, Evergreen and Ash

Go to:

https://linktr.ee/sofiasimpsonauthor

Acknowledgements

First of all, I'd like to give all the glory to Jesus for the making of this book. Without His daily guidance, this book would never have happened.

For the people in my life, I'd like to first thank my hubby. His support through my writing journey has been nothing short of amazing and miraculous. He allows me to do this writing life full time and for that I couldn't be more humbly thankful. I love you, hunny.

I cannot forget my two sons, who are my loudest cheerleaders and sounding boards. Thank you Matthew and Nicky. I love you both to distraction.

Outside of my family, I'd like to thank my amazing and inspiring editor who worked tirelessly to bring this manuscript to the shape you've read it. You don't want to see what she see's, believe you me. She is not only hardworking, but extremely talented at what she does. She turns a sloppy stew into a gourmet meal. Thank you Jessica Gwyn!

I'd also like to thank EAH Creative for the gorgeous cover you see on the front of this book. Emilie, you are a creative genius. Period.

To my Street Team, you gals are stupendous, amazing, illustrious and gorgeous! I cannot thank you enough for helping me get this book out to the world and for your support. Some of you have been with me since Terra, book one and for that I couldn't be more grateful! Thank you to each of you.

And to my readers...this would not be fun without you. With God's help, I created this whole world so you could enjoy a clean romance with really cool elements. I hope you enjoyed this story and that you'll stick around and find out what happens in the final installment, book four.

Join my newsletter, follow my Instagram, Facebook and Tiktok at @sofiasimpsonauthor and keep up to date on all book news!

I have to give a shout out to my special readers, Charlotte
June and Alicia. You both support me in different ways,
Charlotte, you love to pass around my books to your
friends, Alicia, you do so much to help me on social media.
I couldn't thank you two enough!
To my writing groups, Lakeland Writers and Word Weavers
online group, you all helped shape this story into what it is.
Thank you for your generous advice and much needed
criticisms.
Dana, thank you for loving my books! I can't wait to hear
what you think of this one!
And lastly, thank you Jenny. My dear friend and confidante,
who's more sister than friend. You've given unending advice
and encouragement, even getting soaked to the bone in a
monsoon at a book event. All to support me and my crazy
wild journey of being an author. Love you friend, thank
you.